OUT OF THE STILLNESS
IT CAME . . .

Then suddenly the grass parted and one of the three-legged creatures was right in front of me. I raised my finger but didn't squeeze.

"Movement!"

"Movement!"

"HOLD YOUR FIRE! Don't shoot!"

"Movement."

"Movement." I looked left and right and as far as I could see, every perimeter guard had one of the blind dumb creatures standing right in front of him.

Maybe the drug I'd taken to stay awake made me more sensitive to whatever they did. My scalp crawled and I felt a formless thing in my mind, the feeling you get when somebody has said something and you didn't quite hear it, want to respond but the opportunity to ask him to repeat it is gone.

The creature sat back on its haunches, leaning forward on the one front leg. Big green bear with a withered arm. Its power threaded through my mind, spiderwebs, echo of night terrors, trying to communicate, trying to destroy me, I couldn't know . . .

—from "Hero"
by Joe W. Haldeman

BOOTCAMP 3000

INTRODUCTION BY GORDON R. DICKSON

WITH CHARLES G. WAUGH AND MARTIN HARRY GREENBERG, EDITORS

ACE BOOKS, NEW YORK

BOOTCAMP 3000

An Ace Book / published by arrangement with
the editors

PRINTING HISTORY
Ace edition / September 1992

ISBN: 0-441-53168-7

Ace Books are published by The Berkley Publishing Group,
200 Madison Avenue, New York, New York 10016.
The name ''ACE'' and the ''A'' logo
are trademarks belonging to Charter Communications, Inc.

PRINTED IN THE UNITED STATES OF AMERICA

10 9 8 7 6 5 4 3 2 1

Contents

Introduction

Gordon R. Dickson

The book you hold in your hands at this moment is made up of very strong stories. By that I mean that they are not merely selected from the best of science fiction, but that they have a common element that makes me, at least, think of them as belonging to the general class of literature as a whole.

There is an anecdote about H. G. Wells and Jules Verne, both of whom wrote in the nineteenth century some of the earliest of what is now labeled science fiction. These men have been cited as examples of very early and excellent science fiction writers. I cannot remember the title of the source of my discovery of the anecdote, so I will give it to you as my memory retains it.

A reviewer of that same nineteenth century, who was giving his opinion of a story by H. G. Wells, and speaking very highly of it, put himself on record as stating that Wells was certainly the best of those who had written scientific fiction. There was no one that could compare to him.

Someone apparently clipped this review from the newspaper and mailed it to Jules Verne, in France.

Jules Verne wrote the newspaper a letter (which the newspaper published) in which he expressed himself rather strongly:

". . . H. G. Wells is not the greatest writer of scientific fiction," wrote Verne, "I am the greatest writer of scientific fiction. H. G. Wells knows nothing of science and shows his lack of knowledge . . ." etc.

Someone else clipped this letter, once it was published, and mailed it to H. G. Wells.

H. G. Wells wrote back to the newspaper:

"Mr. Verne is quite correct," he wrote, "I am not a writer of scientific fiction. I am a socialist."

Somewhere near the end of the nineteen fifties, I happened to tell that story and to mention that different types of fiction were ideally suited to different subjects. For example, one of the things that science fiction was ideally suited for was propagandizing. I mentioned as examples Aldous Huxley's *Brave New World* and George Orwell's *1984*.

The editor agreed with me—he could hardly disagree, seeing that both books had sold tremendously, although they had come out with several decades between them.

Unfortunately, a little carried away by the success of this statement, I incautiously went on to say that I disliked the term "genre" applied to science fiction, since no two science fiction writers explored the same fictional territory—as was commonly the case with stories in a particular genre—and that the best of science fiction certainly should be considered as simply part of the mainstream of literature—as it was considered to be back in the time of Jules Verne and H. G. Wells. This, because the same attributes that made it an ideal vehicle for propaganda made it an ideal vehicle for examining some aspect of the human character or experience.

The editor disagreed, strongly.

"You're talking about philosophy," he said. "What people want from science fiction is action, adventure and entertainment! They don't look for these things on bookstore shelves that hold books on philosophy; and they don't look for or want philosophy in their books of science fiction!"

Of course, we were talking about two different animals. What my editor had in mind, I later realized, was the dull sort of book in which the fiction existed only to provide a sort of platform for a series of lectures on some philosophical point.

What I thought we were talking about were stories of action and adventure, but which also, as a whole, reflected some real and important element in human individuals or society. I should have said so instead of using the word "philosophy" without explanation. As it was, quite naturally, in the ensuing argument, we were unable to agree; and we did not.

This editor, incidentally, was a very good editor and had bought the sort of stories I was talking about, but I had led him astray by using the word "philosophy" as my label.

That, of course, is the trouble with labels. Jules Verne had called himself a writer of scientific fiction, and H. G. Wells had called himself a socialist—and they had both been right. But my editor had been wrong in thinking that they had both been writing out of the same small literary niche. Verne had written his books to try and lead his readers toward an appreciation of the possibilities of science. Wells had written his to lend the reader to an appreciation of possible developments of human society.

The stories in this book all turn upon a vital decision, which illuminates some aspect of human behavior or human society. This does not mean that in any way the science in them, although it is an integral part of the fiction of each story, exists merely as a platform for that illumination.

Non-fictional philosophy argues a point. Good science fiction demonstrates one.

Joe Haldeman's novella *Hero* involves a great deal of correct science, correctly used—not surprisingly, since his primary degree was in astronomy and physics. It also, later, developed to its full length, won the Hugo Award for best novel of the year in 1976, at the World Science Fiction Convention.

My own degree was in English literature; but though unlike Haldeman, I never saw combat, like him I went through the basic training of a combat engineer (essentially, an infantryman who also builds bridges, roads, and anything else an army must build for itself), and I can personally testify to the painful realism of the training he shows his characters undergo.

Haldeman's story, in other words, uses absolute realism as a form for a story that demonstrates his attitude toward what armies and war do to the individual. Harry Harrison, in his story, demonstrates his attitude toward the same things. Both use army training and first encounter with the enemy as part of the picture they draw. But Harrison uses satire as a form—and the two stories are entirely unconnected and in no way alike, except in being successful in what they set out to do.

In what they set out to do, both are fine examples of science fiction, and also literature. As H. G. Wells' *Men Like Gods* was literature rather than science fiction. As the children's story of the three little pigs and the big bad wolf is literature, in that it demonstrates that industriousness can make the difference between survival and non-survival.

The point of all this is that all the stories in this book are first and foremost enjoyable as stories. They are enjoyable because they are good science fiction. But they are also enjoyable because they are good literature; and you can read them either as one or the other, or both, as you wish.

In short, what I am tempted to say here is that these are cases in which you can have your cake and eat it, too.

HERO

Joe W. Haldeman

I

"Tonight we're going to show you eight silent ways to kill a man." The guy who said that was a sergeant who didn't look five years older than I. Ergo, as they say, he couldn't possibly ever have killed a man, not in combat, silently or otherwise.

I already knew eighty ways to kill people, though most of them were pretty noisy. I sat up straight in my chair and assumed a look of polite attention and fell asleep with my eyes open. So did most everybody else. We'd learned that they never schedule anything important for these after-chop classes.

The projector woke me up and I sat through a short movie showing the "eight silent ways." Some of the actors must have been brainwipes, since they were actually killed.

After the movie a girl in the front row raised her hand. The sergeant nodded at her and she rose to parade rest. Not bad looking, but kind of chunky about the neck and shoulders. Everybody gets that way after carrying a heavy pack around for a couple of months.

"Sir"—we had to call sergeants "sir" until graduation—"most of those methods, really, they looked . . . kind of silly."

"For instance?"

"Like killing a man with a blow to the kidneys, from an entrenching tool. I mean, when would you *actually* just have an entrenching tool, and no gun or knife? And why not just bash him over the head with it?"

"He might have a helmet on," he said reasonably.

"Besides, Taurans probably don't even *have* kidneys!"

He shrugged. "Probably they don't." This was 1997, and we'd never seen a Tauran: hadn't even found any pieces of Taurans

1

bigger than a scorched chromosome. "But their body chemistry is similar to ours, and we have to assume they're similarly complex creatures. They *must* have weaknesses, vulnerable spots. You have to find out where they are.

"That's the important thing." He stabbed a finger at the screen. "That's why those eight convicts got caulked for your benefit . . . you've got to find out how to kill Taurans, and be able to do it whether you have a megawatt laser or just an emery board."

She sat back down, not looking too convinced.

"Any more questions?" Nobody raised a hand.

"O.K.—tench-hut!" We staggered upright and he looked at us expectantly.

"Screw you, sir," came the tired chorus.

"Louder!"

"SCREW YOU, SIR!"

One of the army's less-inspired morale devices.

"That's better. Don't forget, predawn maneuvers tomorrow. Chop at 0330, first formation, 0400. Anybody sacked after 0340 gets one stripe. Dismissed."

I zipped up my coverall and went across the snow to the lounge for a cup of soya and a joint. I'd always been able to get by on five or six hours of sleep, and this was the only time I could be by myself, out of the army for a while. Looked at the newsfax for a few minutes. Another ship got caulked, out by Aldebaran sector. That was four years ago. They were mounting a reprisal fleet, but it'll take four years more for them to get out there. By then, the Taurans would have every portal planet sewed up tight.

Back at the billet, everybody else was sacked and the main lights were out. The whole company'd been dragging ever since we got back from the two-week lunar training. I dumped my clothes in the locker, checked the roster and found out I was in bunk 31. Damn it, right under the heater.

I slipped through the curtain as quietly as possible so as not to wake up my bunkmate. Couldn't see who it was, but I couldn't have cared less. I slipped under the blanket.

"You're late, Mandella," a voice yawned. It was Rogers.

"Sorry I woke you up," I whispered.

"'Sallright." She snuggled over and clasped me spoon-fashion. She was warm and reasonably soft. I patted her hip in what I hoped was a brotherly fashion. "Night, Rogers."

"G'night, Stallion." She returned the gesture, a good deal more pointedly.

Why do you always get the tired ones when you're ready and the randy ones when you're tired? I bowed to the inevitable.

II

"Awright, let's get some *back* inta that! Stringer team! Move it up—move up!"

A warm front had come in about midnight and the snow had turned to sleet. The permaplast stringer weighed five hundred pounds and was a bitch to handle, even when it wasn't covered with ice. There were four of us, two at each end, carrying the plastic girder with frozen fingertips. Rogers and I were partners.

"Steel!" the guy behind me yelled, meaning that he was losing his hold. It wasn't steel, but it was heavy enough to break your foot. Everybody let go and hopped away. It splashed slush and mud all over us.

"Damn it, Petrov," Rogers said, "why didn't you go out for Star Fleet, or maybe the Red Cross? This damn thing's not that damn heavy." Most of the girls were a little more circumspect in their speech.

"Awright, get a *move* on, stringers—Epoxy team! Dog 'em! Dog 'em!"

Our two epoxy people ran up, swinging their buckets. "Let's go, Mandella. I'm freezin'."

"Me, too," the girl said earnestly.

"One—two—heave!" We got the thing up again and staggered toward the bridge. It was about three-quarters completed. Looked as if the Second Platoon was going to beat us. I wouldn't give a damn, but the platoon that got their bridge built first got to fly home. Four miles of muck for the rest of us, and no rest before chop.

We got the stringer in place, dropped it with a clank, and fitted the static clamps that held it to the rise-beams. The female half of the epoxy team started slopping glue on it before we even had it secured. Her partner was waiting for the stringer on the other side. The floor team was waiting at the foot of the bridge, each one holding a piece of the light stressed permaplast over his head, like an umbrella. They were dry and clean. I wondered aloud what they had done to deserve it, and Rogers suggested a couple of colorful, but unlikely possibilities.

We were going back to stand by the next stringer when the Field First—he was named Dougelstein, but we called him "Awright"—

blew a whistle and bellowed, "Awright, soldier boys and girls, ten minutes. Smoke 'em if you got 'em." He reached into his pocket and turned on the control that heated our coveralls.

Rogers and I sat down on our end of the stringer and I took out my weed box. I had lots of joints, but we weren't allowed to smoke them until after night-chop. The only tobacco I had was a cigarro butt about three inches long. I lit it on the side of the box; it wasn't too bad after the first couple of puffs. Rogers took a puff to be sociable, but made a face and gave it back.

"Were you in school when you got drafted?" she asked.

"Yeah. Just got a degree in Physics. Was going after a teacher's certificate."

She nodded soberly. "I was in Biology. . . ."

"Figures." I ducked a handful of slush. "How far?"

"Six years, bachelor's and technical." She slid her boot along the ground, turning up a ridge of mud and slush the consistency of freezing ice milk. "Why the hell did this have to happen?"

I shrugged. It didn't call for an answer, least of all the answer that the UNEF kept giving us. Intellectual and physical elite of the planet, going out to guard humanity against the Tauran menace. It was all just a big experiment. See whether we could goad the Taurans into ground action.

Awright blew the whistle two minutes early, as expected, but Rogers and I and the other two stringers got to sit for a minute while the epoxy and floor teams finished covering our stringer. It got cold fast, sitting there with our suits turned off, but we remained inactive, on principle.

I really didn't see the sense of us having to train in the cold. Typical army half-logic. Sure, it was going to be cold where we were going; but not ice-cold or snow-cold. Almost by definition, a portal planet remained within a degree or two of absolute zero all the time, since collapsars don't shine—and the first chill you felt would mean that you were a dead man.

Twelve years before, when I was ten years old, they had discovered the collapsar jump. Just fling an object at a collapsar with sufficient speed, and it pops out in some other part of the galaxy. It didn't take long to figure out the formula that predicted where it would come out; it just traveled along the same "line"—actually an Einsteinian geodesic—it would have followed if the collapser hadn't been in the way—until it reaches another collapsar field, whereupon it reappears, repelled with the same speed it had approaching the original collapsar. Travel time between the two collapsars is exactly zero.

It made a lot of work for mathematical physicists, who had to redefine simultaneity, then tear down general relativity and build it back up again. And it made the politicians very happy, because now they could send a shipload of colonists to Fomalhaut for less than it once cost to put a brace of men on the Moon. There were a lot of people the politicians would just love to see on Fomalhaut, implementing a glorious adventure instead of stirring up trouble at home.

The ships were always accompanied by an automated probe that followed a couple of million miles behind. We knew about the portal planets, little bits of flotsam that whirled around the collapsars; the purpose of the drone was to come back and tell us in the event that a ship had smacked into a portal planet at .999 of the speed of light.

That particular catastrophe never happened, but one day a drone did come limping back alone. Its data were analyzed, and it turned out that the colonists' ship had been pursued by another vessel and destroyed. This happened near Aldebaran, in the constellation Taurus, but since "Aldebaranian" is a little hard to handle, they named the enemy Taurans.

Colonizing vessels thenceforth went out protected by an armed guard. Often the armed guard went out alone, and finally the colonization effort itself slowed to a token trickle. The United Nations Exploratory and Colonization Group got shortened to UNEF, United Nations Exploratory Force, emphasis on the "force."

Then some bright lad in the General Assembly decided that we ought to field an army of footsoldiers to guard the portal planets of the nearer collapsars. This led to the Elite Conscription Act of 1996 and the most rigorously selected army in the history of warfare.

So here we are, fifty men and fifty women, with IQ's over 150 and bodies of unusual health and strength, slogging elitely through the mud and slush of central Missouri, reflecting on how useful our skill in building bridges will be, on worlds where the only fluid will be your occasional standing pool of liquid helium.

III

About a month later, we left for our final training exercise; maneuvers on the planet Charon. Though nearing perihelion it was still more than twice as far from the sun as Pluto.

The troopship was a converted "cattlewagon," made to carry two hundred colonists and assorted bushes and beasts. Don't think it was roomy, though, just because there were half that many of us. Most of the excess space was taken up with extra reaction mass and ordnance.

The whole trip took three weeks, accelerating at 2 Gs halfway; decelerating the other half. Our top speed, as we roared by the orbit of Pluto, was around one twentieth of the speed of light—not quite enough for relativity to rear its complicated head.

Three weeks of carrying around twice as much weight as normal . . . it's no picnic. We did some cautious exercises three times a day, and remained horizontal as much as possible. Still, we had several broken bones and serious dislocations. The men had to wear special supporters. It was almost impossible to sleep, what with nightmares of choking and being crushed, and the necessity of rolling over periodically to prevent blood pooling and bedsores. One girl got so fatigued that she almost slept through the experience of having a rib rub through to the open air.

I'd been in space several times before, so when we finally stopped decelerating and went went into free fall, it was nothing but a relief. But some people had never been out, except for our training on the Moon, and succumbed to the sudden vertigo and disorientation. The rest of us cleaned up after them, floating through the quarters with sponges and inspirators to suck up globules of partly-digested "Concentrate, High-protein, Low-residue, Beef Flavor (Soya)."

A shuttle took us down to the surface in three trips. I waited for the last one, along with everybody else who wasn't bothered by free fall.

We had a good view of Charon, coming down from orbit. There wasn't much to see, though. It was just a dim, off-white sphere with a few smudges on it. We landed about two hundred meters from the base. A pressurized crawler came out and mated with the ferry, so we didn't have to suit up. We clanked and squeaked up to the main building, a featureless box of grayish plastic.

Inside, the walls were the same inspired color. The rest of the company was sitting at desks, chattering away. There was a seat next to Freeland.

"Jeff—feeling better?" He still looked a little pale.

"If the gods had meant for man to survive in free fall, they would have given him a cast-iron glottis. Somewhat better. Dying for a smoke."

"Yeah."

"*You* seemed to take it all right. Went up in school, didn't you?"

"Senior thesis in vacuum welding, yeah, three weeks in Earth orbit." I sat back and reached for my weed box, for the thousandth time. It still wasn't there, of course. The Life Support Unit didn't want to handle nicotine and THC.

"Training was bad enough," Jeff groused, "but *this* crap—"

"I don't know." I'd been thinking about it. "It might just all be worth it."

"Hell, no—this is a *space* war, let Star Fleet take care of it . . . they're just going to send us out and either we sit for fifty years on some damn ice cube of a portal planet, or we get. . . ."

"Well, Jeff, you've got to look at it the other way, too. Even if there's only one chance in a thousand that we'll be doing some good, keeping the Taurans. . . ."

"Tench-hut!" We stood up in a raggety-ass fashion, by twos and threes. The door opened and a full major came in. I stiffened a little. He was the highest-ranking officer I'd ever seen. He had a row of ribbons stitched into his coveralls, including a purple stripe meaning he'd been wounded in combat, fighting in the old American army. Must have been that Indochina thing, but it had fizzled out before I was born. He didn't look that old.

"Sit, sit." He made a patting motion with his hand. Then he put his hands on his hips and scanned the company with a small smile on his face. "Welcome to Charon. You picked a lovely day to land; the temperature outside is a summery eight point one five degrees Absolute. We expect little change for the next two centuries or so." Some of us laughed half-heartedly.

"You'd best enjoy the tropical climate here at Miami Base, enjoy it while you can. We're on the center of sunside here, and most of your training will be on darkside. Over there, the temperature drops to a chilly two point zero eight.

"You might as well regard all the training you got on Earth and the Moon as just a warm-up exercise, to give you a fair chance of surviving Charon. You'll have to go through your whole repertory here: tools, weapons, maneuvers. And you'll find that, at these temperatures, tools don't work the way they should, weapons don't want to fire. And people move v-e-r-y cautiously."

He studied the clipboard in his hand. "Right now, you have forty-nine women and forty-eight men. Two deaths, one psychiatric release. Having read an outline of your training program, I'm frankly surprised that so many of you pulled through.

"But you might as well know that I won't be displeased if as few as fifty of you graduate from this final phase. And the only way not to graduate is to die. Here. The only way anybody gets back to Earth—including me—is after a combat tour.

"You will complete your training in one month. From here you go to Stargate collapsar, a little over two lights away. You will stay at the settlement on Stargate I, the largest portal planet, until replacements arrive. Hopefully, that will be no more than a month; another group is due here as soon as you leave.

"When you leave Stargate, you will be going to a strategically important collapsar, set up a military base there, and fight the enemy, if attacked. Otherwise, maintain the base until further orders.

"The last two weeks of your training will consist of constructing such a base, on darkside. There you will be totally isolated from Miami Base: no communication, no medical evacuation, no resupply. Sometime before the two weeks are up, your defense facilities will be evaluated in an attack by guided drones. They will be armed.

"All of the permanent personnel here on Charon are combat veterans. Thus, all of us are forty to fifty years of age, but I think we can keep up with you. Two of us will be with you at all times, and will accompany you at least as far as Stargate. They are Captain Sherman Stott, your company commander, and Sergeant Octavio Cortez, your first sergeant. Gentlemen?"

Two men in the front row stood easily and turned to face us. Captain Stott was a little smaller than the major, but cut from the same mold; face hard and smooth as porcelain, cynical half-smile, a precise centimeter of beard framing a large chin, looking thirty at the most. He wore a large, gunpowder-type pistol on his hip.

Sergeant Cortez was another story. His head was shaved and the wrong shape; flattened out on one side where a large piece of skull had obviously been taken out. His face was very dark and seamed with wrinkles and scars. Half his left ear was missing and his eyes were as expressive as buttons on a machine. He had a moustache-and-beard combination that looked like a skinny white caterpillar taking a lap around his mouth. On anybody else, his schoolboy smile might look pleasant, but he was about the ugliest, meanest-looking creature I'd ever seen. Still, if you didn't look at his head and considered the lower six feet or so, he could pose as the "after" advertisement for a body-building spa. Neither Stott nor Cortez wore any ribbons. Cortez had a small pocketlaser suspended in a magnetic rig, sideways, under his left armpit. It had wooden grips that were worn very smooth.

"Now, before I turn you over to the tender mercies of these two gentlemen, let me caution you again.

"Two months ago there was not a living soul on this planet, a working force of forty-five men struggled for a month to erect this base. Twenty-four of them, more than half, died in the construction of it. This is the most dangerous planet men have ever tried to live on, but the places you'll be going will be this bad and worse. Your cadre will try to keep you alive for the next month. Listen to them . . . and follow their example; all of them have survived here for longer than you'll have to. Captain?" The captain stood up as the major went out the door.

"Tench-*hut!*" The last syllable was like an explosion and we all jerked to our feet.

"Now I'm only gonna say this *once* so you better listen," he growled. "We *are* in a combat situation here and in a combat situation there is only *one* penalty for disobedience and insubordination." He jerked the pistol from his hip and held it by the barrel, like a club. "This is an Army model 1911 automatic *pistol* caliber .45 and it is a primitive, but effective, weapon. The sergeant and I are authorized to use our weapons to kill to enforce discipline. Don't make us do it because we will. We *will*." He put the pistol back. The holster snap made a loud crack in the dead quiet.

"Sergeant Cortez and I between us have killed more people than are sitting in this room. Both of us fought in Vietnam on the American side and both of us joined the United Nations International Guard more than ten years ago. I took a break in grade from major for the privilege of commanding this company, and First Sergeant Cortez took a break from sub-major, because we are both *combat* soldiers and this is the first *combat* situation since 1974.

"Keep in mind what I've said while the First Sergeant instructs you more specifically in what your duties will be under this command. Take over, Sergeant." He turned on his heel and strode out of the room, with the little smile on his face that hadn't changed one millimeter during the whole harangue.

The First Sergeant moved like a heavy machine with lots of ball bearings. When the door hissed shut he swiveled ponderously to face us and said, "At ease, siddown," in a surprisingly gentle voice. He sat on a table in the front of the room. It creaked—but held.

"Now the captain talks scary and I look scary, but we both mean well. You'll be working pretty closely with me, so you better get used to this thing I've got hanging in front of my brain. You probably won't see the captain much, except on maneuvers."

He touched the flat part of his head. "And speaking of brains, I still have just about all of mine, in spite of Chinese efforts to the contrary. All of us old vets who mustered into UNEF had to pass the same criteria that got you drafted by the Elite Conscription Act. So I suspect all of you are smart and tough—but just keep in mind that the captain and I are smart and tough *and* experienced.

He flipped through the roster without really looking at it. "Now, as the captain said, there'll be only one kind of disciplinary action on maneuvers. Capital punishment. But normally *we* won't have to kill you for disobeying. Charon'll save us the trouble.

"Back in the billeting area, it'll be another story. We don't much care what you do inside, but once you suit up and go outside, you've gotta have discipline that would shame a Centurian. There will be situations where one stupid act could kill us all.

"Anyhow, the first thing we've gotta do is get you fitted to your fighting suits. The armorer's waiting at your billet; he'll take you one at a time. Let's go."

IV

"Now I know you got lectured and lectured on what a fighting suit can do, back on Earth." The armorer was a small man, partially bald, with no insignia of rank on his coveralls. Sergeant Cortez told us to call him "sir," since he was a lieutenant.

"But I'd like to reinforce a couple of points, maybe add some things your instructors Earthside weren't clear about, or couldn't know. Your First Sergeant was kind enough to consent to being my visual aid. Sergeant?"

Cortez slipped out of his coveralls and came up to the little raised platform where a fighting suit was standing, popped open like a man-shaped clam. He backed into it and slipped his arms into the rigid sleeves. There was a click and the thing swung shut with a sigh. It was bright green with CORTEZ stenciled in white letters on the helmet.

"Camouflage, Sergeant." The green faded to white, then dirty gray. "This is good camouflage for Charon, and most of your portal planets," said Cortez, from a deep well. "But there are several other combinations available." The gray dappled and brightened to a combination of greens and browns: "Jungle." Then smoothed out to a hard light ochre: "Desert." Dark brown, darker, to a deep flat black: "Night or space."

"Very good, Sergeant. To my knowledge, this is the only feature of the suit which was perfected after your training. The control is around your left wrist and is admittedly awkward. But once you find the right combination, it's easy to lock in.

"Now, you didn't get much in-suit training Earthside because we didn't want you to get used to using the thing in a friendly environment. The fighting suit is the deadliest personal weapon ever built, and with no weapon is it easier for the user to kill himself through carelessness. Turn around, Sergeant.

"Case in point." He tapped a square protuberance between the shoulders. "Exhaust fins. As you know the suit tries to keep you at a comfortable temperature no matter what the weather's like outside. The material of the suit is as near to a perfect insulator as we could get, consistent with mechanical demands. Therefore, these fins get *hot*—especially hot, compared to darkside temperatures—as they bleed off the body's heat.

"All you have to do is lean up against a boulder of frozen gas; there's lots of it around. The gas will sublime off faster than it can escape from the fins; in escaping, it will push against the surrounding 'ice' and fracture it . . . and in about one hundredth of a second, you have the equivalent of a hand grenade going off right below your neck. You'll never feel a thing.

"Variations on this theme have killed eleven people in the past two months. And they were just building a bunch of huts.

"I assume you know how easily the waldo capabilities can kill you or your companions. Anybody want to shake hands with the sergeant?" He stepped over and clasped his glove. "He's had lots of practice. Until *you* have, be extremely careful. You might scratch an itch and wind up bleeding to death. Remember, semi-logarithmic response: two pounds' pressure exerts five pounds' force; three pounds gives ten; four pounds, twenty-three; five pounds, forty-seven. Most of you can muster up a grip of well over a hundred pounds. Theoretically, you could rip a steel girder in two with that, amplified. Actually, you'd destroy the material of your gloves and, at least on Charon, die very quickly. It'd be a race between decompression and flash-freezing. You'd be the loser.

"The leg waldos are also dangerous, even though the amplification is less extreme. Until you're really skilled, don't try to run, or jump. You're likely to trip, and that means you're likely to die.

"Charon's gravity is three-fourths of Earth normal, so it's not too bad. But on a really small world, like Luna, you could take a running jump and not come down for twenty minutes, just keep sailing over the horizon. Maybe bash into a mountain at eighty meters per second. On a small asteroid, it'd be no trick at all to run up to escape velocity and be off on an informal tour of intergalactic space. It's a slow way to travel.

"Tomorrow morning, we'll start teaching you how to stay alive inside of this infernal machine. The rest of the afternoon and evening, I'll call you one at a time to be fitted. That's all, Sergeant."

Cortez went to the door and turned the stopcock that let air into the air lock. A bank of infrared lamps went on to keep the air from freezing inside it. When the pressures were equalized, he shut the stopcock, unclamped the door and stepped in, clamping it shut behind him. A pump hummed for about a minute, evacuating the air lock, then he stepped out and sealed the outside door. It was pretty much like the ones on Luna.

"First I want Private Omar Almizar. The rest of you can go find your bunks. I'll call you over the squawker."

"Alphabetical order, sir?"

"Yep. About ten minutes apiece. If your name begins with Z, you might as well get sacked."

That was Rogers. She probably *was* thinking about getting sacked.

V

The sun was a hard white point directly overhead. It was a lot brighter than I had expected it to be; since we were eighty AUs out, it was only 1/6400th as bright as it is on Earth. Still, it was putting out about as much light as a powerful streetlamp.

"This is considerably more light than you'll have on a portal planet," Captain Stott's voice crackled in our collective ear. "Be glad that you'll be able to watch your step."

We were lined up, single file, on a permaplast sidewalk connecting the billet and the supply hut. We'd practiced walking inside, all morning, and this wasn't any different except for the exotic scenery. Though the light was rather dim, you could see all the way to the horizon quite clearly, with no atmosphere in the way. A black cliff that looked too regular to be natural stretched from one horizon to the other, passing within a kilometer of us. The ground was obsidian-black, mottled with patches of white, or bluish, ice. Next to the supply hut was a small mountain of snow in a bin marked OXYGEN.

The suit was fairly comfortable, but it gave you the odd feeling of being simultaneously a marionette and a puppeteer. You apply the impulse to move your leg and the suit picks it up and magnifies it and moves your leg for you.

"Today we're only going to walk around the company area and nobody will *leave* the company area." The captain wasn't wearing his .45, but he had a laser-finger like the rest of us. And his was probably hooked up.

Keeping an interval of at least two meters between each person, we stepped off the permaplast and followed the captain over the smooth rock. We walked carefully for about an hour, spiraling out, and finally stopped at the far edge of the perimeter.

"Now everybody pay close attention. I'm going out to that blue slab of ice"—it was a big one, about twenty meters away—"and show you something that you'd better know if you want to live."

He walked out a dozen confident steps. "First I have to heat up a rock—filters down." I slapped the stud under my armpit and the filter slid into place over my image converter. The captain pointed his finger at a black rock the size of a basketball and gave it a short burst. The glare rolled a long shadow of the captain over us and beyond. The rock shattered into a pile of hazy splinters.

"It doesn't take long for these to cool down." He stopped and picked up a piece. "This one is probably twenty or twenty-five degrees. Watch." He tossed the "warm" rock on the ice slab. It skittered around in a crazy pattern and shot off the side. He tossed another one, and it did the same.

"As you know you are not quite *perfectly* insulated. These rocks are about the temperature of the soles of your boots. If you try to stand on a slab of hydrogen the same thing will happen to you. Except that the rock is *already* dead.

"The reason for this behavior is that the rock makes a slick interface with the ice—a little puddle of liquid hydrogen—and rides a few molecules above the liquid on a cushion of hydrogen vapor. This makes the rock, or *you,* a frictionless bearing as far as the ice is concerned and you *can't* stand up without any friction under your boots.

"After you have lived in your suit for a month or so you *should* be able to survive falling down, but right *now* you just don't know enough. Watch.''

The captain flexed and hopped up onto the slab. His feet shot out from under him and he twisted around in midair, landing on hands and knees. He slipped off and stood on the ground.

''The idea is to keep your exhaust fins from making contact with the frozen gas. Compared to the ice they are as hot as a blast furnace and contact with any weight behind it will result in an explosion.''

After that demonstration, we walked around for another hour or so, and returned to the billet. Once through the air lock, we had to mill around for a while, letting the suits get up to something like room temperature. Somebody came up and touched helmets with me.

''William?'' She had MC COY stenciled above her faceplate.

''Hi, Sean. Anything special?''

''I just wondered if you had anyone to sleep with tonight.''

That's right; I'd forgotten, there wasn't any sleeping roster here. Everybody just chose his own partner. ''Sure, I mean, uh, no . . . no, I haven't asked anybody, sure, if you want to. . . .''

''Thanks, William. See you later.'' I watched her walk away and thought that if anybody could make a fighting suit look sexy, it'd be Sean. But even Sean couldn't.

Cortez decided we were warm enough and led us to the suit room where we backed the things into place and hooked them up to the charging plates—each suit had a little chunk of plutonium that would power it for several years, but we were supposed to run on fuel cells as much as possible. After a lot of shuffling around, everybody finally got plugged in and we were allowed to unsuit, ninety-seven naked chickens squirming out of bright green eggs. It was *cold*—the air, the floor, and especially the suits—and we made a pretty disorderly exit toward the lockers.

I slipped on tunic, trousers and sandals and was still cold. I took my cup and joined the line for soya, everybody jumping up and down to keep warm.

''How c-cold, do you think, it is, M-Mandella?'' That was McCoy.

''I don't, even want, to think, about it.'' I stopped jumping and rubbed myself as briskly as possible, while holding a cup in one hand. ''At least as cold as Missouri was.''

''Ung . . . wish they'd, get some damn heat in, this place.'' It always affects the small girls more than anybody else. McCoy was the littlest one in the company, a waspwaist doll barely five feet high.

"They've got the airco going. It can't be long now."

"I wish I, was a big, slab of, meat like, you."

I was glad she wasn't.

VI

We had our first casualty on the third day, learning how to dig holes.

With such large amounts of energy stored in a soldier's weapons, it wouldn't be practical for him to hack out a hole in the frozen ground with the conventional pick and shovel. Still, you can launch grenades all day and get nothing but shallow depressions—so the usual method is to bore a hole in the ground with the hand laser, drop a timed charge in after it's cooled down and, ideally, fill the hole with stuff. Of course, there's not much loose rock on Charon, unless you've already blown a hole nearby.

The only difficult thing about the procedure is getting away. To be safe, we were told, you've got to either be behind something really solid, or be at least a hundred meters away. You've got about three minutes after setting the charge, but you can't just spring away. Not on Charon.

The accident happened when we were making a really deep hole, the kind you want for a large underground bunker. For this, we had to blow a hole, then climb down to the bottom of the crater and repeat the procedure again and again until the hole was deep enough. Inside the crater we used charges with a five-minute delay, but it hardly seemed enough time—you really had to go slow, picking your way up the crater's edge.

Just about everybody had blown a double hole; everybody but me and three others. I guess we were the only ones paying really close attention when Bovanovitch got into trouble. All of us were a good two hundred meters away. With my image converter turned up to about forty power, I watched her disappear over the rim of the crater. After that I could only listen in on her conversation with Cortez.

"I'm on the bottom, Sergeant." Normal radio procedure was suspended for these maneuvers; only the trainee and Cortez could broadcast.

"O.K., move to the center and clear out the rubble. Take your time. No rush until you pull the pin."

"Sure, Sergeant." We could hear small echoes of rocks clattering; sound conduction through her boots. She didn't say anything for several minutes.

"Found bottom." She sounded a little out of breath.

"Ice, or rock?"

"Oh, it's rock, Sergeant. The greenish stuff."

"Use a low setting, then. One point two, dispersion four."

"God darn it, Sergeant, that'll take forever."

"Yeah, but that stuff's got hydrated crystals in it—heat it up too fast and you might make it fracture. And we'd just have to leave you there, girl."

"O.K., one point two dee four." The inside edge of the crater flickered red with reflected laser light.

"When you get about half a meter deep, squeeze it up to dee two."

"Roger." It took her exactly seventeen minutes, three of them at dispersion two. I could imagine how tired her shooting arm was.

"Now rest for a few minutes. When the bottom of the hole stops glowing, arm the charge and drop it in. Then *walk* out. Understand? You'll have plenty of time."

"I understand, Sergeant. Walk out." She sounded nervous. Well, you don't often have to tiptoe away from a twenty microton tachyon bomb. We listened to her breathing for a few minutes.

"Here goes." Faint slithering sound of the bomb sliding down.

"Slow and easy now, you've got five minutes."

"Y-yeah. Five." Her footsteps started out slow and regular. Then, after she started climbing the side, the sounds were less regular; maybe a little frantic. And with four minutes to go—

"Crap!" A loud scraping noise, then clatters and bumps.

"What's wrong, Private?"

"Oh, crap." Silence. "Crap!"

"Private, you don't wanna get shot, you *tell me what's wrong!*"

"I . . . I'm stuck, damn rockslide . . . DO SOMETHING I can't move. I can't move I, I—"

"Shut up! How deep?"

"Can't move my crap, my damn legs HELP ME—"

"Then damn it use your arms—push!—you can move a ton with each hand." Three minutes.

Then she stopped cussing and started to mumble, in Russian, I guess, a low monotone. She was panting and you could hear rocks tumbling away.

"I'm free." Two minutes.

"Go as fast as you can." Cortez's voice was flat, emotionless.

At ninety seconds she appeared crawling over the rim. "Run, girl . . . you better run." She ran five or six steps and fell, skidded a few meters and got back up, running; fell again, got up again—

It looked like she was going pretty fast, but she had only covered about thirty meters when Cortez said, "All right, Bovanovitch, get down on your stomach and lie still." Ten seconds, but she didn't hear him, or she wanted to get just a little more distance, and she kept running, careless leaping strides and at the high point of one leap there was a flash and a rumble and something big hit her below the neck and her headless body spun off end over end through space, trailing a red-black spiral of flash-frozen blood that settled gracefully to the ground, a path of crystal powder that nobody disturbed while we gathered rocks to cover the juiceless thing at the end of it.

That night Cortez didn't lecture us, didn't even show up for night-chop. We were all very polite to each other and nobody was afraid to talk about it.

I sacked with Rogers; everybody sacked with a good friend, but all she wanted to do was cry, and she cried so long and so hard that she got me doing it, too.

VII

"Fire team A—move out!" The twelve of us advanced in a ragged line toward the simulated bunker. It was about a kilometer away, across a carefully prepared obstacle course. We could move pretty fast, since all of the ice had been cleared from the field, but even with ten days' experience we weren't ready to do more than an easy jog.

I carried a grenade launcher, loaded with tenth-microton practice grenades. Everybody had their laser-fingers set at point oh eight dee one; not much more than a flashlight. This was a *simulated* attack—the bunker and its robot defender cost too much to be used once and thrown away.

"Team B follow. Team leaders, take over."

We approached a clump of boulders at about the halfway mark, and Potter, my team leader, said "Stop and cover." We clustered behind the rocks and waited for team B.

Barely visible in their blackened suits, the dozen men and women whispered by us. As soon as they were clear, they jogged left, out of our line of sight.

"Fire!" Red circles of light danced a half-click downrange, where the bunker was just visible. Five hundred meters was the limit for these practice grenades; but I might luck out, so I lined the launcher up on the image of the bunker, held it at a 45° angle and popped off a salvo of three.

Return fire from the bunker started before my grenades even landed. Its automatic lasers were no more powerful than the ones we were using, but a direct hit would deactivate your image converter, leaving you blind. It was setting down a random field of fire, not even coming close to the boulders we were hiding behind.

Three magnesium-bright flashes blinked simultaneously, about thirty meters short of the bunker. "Mandella! I thought you were supposed to be *good* with that thing."

"Damn it, Potter—it only throws half a click. Once we get closer, I'll lay 'em right on top, every time."

"*Sure* you will." I didn't say anything. She wouldn't be team leader forever. Besides, she hadn't been such a bad girl before the power went to her head.

Since the grenadeier is the assistant team leader, I was slaved into Potter's radio and could hear B team talk to her.

Potter's, this is Freeman, Losses?"

"Potter here—no, looks like they were concentrating on you."

"Yeah, we lost three. Right now we're in a depression about eighty, a hundred meters down from you. We can give cover whenever you're ready."

"O.K., start." Soft click: "A team follow me." She slid out from behind the rock and turned on the faint pink beacon beneath her powerpack. I turned on mine and moved out to run alongside of her and the rest of the team fanned out in a trailing wedge. Nobody fired while B team laid down a cover for us.

All I could hear was Potter's breathing and the soft *crunch-crunch* of my boots. Couldn't see much of anything, so I tongued the image converter up to a log two intensification. That made the image kind of blurry but adequately bright. Looked like the bunker had B team pretty well pinned down; they were getting quite a roasting. All of their return fire was laser; they must have lost their grenadier.

"Potter, this is Mandella. Shouldn't we take some of the heat off B team?"

"Soon as I can find us good enough cover. Is that all right with you? Private?" She'd been promoted to corporal for the duration of the exercise.

We angled to the right and laid down behind a slab of rock. Most of the others found cover nearby, but a few had to just hug the ground.

"Freeman, this is Potter."

"Potter, this is Smithy. Freeman's out; Samuels is out. We only have five men left. Give us some cover so we can get. . . ."

"Roger, Smithy."—*click*—"Open up, A team. The B's are really hurtin'."

I peeked out over the edge of the rock. My rangefinder said that the bunker was about three hundred fifty meters away, still pretty far. I aimed just a smidgeon high and popped three, then down a couple of degrees and three more. The first ones overshot by about twenty meters, then the second salvo flared up directly in front of the bunker. I tried to hold on that angle and popped fifteen, the rest of the magazine, in the same direction.

I should have ducked down behind the rock to reload, but I wanted to see where the fifteen would land, so I kept my eyes on the bunker while I reached back to unclip another magazine. . . .

When the laser hit my image converter there was a red glare so intense it seemed to go right through my eyes and bounce off the back of my skull. It must have been only a few milliseconds before the converter overloaded and went blind, but the bright green afterimage hurt my eyes for several minutes.

Since I was officially "dead," my radio automatically cut off and I had to remain where I was until the mock battle was over. With no sensory input besides the feel of my own skin—and it ached where the image converter had shone on it—and the ringing in my ears, it seemed like an awfully long time. Finally, a helmet clanked against mine.

"You O.K., Mandella?" Potter's voice.

"Sorry, I died of boredom twenty minutes ago."

"Stand up and take my hand." I did so and we shuffled back to the billet. It must have taken over an hour. She didn't say anything more, all the way back—it's a pretty awkward way to communicate—but after we'd cycled through the air lock and warmed up, she helped me undo my suit. I got ready for a mild tongue-lashing, but when the suit popped open, before I could even get my eyes adjusted to the light, she grabbed me around the neck and planted a wet kiss on my mouth.

"Nice shooting, Mandella."

"Huh?"

"The last salvo before you got hit—four direct hits; the bunker decided it was knocked out, and all we had to do was walk the rest of the way."

"Great." I scratched my face under the eyes and some dry skin flaked off. She giggled.

"You should see yourself, you look like. . . ."

"All personnel report to the assembly area." That was the captain's voice. Bad news.

She handed me a tunic and sandals. "Let's go."

The assembly area/chop hall was just down the corridor. There was a row of roll-call buttons at the door; I pressed the one beside my name. Four of the names were covered with black tape. That was good, we hadn't lost anybody else during today's maneuvers.

The captain was sitting on the raised dais, which at least meant we didn't have to go through the tench-hut bullshit. The place filled up in less than a minute; a soft chime indicated the roll was complete.

Captain Stott didn't stand up. "You did *fairly* well today, nobody got killed and I expected some to. In that respect you exceeded my expectations but in *every* other respect you did a poor job.

"I am glad you're taking care of yourself because each of you represents an investment of over a million dollars and one fourth of a human life.

"But in this simulated battle against a *very* stupid robot enemy, thirty-seven of you managed to walk into laser fire and be killed in a *sim*ulated way and since dead people require no food *you* will require no food, for the next three days. Each person who was a casualty in this battle will be allowed only two liters of water and a vitamin ration each day."

We knew enough not to groan or anything, but there were some pretty disgusted looks, especially on the faces that had singed eyebrows and a pink rectangle of sunburn framing their eyes.

"Mandella."

"Sir?"

"You are far and away the worst burned casualty. Was your image converter set on normal?"

Oh, crap. "No, sir. Log two."

"I see. Who was your team leader for the exercise?"

"Acting Corporal Potter, sir."

"Private Potter, did you order him to use image intensification?"

"Sir, I . . . I don't remember."

"You don't. Well as a memory exercise you may join the dead people. Is that satisfactory?"

"Yes, sir."

"Good. Dead people get one last meal tonight, and go on no rations starting tomorrow. Are there any questions?" He must have been kidding. "All right. Dismissed."

I selected the meal that looked as if it had the most calories and took my tray over to sit by Potter.

"That was a quixotic damn thing to do. But thanks."

"Nothing. I've been wanting to lose a few pounds anyway." I couldn't see where she was carrying any extra.

"I know a good exercise," I said. She smiled without looking up from her tray. "Have anybody for tonight?"

"Kind of thought I'd ask Jeff. . . ."

"Better hurry, then. He's lusting after Uhuru." Well, that was mostly true. Everybody did.

"I don't know. Maybe we ought to save our strength. That third day. . . ."

"Come on," I scratched the back of her hand lightly with a fingernail. "We haven't sacked since Missouri. Maybe I've learned something new."

"Maybe you have." She tilted her head up at me in a sly way. "O.K."

Actually, she was the one with the new trick. The French corkscrew, she called it. She wouldn't tell me who taught it to her, though. I'd like to shake his hand.

VIII

The two weeks' training around Miami Base eventually cost us eleven lives. Twelve, if you count Dahlquist. I guess having to spend the rest of your life on Charon, with a hand and both legs missing, is close enough to dying.

Little Foster was crushed in a landslide and Freeland had a suit malfunction that froze him solid before we could carry him inside.

Most of the other deaders were people I didn't know all that well. But they all hurt. And they seemed to make us more scared rather than more cautious.

Now darkside. A flier brought us over in groups of twenty, and set us down beside a pile of building materials, thoughtfully immersed in a pool of helium II.

We used grapples to haul the stuff out of the pool. It's not safe to go wading, since the stuff crawls all over you and it's hard to tell what's underneath; you could walk out onto a slab of hydrogen and be out of luck.

I'd suggested that we try to boil away the pool with our lasers, but ten minutes of concentrated fire didn't drop the helium level appreciably. It didn't boil, either; helium II is a "superfluid," so what evaporation there was had to take place evenly, all over the surface. No hot spots, so no bubbling.

We weren't supposed to use lights, to "avoid detection." There was plenty of starlight, with your image converter cranked up to log three or four, but each stage of amplification meant some loss of detail. By log four, the landscape looked like a crude monochrome painting, and you couldn't read the names on people's helmets unless they were right in front of you.

The landscape wasn't all that interesting, anyhow. There were half a dozen medium-sized meteor craters—all with exactly the same level of helium II in them—and the suggestion of some puny mountains just over the horizon. The uneven ground was the consistency of frozen spiderwebs; every time you put your foot down, you'd sink half an inch with a squeaking crunch. It could get on your nerves.

It took most of a day to pull all the stuff out of the pool. We took shifts napping, which you could do either standing up, sitting, or lying on your stomach. I didn't do well in any of those positions, so I was anxious to get the bunker built and pressurized.

We couldn't build the thing underground—it'd just fill up with helium II—so the first thing to do was to build an insulating platform, a permaplast-vacuum sandwich three layers tall.

I was an acting corporal, with a crew of ten people. We were carrying the permaplast layers to the building site—two people can carry one easily—when one of "my" men slipped and fell on his back.

"Damn it, Singer, watch your step." We'd had a couple of deaders that way.

"Sorry, Corporal. I'm bushed, just got my feet tangled up."

"Yeah, just watch it." He got back up all right, and with his partner placed the sheet and went back to get another.

I kept my eye on him. In a few minutes he was practically staggering, not easy to do with that suit of cybernetic armor.

"Singer! After you set that plank, I want to see you."

"O.K." He labored through the task and mooched over.

"Let me check your readout." I opened the door on his chest to expose the medical monitor. His temperature was two degrees high; blood pressure and heart rate both elevated. Not up to the red line, though.

"You sick or something?"

"Hell, Mandella, I feel O.K., just tired. Since I fell I've been a little dizzy."

I chinned the medic's combination. "Doc, this is Mandella. You wanna come over here for a minute?"

"Sure, where are you?" I waved and he walked over from poolside.

"What's the problem?" I showed him Singer's readout.

He knew what all the other little dials and things meant, so it took him a while. "As far as I can tell, Mandella . . . he's just hot."

"Hell, I coulda told you that," said Singer.

"Maybe you better have the armorer take a look at his suit." We had two people who'd taken a crash course in suit maintenance; they were our "armourers."

I chinned Sanchez and asked him to come over with his tool kit.

"Be a couple of minutes, Corporal. Carryin' a plank."

"Well, put it down and get on over here." I was getting an uneasy feeling. Waiting for him, the medic and I looked over Singer's suit.

"Uh-oh," Doc Jones said. "Look at this." I went around to the back and looked where he was pointing. Two of the fins on the heat exchanger were bent out of shape.

"What is wrong?" Singer asked.

"You fell on your heat exchanger, right?"

"Sure, Corporal—that's it, it must not be working right."

"I don't think it's working at *all*," said Doc.

Sanchez came over with his diagnostic kit and we told him what had happened. He looked at the heat exchanger, then plugged a couple of jacks into it and got a digital readout from a little monitor in his kit. I didn't know what it was measuring, but it came out zero to eight decimal places.

Heard a soft click, Sanchez chinning my private frequency. "Corporal, this guy's a deader."

"What? Can't you fix the damn thing?"

"Maybe . . . maybe I could, if I could take it apart. But there's no way. . . ."

"Hey! Sanchez?" Singer was talking on the general freak. "Find out what's wrong?" He was panting.

Click. "Keep your pants on, man, we're working on it." *Click.* "He won't last long enough for us to get the bunker pressurized. And I can't work on the heat exchanger from outside of the suit."

"You've got a spare suit, haven't you?"

"Two of 'em, the fit-anybody kind. But there's no place . . . say. . . ."

"Right. Go get one of the suits warmed up." I chinned the general freak. "Listen, Singer, we've gotta get you out of that thing. Sanchez has a spare unit, but to make the switch, we're gonna have to build a house around you. Understand?"

"Huh-uh."

"Look, we'll just make a box with you inside, and hook it up to the life-support unit. That way you can breathe while you make the switch."

"Soun's pretty compis . . . complicated t'me."

"Look, just come along. . . ."

"I'll be all right, man, jus' lemme res'. . . ."

I grabbed his arm and led him to the building site. He was really weaving. Doc took his other arm and between us, we kept him from falling over.

"Corporal Ho, this is Corporal Mandella." Ho was in charge of the life-support unit.

"Go away, Mandella, I'm busy."

"You're going to be busier." I outlined the problem to her. While her group hurried to adapt the LSU—for this purpose, it need only be an air hose and heater—I got my crew to bring around six slabs of permaplast, so we could build a big box around Singer and the extra suit. It would look like a huge coffin, a meter square and six meters long.

We set the suit down on the slab that would be the floor of the coffin. "O.K., Singer, let's go."

No answer.

"Singer!" He was just standing there. Doc Jones checked his readout.

"He's out, man, unconscious."

My mind raced. There might just be room for another person in the box. "Give me a hand here." I took Singer's shoulders and Doc took his feet, and we carefully laid him out at the feet of the empty suit.

Then I laid down myself, above the suit. "O.K., close 'er up."

"Look, Mandella, if anybody goes in there, it oughta be me."

"No, Doc. *My* job. My man." That sounded all wrong. William Mandella, boy hero.

They stood a slab up on edge—it had two openings for the LSU input and exhaust—and proceeded to weld it to the bottom plank with a narrow laser beam. On Earth, we'd just use glue, but here the only fluid was helium, which has lots of interesting properties, but is definitely not sticky.

After about ten minutes we were completely walled up. I could feel the LSU humming. I switched on my suit light—the first time since we landed on darkside—and the glare made purple blotches dance in front of my eyes.

"Mandella, this is Ho. Stay in your suit at least two or three minutes. We're putting hot air in, but it's coming back just this side of liquid." I lay and watched the purple fade.

"O.K., it's still cold, but you can make it." I popped my suit. It wouldn't open all the way, but I didn't have too much trouble getting out. The suit was still cold enough to take some skin off my fingers and butt as I wiggled out.

I had to crawl feet-first down the coffin to get to Singer. It got darker fast, moving away from my light. When I popped his suit a rush of hot stink hit me in the face. In the dim light his skin was dark red and splotchy. His breathing was very shallow and I could see his heart palpitating.

First, I unhooked the relief tubes—an unpleasant business—then the bio sensors, and then I had the problem of getting his arms out of their sleeves

It's pretty easy to do for yourself. You twist this way and turn that way and the arm pops out. Doing it from the outside is a different matter: I had to twist his arm and then reach under and move the suit's arm to match—and it takes muscle to move a suit around from the outside.

Once I had one arm out it was pretty easy: I just crawled forward, putting my feet on the suit's shoulders, and pulled on his free arm. He slid out of the suit like an oyster slipping out of its shell.

I popped the spare suit and after a lot of pulling and pushing, managed to get his legs in. Hooked up the bio sensors and the front relief tube. He'd have to do the other one himself, it's too complicated. For the nth time I was glad not to have been born female; they have to have two of those damned plumber's friends, instead of just one and a simple hose.

I left his arms out of the sleeves. The suit would be useless for any kind of work, anyhow; waldos have to be tailored to the individual.

His eyelids fluttered. "Man . . . della. Where . . . the hell. . . ."

I explained, slowly, and he seemed to get most of it. "Now I'm gonna close you up and go get into my suit. I'll have the crew cut the end off this thing and I'll haul you out. Got it?"

He nodded. Strange to see that—when you nod or shrug in a suit, it doesn't communicate anything.

I crawled into my suit, hooked up the attachments and chinned the general freak. "Doc, I think he's gonna be O.K. Get us out of here now."

"Will do." Ho's voice. The LSU hum was replaced by a chatter, then a throb; evacuating the box to prevent an explosion.

One corner of the seam grew red, then white and a bright crimson beam lanced through, not a foot away from my head. I scrunched back as far as I could. The beam slid up the seam and around three corners, back to where it started. The end of the box fell away slowly, trailing filaments of melted 'plast.

"Wait for the stuff to harden, Mandella."

"Sanchez, I'm not that stupid."

"Here you go." Somebody tossed a line to me. That *would* be smarter than dragging him out by myself. I threaded a long bight under his arms and tied it behind his neck. Then I scrambled out to help them pull, which was silly—they had a dozen people already lined up to haul.

Singer got out all right and was actually sitting up while Doc Jones checked his readout. People were asking me about it and congratulating me when suddenly Ho said "Look!" and pointed toward the horizon.

It was a black ship, coming in fast. I just had time to think it wasn't fair, they weren't supposed to attack until the last few days, and then the ship was right on top of us.

IX

We all flopped to the ground instinctively, but the ship didn't attack. It blasted braking rockets and dropped to land on skids. Then it skied around to come to a rest beside the building site.

Everybody had it figured out and was standing around sheepishly when the two suited figures stepped out of the ship.

A familiar voice crackled over the general freak. "Every *one* of you saw us coming in and not *one* of you responded with laser fire. It wouldn't have done any good but it would have indicated a certain amount of fighting spirit. You have a week or less before the real thing and since the sergeant and *I* will be here *I* will insist that you show a little more will to live. Acting Sergeant Potter."

"Here, sir."

"Get me a detail of twelve men to unload cargo. We brought a hundred small robot drones for *target* practice so that you might have at least a fighting chance, when a live target comes over.

"Move *now;* we only have thirty minutes before the ship returns to Miami."

I checked, and it was actually more like forty minutes.

Having the captain and sergeant there didn't really make much difference; we were still on our own, they were just observing.

Once we got the floor down, it only took one day to complete the bunker. It was a gray oblong, featureless except for the air-lock blister and four windows. On top was a swivel-mounted bevawatt laser. The operator—you couldn't call him a "gunner"—sat in a chair holding dead-man switches in both hands. The laser wouldn't fire as long as he was holding one of those switches. If he let go, it would automatically aim for any moving aerial object and fire at will. Primary detection and aiming was by means of a kilometer-high antenna mounted beside the bunker.

It was the only arrangement that could really be expected to work, with the horizon so close and the human reflexes so slow. You couldn't have the thing fully automatic, because in theory, friendly ships might also approach.

The aiming computer could choose up to twelve targets, appearing simultaneously—firing at the largest ones first. And it would get all twelve in the space of half a second.

The installation was partly protected from enemy fire by an efficient ablative layer that covered everything except the human operator. But then they *were* dead-man switches. One man above guarding eighty inside. The army's good at that kind of arithmetic.

Once the bunker was finished, half of us stayed inside at all times—feeling very much like targets—taking turns operating the laser, while the other half went on maneuvers.

About four clicks from the base was a large "lake" of frozen hydrogen; one of our most important maneuvers was to learn how to get around on the treacherous stuff.

It really wasn't too difficult. You couldn't stand up on it, so you had to belly down and slide.

If you had somebody to push you from the edge, getting started was no problem. Otherwise, you had to scrabble with your hands and feet, pushing down as hard as was practical, until you started moving, in a series of little jumps. Once started, you would keep going until you ran out of ice. You could steer a little bit by digging in, hand and foot, on the appropriate side, but you couldn't slow to a stop that way. So it was a good idea not to go too fast, and to be positioned in such a way that your helmet didn't absorb the shock of stopping.

We went through all the things we'd done on the Miami side; weapons practice, demolition, attack patterns. We also launched drones at irregular intervals, toward the bunker. Thus, ten or fifteen times a day, the operators got to demonstrate their skill in letting go of the handles as soon as the proximity light went on.

I had four hours of that, like everybody else. I was nervous until the first "attack," when I saw how little there was to it. The light went on, I let go, the gun aimed and when the drone peeped over the horizon—*zzt!* Nice touch of color, the molten metal spraying through space. Otherwise not too exciting.

So none of us were worried about the upcoming "graduation exercise," thinking it would be just more of the same.

Miami Base attacked on the thirteenth day with two simultaneous missiles streaking over opposite sides of the horizon at some forty kilometers per second. The laser vaporized the first one with no trouble, but the second got within eight clicks of the bunker before it was hit.

We were coming back from maneuvers, about a click away from the bunker. I wouldn't have seen it happen if I hadn't been looking directly at the bunker the moment of the attack.

The second missile sent a shower of molten debris straight toward the bunker. Eleven pieces hit, and, as we later reconstructed it, this is what happened.

The first casualty was Uhuru, pretty Uhuru inside the bunker, who was hit in the back and head and died instantly. With the drop in pressure, the LSU went into high gear. Friedman was standing in front of the main airco outlet and was blown into the opposite wall hard enough to knock him unconscious; he died of decompression before the others could get him to his suit.

Everybody else managed to stagger through the gale and get into their suits, but Garcia's suit had been holed and didn't do him any good.

By the time we got there, they had turned off the LSU and were welding up the holes in the wall. One man was trying to scrape up the unrecognizable mess that had been Uhuru. I could hear him sobbing and retching. They had already taken Garcia and Friedman outside for burial. The captain took over the repair detail from Potter. Sergeant Cortez led the sobbing man over to a corner and came back to work on cleaning up Uhuru's remains, alone. He didn't order anybody to help and nobody volunteered.

X

As a graduation exercise, we were unceremoniously stuffed into a ship—*Earth's Hope,* the same one we rode to Charon—and bundled off to Stargate at a little more than 1 G.

The trip seemed endless, about six months subjective time, and boring, but not as hard on the carcass as going to Charon had been. Captain Stott made us review our training orally, day by day, and we did exercises every day until we were worn to a collective frazzle.

Stargate I was like Charon's darkside, only more so. The base on Stargate I was smaller than Miami Base—only a little bigger than the one we constructed on darkside—and we were due to lay over a week to help expand the facilities. The crew there was very glad to see us; especially the two females, who looked a little worn around the edges.

We all crowded into the small dining hall, where Submajor Williamson, the man in charge of Stardust I, gave us some disconcerting news:

"Everybody get comfortable. Get off the tables, though, there's plenty of floor.

"I have some idea of what you just went through, training on Charon. I won't say it's all been wasted. But where you're headed, things will be quite different. Warmer."

He paused to let that soak in.

"Aleph Aurigae, the first collapsar ever detected, revolves around the normal star Epsilon Aurigae, in a twenty-seven-year orbit. The enemy has a base of operations, not on a regular portal planet of Aleph, but on a planet in orbit around Epsilon. We don't know much about the planet: just that it goes around Epsilon once ever seven hundred forty-five days, is about three fourths the size of Earth, and has an albedo of 0.8, meaning it's probably covered with clouds. We can't say precisely how hot it will be, but judging from its distance from Epsilon, it's probably rather hotter than Earth. Of course, we don't know whether you'll be working . . . fighting on lightside or darkside, equator or poles. It's highly unlikely that the atmosphere will be breathable—at any rate, you'll stay inside your suits.

"Now you know exactly as much about where you're going as I do. Questions?"

"Sir," Stein drawled, "now we know where we're goin' . . . anybody know what we're goin' to do when we get there?"

Williamson shrugged. "That's up to your captain—and your sergeant, and the captain of *Earth's Hope,* and *Hope*'s logistic computer. We just don't have enough data yet, to project a course of action for you. It may be a long and bloody battle, it may be just a case of walking in to pick up the pieces. Conceivably, the Taurans might want to make a peace offer"—Cortez snorted— "in which case you would simply be part of our muscle, our bargaining power." He looked at Cortez mildly. "No one can say for sure."

The orgy that night was kind of amusing, but it was like trying to sleep in the middle of a raucous beach party. The only area big enough to sleep all of us was the dining hall; they draped a few bedsheets here and there for privacy, then unleashed Stargate's eighteen sex-starved men on our women, compliant and promiscuous by military custom—and law—but desiring nothing so much as sleep on solid ground.

The eighteen men acted as if they were compelled to try as many permutations as possible, and their performance was impressive—in a strictly quantitative sense, that is.

The next morning—and every other morning we were on

Stargate I—we staggered out of bed and into our suits, to go outside and work on the "new wing." Eventually, Stargate would be tactical and logistic headquarters for the war, with thousands of permanent personnel, guarded by half-a-dozen heavy cruisers in *Hope*'s class. When we started, it was two shacks and twenty people; when we left, it was four shacks and twenty people. The work was a breeze, compared to darkside, since we had all the light we needed, and got sixteen hours inside for every eight hours' work. And no drone attacks for a final exam.

When we shuttled back up to the *Hope,* nobody was too happy about leaving—though some of the more popular females declared it'd be good to get some rest—Stargate was the last easy, safe assignment we'd have before taking up arms against the Taurans. And as Williamson had pointed out the first day, there was no way of predicting what that would be like.

Most of us didn't feel too enthusiastic about making a collapsar jump, either. We'd been assured that we wouldn't even feel it happen, just free fall all the way.

I wasn't convinced. As a physics student, I'd had the usual courses in general relativity and theories of gravitation. We only had a little direct data at that time—Stargate was discovered when I was in grade school—but the mathematical model seemed clear enough.

The collapsar Stargate was a perfect sphere about three kilometers in radius. It was suspended forever in a state of gravitational collapse that should have meant its surface was dropping toward its center at nearly the speed of light. Relativity propped it up, at least gave it the illusion of being there . . . the way all reality becomes illusory and observer-oriented when you study general relativity, or Buddhism.

At any rate, there would be a theoretical point in spacetime when one end of our ship was just above the surface of the collapsar, and the other end was a kilometer away—in our frame of reference. In any sane universe, this would set up tidal stresses and tear the ship apart, and we would be just another million kilograms of degenerate matter on the theoretical surface, rushing headlong to nowhere for the rest of eternity; or dropping to the center in the next trillionth of a second. You pays your money and you takes your frame of reference.

But they were right. We blasted away from Stargate I, made a few course corrections and then just dropped, for about an hour.

Then a bell rang and we sank into our cushions under a steady two gravities of deceleration. We were in enemy territory.

XI

We'd been decelerating at two gravities for almost nine days when the battle began. Lying on our couches being miserable, all we felt were two soft bumps, missiles being released. Some eight hours later, the squawkbox crackled: "Attention, all crew. This is the captain." Quinsana, the pilot, was only a lieutenant, but was allowed to call himself captain aboard the vessel, where he outranked all of us, even Captain Stott. "You grunts in the cargo hold can listen, too.

"We just engaged the enemy with two fifty-bevaton tachyon missiles, and have destroyed both the enemy vessel and another object which it had launched approximately three microseconds before.

"The enemy has been trying to overtake us for the past one hundred seventy-nine hours, ship time. At the time of the engagement, the enemy was moving at a little over half the speed of light, relative to Aleph, and was only about thirty AU's from *Earth's Hope*. It was moving at .47c relative to us, and thus we would have been coincident in spacetime"—rammed!—"in a little more than nine hours. The missiles were launched at 0719 ship's time, and destroyed the enemy at 1540, both tachyon bombs detonating within a thousand clicks of the enemy objects."

The two missiles were a type whose propulsion system itself was only a barely-controlled tachyon bomb. They accelerated at a constant rate of 100 Gs, and were traveling at a relativistic speed by the time the nearby mass of the enemy ship detonated them.

"We expect no further interference from enemy vessels. Our velocity with respect to Aleph will be zero in another five hours; we will then begin to journey back. The return will take twenty-seven days." General moans and dejected cussing. Everybody knew all that already, of course; but we didn't care to be reminded of it.

So after another month of logycalisthenics and drill, at a constant 2 Gs, we got our first look at the planet we were going to attack. Invaders from outer space, yes, sir.

It was a blinding white crescent basking two AU's from Epsilon. The captain had pinned down the location of the enemy base from fifty AU's out, and we had jockeyed in on a wide arc, keeping the bulk of the planet between them and us. That didn't mean we were sneaking up on them—quite the contrary; they launched three abortive attacks—but it puts us in a stronger defensive position. Until we had to go to the surface, that is. Then only the ship and its Star Fleet crew would be reasonably safe.

Since the planet rotated rather slowly—once every ten and one half days—a "stationary" orbit for the ship had to be one hundred fifty thousand clicks out. This made the people in the ship feel quite secure, with six thousand miles of rock and ninety thousand miles of space between them and the enemy. But it meant a whole second's time lag in communication between us on the ground and the ship's battle computer. A person could get awful dead while that neutrino pulse crawled up and back.

Our vague orders were to attack the base and gain control while damaging a minimum of enemy equipment. We were to take at least one enemy alive. We were under no circumstances to allow *ourselves* to be taken alive, however. And the decision wasn't up to us; one special pulse from the battle computer, and that speck of plutonium in your power planet would fission with all of .01% efficiency, and you'd be nothing but a rapidly expanding, very hot plasma.

They strapped us into six scoutships—one platoon of twelve people in each—and we blasted away from *Earth's Hope* at 8 Gs. Each scoutship was supposed to follow its own carefully random path to our rendezvous point, one hundred eight clicks from the base. Fourteen drone ships were launched at the same time, to confound the enemy's anti-spacecraft system.

The landing went off almost perfectly. One ship suffered minor damage, a near miss boiling away some of the ablative material on one side of the hull, but it'd still be able to make it and return, as long as it kept its speed down while in the atmosphere.

We zigged and zagged and wound up first ship at the rendezvous point. There was only one trouble. It was under four kilometers of water.

I could almost hear that machine, ninety thousand miles away, grinding its mental gears, adding his new bit of data. We proceeded just as if we were landing on solid ground: braking rockets, falling, skids out, hit the water, skip, hit the water, skip, hit the water, sink.

It would have made sense to go ahead and land on the bottom—we were streamlined, after all, and water just another fluid—but the hull wasn't strong enough to hold up a four-kilometer column of water. Sergeant Cortez was in the scoutship with us.

"Sarge, tell that computer to *do* something! We're gonna get. . . ."

"Oh, shut up, Mandella. Trust in th' lord." "Lord" was definitely lower-case when Cortez said it.

There was a loud bubbly sigh, then another and a slight increase in pressure on my back that meant the ship was rising. "Flotation bags?" Cortez didn't deign to answer, or didn't know.

That must have been it. We rose to within ten or fifteen meters of the surface and stopped, suspended there. Through the port I could see the surface above, shimmering like a mirror of hammered silver. I wondered what it could be like, to be a fish and have a definite roof over your world.

I watched another ship splash in. It made a great cloud of bubbles and turbulence, then fell—slightly tailfirst—for a short distance before large bags popped out under each delta wing. Then it bobbed up to about our level and stayed.

Soon all the ships were floating within a few hundred meters of us, like a school of ungainly fish.

"This is Captain Stott. Now listen carefully. There is a beach some twenty-eight clicks from your present position, in the direction of the enemy. You will be proceeding to this beach by scoutship and from there will mount your assault on the Tauran position." That was *some* improvement; we'd only have to walk eight clicks.

We deflated the bags, blasted to the surface and flew in a slow, spread-out formation to the beach. It took several minutes. As the ship scraped to a halt I could hear pumps humming, making the cabin pressure equal to the air pressure outside. Before it had quite stopped moving, the escape slot beside my couch slid open. I rolled out onto the wing of the craft and jumped to the ground. Ten seconds to find cover—I sprinted across loose gravel to the "treeline," a twisty bramble of tall sparse bluish-green shrubs. I dove into the briar path and turned to watch the ships leave. The drones that were left rose slowly to about a hundred meters, then took off in all directions with a bone-jarring roar. The real scoutships slid slowly back into the water. Maybe that was a good idea.

It wasn't a terribly attractive world, but certainly would be easier to get around in than the cryogenic nightmare we were trained for. The sky was a uniform dull silver brightness that merged with the mist over the ocean so completely as to make it impossible to tell where water ended and air began. Small wavelets licked at the black gravel shore, much too slow and graceful in the three-quarters Earth normal gravity. Even from fifty meters away, the rattle of billions of pebbles rolling with the tide was loud in my ears.

The air temperature was 79° Centigrade, not quite hot enough for the sea to boil, even though the air pressure was low compared to Earth's. Wisps of steam drifted quickly upward from the line where water met land. I wondered how long a man would survive, exposed here without a suit. Would the heat or the low oxygen—partial pressure one-eighth Earth normal—kill him first? Or was there some deadly microorganism that would beat them both. . . .

"This is Cortez. Everybody come over and assemble by me." He was standing on the beach a little to the left of me, waving his hand in a circle over his head. I walked toward him through the shrubs. They were brittle, unsubstantial, seemed paradoxically dried-out in the steamy air. They wouldn't offer much in a way of cover.

"We'll be advancing on a heading .05 radians east of north. I want Platoon One to take point. Two and Three follow about twenty meters behind, to the left and right. Seven, command platoon, is in the middle, twenty meters behind Two and Three. Five and Six, bring up the rear, in a semicircular closed flank. Everybody straight?" Sure, we could do that "arrowhead" maneuver in our sleep. "O.K., let's move out."

I was in Platoon Seven, the "command group." Captain Stott put me there not because I was expected to give any commands, but because of my training in physics.

The command group was supposedly the safest place, buffered by six platoons: people were assigned to it because there was some tactical reason for them to survive at least a little longer than the rest. Cortez was there to give orders. Chavez was there to correct suit malfuncts. The senior medic, Doc Wilson—the only medic who actually had an MD—was there and so was Theodopolis, the radio engineer: our link with the captain, who had elected to stay in orbit.

The rest of us were assigned to the company group by dint of special training or aptitude that wouldn't normally be considered of a "tactical" nature. Facing a totally unknown enemy, there was no way of telling what might prove important. Thus I was there because I was the closest the company had to a physicist. Rogers was biology. Tate was chemistry. He could crank out a perfect score on the Rhine extrasensory perception test, every time. Bohrs was a polyglot, able to speak twenty-one languages fluently, idiomatically. Petrov's talent was that he had tested out to have not one molecule of xenophobia in his psyche. Keating was a skilled acrobat. Debby Hollister—"Lucky" Hollister—showed a remarkable aptitude for making money, and also had a consistency high Rhine potential.

XII

When we first set out, we were using the "jungle" camouflage combination on our suits. But what passed for jungle in these anemic tropics was too sparse; we looked like a band of conspicuous harlequins trooping through the woods. Cortez had us switch to black, but that was just as bad, as the light from Epsilon came evenly from all parts of the sky, and there were no shadows except us. We finally settled on the dun-colored desert camouflage.

The nature of the countryside changed slowly as we walked north, away from the sea. The throned stalks, I guess you could call them trees, came in fewer numbers but were bigger around and less brittle; at the base of each was a tangled mass of vine with the same blue-green color, which spread out in a flattened cone some ten meters in diameter. There was a delicate green flower the size of a man's head near the top of each tree.

Grass began to appear some five clicks from the sea. It seemed to respect the trees' "property rights," leaving a strip of bare earth around each cone of vine. At the edge of such a clearing, it would grow as timid blue-green stubble; then, moving away from the tree, would get thicker and taller until it reached shoulder-high in some places, where the separation between two trees was unusually large. The grass was a lighter, greener shade than the trees and vines. We changed the color of our suits to the bright green we had used for maximum visibility on Charon. Keeping to the thickest part of the grass, we were fairly inconspicuous.

I couldn't help thinking that one week of training in a South American jungle would have been worth a hell of a lot more than all those weeks on Charon. We wouldn't be so understrength, either.

We covered over twenty clicks each day, buoyant after months under 2 Gs. Until the second day, the only form of animal life we saw was a kind of black worm, finger-sized with hundreds of cilium legs like the bristles of a stiff brush. Rogers said that there obviously had to be some sort of larger creature around, or there would be no reason for the trees to have thorns. So we were doubly on guard, expecting trouble both from the Taurans and the unidentified "large creatures."

Potter's Second Platoon was on point; the general freak was reserved for her, since point would likely be the first platoon to spot any trouble.

"Sarge, this is Potter," we all heard. "Movement ahead."

"Get down then!"

"We are. Don't think they see us."

"First Platoon, go up to the right of point. Keep down. Fourth, get up to the left. Tell me when you get in position. Sixth Platoon, stay back and guard the rear. Fifth and Third, close with the command group."

Two dozen people whispered out of the grass, to join us. Cortez must have heard from the Fourth Platoon.

"Good. How about you, First . . . O.K., fine. How many are there?"

"Eight we can see." Potter's voice.

"Good. When I give the word, open fire. Shoot to kill."

"Sarge . . . they're just animals."

"Potter—if you've known all this time what a Tauran looks like, you should've told us. Shoot to kill."

"But we need. . . ."

"We need a prisoner, but we don't need to escort him forty clicks to his home base and keep an eye on him while we fight. Clear?"

"Yes. Sergeant."

"O.K. Seventh, all you brains and weirds, we're going up and watch. Fifth and Third, come along to guard."

We crawled through the meter-high grass to where the Second Platoon had stretched out in a firing line.

"I don't see anything," Cortez said.

"Ahead and just to the left. Dark green."

They were only a shade darker than the grass. But after you saw the first one, you could see them all, moving slowly around some thirty meters ahead.

"Fire!" Cortez fired first, then twelve streaks of crimson leaped out and the grass wilted back, disappeared and the creatures convulsed and died trying to scatter.

"Hold fire, hold it!" Cortez stood up. "We want to have something left—Second Platoon, follow me." He strode out toward the smoldering corpses, laser finger pointed out front, obscene divining rod pulling him toward the carnage . . . I felt my gorge rising and knew that all the lurid training tapes, all the horrible deaths in training accidents, hadn't prepared me for this sudden reality . . . that I had a magic wand that I could point at a life and make it a smoking piece of half-raw meat; I wasn't a soldier nor even wanted to be one nor ever would want. . . .

"O.K., Seventh, come on up."

While we were walking toward them, one of the creatures moved, a tiny shudder, and Cortez flicked the beam of his laser over it with an almost negligent gesture. It made a hand-deep gash across the creature's middle. It died, like the others, without emitting a sound.

They were not quite as tall as humans, but wider in girth. They were covered with dark green, almost black fur; white curls where the laser had singed. They appeared to have three legs and an arm. The only ornament to their shaggy heads was a mouth, wet black orifice filled with flat black teeth. They were thoroughly repulsive but their worst feature was not a difference from human beings but a similarity . . . wherever the laser had opened a body cavity, milk-white glistening veined globes and coils of organs spilled out, and their blood was dark clotting red.

"Rogers, take a look. Taurans or not?"

Rogers knelt by one of the disemboweled creatures and opened a flat plastic box, filled with glistening dissecting tools. She selected a scalpel. "One way we might be able to find out." Doc Wilson watched over her shoulder as she methodically slit the membrane covering several organs.

"Here." She held up a blackish fibrous mass between two fingers, a parody of daintiness through all that armor.

"So?"

"It's grass, Sergeant. If the Taurans can eat grass and breathe the air, they certainly found a planet remarkably like their home." She tossed it away. "They're animals, Sergeant, just damn animals."

"I don't know," Doc Wilson said. "Just because they walk around on all fours, threes maybe, and are able to eat grass. . . ."

"Well, let's check out the brain." She found one that had been hit on the head and scraped the superficial black char from the wound. "Look at that."

It was almost solid bone. She tugged and ruffled the hair all over the head of another one. "What the hell does it use for sensory organs? No eyes, or ears, or. . . ." She stood up. "Nothing in that head but a mouth and ten centimeters of skull. To protect nothing, not a damn thing."

"If I could shrug, I'd shrug," the doctor said. "It doesn't prove anything—a brain doesn't have to look like a mushy walnut and it doesn't have to be in the head. Maybe that skull isn't bone, maybe *that's* the brain, some crystal lattice. . . ."

"Yeah, but the stomach's in the right place, and if those aren't intestines I'll eat—"

"Look," Cortez said, "this is all real interesting, but all we need to know is whether that thing's dangerous, then we've gotta move on, we don't have all—"

"They aren't dangerous," Rogers began. "They don't. . . ."

"Medic! DOC!" Somebody was waving his arms, back at the firing line. Doc sprinted back to him, the rest of us following.

"What's wrong?" He had reached back and unclipped his medical kit on the run.

"It's Ho, she's out."

Doc swung open the door on Ho's biomedical monitor. He didn't have to look far. "She's dead."

"Dead?" Cortez said. "What the hell. . . ."

"Just a minute." Doc plugged a jack into the monitor and fiddled with some dials on his kit. "Everybody's biomed readout is stored for twelve hours. I'm running it backwards, should be able to—there!"

"What?"

"Four and a half minutes ago—must have been when you opened fire. . . ."

"Well?"

"Massive cerebral hemorrhage. No. . . ." He watched the dials. "No . . . warning, no indication of anything out of the ordinary; blood pressure up, pulse up, but normal under the circumstances . . . nothing to . . . indicate. . . ." He reached down and popped her suit. Her fine oriental features were distorted in a horrible grimace, both gums showing. Sticky fluid ran from under her collapsed eyelids and a trickle of blood still dripped from each ear. Doc Wilson closed the suit back up.

"I've never seen anything like it. It's as if a bomb went off in her skull."

"Oh crap," Rogers said, "she was Rhine-sensitive, wasn't she."

"That's right." Cortez sounded thoughtful. "All right, everybody listen. Platoon leaders, check your platoons and see if anybody's missing, or hurt. Anybody else in Seventh?"

"I . . . I've got a splitting headache, Sarge," Lucky said.

Four others had bad headaches. One of them affirmed that he was slightly Rhine-sensitive. The others didn't know.

"Cortez, I think it's obvious," Doc Wilson said, "that we should give these . . . monsters wide berth, especially shouldn't harm any more of them. Not with five people susceptible to whatever apparently killed Ho."

"Of course, damn it, I don't need anybody to tell me that. We'd better get moving. I just filled the captain in on what happened; he agrees that we'd better get as far away from here as we can, before we stop for the night.

"Let's get back in formation and continue on the same bearing. Fifth Platoon, take over point; Second, come back to the rear. Everybody else, same as before."

"What about Ho?" Lucky said.

"She'll be taken care of. From the ship."

After we'd gone half a click, there was a flash and rolling thunder. Where Ho had been, came a wispy luminous mushroom cloud boiling up to disappear against the gray sky.

XIII

We stopped for the "night"—actually, the sun wouldn't set for another seventy hours—atop a slight rise some ten clicks from where we had killed the aliens. But they weren't aliens, I had to remind myself—*we* were.

Two platoons deployed in a ring around the rest of us, and we flopped down exhausted. Everybody was allowed four hours' sleep and had two hours' guard duty.

Potter came over and sat next to me. I chinned her frequency.

"Hi, Marygay."

"Oh, William," her voice over the radio was hoarse and cracking. "God, it's so horrible."

"It's over now. . . ."

"I killed one of them, the first instant, I shot it right in the, in the . . ."

I put my hand on her knee. The contact made a plastic click and I jerked it back, visions of machines embracing, copulating. "Don't feel singled out, Marygay, whatever guilt there is, belongs evenly to all of us . . . but a triple portion for Cor. . . ."

"You privates quit jawin' and get some sleep. You both pull guard in two hours."

"O.K., Sarge." Her voice was so sad and tired I couldn't bear it. I felt if I could only touch her I could drain off the sadness like a ground wire draining current but we were each trapped in our own plastic world.

"G'night, William."

"Night." It's almost impossible to get sexually excited inside a suit, with the relief tube and all the silver chloride sensors poking you, but somehow this was my body's response to the emotional impotence, maybe remembering more pleasant sleeps with Marygay, maybe feeling that in the midst of all this death, personal death could be soon, cranking up the pro-creative derrick for one last try . . . lovely thoughts like this and I fell asleep and dreamed that I was a machine, mimicking the functions of life, creaking and clanking my clumsy way through the world, people too polite to say anything but giggling behind my back, and the little man who sat inside my head pulling the levers and clutches and watching the dials, he was hopelessly mad and was storing up hurts for the day. . . .

"Mandella—wake up, damn it, your shift!"

I shuffled over to my place on the perimeter to watch for God knows what . . . but I was so weary I couldn't keep my eyes open. Finally I tongued a stimtab, knowing I'd pay for it later.

For over an hour I sat there, scanning my sector left, right, near, far; the scene never changing, not even a breath of wind to stir the grass.

Then suddenly the grass parted and one of the three-legged creatures was right in front of me. I raised my finger but didn't squeeze.

"Movement!"

"Movement!"

"HOLD YOUR FIRE. Don't shoot!"

"Movement."

"Movement." I looked left and right as far as I could see, every perimeter guard had one of the blind dumb creatures standing right in front of him.

Maybe the drug I'd taken to stay awake made me more sensitive to whatever they did. My scalp crawled and I felt a formless *thing* in my mind, the feeling you get when somebody has said something and you didn't quite hear it, want to respond but the opportunity to ask him to repeat it is gone.

The creature sat back on its haunches, leaning forward on the one front leg. Big green bear with a withered arm. Its power threaded through my mind, spiderwebs, echo of night terrors, trying to communicate, trying to destroy me, I couldn't know.

"All right, everybody on the perimeter, fall back, slow. Don't make any quick gestures . . . anybody got a headache or anything?"

"Sergeant, this is Hollister." Lucky.

"They're trying to say something . . . I can almost . . . no, just. . . ."

"Well?"

"All I can get is that they think we're . . . think we're . . . well, *funny.* They aren't afraid."

"You mean the one in front of you isn't. . . ."

"No, the feeling comes from all of them, they're all thinking the same thing. Don't ask me how I know, I just do."

"Maybe they thought it was funny, what they did to Ho."

"Maybe. I don't feel like they're dangerous. Just curious about us."

"Sergeant, this is Bohrs."

"Yeah."

"The Taurans have been here at least a year—maybe they've learned how to communicate with these . . . overgrown teddy-bears. They might be spying on us, might be sending back. . . ."

"I don't think they'd show themselves, if that were the case," Lucky said. "They can obviously hide from us pretty well when they want to."

"Anyhow," Cortez said, "if they're spies, the damage has been done. Don't think it'd be smart to take any action against them. I know you'd all like to see 'em dead for what they did to Ho, so would I, but we'd better be careful."

I didn't want to see them dead, but I'd just as soon not see them in any condition. I was walking backwards slowly, toward the middle of camp. The creature didn't seem disposed to follow.

Maybe he just knew we were surrounded. He was pulling up grass with his arm and munching.

"O.K., all of you platoon leaders, wake everybody up, get a roll count. Let me know if anybody's been hurt. Tell your people we're moving out in one minute."

I don't know what Cortez expected, but of course the creatures just followed right along. They didn't keep us surrounded; just had twenty or thirty following us all the time. Not the same ones, either. Individuals would saunter away, new ones would join the parade. It was pretty obvious that *they* weren't going to tire out.

We were each allowed one stimtab. Without it, no one could have marched an hour. A second pill would have been welcome after the edge started to wear off, but the mathematics of the situation forbade it: we were still thirty clicks from the enemy base; fifteen hours' marching at the least. And though one could stay awake and energetic for a hundred hours on the 'tabs, aberrations of judgment and perception snowballed after the second 'tab, until *in extremis* the most bizarre hallucinations would be taken at face value, and a person would fidget for hours, deciding whether to have breakfast.

Under artificial stimulation the company traveled with great energy for the first six hours, was slowing by the seventh, and ground to an exhausted halt after nine hours and nineteen kilometers. The teddy-bears had never lost sight of us and, according to Lucky, had never stopped "broadcasting." Cortez's decision was that we would stop for seven hours, each platoon taking one hour of perimeter guard. I was never so glad to have been in the Seventh Platoon, as we stood guard the last shift and thus were the only ones to get six hours of uninterrupted sleep.

In the few moments I lay awake after finally lying down, the thought came to me that the next time I closed my eyes could well be the last. And partly because of the drug hangover, mostly because of the past day's horrors, I found that I really just didn't give a damn.

XIV

Our first contact with the Taurans came during my shift.

The teddy-bears were still there when I woke up and replaced Doc Jones on guard. They'd gone back to their original formation, one in front of each guard position. The one who was waiting for me seemed a little larger than normal, but otherwise looked just like all the others. All the grass had been cropped where he was sitting, so he occasionally made forays to the left or right. But he always returned to sit right in front of me, you would say staring if he had had anything to stare with.

We had been facing each other for about fifteen minutes when Cortez's voice rumbled:

"Awright, everybody wake up and get hid!"

I followed instinct and flopped to the ground and rolled into a tall stand of grass.

"Enemy vessel overhead." His voice was almost laconic.

Strictly speaking, it wasn't really overhead, but rather passing somewhat east of us. It was moving slowly, maybe a hundred clicks per hour, and looked like a broomstick surrounded by a dirty soap bubble. The creature riding it was a little more human-looking than the teddy-bears, but still no prize. I cranked my image amplifier up to forty log two for a closer look.

He had two arms and two legs, but his waist was so small you could encompass it with both hands. Under the tiny waist was a large horseshoe-shaped pelvic structure nearly a meter wide, from which dangled two ling skinny legs with no apparent knee joint. Above that waist his body swelled out again, to a chest no smaller than the huge pelvis. His arms looked surprisingly human, except that they were too long and undermuscled. There were too many fingers on his hands. Shoulderless, neckless; his head was a nightmarish growth that swelled like a goiter from his massive chest. Two eyes that looked like clusters of fish eggs, a bundle of tassles instead of a nose, and a rigidly open hole that might have been a mouth sitting low down where his Adam's apple should have been. Evidently the soap bubble contained an amenable environment, as he was wearing absolutely nothing except a ridged hide that looked like skin submerged too long in hot water, then dyed a pale orange. "He" had no external genitalia, nor anything that might hint of mammary glands.

Obviously, he either didn't see us, or thought we were part of the herd of teddy-bears. He never looked back at us, but just continued in the same direction we were headed, .05 rad east of north.

"Might as well go back to sleep now, if you can sleep after looking at *that* thing. We move out at 0435." Forty minutes.

Because of the planet's opaque cloud cover, there had been no way to tell, from space, what the enemy base looked like or how big it was. We only knew its position, the same way we knew the position the scoutships were supposed to land on. So it could easily have been underwater too, or underground.

But some of the drones were reconnaissance ships as well as decoys; and in their mock attacks on the base, one managed to get close enough to take a picture. Captain Stott beamed down a diagram of the place to Cortez—the only one with a visor in his suit—when we were five clicks from the base's "radio" position. We stopped and he called all of the platoon leaders in with the Seventh Platoon to confer. Two teddy-bears loped in, too. We tried to ignore them.

"O.K., the captain sent down some pictures of our objective. I'm going to draw a map; you platoon leaders copy." They took pads and styli out of their leg pockets, while Cortez unrolled a large plastic mat. He gave it a shake to randomize any residual charge, and turned on his stylus.

"Now, we're coming from this direction." He put an arrow at the bottom of the sheet. "First thing we'll hit is this row of huts, probably billets, or bunkers, but who the hell knows . . . our initial objective is to destroy these buildings—the whole base is on a flat plain; there's no way we could really sneak by them."

"Potter here. Why can't we just over them?"

"Yeah, we could do that, and wind up completely surrounded, cut to ribbons. We take the buildings.

"After we do that . . . all I can say is that we'll have to think on our feet. From the aerial reconnaissance, we can figure out the function of only a couple of buildings—and that stinks. We might wind up wasting a lot of time demolishing the equivalent of an enlisted man's bar, ignoring a huge logistic computer because it looks like . . . a garbage dump or something."

"Mandella here," I said. "Isn't that a spaceport of some kind—seems to me we ought to. . . ."

"I'll *get* to that, damn it. There's a ring of these huts all around the camp, so we've got to break through somewhere. This place'll be closest, less chance of giving away our position before we attack.

"There's nothing in the whole place that actually looks like a weapon. That doesn't mean anything, though; you could hide a bevawatt laser in each of those huts.

"Now, about five hundred meters from the huts, in the middle of the base, we'll come to this big flower-shaped structure." Cortez drew a large symmetrical shape that looked like the outline of a flower with seven petals. "What the hell this is, your guess is as good as mine. There's only one of them, though, so we don't damage it any more than we have to. Which means . . . we blast it to splinters if I think it's dangerous.

"Now, as far as your spaceport, Mandella, is concerned—there just isn't one. Nothing.

"That cruiser the *Hope* caulked had probably been left in orbit, like ours has to be. If they have any equivalent of a scoutship, or drone missiles, they're either not kept here or they're well hidden."

"Bohrs here. Then what did they attack with, while we were coming down from orbit?"

"I wish we knew, Private."

"Obviously, we don't have any way of estimating their numbers, not directly. Recon pictures failed to show a single Tauran on the grounds of the base. Meaning nothing, because it *is* an alien environment. Indirectly, though . . . we can count the number of broomsticks.

"There are fifty-one huts, and each has at most one broomstick. Four don't have one parked outside, but we located three at various other parts of the base. Maybe this indicates that there are fifty-one Taurans, one of whom was outside the base when the picture was taken."

"Keating here. Or fifty-one officers."

"That's right—maybe fifty thousand infantrymen stacked in one of these buildings. No way to tell. Maybe ten Taurans, each with five broomsticks, to use according to his mood.

"We've got one thing in our favor, and that's communications. They evidently use a frequency modulation of megahertz electromagnetic radiation."

"Radio!"

"That's right, whoever you are. Identify yourself when you speak. So, it's quite possible that they can't detect our phased-neutrino communications. Also, just prior to the attack, the *Hope* is going to deliver a nice dirty fission bomb; detonate it in the upper atmosphere right over the base. That'll restrict them to line-of-sight communication for some time; even those will be full of static."

"Why don't . . . Tate here . . . why don't they just drop the bomb right in their laps? Would save a lot of. . . ."

"That doesn't even deserve an answer, Private. But the answer is, they might. And you better hope they don't. If they caulk the base, it'll be for the safety of the *Hope. After* we've attacked, and probably before we're far enough away for it to make much difference.

"We keep that from happening by doing a good job. We have to reduce the base to where it can no longer function; at the same time, leave as much intact as possible. And take one prisoner."

"Potter here. You mean, at least one prisoner."

"I mean what I say. One only. Potter . . . you're relieved of your platoon. Send Chavez up."

"All right, Sergeant." The relief in her voice was unmistakable.

Cortez continued with his map and instructions. There was one other building whose function was pretty obvious; it had a large steerable dish antenna on top. We were to destroy it as soon as the grenadiers got in range.

The attack plan was very loose. Our signal to begin would be the flash of the fission bomb. At the same time, several drones would converge on the base, so we could see what their anti-spacecraft defenses were. We would try to reduce the effectiveness of those defenses without destroying them completely.

Immediately after the bomb and the drones, the grenadiers would vaporize a line of seven huts. Everybody would break through the hole into the base . . . and what would happen after that was anybody's guess.

Ideally, we'd sweep from that end of the base to the other, destroying certain targets caulking all but one Tauran. But that was unlikely to happen, as it depended on the Taurans' offering very little resistance.

On the other hand, if the Taurans showed obvious superiority from the beginning, Cortez would give the order to scatter: everybody had a different compass bearing for retreat—we'd blossom out in all directions, the survivors to rendezvous in a valley some forty clicks east of the base. Then we'd see about a return engagement, after the *Hope* softened the base up a bit.

"One last thing," Cortez rasped. "Maybe some of you feel the way Potter evidently does, maybe some of your men feel that way . . . that we ought to go easy, not make this so much of a bloodbath. Mercy is a luxury, a weakness we can't afford to indulge in at this stage of the war. *All* we know about the enemy is that they have killed seven hundred and ninety-eight humans. They haven't shown any restraint in attacking our cruisers, and it'd be foolish to expect any this time, this first ground action.

"*They* are responsible for the lives of all of your comrades who died in training, and for Ho, and for all the others who are surely going to die today. I can't *understand* anybody who wants to spare them. But that doesn't make any difference. You have your orders, and what the hell, you might as well know, all of you have a posthypnotic suggestion that I will trigger by a phrase, just before the battle. It will make your job easier.''

''Sergeant. . . .''

''Shut up. We're short on time; get back to your platoons and brief them. We move out in five minutes.''

The platoon leaders returned to their men, leaving Cortez and the ten of us, plus three teddy-bears, milling around, getting in the way.

XV

We took the last five clicks very carefully, sticking to the highest grass, running across occasional clearings. When we were five hundred meters from where the base was supposed to be, Cortez took the Third Platoon forward to scout, while the rest of us laid low.

Cortez's voice came over the general freak: ''Looks pretty much like we expected. Advance in a file, crawling. When you get to the Third Platoon, follow your squad leader to the left, or right.''

We did that and wound up with a string of eighty-three people in a line roughly perpendicular to the direction of attack. We were pretty well hidden, except for the dozen or so teddy-bears that mooched along the line munching grass.

There was no sign of life inside the base. All of the buildings were windowless, and a uniform shiny white. The huts that were our first objective were large featureless half-buried eggs, some sixty meters apart. Cortez assigned one to each grenadier.

We were broken into three fire teams: Team A consisted of platoons Two, Four, and Six; Team B was One, Three, and Five; the command platoon was Team C.

''Less than a minute now—filters down!—when I say 'fire', grenadiers take out your targets. God help you if you miss.''

There was a sound like a giant's belch and a stream of five or six iridescent bubbles floated up from the flower-shaped building. They rose with increasing speed to where they were almost out of sight, then shot off to the south, over our heads. The ground was suddenly bright and for the first time in a long time, I saw my shadow, a long one pointed north. The bomb had gone off prematurely. I just had time to think that it didn't make too much difference; it'd still make alphabet soup out of their communications. . . .

"Drones!" A ship came screaming in just above tree level, and a bubble was in the air to meet it. When they contacted, the bubble popped and the drone exploded into a million tiny fragments. Another one came from the opposite side and suffered the same fate.

"FIRE!" Seven bright glares of 500-microton grenades and a sustained concussion that I'm sure would have killed an unprotected man.

"Filters up." Gray haze of smoke and dust. Clods of dirt falling with a sound like heavy raindrops.

"Listen up:

> " 'Scots, wha hae wi' Wallace bled;
> Scots, wham Bruce has aften led,
> Welcome to your gory bed,
> Or to victory!' "

I hardly heard him, for trying to keep track of what was going on in my skull. I knew it was just posthypnotic suggestion, even remembered the session in Missouri when they'd implanted it, but that didn't make it any less compelling. My mind reeled under the strong pseudo-memories; shaggy hulks that were Taurans—not at all what we now knew they looked like—boarding a colonist's vessel, eating babies while mothers watched in screaming terror—the colonists never took babies; they wouldn't stand the acceleration—then raping the women to death with huge veined purple members—ridiculous that they would feel desire for humans—holding the men down while they plucked flesh from their living bodies and gobbled it. . . . a hundred grisly details as sharply remembered as the events of a minute ago, ridiculously overdone and logically absurd; but while my conscious mind was reflecting the silliness, somewhere much deeper, down in that sleeping giant where we keep our real motives and morals, something was thirsting for alien blood, secure in the conviction that the noblest thing a man could do would be to die killing one of those horrible monsters. . . .

I knew it was all purest soya, and I hated the men who had taken such obscene liberties with my mind, but still I could hear my teeth grinding, feel cheeks frozen in a spastic grin, blood-lust . . . a teddy-bear walked in front of me, looking dazed. I started to raise my laserfinger, but somebody beat me to it and the creature's head exploded in a cloud of gray splinters and blood.

Lucky groaned, half-whining, "Dirty . . . filthy bastards." Lasers flared and crisscrossed and all of the teddy-bears fell dead.

"*Watch* it, damn it," Cortez screamed. "*Aim* those things, they aren't toys!"

"Team A, move out—into the craters to cover B."

Somebody was laughing and sobbing. "What the crap is wrong with *you*, Petrov?" First time I could remember Cortez cussing.

I twisted around and saw Petrov, behind and to my left, lying in a shallow hole, digging frantically with both hands, crying and gurgling.

"Crap," Cortez said. "Team B! Past the craters ten meters, get down in a line. Team C—into the craters with A."

I scrambled up and covered the hundred meters in twelve amplified strides. The craters were practically large enough to hide a scoutship, some ten meters in diameter. I jumped to the opposite side of the hole and landed next to a fellow named Chin. He didn't even look around when I landed, just kept scanning the base for signs of life.

"Team A—past Team B ten meters, down in line." Just as he finished, the building in front of us burped and a salvo of the bubbles fanned out toward our lines. Most people saw it coming and got down, but Chin was just getting up to make his rush and stepped right into one.

It grazed the top of his helmet, and disappeared with a faint pop. He took one step backwards and toppled over the edge of the crater, trailing an arc of blood and brains. Lifeless, spreadeagled, he slid halfway to the bottom, shoveling dirt into the perfectly symmetrical hole where the bubble had chewed through plastic, hair, skin, bone and brain indiscriminately.

"Everybody hold it. Platoon leaders, casualty report . . . check . . . check, check . . . check, check, check . . . check. We have three deaders. Wouldn't be *any* if you'd have kept low. So everybody grab dirt when you hear that thing go off. Team A, complete the rush."

They completed the maneuver without incident. "O.K. Team C, rush to where B . . . hold it! Down!"

Everybody was already hugging the ground. The bubbles slid

by in a smooth arc about two meters off the ground. They went serenely over our heads and, except for one that made toothpicks out of a tree, disappeared in the distance.

"B, rush past A ten meters. C, take over B's place. You B grenadiers see if you can reach the Flower."

Two grenades tore up the ground thirty or forty meters from the structure. In a good imitation of panic, it started belching out a continuous stream of bubbles—still, none coming lower than two meters off the ground. We kept hunched down and continued to advance.

Suddenly, a seam appeared in the building, widened to the size of a large door, and Taurans came swarming out.

"Grenadiers, hold your fire. B team, laser fire to the left and right, keep 'em bunched up. A and C, rush down the center."

One Tauran died trying to turn through a laser beam. The others stayed where they were.

In a suit, it's pretty awkward to run and try to keep your head down, at the same time. You have to go from side to side, like a skater getting started; otherwise you'll be airborne. At least one person, somebody in A team, bounced too high and suffered the same fate as Chin.

I was feeling pretty fenced-in and trapped, with a wall of laser fire on each side and a low ceiling that meant death to touch. But in spite of myself, I felt happy, euphoric at finally getting the chance to kill some of those villainous baby-eaters.

They weren't fighting back, except for the rather ineffective bubbles—obviously not designed as an antipersonnel weapon—and they didn't retreat back into the building, either. They just milled around, about a hundred of them, and watched us get closer. A couple of grenades would caulk them all, but I guess Cortez was thinking about the prisoner.

"O.K., when I say 'go', we going to flank 'em. B team will hold fire . . . Second and Fourth to the right, Sixth and Seventh to the left. B team will move forward in the line to box them in.

"Go!" We peeled off to the left. As soon as the lasers stopped, the Taurans bolted, running in a group on a collision course with our flank.

"A Team, down and fire! Don't shoot until you're sure of your aim—if you miss you might hit a friendly. And fer Chris'sake save me one!"

It was a horrifying sight, that herd of monsters bearing down on us. They were running in great leaps—the bubbles avoiding them—and they all looked like the one we saw earlier, riding the broomstick; naked except for an almost transparent sphere around their whole bodies, that moved along with them. The right flank started firing, picking off individuals in the rear of the pack.

Suddenly a laser flared through the Taurans from the other side, somebody missing his mark. There was a horrible scream and I looked down the line to see someone, I think it was Perry, writhing on the ground, right hand over the smoldering stump of his left arm, seared off just below the elbow. Blood sprayed through his fingers and the suit, its camouflage circuits scrambled, flickered black-white-jungle-desert-green-gray. I don't know how long I stared—long enough for the medic to run over and start giving aid—but when I looked up the Taurans were almost on top of me.

My first shot was wild and high, but it grazed the top of the leading Tauran's protective bubble. The bubble disappeared and the monster stumbled and fell to the ground, jerking spasmodically. Foam gushed out of his mouth-hole, first white, then streaked with red. With one last jerk he became rigid and twisted backwards, almost to the shape of a horseshoe. His long scream, a high-pitched whistle, stopped just as his comrades trampled over him and I hated myself for smiling.

It was slaughter, even though our flank was outnumbered five to one. They kept coming without faltering, even when they had to climb over the drift of bodies and parts of bodies that piled up high, parallel to our flank. The ground between us was slick red with Tauran blood—all God's children got hemoglobin—and, like the teddy-bears, their guts looked pretty much like guts to my untrained eye. My helmet reverberated with hysterical laughter while we cut them to gory chunks. I almost didn't hear Cortez.

"Hold your fire—I said HOLD IT damn it! *Catch* a couple of the bastards, they won't hurt you."

I stopped shooting and eventually so did everybody else. When the next Tauran jumped over the smoking pile of meat in front of me, I dove to tackle him around those spindly legs.

It was like hugging a big, slippery balloon. When I tried to drag him down, he just popped out of my arms and kept running.

We managed to stop one of them by the simple expedient of piling half-a-dozen people on top of him. By that time the others had run through our line and were headed for the row of large cylindrical tanks that Cortez had said were probably for storage. A little door had opened in the base of each one.

"We've *got* our prisoner," Cortez shouted. *"Kill!"*

They were fifty meters away and running hard, difficult targets. Lasers slashed around them, bobbing high and low. One fell, sliced in two, but the others, about ten of them, kept going and were almost to the doors when the grenadiers started firing.

They were still loaded with 500-mike bombs, but a near miss wasn't enough—the concussion would just send them flying, unhurt in their bubbles.

"The buildings! Get the damn buildings!" The grenadiers raised their aim and let fly, but the bombs only seemed to scorch the white outside of the structures until, by chance, one landed in a door. That split the building just as it had a seam; the two halves popped away and a cloud of machinery flew into the air, accompanied by a huge pale flame that rolled up and disappeared in an instant. Then the others all concentrated on the doors, except for potshots at some of the Taurans; not so much to get them as to blow them away before they could get inside. They seemed awfully eager.

All this time, we were trying to get the Taurans with laser fire, while they weaved and bounced around trying to get into the structures. We moved in as close to them as we could without putting ourselves in danger from the grenade blasts—that was still too far away for good aim.

Still, we were getting them one by one, and managed to destroy four of the seven buildings. Then, when there were only two aliens left, a nearby grenade blast flung one of them to within a few meters of a door. He dove in and several grenadiers fired salvos after him, but they all fell short, or detonated harmlessly on the side. Bombs were falling all around, making an awful racket, but the sound was suddenly drowned out by a great sigh, like a giant's intake of breath, and where the building had been was a thick cylindrical cloud of smoke, solid-looking, dwindling away into the stratosphere, straight as if laid down by a ruler. The other Tauran had been right at the base of the cylinder; I could see pieces of him flying. A second later, a shock wave hit us and I rolled helplessly, pinwheeling, to smash into the pile of Tauran bodies and roll beyond.

I picked myself up and panicked for a second when I saw there was blood all over my suit—when I realized it was only alien blood, I relaxed but felt unclean.

"*Catch* the bastard! Catch him!" In the confusion, the Tauran—now the only one left alive—had got free and was running for the grass. One platoon was chasing after him, losing ground, but then all of B team ran over and cut him off. I jogged over to join in the fun.

There were four people on top of him, and fifty people watching.

"Spread out, damn it! There might be a thousand more of them waiting to get us in one place." We dispersed, grumbling. By unspoken agreement we were all sure that there were no more live Taurans on the face of the planet.

Cortez was walking toward the prisoner while I backed away. Suddenly the four men collapsed in a pile on top of the creature . . . even from my distance I could see the foam spouting from his mouth-hole. His bubble had popped. Suicide.

"Damn!" Cortez was right there. "Get off that bastard." The four men got off and Cortez used his laser to slice the monster into a dozen quivering chunks. Heartwarming sight.

"That's all right, though, we'll find another one—everybody! Back in the arrowhead formation. Combat assault, on the Flower."

Well, we assaulted the Flower, which had evidently run out of ammunition—it was still belching, but no bubbles—and it was empty. We just scurried up ramps and through corridors, fingers at the ready, like kids playing soldier. There was nobody home.

The same lack of response at the antenna installation, the "Salami," and twenty other major buildings, as well as the forty-four perimeter huts still intact. So we had "captured" dozens of buildings, mostly of incomprehensible purpose, but failed in our main mission; capturing a Tauran for the xenologists to experiment with. Oh, well, they could have all the bits and pieces of the creatures they'd ever want. That was something.

After we'd combed every last square centimeter of the base, a scoutship came in with the real exploration crew, Star Fleet scientists. Cortez said, "All right, snap out of it," and the hypnotic compulsion fell away.

At first it was pretty grim. A lot of people, like Lucky and Marygay, almost went crazy with the memories of bloody murder multiplied a hundred times. Cortez ordered everybody to take a sedtab, two for the ones most upset. I took two without being specifically ordered to do so.

Because it *was* murder, unadorned butchery—once we had the antispacecraft weapon doped out, we weren't in any danger. The Taurans didn't seem to have any conception of person-to-person fighting. We just herded them up and slaughtered them, in the first encounter between mankind and another intelligent species. What might have happened if we had sat down and tried to communicate? Maybe it was the second encounter, counting the teddybears. But they got the same treatment.

I spent a long time after that, telling myself over and over that it hadn't been *me* who so gleefully carved up those frightened, stampeding creatures. Back in the Twentieth Century, they established to everybody's satisfaction that "I was just following orders" was an inadequate excuse for inhuman conduct . . . but what can you do when the orders come from deep down in that puppet master of the unconscious?

Worst of all was the feeling that perhaps my actions weren't all that inhuman. Ancestors only a few generations back would have done the same thing, even to their fellowmen, without any hypnotic conditioning.

So I was disgusted with the human race, disgusted with the army, and horrified at the prospect of living with myself for another century or so . . . well, there was always brainwipe.

The ship that the lone Tauran survivor had escaped in had got away, clean, the bulk of the planet shielding it from *Earth's Hope* while it dropped into Aleph's collapsar field. Escaped to home, I guessed, wherever that was, to report what twenty men with hand-weapons could do to a hundred fleeing on foot, unarmed.

I suspected that the next time humans met Taurans in ground combat, we would be more evenly matched. And I was right.

THE SHORT ONES

Raymond E. Banks

Valsek came out of his hut and looked at the sky. As usual it was milk-white, but grayed down now to predawn somberness.

"Telfus!"

The sleepy face of his hired man peered over a rock, behind which he had slept.

"We must plow today," said Valsek. "There'll be no rain."

"Did a god tell you this?" asked Telfus, a groan in his voice.

Valsek stumbled over a god-wire before he could answer. Another exposed god-wire! Important things were stirring and he had to drive this farm-hand clod to his labor.

"If you are to sleep in my field and eat at my table, you must work," said Valsek angrily. He bent to examine the god-wire. The shock to his hands told him there was a feeble current running in it which made his magnetic backbone tingle. Vexing, oh vexing, to know that current ran through the wire and through you, but not to know whether it was the current of the old god, Melton, or the new god, Hiller!

"Bury this god-wire at once," he told Telfus. "It isn't neat to have the god-wires exposed. How can I make contact with Hiller when he can see my fields unplowed and my god-wires exposed? He will not choose me Spokesman."

"Did this Hiller come to you in the night?" asked Telfus politely.

"In a way, in a way," said the prophet testily. It was hard to know. It was time for a new god, but you could miss it by weeks.

Valsek's wife came over the hill, carrying a pail of milk warm from the goat.

"Was there a sign last night?" she asked, pausing before the hut.

Valsek gave his wife a cold stare. "Naturally there was a sign," he said. "I do not sleep on the cold stone of the barn floor because it pleases my bones. I have had several portents from Hiller."

His wife looked resigned. "Such as?"

Short Ones! Valsek felt contempt inside of him. All of the Short Ones were fools. It was the time for a new god, and they went around milking goats and asking about signs. Short Ones! (And what god had first revealed to them that name? And why, when they were the tallest living beings in all the world?)

"The wind blew last night," he said.

"The wind blows every night," she said.

He presented his hard conviction to the cutting blade of her scorn.

"About midnight it rained," he persisted. "I had just got through suggesting rain to the new god, Hiller."

"Now was that considerate?" asked Telfus, still leaning on his rock. "Your only hired hand asleep in the fields outside and you ask for rain."

"There is no Hiller," said Valsek's wife, tightening her lips. "It rains every midnight this time of year. And there will be no corn if you keep sleeping in the barn, making those stupid clay images and avoiding work."

"Woman," said Valsek, "god-business is important. If Hiller chooses me for Spokesman to all the Short Ones we shall be rich."

But his wife was tired, perhaps because she had had to pull the plow yesterday for Telfus. "Ask Hiller to send us a bushel of corn," she said coldly. "Then I will come into the barn and burn a manure stick to him."

She went into the hut, letting the door slam.

"If it is permitted to sleep in the barn," said Telfus, "I will help you fashion your clay idols. Once in King Giron's courtyard I watched an artist fashion a clay idol for Melton, and I think I might have a hand for it, if it is permitted to sleep in the barn."

Blasphemers! Worldly blasphemers! "It is not permitted to sleep in the barn," said Valsek. "I have spent many years in the barn, reaching out for each new god as he or she came, and though I have not yet made contact, it is a dedicated place. You have no touch for prophecy."

"I have seen men go mad, each trying to be picked Spokesman to the gods for the Short Ones," said Telfus. "The chances are much against it. And consider the fate of the Spokesman once the year of his god is over."

Valsek's eyes flashed angrily. "Consider the fate of the Spokesman in his prime. Power, rich power in the time of your god, you fool, if you are Spokesman. And afterwards many Spokesmen become members of the Prophets' Association—with a pension. Does life hold more?"

Telfus decided not to remind his employer that usually the new Spokesman felt it necessary to execute the old Spokesman of the used-up god.

"Perhaps it is only that my knees are too tender for god-business," he said, sighing against the rock.

"Quiet now," said Valsek. "It is time for dawn. I have asked Hiller for a portent, to show his choice of me as Spokesman. A dawn portent."

They turned to watch the dawn. Even Valsek's wife came out to watch, for Valsek was always asking for a dawn portent. It was his favorite suggestion to the gods.

Dawn came. There was a flicker of flashing, magic lights, much, much faster than the slow flame of a tallow taper that the Short Ones used for light. One-two-three-four-five, repeated, one-two-three-four-five. And then the day was upon them. In an instant the gray turned to milk-white and the day's heat fell.

"Ah!" cried Valsek. "The dawn light flashed six times. Hiller is the new god. I am his Spokesman! I must hurry to the market place in town with my new idol!"

Telfus and the wife exchanged looks. Telfus was about to point out that there had been only the usual five lights of dawn, but the wife shook her head. She pointed a scornful finger to the horizon where a black pall of smoke lingered in the sky.

"Yesterday there were riots," she said. "Fighting and the burning of things. If you take your new idol to the market place, you will insult either the followers of King Giron or the followers of Melton. One or the other, they will carve your heart out, old man!"

But it was no use. Valsek had rushed back into the barn to burn a manure stick to Hiller and start his journey, on the strength of the lights of dawn.

Valsek's wife stared down at her work-stained hands and sighed. "Now I suppose I should prepare a death sheet for him," she said.

"No," said Telfus, wearily picking up the harness from the ground. "They will only laugh at him and he will live forever while you and I die from doing the world's work. Come, Mrs.

Valsek, assume the harness, so that I may walk behind and plow a careful furrow in his fields.''

Time: One month earlier . . . or half an hour.
  Place: The Pentagon, Washington, D.C.
  The Life Hall.
  In the vast, gloomy auditorium the scurryings and scuttlings of the Short Ones rose to a climax beneath the opaque, milky glass that covered the colony. Several spectators rose in their seats. At the control panel, Charles Melton also rose.
  ''The dials!'' cried his adviser.
  But Melton was past tending the dials. He jerked the control helmet off his head a second too late. A blue flash from the helmet flickered in the dark room. Short circuit!
  Melton leaned over the glass, trying to steady himself, and vomited blood. Then a medical attendant came and escorted him away, as his adviser assumed the dials and his helmet.
  A sigh from the spectators. They bent and peered at Melton from the seats above his level, like medical students in an operating theátre. The political career of Charles Melton was over: he had failed the Life Hall Test.
  A technician tapped some buttons and the lighted sign, visible to all, changed:

TEST 39167674
HILLER, RALPH, ASSISTANT SECRETARY OF DEFENSE, USA
TEST TIME: 6 HOURS
OBJECTIVE: BLUE CERTIFICATE TO PROVE LEADERSHIP QUALITIES
ADVISER: DR. CYNTHIA WOLLRATH

Cynthia Wollrath!
  Ralph Hiller turned from the door of the Ready Room and paced. What rotten luck he was having! To begin with, his test started right after some inadequate Judge-applicant had failed badly and gotten the Short Ones all upset. On top of that, they had assigned his own former wife to be adviser. How unethical can you get?
  He was sure now that his enemies in the Administration had given him a bad test position and picked a prejudiced adviser to insure his failure—that was typical of the Armstrong crowd. He felt the hot anger on his face. They weren't going to get away with this. . . .

Cynthia came into the Ready Room then, dressed in the white uniform of the Life Hall Staff, and greeted him with a cool, competent nod.

"I'm rather surprised that I've been given a prejudiced adviser," he said.

"I'm sorry. The Board considered me competent to sit in on this test."

"Did you tell them that we were once married?"

She sighed. "No. You did that in at least three memorandums, I believe. Shall we proceed with the briefing?"

"The Board knows you dislike me," he said. "They know I could lose my sanity in there. You could foul me up and no one would be the wiser. I won't stand for it."

Her eyes were carefully impartial. "I don't dislike you. And I rather think that the Board chose me because they felt that it would help you out. They feel I know your personality, and in something as dangerous as the Life Hall Tests they try to give all the applicants a break."

"My father died in that chair," he said. "My uncle——"

"You aren't your father. Nor your uncle. Shall we start? We're late. This is a Short One——"

She held up a figure, two inches high, a perfectly formed little man, a dead replica of the life below. In her other hand she held a metal sliver that looked like a three-quarter-inch needle. "The Short Ones are artificial creatures of living protoplasm, except for this metallic backbone imbedded in each. It is magnetic material——"

"I want a postponement."

"Bruce Gerard of the *Times* is covering this test," she said patiently. "His newspaper is not favorable to the Administration. He would like to report a postponement in a Life Hall Test by an important Administration figure. Now, Ralph, we really must get on with this. There are many other testees to follow you to the chair."

He subsided. He held his temper in. That temper that had killed his father, almost destroyed his uncle. That temper that would be put to the most severe test known to men for the next few hours. He found it difficult to concentrate on her words.

"—wires buried in the ground of the Colony, activate the Short Ones—a quarter of a million Short Ones down there—one of our minutes is a day to them—your six hours of testing cover a year of their lives—"

He knew all that. A Blue Certificate Life Hall Test was rather like an execution and you studied up on it long before. Learned how science had perfected this tiny breed. How there had been opposition to them until the beginnings of the Life Hall. In today's world the Short Ones protected the people from inefficient and weak leaders. To hold an important position, such as his Cabinet job, you had to have a Life Hall Certificate. You had to prove out your leadership wisdom over the roiling, boiling generations of Short Ones before you could lead mankind. The test was rightfully dangerous; the people could expect their leaders to have true ability if they passed the test, and the false leaders and weaklings either never applied, or were quickly broken down by the Short Ones.

"Let's go," said Cynthia.

There was a stir from the audience as they entered the auditorium. They recognized him. Many who had been resting with their spectator helmets off reassumed them. A wave of tense expectancy seemed to come from them. The people knew about the failure of his father and his uncle. This looked like a blood test and it was fascinating to see a blood test.

Ralph took his position in the chair with an inward sigh. It was too late now to change anything. He dare not embarrass the Administration before a hostile reporter. He let Cynthia show him the inside of the Director's helmet with its maze of wires.

"Since their time runs so fast, you can't possibly read out each and every mind of the Short Ones down there," she said. "You can handle perhaps half a dozen. Step-down transformers will allow you to follow their lives. They are your leaders and representatives down in the world of the Short Ones.

"These knob hand dials are your mechanical controls down there. There are hydraulic linkages which give you power to change the very seas, cause mountains to rise and valleys to form. Their weather is in your control, for when you think of weather, by an electronic signal through the helmet, you cause rain or sun, wind or stillness. The left hand dial is destructive, the right hand dial is constructive. As the current flows throughout the system, your thoughts and wishes are impressed upon the world of the Short Ones, through your leaders. You can back up your edicts by smashing the very ground under their feet. Should you desire to kill, a flick of the dial saturates the magnetized backbone of the unfortunate Short One, and at full magnetization all life ceases for them.

"Unfortunately, you are directing a dangerous amount of power in this system which courses within a fraction of an inch of your head in the control helmet. At each death down there a tiny amount less current is needed to control the Short Ones. At many deaths this wild current, no longer being drawn by the dead creatures, races through the circuits. Should too many die, you will receive a backlash of wild current before I can——"

Ralph nodded, put on the helmet and let the scurryings and scuttlings of the Short Ones burst in on his mind.

He sat straight, looking out over a sheet of milky glass fifty feet across that covered the world below. He was sinking mentally into their world. With him, but fully protected, the spectators put on their helmets to sink into the Colony and witness the events below as he directed them.

The eerie light from the glass shone on the face of the medical attendant standing ready.

Ralph reached out his hands to start his test and gave himself a final admonition about his temper. At all costs he must curb it.

There is a temper that destroys and also one that demands things done by other men. Ralph had used his sternness well for most of the years of his life, but there had been times, bad times, when that fiery temperament had worked against him.

Like his marriage to Cynthia, ten years before. She had had a cool, scientific detachment about life which had attracted him. She had been a top student of psychology on the campus. At first her cool detachment had steadied him and enabled him to get started in his political career. But then it began to haunt him—her reasonableness against his storms; he had a growing compulsion to smash through her calmness and subjugate her to his will.

He had hurt her badly once.

He still felt the flame of embarrassment when he remembered her face in the bedroom, staring down at the nakedness of the other woman, staring at his own nakedness, as the adulterers lay on her bed, and the shivery calmness of his own nervous system at the expected interruption. And his words across the years:

"Why not? You seem to be sterile."

Foolish, hot ego of youth. He had meant to stir and shock a very proper Cynthia, and he had done so. Her moan of rage and hurt had made him for that triumphant moment the flamethrower he was destined to be.

He hadn't counted on a divorce, but then it was impossible for him to give up his victory. He was Ralph Hiller, a man who asked no favors——

Ah, that was ten years ago when he was barely twenty-five! Many times since the divorce he'd wished for her quiet calmness. She had stayed in the arms of science, never marrying again, preferring the well-lighted lab to the dark halls of passion. But such an act could rankle and burn over the years. . . .

The affairs of the Short Ones pressed impatiently on him, and he turned to his job with unsteady nerves.

When Valsek appeared, towing his clay idol of Hiller on a handcart, the soldiers were too drunk to be cruel to him. They merely pricked his buttocks with their swords and laughed at him. And the priests of Melton, likewise sated with violence, simply threw stones at him and encouraged the loiterers to upend the cart and smash the grinning nonentity of clay. Hiller indeed! Would a new god creep into their lives on a handcart pulled by a crazy old man? Go away, old man, go away.

Back at the farm Valsek found Telfus finishing up a new idol.

"You knew?" he asked sadly.

"It was somehow written in my mind that you would need a new idol," said Telfus. "I am quite enthusiastic about this new god, and if I may be permitted to sleep in the barn, I am sure that I would get the feel of him and help you do good works in his name."

"It is not permitted to sleep in the barn," grunted Valsek, easing his tender backside on a haypile. "Also I take notice that the plowing has stopped."

"Your wife fainted in the fields," said Telfus. "I could not bring myself to kick her back to consciousness as you ordered because I have a bad leg from sleeping on the ground. I have slept on the ground many, many years and it is not good for the leg."

The fire of fanaticism burned in Valsek's eyes. "Bother your leg," he said. "Place my new idol on the handcart; there are other towns and other ears to listen, and Hiller will not fail me."

In a short time Valsek had used up several of the idols to Hiller in various towns and was required to rest from the injuries given him by the scornful priests, the people and the soldiers.

"When I beg," said Telfus, "I place myself before the door of a rich man, not a poor one. Would it not be wisdom to preach before King Giron himself rather than the lesser figures? Since Melton is his enemy, the King might welcome a new god."

"You are mad," said Valsek. "Also, I do not like your latest idols. You are shirking on the straw which holds the clay together. I suspect you of eating my straw."

Telfus looked pained. "I would not dream of eating Hiller's straw," he said, "any more than I would dream of sleeping in the barn without permission. It is true, however, that your wife and goat occasionally get hungry."

Valsek waved a hand. "Prepare a knapsack. It has occurred to me that I should go to the very courtyard of the King himself and tell him of Hiller. After all, does a beggar beg at the door of a poor man?"

Telfus nodded. "An excellent idea, one I should've thought of."

"Prepare the knapsack," ordered Valsek. "We will go together."

At the gate of the palace itself, Telfus stopped. "Many Short Ones have died," he said, "because in the midst of a hazardous task they left no avenue of escape open. Therefore I shall entertain the guards at the gate with my juggling while you go on in. Should it be necessary for you to fly, I will keep the way open."

Valsek frowned. "I had planned for you to pull the idol-cart for me, Telfus, so that I might make a better impression."

"An excellent idea!" said Telfus. "But, after all, you have the company of Hiller, which is worth a couple of regiments. And I have a bad leg, and Hiller deserves a better appearance than to be pulled before a King by a limping beggar. Therefore I will remain at the gates and keep the way open for you."

Valsek took the cart rope from Telfus, gave him a look of contempt and swept into the courtyard of King Giron.

King Giron, who had held power for more than a year now, stared out of his lofty bedroom window and listened to the words of Valsek carried on the wind from the courtyard below, as he preached to the loiterers. He turned white; in just such a fashion had he preached Melton the previous year. True, he had no longer believed in Melton, but, since he was writing a bible for the worship of King Giron, a new god didn't fit into his plans. He ordered the guards to bring the man before him.

"Make a sign, old man," he directed. "If you represent a new god, have him make a sign if, as you say, Melton is dead and Hiller is the new god."

Valsek threw himself down and groveled to Hiller and asked for a sign. He crooned over Telfus' latest creation, asking for a sign. There was none. Ralph was being careful.

"But Hiller lives!" cried Valsek as the guards dragged him upright and King Giron smiled cynically. "Melton is dead! You can't get a sign from Melton either! Show me a sign from Melton!"

The two men stared at each other. True, Melton was gone. The King misdoubted that Melton had ever existed, except in the furious fantasies of his own mind which had been strong enough to convince other people. Here now was a test. If he could destroy the old man, that would prove him right—that the gods were all illusion and that the Short Ones could run their own affairs.

The King made a cutting sign across his own throat. The guards threw Valsek to his knees and one of them lifted a sharp, shining blade.

"Now cut his throat quickly," ordered the King, "because I find him a very unlikely citizen."

"Hiller," moaned Valsek, "Hiller, I've believed in you and still do. Now you must save me, for it is the last moment of my miserable life. Believe in me, Hiller!"

Sweat stood out on Ralph's brow. He had held his temper when the old man had been rejected by the others. He had hoped for a better Spokesman than this fanatic, but the other Short Ones were confused by King Giron's defiance of all gods and Valsek was his only active disciple. He would have to choose the old man after all, and, in a way, the fanatical old man did have spirit. . . . Then he grinned to himself. Funny how these creatures sneaked into your ego. And deadly, no doubt!

The sword of the guard began to descend. Ralph, trying hard to divine the far-reaching consequences of each act he would perform, made his stomach muscles grip to hold himself back. He didn't mean to pass any miracles, because once you started it became an endless chain. And this was obviously the trap of the test.

Then King Giron clapped his hands in glee and a particle of Ralph's anger shot through the tight muscles. His hand on the dial twitched.

The sword descended part way and then hung motionless in the air. The guards cried out in astonishment, as did Ralph up above. King Giron stopped laughing and turned very white.

"Thrust this man out of the gate," he ordered hoarsely. "Get him out of my sight."

At the gate Telfus, who had been watching the miracle as openmouthed as the soldiers, eagerly grasped the rope of the handcart and started off.

"What has become of your sore leg?" asked Valsek, relaxed after his triumph.

"It is well rested," said Telfus shortly.

"You cannot maintain that pace," said Valsek. "As you said this morning, it is a long, weary road back home."

"We must hurry," said Telfus. "We will ignore the road." His muscles tensed as he jerked the cart over the bumpy field. "Hiller would want us to hurry and make more idols. Also we must recruit. We must raise funds, invent insignia, symbols. We have much to do, Valsek. Hurry!"

Ralph relaxed a little and looked at Cynthia beside him. Her fair skin glowed in the subdued light of the Hall. There was a tiny, permanent frown on her forehead, but the mouth was expressionless. Did she expect he would lash out at the first opposition to his control? He would show her and Gerard and the rest of them. . . .

They called Valsek the Man the King Couldn't Kill. They followed him wherever he went and listened to him preach. They brought him gifts of clothes and food which Telfus indicated would not be unpleasing to such a great man, and his wife and servant no longer had to work in the fields. He dictated a book, *Hiller Says So,* to Telfus, and the book grew into an organization which rapidly became political and then began to attract the military. They made his barn a shrine and built him a mud palace where the old hut had stood. Telfus kept count with manure sticks of the numbers who came, but presently there weren't enough manure sticks to count the thousands.

Throughout the land the cleavage grew, people deciding and dividing, deciding and dividing. If you didn't care for King Giron, you fell under the sway of Hillerism. But if you were tired of the strange ways of the gods, you clung to Gironism in safety, for this new god spoke seldom and punished no one for blasphemy.

King Giron contented himself with killing a few Hillerites. He was fairly certain that the gods were an illusion. Was there anything more wonderful than the mountains and trees and grass that grew on the plains? As for the god-wires, they were no more nor less wonderful, but to imagine they meant any more than a tree was to engage in superstition. He had once believed that Melton existed but the so-called signs no longer came, and by denying the gods—it was very simple—the miracles seemed to have ceased. True, there was the event when the guard had been unable to cut Valsek's throat, but then the man had a history of a rheumatic father, and the coincidence of his frozen arm at the proper moment was merely a result of the man's natural weakness and the excitement of the occasion.

"We shall let the Hillerites grow big enough," King Giron told his advisers. "Then we shall march on them and execute them and when that is done, the people will understand that there is no god except King Giron, and we shall be free of godism forever."

For his part, Valsek couldn't forget that his palace was made of mud, while Giron's was made of real baked brick.

"Giron insults you!" cried Valsek from his barntemple to Hiller. "His men have the finest temples in the city, the best jobs, the most of worldly goods. Why is this?"

"Giron represents order," Ralph directed through his electronic circuits. "It is not time to upset the smoothness of things."

Valsek made an impudent gesture. "At least give us miracles. I have waited all my life to be Spokesman, and I can have no miracles! The priests who deserted Melton for you are disgusted with the lack of miracles. Many turn to the new religion, Gironism."

"I don't believe in miracles."

"Fool!" cried Valsek.

In anger Ralph twisted the dial. Valsek felt himself lifted by a surge of current and dashed to the floor.

"Thanks," he said sadly.

Ralph shot a look at Cynthia. A smile, almost dreamy, of remembrance was on her lips. Here comes the old Ralph, she was thinking. Ralph felt himself tense so hard his calf muscles ached. "No more temper now, none," he demanded of himself.

Giron discovered that his *King's Book of Worship* was getting costly. More and more hand-scribes were needed to spread the worship of Gironism, and to feed them he had to lay heavier taxes on the people. He did so. The people responded by joining the Hillerites in great numbers, because even those who agreed with Giron about the illusory existence of the gods preferred Hiller's lower tax structure. This angered the King. A riot began in a minor city, and goaded by a determined King Giron, it flowered into an armed revolt and flung seeds of civil war to all corners of the land.

Telfus, who had been busy with organizational matters, hurried back to the mud palace.

"I suspect Hiller does not care for war," he said bitterly. "Giron has the swords, the supplies, the trained men. We have nothing. Therefore would it not be wise for us to march more and pray less—since Hiller expects us to take care of themselves?"

Valsek paced the barn. "Go hide behind a rock, beggar. Valsek fears no man, no arms."

"But Giron's troops are organizing——"

"The children of Hiller need no troops," Valsek intoned.

Telfus went out and stole, begged or borrowed all of the cold steel he could get. He began marching the men in the fields.

"What—troops!" frowned Valsek. "I ordered against it."

"We are merely practicing for a pageant," growled Telfus. "It is to please the women and children. We shall re-enact your life as a symbol of marching men. Is this permitted?"

"You may do that," nodded Valsek, appeased.

The troops of Giron came like a storm. Ralph held out as he watched the Gironists destroy the homes of the Hillers, deflower the Hiller women, kill the children of Hillers. And he waited. . . .

Dismayed, the Hillerites fell back on Valsek's bishopric, the mud palace, and drew around the leader.

Valsek nervously paced in the barn. "Perhaps it would be better to kill a few of the Gironists," he suggested to Ralph, "rather than wait until we are dead, for there may be no battles in heaven."

There was silence from above.

The Gironist troops drew up before the palace, momentarily stopped by the Pageant Guards of Telfus. You had to drive a god, thought Valsek. With a sigh, he made his way out of the besieged fortress and presented himself to the enemy. He had nothing to offer but himself. He had brought Hillerism to the land and he alone must defend it if Hiller would not.

King Giron smiled his pleasure at the foolish old man who was anxious to become a martyr. Was there ever greater proof of the falseness of the gods? Meekly Valsek bowed before the swords of King Giron's guardsmen.

"I am faithful to Hiller," said Valsek, "and if I cannot live with it, then I will die for it."

"That's a sweet way to go," said King Giron, "since you would be killed anyway. Guards, let the swords fall."

Ralph stared down at the body of Valsek. He felt a thin pulse of hate beating at his temples. The old man lay in the dust murdered by a dozen sword wounds, and the soldiers were cutting the flesh from the bones in joy at destroying the fountainhead of Hillerism. Then the banners lifted, the swords and lances were raised, the cry went down the ranks and the murderous horde swept upon the fortress of the fallen Valsek. A groan of dismay came from the Pageant troops when the Hillerites saw the severed head of Valsek borne before the attackers.

Ralph could hardly breathe. He looked up, up at the audience as they stirred, alive to the trouble he was in. He stared at Cynthia. She wet her lips, looking down, leaning forward. "Watch the power load," she whispered; "there will soon be many dead." Her white fingers rested on a dial.

Now, he thought bitterly, I will blast the murderers of Valsek and uphold my ego down there by destroying the Gironists. I will release the blast of energy held in the hand of an angry god—

And I shall pass the critical point and there will be a backlash and the poor ego-destroyed human up here will come screaming out of his Director's chair with a crack in his skull.

Not me!

Ralph's hands felt sweaty on the dials as he heard the far-off cries of the murders being wrought among the Hillerites. But he held his peace while the work was done, stepping down the system energy as the Short Ones died by the hundreds. The Hillerites fell. They were slaughtered without mercy by King Giron. Then the idols to Hiller were destroyed. Only one man, severely wounded, survived the massacre.

Telfus . . .

That worthy remembered the rock under which he had once slept when he plowed Valsek's fields. He crept under the rock now, trying to ignore his nearly severed leg. Secure, he peered out on the field of human misery.

"A very even-tempered god indeed," he told himself, and then fainted.

There was an almost audible cry of disappointment from the human audience in the Life Hall above Ralph's head. He looked up and Cynthia looked up too. Obviously human sentiment demanded revenge on the ghastly murderers of King Giron's guard. What sort of Secretary of Defense would this be who would let his "side" be so destroyed?

He noted that Bruce Gerard frowned as he scribbled notes. The Life Hall critic for the *Times*, spokesman for the intellectuals. Ralph would be ticked off proper in tomorrow's paper:

"Blunt-jawed, domineering Ralph Hiller, Assistant Secretary of Defense, turned in a less than jolly Life Hall performance yesterday for the edification of the thoughtful. His pallid handling of the proteins in the Pentagon leads one to believe that his idea of the best defense is signified by the word *refrainment,* a refinement on containment. Hiller held the seat long enough to impress his warmth upon it, the only good impression he made. By doing nothing at all and letting his followers among the Short Ones be slaughtered like helpless ants, he was able to sit out the required time and gain the valuable certificate that all politicos need. What this means for the defense of America, however, is another thing. One pictures our land in ashes, our people badly smashed and the porticoed jaw of Mr. Hiller opening to say, as he sits with folded hands, 'I am aware of all that is going on. You should respect my awareness.'"

Ralph turned to Cynthia.

"I have undercontrolled, haven't I?"

She shook her head. "I am forbidden to suggest. I am here to try to save you from the Short Ones and the Short Ones from you in case of emergency. I can now state that you have about used up your quota of violent deaths and another holocaust will cause the Board to fail you for mismanagement."

Ralph sighed. He had feared overcontrol and fallen into the error of undercontrol. God, it was frustrating. . . .

Ralph was allowed a half-hour lunch break while Cynthia took over the board. He tried to devise a safe way of toppling King Giron but could think of none. The victory was Giron's. If Giron was content, Ralph could do nothing. But if Giron tried any more violence—Ralph felt the blood sing in his ears. If he was destined to fail, he would make a magnificent failure of it!

Then he was back at the board beside Cynthia and under the helmet and the world of the Short Ones closed in on him. The scenes of the slaughter remained with him vividly, and he sought Telfus, the sole survivor, now a man with one eye and a twisted leg who nevertheless continued to preach Hillerism and tell about the god who was big enough to let Short Ones run their own affairs. He was often laughed at, more often stoned, but always he gathered a few adherents.

Telfus even made friends with a Captain of Giron's guard.

"Why do you persist in Hillerism?" asked the Captain. "It is obvious that Hiller doesn't care for his own priests enough to protect them."

"Not so," said Telfus. "He cares so much that he will trust them to fall on their knees or not, as they will, whereas the old gods were usually striking somebody dead in the market place because of some fancied insult. I cannot resist this miracle-less god. Our land has been sick with miracles."

"Still you'll need one when Giron catches up with you."

"Perhaps tomorrow. But if you give me a piece of silver for Hiller, I will sleep in an inn tonight and dream your name to him."

Ralph sought out King Giron.

That individual seemed sleek and fat now, very self-confident. "Take all of the statues of Hiller and Melton and any other leftover gods and smash them," ordered the King. "The days of the gods are over. I intend to speed up the building of statues to myself, now that I control the world."

The idols to the King went up in the market places. The people concealed doubt and prayed to him because his military was strong. But this pretense bothered Giron.

"The people cannot believe I'm divine," said King Giron. "We need a mighty celebration. A ritual to prove it. I've heard from a Guard Captain of Telfus, this one-eyed beggar who still clings to Hiller. I want him brought to my palace for a celebration. I want the last survivor of the Hiller massacre dressed in a black robe and sacrificed at my celebration. Then the people will understand that Gironism defies all gods and is eternal."

Ralph felt a dryness on the inside of his mouth. He watched the guards round up the few adherents of Hillerism and bring them to the palace. He watched the beginnings of the celebration to King Giron.

There was irony, he thought. Just as violence breeds violence, so non-violence breeds violence. Now the whole thing had to be done over again, only now the insolence of the Gironists dug into Ralph like a scalpel on a raw nerve.

Rank upon rank of richly clad soldiers, proud merchants, laughing Gironists crowded together in the center of the courtyard where the one-eyed man and a dozen of his tattered followers faced death.

"Now, Guards," said King Giron, "move out and kill them. Place the sword firmly at the neck and cleave them down the middle. Then there will be twice as many Hillers!"

Cheers! Laughter! Oh, droll, divine King Giron!

Ralph felt the power surging in the dial under his hand, ready but not yet unleashed. He felt the dizzying pull of it, the knowledge that he could rip the flesh apart and strip the bones of thousands of Gironists. The absolute power to blast the conceited ruler from his earth. To smash bodies, stone, sand, vegetation, all—absolute, absolute power ready to use.

And King Giron laughed as the swordsman cleft the first of the beggarly Hillers.

Ralph was a seething furnace of rage. "Go! Go! Go!" his mind told his hands.

Then Cynthia did a surprising thing. "Take your hands off the dials," she said. "You're in a nasty spot. I'm taking over."

His temples throbbed but with an effort he removed his hands from the dials. Whether she was helping him or hurting him, he didn't know, but she had correctly judged that he had reached his limit.

One by one the followers of Hillerism died. He saw the vein along her throat throb, and he saw her fingers tremble on the dials she tried to hold steady. A flush crept up her neck. Participation in the world below was working on her too. She could see no way out and he understood it.

The cruel, fat dictator and his unctuous followers, the poor, set-upon martyrs—even the symbol of Telfus, his last followers, being a crippled and helpless man. A situation like this could trigger a man into unleashing a blasting fury that would overload the circuits and earn him revenge only at the cost of a crack in his skull. In real life, a situation of white-hot seething public emotion would make a government official turn to his H-bombs with implacable fury and strike out with searing flames that would wash the world clean, taking the innocent along with the guilty, unblocking great segments of civilization, radioactivating continents and sending the sea into an eternal boil.

And yet—GOD DAMN IT, YOU HAD TO STOP THE GIRONS!

Cynthia broke. She was too emotionally involved to restrain herself. She bit her lips and withdrew her hands from the dials with a moan.

But the brief interruption had helped Ralph as he leaned forward and took the dials in her place. His anger had subsided suddenly into a clear-minded determination.

He thought-waved Telfus. "I fear that you must go," he said. "I thank you for keeping the faith."

"You've been a most peculiar god," said Telfus, warily watching the last of his friends die. His face was white; he knew he was being saved for the last.

"Total violence solves nothing."

"Still it would be nice to kick one of these fellows in the shins," said Telfus, the sweat pouring from his face. "In the natural order of things an occasional miracle cannot hurt."

"What would you have me do?"

Telfus passed a hand over his face. "Hardly a moment for thoughtful discussion," he groaned. He cried out in passionate anguish as his closest friend died. Ralph let the strong emotions of Telfus enter his mind, and then gradually Telfus caught hold of himself.

"Well," he said, "if I could only see King Giron die . . ."

"Never mind the rest?" asked Ralph.

"Never mind the rest," said Telfus. "Men shouldn't play gods."

"How right you are!" cried Ralph.

"Telfus!" cried King Giron. "You see now how powerful I am! You see now that there are no more gods!"

"I see a fool," said Telfus as the guard's sword fell. The guard struck low to prolong the death for the King's enjoyment and Telfus rolled on the ground trying to hold the blood in his body. The nobles cheered and King Giron laughed and clapped his hands in glee. The guards stood back to watch the death throes of Telfus.

But Telfus struggled to a sitting position and cried out in a voice that was strangely powerful as if amplified by the voice of a god.

"I've been permitted one small miracle," he said. "Under Hiller these favors are hard to come by."

There was an electric silence. Telfus pointed his empty hand at King Giron with the forefinger extended, like a gun. He dropped his thumb.

"Bang," he said.

At that moment Ralph gave vent to his pent-up steam of emotions in one lightning-quick flip of the dial of destruction, sent out with a prayer. A microsecond jab. At that the earth rocked and there was a roaring as the nearby seas changed the shoreline.

But King Giron's head split open and his insides rushed out like a fat, ripe pea that had been opened and shucked by a celestial thumb. For a second the empty skin and bones stood in semblance of a man and then gently folded to the ground.

"Not bad," said Telfus. "Thanks." He died.

It was interesting to watch the Gironists. Death—death in battle or natural death—was a daylight-common thing. Dignified destruction is a human trade. But the unearthly death of the King brought about by the lazy fingering of the beggar—what person in his time would forget the flying guts and empty, upright skin of the man who lived by cruelty and finally had his life shucked out?

Down below in the courtyard the Gironists began to get rid of their insignia. One man dropped Giron's book into a fire. Another softly drew a curtain over the idol of Giron. Men slunk away to ponder the non-violent god who would always be a shadow at their shoulder—who spoke seldom but when he spoke was heard for all time. Gironism was dead forever.

Up above a bell rang and Ralph jerked up from his contemplation with surprise to hear the rainlike sound, the applause and the approval of the audience in the Life Hall. Even Gerard was leaning over the press-box rail and grinning and nodding his head in approval, like a fish.

Ralph still had some time in the chair, but there would be no more trouble with the Short Ones. Already off somewhere a clerk was filling out the certificate.

He turned to Cynthia. "You saved me by that interruption."

"You earned your way," she said.

"I've learned much," he said. "If a god calls upon men for faith, then a god must return it with trust, and it was Telfus, not I, whom I trusted to solve the problem. After all, it was his life, his death."

"You've grown," she said.

"We have grown," he said, taking her hand under the table and not immediately letting go.

TRANSFUSION

Chad Oliver

The machine stopped.

There was no sound at all now, and the green light on the control panel blinked like a mocking eye. With the easy precision born of long routine, Ben Hazard did what had to be done. He did it automatically, without real interest, for there was no longer any hope.

He punched a figure into the recorder: 377

He computed the year, using the Gottwald-Hazard Correlation, and added that to the record: 254,000 B.C.

He completed the form with the name of the site: Choukoutien.

Then, with a lack of anticipation that eloquently reminded him that this was the three hundred seventy-seventh check instead of the first, Ben Hazard took a long preliminary look through the viewer. He saw nothing that interested him.

Careful as always before leaving the Bucket, he punched in the usual datum: Viewer Scan Negative.

He unlocked the hatch at the top of the Bucket and climbed out of the metallic gray sphere. It was not raining, for a change, and the sun was warm and golden in a clean blue sky.

Ben Hazard stretched his tired muscles and rested his eyes on the fresh green of the tangled plants that grew along the banks of the lazy stream to his right. The grass in the little meadow looked cool and inviting, and there were birds singing in the trees. He was impressed as always by how little this corner of the world had changed in fifty years. It was very much as it had been a thousand years ago, or two thousand, or three . . .

It was just a small corner of nowhere, lost in the mists of time, waiting for the gray sheets of ice to come again.

It was just a little stream, bubbling along and minding its own business, and a lonely limestone hill scarred with the dark staring eyes of rock shelters and cave entrances.

There was nothing different about it.

It took Man to change things in a hurry, and Man wasn't home. That was the problem.

Ben took the six wide-angle photographs of the terrain that he always took. There were no animals within camera range this trip. He clambered through the thick brown brush at the base of the limestone hill and climbed up the rough rocks to the cave entrance. It was still open, and he knew its location by heart.

He well remembered the thrill he had felt the first time he had entered this cave. His heart had hammered in his chest and his throat had been so dry that he couldn't swallow. His mind had been ablaze with memories and hopes and fears, and it had been the most exciting moment of his life.

Now, only the fear remained—and it was a new kind of fear, the fear of what he *wouldn't* find.

His light blazed ahead of him as he picked his way along the winding passage of the cave. He disturbed a cloud of indignant bats, but there was no other sign of life. He reached the central cavern, dark and hushed and hidden under the earth, and flashed his light around carefully.

There was nothing new.

He recognized t he familiar bones of wolf, bear, tiger, and camel. He photographed them again, and did manage to find the remains of an ostrich that he had not seen before. He took two pictures of that.

He spent half an hour poking around in the cavern, checking all of the meticulously recorded sites, and then made his way back to the sunlit entrance.

The despair welled up in him, greater than before. Bad news, even when it is expected, is hard to take when it is confirmed. And there was no longer any real doubt.

Man wasn't home.

Ben Hazard wasn't puzzled any longer. He was scared and worried. He couldn't pass the buck to anyone else this time. He had come back to see for himself, and he had seen.

Imagine a man who built a superb computer, a computer that could finally answer the toughest problems in his field. Suppose the ultimate in computers, and the ultimate in coded tapes; a machine—however hypothetical—that was never wrong. Just for kicks, suppose that the man feeds in an easy one: *What is two plus three?*

If the computer answers *six,* then the man is in trouble. Of course, the machine might be multiplying rather than adding—

But if the computer answers *zero* or *insufficient data,* what then?

Ben Hazard slowly walked back to the Bucket, climbed inside, and locked the hatch.

He filed his films under the proper code number.

He pushed in the familiar datum: Field Reconnaissance Negative.

He sat down before the control board and got ready.

He was completely alone in the small metallic sphere; he could see every inch of it. He *knew* that he was alone. And yet, as he had before, he had the odd impression that there was someone with him, someone looking over his shoulder . . .

Ben Hazard had never been one to vault into the saddle and gallop off in all directions. He was a trained scientist, schooled to patience. He did not understand the soundless voice that kept whispering in his mind: *Hurry, hurry, hurry—*

"Boy," he said aloud, "you've been in solitary too long."

He pulled himself together and reached for the controls. He was determined to run out the string—twenty-three checks to go now—but he already knew the answer.

Man wasn't home.

When Ben Hazard returned to his original year of departure, which was 1982, he stepped out of the Bucket at New Mexico Station—for the machine, of necessity, moved in space as well as time. As a matter of fact, the spatial movement of the Bucket was one of the things that made it tough to do an intensive periodic survey of any single spot on the Earth's surface; it was hard to hold the Bucket on target.

According to his own reckoning, and in terms of physiological time, he had spent some forty days in his check of Choukoutien in the Middle Pleistocene. Viewed from the other end of New Mexico Station, he had been gone only five days.

The first man he saw was a big M.P. corporal.

"I'll need your prints and papers, sir," the M.P. said.

"Dammit, Ames." Ben handed over the papers and stuck his thumbs in the scanner. "Don't you know me by now?"

"Orders sir."

Ben managed a tired smile. After all, the military implications of time travel were staggering, and care was essential. If you could move back in time only a few years and see what the other side had done, then you could counter their plans in the present. Since the old tribal squabbles were still going full blast, Gottwald had had to pull a million strings in order to get his hands on some of the available Buckets.

"Sorry, Ames. You look pretty good to me after a month or so of old camel bones."

"Nice to have you back, Dr. Hazard," the M.P. said neutrally.

After he had been duly identified as Benjamin Wright Hazard, Professor of Anthropology at Harvard and Senior Scientist on the Joint Smithsonian-Harvard-Berkeley Temporal Research Project, he was allowed to proceed. Ben crossed the crowded floor of the room they called Grand Central Station and paused a moment to see how the chimps were getting along.

There were two of them, Charles Darwin and Cleopatra, in separate cages. The apes had been the first time travelers, and were still used occasionally in testing new Buckets. Cleopatra scratched herself and hooted what might have been a greeting, but Charles Darwin was busy with a problem. He was trying to fit two sticks together so he could knock down a banana that was hanging just out of reach. He was obviously irritated, but he was no quitter.

"I know just how you feel, Charles," Ben said.

Charles Darwin pursed his mobile lips and redoubled his efforts.

What they won't do for one lousy banana.

Ben looked around for Nate York, who was working with the chimps, and spotted him talking to a technician and keeping track of his experiment out of the corner of his eye. Ben waved and went on to the elevator.

He rode up to the fourth floor and walked into Ed Stone's office. Ed was seated at his desk and he looked very industrious as he studied the dry white skull in front of him. The skull, however, was just a paper weight; Ed had used it for years.

Ed stood up, grinned, and stuck out his hand. "Sure glad you're back, Ben. Any luck?"

Ben shook hands and straddled a chair. He pulled out his pipe, filled it from a battered red can, and lit it gratefully. It felt good to be back with Ed. A man doesn't find too many other men he can really talk to in his lifetime, and Ed was definitely Number One. Since they were old friends, they spoke a private language.

"He was out to lunch," Ben said.

"For twenty thousand years?"

"Sinanthropus has always been famous for his dietary eccentricities."

Ed nodded to show that he caught the rather specialized joke—Sinanthropus had been a cannibal—and then leaned forward, his elbows on the desk. "You satisfied now?"

"Absolutely."

"No margin for error?" Ed insisted.

"None. I didn't really doubt Thompson's report, but I wanted to make certain. Sinanthropus isn't there. Period."

"That tears it then. We're up the creek for sure."

"Without a paddle."

"Without even a canoe." Ben puffed on his pipe. "Blast it, Ed, where *are* they?"

"You tell me. Since you left, Gottwald and I have gotten exactly nowhere. The way it looks right now, man hasn't got any ancestors—and that's crazy."

It's more than crazy, Ben thought. It's frightening. When you stop to think about it, man is a lot more than just an individual. Through his children, he extends on into the future. Through his ancestors, he stretches back far into the past. It is immortality of a sort. And when you chop off one end—

"I'm scared," he said. "I don't mind admitting it. There's an answer somewhere, and we've got to find it."

"I know how you feel, Ben. If this thing means what it seems to mean, then all science is just so much hot air. There's no cause and effect, no evidence, no reason. Man isn't what he thinks he is at all. We're just frightened animals sitting in a cave gaping at the darkness outside. Don't think I don't feel it, too. But what are we going to *do?*"

Ben stood up and knocked out his pipe. "Right now, I'm going home and hit the sack; I'm dead. Then the three of us—you and I and Gottwald—are going to sit down and hash this thing out. Then we'll at least know where we are."

"Will we?"

"We'd better."

He walked to the elevator and rode down to the ground floor of New Mexico Station. He had to identify himself twice more before he finally emerged into the glare of the desert sunlight. The situation struck him as the height of irony: here they were worried about spies and fancy feuds, when all the time—

What?

He climbed into his car and started for home. The summer day was bright and hot, but he felt as though he were driving down an endless tunnel of darkness, an infinite black cave to nowhere.

The voice whispered in his brain: *Hurry, hurry—*

His home was a lonely one, lonely with a special kind of emptiness. All his homes seemed deserted now that Anne was gone, but he liked this one better than most.

It was built of adobe with heavy exposed roof beams, cool in the summer and warm in winter. The Mexican tile floor was artfully broken up by lovely Navaho rugs—the rare Two Gray Hills kind in subdued and intricate grays and blacks and whites. He had brought many of his books with him from Boston and their familiar jackets lined the walls.

Ben was used to loneliness, but memories died hard. The plane crash that had taken Anne from him had left an emptiness in his heart. Sometimes, late in the evening, he thought he heard her footsteps in the kitchen. Often, when the telephone rang, he waited for her to answer it.

Twenty years of marriage are hard to forget.

Ben took a hot shower, shaved, and cooked himself a steak from the freezer. Then he poured a healthy jolt of Scotch over two ice cubes and sat down in the big armchair, propping his feet on the padded bench. He was still tired, but he felt more like a human being.

His eyes wandered to his books. There was usually something relaxing about old books and long-read titles, something reassuring. It had always been that way for him, but not any longer.

The titles jeered at him: *Mankind So Far, Up from the Ape, History of the Primates, Fossil Men, The Story of Man, Human Origins, The Fossil Evidence for Human Evolution, History of the Vertebrates* . . .

Little man, what now?

"We seem to have made a slight mistake, as the chemist remarked when his lab blew up," Ben said aloud.

Yes, but where could they have gone wrong?

Take Sinanthropus, for example. The remains of forty different Sinanthropus individuals had been excavated from the site of Choukoutien in China by Black and Weidenreich, two excellent men. There was plenty of material and it had been thoroughly studied. Scientists knew when Sinanthropus had lived in the Middle Pleistocene, where he lived, and how he lived. They even had the hearths where he cooked his food, the tools he used, the animals he killed. They knew what he looked like. They knew how he was related to his cousin, Pithecanthropus Erectus, and to modern men. There was a cast of his skull in every anthropology museum in the world, a picture of him in every textbook.

There was nothing mysterious about Sam Sinanthropus. He was one of the regulars.

Ben and Gottwald had nailed the date to the wall at 250,000 B.C. After Thompson's incredible report, Ben himself had gone back in time to search for Sinanthropus. Just to make certain, he had checked through twenty thousand years.

Nobody home.

Sinanthropus wasn't there.

That was bad enough.

But *all* the early human and pre-human fossils were missing.

There *were* no men back in the Pleistocene.

No Australopithecus, no Pithecanthropus, no Neanderthal, no nothing.

It was impossible.

At first, Ben had figured that there must be an error somewhere in the dating of the fossils. After all, a geologist's casual "Middle Pleistocene" isn't much of a target, and radiocarbon dating was no good that far back. But the Gottwald-Hazard Correlation had removed that possibility.

The fossil men simply were not there.

They had disappeared. Or they had never been there. Or—

Ben got up and poured himself another drink. He needed it.

When the Winfield-Homans equations had cracked the time barrier and Ben had been invited by old Franz Gottwald to take part in the Temporal Research Project, Ben had leaped at the opportunity. It was a scientist's dream come true.

He could actually go back and *see* the long-vanished ancestors of the human species. He could listen to them talk, watch their kids, seek them make their tools, hear their songs. No more sweating with a few broken bones. No more puzzling over flint artifacts. No more digging in ancient firepits.

He had felt like a man about to sit down to a Gargantuan feast.

Unhappily, it had been the cook's night out. There was nothing to eat.

Every scientist knows in his heart that his best theories are only educated guesses. There is a special Hall of Fame reserved for thundering blunders: the flat Earth, the medical humors, the unicorn.

Yes, and don't forget Piltdown Man.

Every scientist expects to revise his theories in the light of new knowledge. That's what science means. But he doesn't expect to find out that it's *all* wrong. He doesn't expect his Manhattan Project to show conclusively that uranium doesn't actually exist.

Ben finished his drink. He leaned back and closed his eyes. There had to be an answer somewhere—or somewhen. *Had* to be. A world of total ignorance is a world of terror; anything can happen.

Where was Man?

And why?

He went to bed and dreamed of darkness and ancient fears. He dreamed that he lived in a strange and alien world, a world of fire and blackness and living shadows—

When he woke up the next morning, he wasn't at all sure that he had been dreaming.

Among them, an impartial observer would have agreed, the three men in the conference room at New Mexico Station knew just about all there was to know concerning early forms of man. At the moment, in Ben's opinion, they might as well have been the supreme experts on the Ptolemaic theory of epicycles.

They were three very different men.

Ben Hazard was tall and lean and craggy-featured, as though the winds of life had weathered him down to the tough, naked rock that would yield no further. His blue eyes had an ageless quality about them, the agelessness of deep seas and high mountains, but they retained an alert and restless curiosity that had changed little from the eyes of an Ohio farm boy who had long ago wondered at the magic of the rain and filled his father's old cigar boxes with strange stones that carried the imprints of plants and shells from the dawn of time.

Ed Stone looked like part of what he was: a Texan, burned by the sun, his narrow gray eyes quiet and steady. He was not a big man, and his soft speech and deliberate movements gave him a deceptive air of lassitude. Ed was an easy man to underestimate;

he wasted no time on frills or pretense, but there was a razor-sharp brain in his skull. He was younger than Ben, not yet forty, but Ben trusted his judgment more than he did his own.

Franz Gottwald, old only in years, was more than a man now; he was an institution. They called him the dean of American anthropology, but not to his white-bearded face; Franz had small respect for deans. They stood when he walked into meetings, and Franz took it as his due—he had earned it, but it concerned him no more than the make of the car he drove. Ben and Ed had both studied under Franz, and they still deferred to him, but the relationship was a warm one. Franz had been born in Germany—he never spoke about his life before he had come to the United States at the age of thirty—and his voice was still flavored by a slight accent that generations of graduate students had tried to mimic without much success. He was the Grand Old Man.

"Well?" asked Dr. Gottwald when Ben had finished his report. "What is the next step, gentlemen?"

Ed Stone tapped on the polished table with a yellow pencil that showed distinct traces of gnawing. "We've got to accept the facts and go on from there. We know what the situation is, and we think that we haven't made any whopping mistakes. In a nutshell, man has vanished from his own past. What we need is an explanation, and the way to get it is to find some relatively sane hypothesis that we can *test*, not just kick around. Agreed?"

"Very scientific, Edward," Gottwald said, stroking his neat white beard.

"O.K.," Ben said. "Let's work from what we know. Those skeletons *were* in place in Africa, in China, in Europe, in Java—they had to be there because that's where they were originally dug up. The bones are real, I've held them in my hands, and they're still in place in the museums. No amount of twaddle about alternate time-tracks and congruent universes is going to change that. Furthermore, unless Franz and I are the prize dopes of all time, the dating of those fossils is accurate in terms of geology and the associated flora and fauna and whatnot. The Buckets work; there's no question about that. So why can't we find the men who left the skeletons, or even the bones themselves in their original sites?"

"That's a question with only one possible answer," Ed said.

"Check. Paradoxes aside—and there are no paradoxes if you have enough accurate information—the facts have to speak for themselves. *We don't find them because they are not there.* Next question: where the devil are they?''

Ed leaned forward, chewing on his pencil. ''If we forget about their geological context, none of those fossils are more than a few hundred years old. I mean, that's whey they were found. Even Neanderthal only goes back to around 1856 or thereabouts. Science itself is an amazingly recent phenomenon. So—''

''You mean Piltdown?'' Gottwald suggested, smiling.

''Maybe.''

Ben filled his pipe and lit it. ''I've thought about that, too. I guess all of us have. If one fossil man was a fake, why not all of them? But it won't hold water, and you know it. For one thing, it would have required a world-wide conspiracy, which is nonsense. For another—sheer manpower aside—the knowledge that would have been required to fake all those fossils simply did not exist at the time they were discovered. Piltdown wouldn't have lasted five minutes with fluorine dating and decent X-rays, and no one can sell me on the idea that men like Weidenreich and Von Koenigswald and Dart were fakers. Anyhow, that idea would leave us with a problem tougher than the one we're trying to solve—where did man come from if he had no past, no ancestors? I vote we exorcise that particular ghost.''

''Keep going,'' Gottwald said.

Ed took it up. ''Facts, Ben. Leave the theories for later. If neither the bones nor the men were present back in the Pleistocene where they belong, but the bones were present to be discovered later, then they *have* to appear somewhere in between. Our problem right now is *when.*''

Ben took his pipe out of his mouth and gestured with it, excited now. ''We can handle that one. Dammit, *all* of our data can't be haywire. Look: for most of his presumed existence, close to a million years, man was a rare animal—all the bones of all the fossil men ever discovered wouldn't fill up this room we're sitting in; all the crucial ones would fit in a broom closet. O.K.? But by Neolithic times, with agricultural villages, there were men everywhere, even here in the New World. That record is clear. So those fossils *had* to be in place by around eight thousand years ago. All we have to do—''

''Is to work back the other way,'' Ed finished, standing up. ''By God, that's it! We can send teams back through history, checking at short intervals until we *see* how it started. As long as the bones are where they should be, fine. When they disappear—and they have to disappear, because we know they're not there earlier—we'll reverse our field and check it hour by hour if necessary. Then we'll know what happened. After that, we can kick the theories around until we're green in the face.''

"It'll work," Ben said, feeling like a man walking out of a heavy fog. "It won't be easy, but it can be done. Only—"

"Only what?" Gottwald asked.

"Only I wonder what we'll find. I'm a little afraid of what we're going to see."

"One thing sure," Ed said.

"Yes?"

"This old world of ours will never be the same. Too bad—I kind of liked it the way it was."

Gottwald nodded, stroking his beard.

For months, Ben Hazard virtually lived within the whitewashed walls of New Mexico Station. He felt oddly like a man fighting a rattlesnake with his fists at some busy intersection, while all about him people hurried by without a glance, intent on their own affairs.

What went on in New Mexico Station was, of course, classified information. In Ben's opinion, this meant that there had been a ludicrous reversion to the techniques of magic. Facts were stamped with the sacred symbol of *CLASSIFIED,* thereby presumably robbing them of their power. Nevertheless, the world outside didn't know what the score was, and probably didn't care, while inside the Station—

History flickered by, a wonderful and terrible film.

Man was its hero and its villain—but for how long?

The teams went back, careful to do nothing and to touch nothing. The teams left Grand Central and pushed back, probing, searching . . .

Back past the Roman legions and the temples of Athens, back beyond the pyramids of Egypt and the marvels of Ur, back through the sunbaked villages of the first farmers, back into the dark shadows of pre-history—

And the teams found nothing.

At every site they could reach without revealing their presence, the bones of the early men were right where they should have been, waiting patiently to be unearthed.

Back past 8,000 B.C.

Back past 10,000.

Back past 15,000—

And then, when the teams reached 25,000 B.C., it happened. Quite suddenly, in regions as far removed from one another as France and Java, the bones disappeared.

And not just the bones.

Man himself was gone.

The world, in some ways, was as it had been—or was to be. The gray waves still tossed on the mighty seas, the forests were cool and green under clean blue skies, the sparkling sheets of snow and ice still gleamed beneath a golden sun.

The Earth was the same, but it was a strangely empty world without men. A desolate and somehow fearful world, hushed by long silences and stroked coldly by the restless winds . . .

"That's it," Ben said. "Whatever it was, we know when it happened—somewhere between 23,000 and 25,000 at the end of the Upper Paleolithic. I'm going back there."

"*We're* going back there," Ed corrected him. "If I sit this one out I'll be ready for the giggle factory."

Ben smiled, not trying to hide his relief. "I think I could use some company this trip."

"It's a funny feeling, Ben."

"Yes." Ben Hazard glanced toward the waiting Buckets. "I've seen a lot of things in my life, but I never thought I'd see the Beginning."

The machine stopped and the green light winked.

Ed checked the viewer while Ben punched data into the recorder.

"Nothing yet," Ed said. "It's raining."

"Swell." Ben unlocked the hatch and the two men climbed out. The sky above them was cold and gray. An icy rain was pouring down from heavy, low-hanging clouds. There was no thunder. Apart from the steady hiss of the rain, France in the year 24,571 B.C. was as silent as a tomb. "Let's get this thing covered up."

They hauled out the plastic cover, camouflaged to blend with the landscape, and draped it over the metallic gray sphere. They had been checking for eighteen days without results, but they were taking no chances.

They crossed the narrow valley through sheets of rain, their boots sinking into the soaked ground with every step. They climbed up the rocks to the gaping black hole of the cave entrance and worked their way in under the rock ledge, out of the rain. They switched on their lights, got down on their hands and knees, and went over every inch of the dry area just back of the rock overhang.

Nothing.

The gray rain pelted the hillside and became a torrent of water that splashed out over the cave entrance in a hissing silver waterfall. It was a little warmer in the cave, but dark and singularly uninviting.

"Here we go again," Ed muttered. "I know this blasted cave better than my own backyard."

"I'd like to see that backyard of yours about now. We could smoke up some chickens in the barbecue pit and sample some of Betty's tequila sours."

"Right now I'd just settle for the tequila. If we can't figure this thing out any other way we might just as well start looking in the old bottle."

"Heigh-ho," Ben sighed, staring at the waiting cave. "Enter one dwarf and one gnome, while thousands cheer."

"I don't hear a thing."

Ed took the lead and they picked and crawled their way back through the narrow passages of the cave, their lights throwing grotesque black shadows that danced eerily on the spires and pillars of ancient, dripping stone. Ben sensed the weight of the great rocks above him and his chest felt constricted. It was hard to breathe, hard to keep going.

"Whatever I am in my next incarnation," he said, "I hope it isn't a mole."

"You won't even make the mammals," Ed assured him.

They came out into a long, twisted vault. It was deep in the cave, far from the hidden skies and insulated from the pounding of the rain. They flashed their lights over the walls, across the dry gray ceiling, into the ageless silence.

Nothing.

No cave paintings.

It was as though man had never been, and never was to be.

"I'm beginning to wonder whether *I'm* real," Ed said.

"Wait a minute." Ben turned back toward the cave entrance, his body rigid. "Did you hear something?"

Ed held his breath and listened. "Yeah. There it is again."

It was faint and remote as it came to them in the subterranean vault, but there was no mistaking it.

A sound of thunder, powerful beyond belief.

Steady, now.

Coming closer.

And there had been no thunder in that cold, hissing rain . . .

"Come on." Ben ran across the cavern and got down on his hands and knees to crawl back through the twisting passage that led to the world outside. "There's something out there."

"What is it?"

Ben didn't stop. He clawed at the rocks until his hands were bloody. "I think the lunch hour's over," he panted. "I think Man's coming home."

Like two frightened savages, they crouched in the cave entrance and looked out across the rain-swept valley. The solid stone vibrated under their feet and the cold gray sky was shattered by blasting roars.

One thing was certain: that was no natural thunder.

"We've got to get out of here," Ben yelled. "We've got to hide before—"

"Where? The Bucket?"

"That's the best bet. It's almost invisible in this rain, and we can see through the viewer."

"Right. Run for it!"

The scrambled down among the slick rocks and ran across the wet grass and mud of the valley floor. It was cold and the rain pelted their faces in icy gray sheets. The deafening roar grew even louder, falling down from the leaden sky.

Fumbling in their haste, they jerked up a corner of the plastic cover so that the viewer could operate. Then they squirmed and wriggled under the plastic, dropped through the hatch, and sealed the lock. They dripped all over the time sphere but there was no time to bother about it. Even inside the Bucket they could feel the ocean of sound around them.

Ben cut in the recorder. "Start the cameras."

"Done."

"Hang on—"

The shattering roar reached an ear-splitting crescendo. Suddenly, there was something to see.

Light.

Searing white flame stabbing down from the gray skies.

They saw it: Gargantuan, lovely, huge beyond reason.

Before their eyes, like a vast metal fish from an unknown and terrible sea, the spaceship landed in the rain-soaked valley of Paleolithic France.

The long silence came again.

Fists clenched, Ben Hazard watched the *Creation*.

The great ship towered in the rain, so enormous that it was hard to imagine that it had ever moved. It might have been there always, but it was totally alien, out of place in its setting of hills and earth and sodden grasses.

Circular ports opened in the vast ship like half a hundred awakening eyes. Bright warm yellow light splashed out through the rain. Men—strangely dressed in dark, close-fitting tunics—floated out of the ship and down to the ground on columns of the yellow light.

The men were human, no different physically from Ben or Ed.

Equipment of some sort drifted down the shafts of light: strange spider-legged machines, self-propelled crates that gleamed in the light, shielded stands that might have been for maps or charts, metallic robots that were twice the size of a man.

It was still raining, but the men ignored it. The yellow light deflected the rain—Ben could see water dripping down the yellow columns as though solid tubes had been punched through the air—and the rain was also diverted from the men and their equipment.

The men from the ship moved quickly, hardly pausing to glance around them. They fanned out and went to work with the precision of trained specialists who knew exactly what they were doing.

Incredible as it was, Ben thought that he knew what they were doing too.

The spider-legged machines stayed on the valley floor, pulsing. Most of the men, together with three of the robots and the bulk of the self-propelled crates, made their way up to the cave Ben and Ed had just left and vanished inside.

"Want to bet on what's in those crates?" Ben whispered.

"Haven't the faintest idea, but two-bits says you spell it b-o-n-e-s."

The great ship waited, the streams of yellow light still spilling out into the rain. Five men pored over the shielded stands, looking for all the world like engineers surveying a site. Others worked over the spider-legged machines, setting up tubes of the yellow light that ran from the machines to the rocky hills. Two of the robots, as far as Ben could see, were simply stacking rocks into piles.

After three hours, when it was already growing dark, the men came back out of the cave. The robots and the crates were reloaded through the ship's ports and the uniformed men themselves boarded the ship again.

Night fell. Ben stretched to ease his cramped muscles, but he didn't take his eyes from the viewer for a second.

The rain died down to a gentle patter and then stopped entirely. The overcast lifted and slender white clouds sailed through the wind-swept sky. The moon rose, fat and silver, its radiance dimming the burning stars.

The impossible ship, towering so complacently beneath the moon of Earth, was a skyscraper of light. It literally hummed with activity. Ben would have given a lot to know what was going on inside that ship, but there was no way to find out.

The pulsing spider-legged machines clicked and buzzed in the cold of the valley night. Rocks were conveyed along tubes of the yellow light to the machines, which were stamping something out by the hundreds of thousands. Something . . .

Artifacts?

The long, uncanny night ended. Ben and Ed watched in utter fascination, their fears almost forgotten, sleep never even considered.

Dawn streaked the eastern sky, touching the clouds with fingers of rose and gold. A light breeze rustled the wet, heavy grasses. Water still dripped from the rocks.

The uniformed men came back out of the ship, riding down on the columns of yellow light. The robots gathered up some immense logs and stacked them near the mouth of the cave. They treated the wood with some substance to dry it, then ignited a blazing fire.

Squads of men moved over the valley floor, erasing all traces of their presence. One of them got quite close to the Bucket and Ben felt a sudden numbing chill. What would happen if they were seen? He was no longer worried about himself. But what about all the men who were to live on the Earth? Or—

The squad moved away.

Just as the red sun lifted behind the hills, while the log fire still blazed by the cave, the ship landed the last of its strange cargo.

Human beings.

Ben felt the sweat grow clammy in the palms of his hands.

They floated down the shafts of yellow light, shepherded by the uniformed men. There were one hundred of them by actual count, fifty men and fifty women. There were no children. They were a tall, robust people, dressed in animal skins. They shivered in the cold and seemed dazed and uncomprehending. They had to be led by the hand, and several had to be carried by the robots.

The uniformed men took them across the wet valley, a safe distance away from the ship. They huddled together like sheep, clasping one another in sexless innocence. Their eyes turned from the fire to the ship, understanding neither. Like flowers, they lifted their heads to the warmth of the sun.

It was a scene beyond age; it had always been. There were the rows of uniformed men, standing rigidly at attention. And there were the clustered men in animal skins, waiting without hope, without regret.

An officer—Ben thought of him that way, though his uniform was no different from the others—stepped forward and made what seemed to be a speech. At any rate, he talked for a long time—nearly an hour. It was clear that the dazed people did not understand a word of what he was saying, and that, too, was older than time.

It's a ceremony, Ben thought. *It must be some kind of ritual. I hadn't expected that.*

When it was over, the officer stood for a long minute looking at the huddle of people. Ben tried to read his expression in the viewer, but it was impossible. It might have been regret. It might have been hope. It might have been only curiosity.

It might have been anything.

Then, at a signal, the uniformed men turned and abandoned the others. They walked back to their waiting ship and the columns of yellow light took them inside. The ports closed.

Ten minutes later, the ship came to life.

White flame flared beneath its jets and the earth trembled. The terrible roar came again. The people who had been left behind fell to the ground, covering their ears with their hands. The great ship lifted slowly into the blue sky, then faster and faster—

It was gone, and only the sound remained, the sound of thunder . . .

In time, that, too, was gone.

Ben watched his own ancestors with an almost hypnotic fascination. They did not move.

Get up, get up—

The skin-clad people stood up shakily after what seemed to be hours. They stared blankly at one another. As though driven by some vague instinct that spoke through their shock, they turned and looked at the blazing fire that burned by the mouth of the cave.

Slowly, one by one, they pulled themselves over the rocks to the fire. They stood before it, seeking a warmth they could not understand.

The sun climbed higher into the sky, flooding the rain-clean world with golden light.

The people stood for a long time by the cave entrance, watching the fire burn down. They did nothing and said nothing.

Hurry, hurry. The voice spoke again in Ben's brain. He shook his head. Was he thinking about those dazed people out there, or was someone thinking about *him?*

Gradually, some of them seemed to recover their senses. They began to move about purposefully—still slowly, still uncertainly, like men coming out from under an anaesthetic. One man picked up a fresh log and threw it on the fire. Another crouched down and fingered a chipped piece of flint he found on a rock. Two women stepped behind the fire and started into the dark cave.

Ben turned away from the viewer, his unshaven face haggard. "Meet Cro-Magnon," he said, waving his hand.

Ed lit a cigarette, his first in eighteen hours. His hand was shaking. "Meet everybody, you mean. Those jokers planted the other boys—Neanderthal and whatnot—back in the cave before they landed the living ones."

"We came out of that ship too, Ed."

"I know—but where did the *ship* come from? And why?"

Ben took a last long look at the people huddled around the fire. He didn't feel like talking. He was too tired to think. None of it made any sense.

What kind of people could *do* a thing like that?

And if they hadn't—

"Let's go home," Ed said quietly.

They went out and removed the plastic cover, and then set the controls for New Mexico Station in a world that was no longer their own.

Old Franz Gottwald sat behind his desk. His white suit was freshly pressed and his hair was neatly combed. He stroked his beard in the old familiar gesture, and only the gleam in his eyes revealed the excitement within him.

"It has always been my belief, gentlemen, that there is no substitute for solid thinking based on verified facts. There is a time for action and there is a time for thought. I need hardly remind you that action without thought is pointless; it is the act of an animal, the contraction of an earthworm. We have the facts we need. You have been back for three days, but the thinking is yet to be done."

"We've been beating our brains out," Ben protested.

"That may be, Ben, but a man can beat his brains out with a club. It is not thinking."

"*You* try thinking," Ed said, grinding out his cigarette.

Gottwald smiled. "You are too old to have your thinking done for you, Edward. I have given you all I can give. It is your turn now."

Ben sat down in his chair and lit his pipe. He took his time doing it, trying to clear his mind. He had to forget those frightened people huddled around a fire in the mists of time, had to forget the emotions he had felt when the great ship had left them behind. Gottwald was right, as always.

The time had come for thought.

"O.K.," he said. "We all know the facts. Where do we go from here?"

"I would suggest to you, gentlemen, that we will get no answers until we begin to ask the right questions. That is elementary, if I may borrow from Mr. Holmes."

"You want questions?" Ed laughed shortly. "Here's one, and it's a dilly. 'There's a hole in all this big enough to drive the American Anthropological Association through in a fleet of trucks.' What about the apes?"

Ben nodded. "You quoted Conan Doyle, Franz, so I'll borrow a line from another Englishman—Darwin's pal Huxley. 'Bone for bone, organ for organ, man's body is repeated in the body of the ape.' Hell, we all know that. There are differences, sure, but the apes are closer to men than they are to monkeys. If man didn't evolve on Earth—"

"You've answered your own question, Ben."

"Of course!" Ed fished out another cigarette. "If man didn't evolve on Earth, then neither did the apes. That ship—or some ship—brought them both. But that's impossible."

"Impossible?" Franz asked.

"Maybe not," Ben said slowly. "After all, there are only four living genera of apes—two in Africa and two in Asia. We could even leave out the gibbon; he's a pretty primitive customer. It *could* have been done.''

"Not for all the primates," Ed insisted. "Not for all the monkeys and lemurs and tarsiers, not for all the fossil primate bones. It would have made Noah's ark look like a rowboat.''

"I would venture the suggestion that your image is not very apt," Gottwald said. "That ship *was* big enough to make any of our ships look like rowboats.''

"Never mind," Ben said, determined not to get sidetracked. "It doesn't matter. Let's assume that the apes were seeded, just as the men were. The other primates could have evolved here without interference, just as the other animals did. That isn't the real problem.''

"I wonder," Ed said. "Could that ship have come out of *time* as well as space? After all, if we have time travel they must have it. They could do anything—''

"Bunk," Gottwald snorted. "Don't let yourself get carried away. Edward. Anything is *not* possible. A scientific law is a scientific law, no matter who is working with it, or where, or when. We know from the Winfield-Homans Equations that it is impossible to go back into time and alter it in any way, just as it is impossible to go into the future which does not yet exist. There are no paradoxes in time travel. Let's not make this thing harder than it is by charging off into all the blind alleys we can think of. Ben was on the right track. What is the real problem here?''

Ben sighed. He saw the problem all too clearly. "It boils down to this, I think. *Why* did they plant those fossils—and probably the apes too? I can think of fifty reasons why they might have seeded man like themselves on a barren planet—population pressure and so forth—but why go to all the trouble of planting a false evolutionary picture for them to dig up later?''

"Maybe it isn't false," Ed said slowly.

Franz Gottwald smiled. "Now you're *thinking,* Edward.''

"Sorry, Ed. I don't follow you. You saw them plant those bones. If that isn't a prime example of salting a site, then what the devil is it?''

"Don't shoot, pal. I was trying to say that the fossils could have been planted and *still* tell a true story. Maybe I'm just an old codger set in his ways, but I can't believe that human evolution is a myth. And there's a clincher, Ben: why bother with the apes if there is no relationship?"

"I still don't see—"

"He means," Gottwald said patiently, "that the fossil sequence is a true one—*some place else.*"

Ed nodded. "Exactly. The evolutionary series is the genuine article, but man developed on their world rather than on ours. When they seeded men on Earth, they also provided them with a kind of history book—if they could read it."

Ben chewed on his pipe. It made sense, to the extent that anything made sense any more. "I'll buy that. But where does it leave us?"

"Still up that well-known creek. Every answer we get just leads back to the same old question. *Why* did they leave us a history book?"

"Answer that one," Gottwald said, "and you win the gold cigar."

Ben got to his feet. His head felt as though it were stuffed with dusty cotton.

"Where are you going?"

"I'm going fishing. As long as I'm up the creek I might as well do something useful. I'll see you later."

"I hope you catch something," Ed said.

"So do I," Ben Hazard said grimly.

The car hummed sleepily across the monotonous flatlands of New Mexico, passed through the gently rolling country that rested the eye, and climbed into the cool mountains where the pines grew tall and the grass was a thick dark green in the meadows.

Ben loved the mountains. As he grew older, they meant more and more to him. The happiest times of his life had been spent up next to the sky, where the air was crisp and the streams ran clear. He needed the mountains, and he always returned to them when the pressure was too much to bear.

He turned off the main road and jolted over a gravel trail; paved roads and good fishing were mutually exclusive, like cities and sanity. He noted with approval that the clouds were draping the mountain peaks, shadowing the land below. When the sun was too bright the fish could see a man coming.

He took a deep breath, savoring the tonic of the air.

Relax, that's the ticket.

He checked to see that no interloper had discovered his favorite stretch of water, then parked his car by the side of Mill Creek, a gliding stream of crystal-clean water that tumbled icily out of the mountains and snaked its lazy way through the long green valley. He grinned like a kid with his first cane pole.

Ben pulled on his waders, assembled his rod with practiced skill, and tied on his two pet flies—a Gray Hackle Yellow and a Royal Coachman. He hung his net over one shoulder and his trout basket over the other, lit his pipe, and waded out into the cold water of Mill Creek.

He felt wonderful. He hooked a nice brook trout within five minutes, taking him from a swirl of dark water shadowed by the blank of the stream. He felt the knots and the tensions flow out of him like melting snow, and that was the first step.

He *had* to relax. There was no other way.

Consider the plight of a baseball player in a bad slump. He gives it all he has, tries twice as hard as usual, but everything he does backfires. His hits don't fall in, he misses the easy grounders. He lies awake at night and worries.

"Relax, Mac," his manager tells him. "All you gotta do is *relax*. Take it easy."

Sure, but how?

It was the same with a tough scientific problem. Ben had long ago discovered that persistent and orderly logic could take him only so far. There came a time when no amount of forced thinking would get the job done.

The fresh insights and the new slants seldom came to him when he went after them, no matter how hard he tried. In fact, the more he sweated over a problem the more stubbornly recalcitrant his mind became. The big ideas, and the good ones, came to him in a flash of almost intuitive understanding—a flash that was conditioned by what he knew, of course, but a flash that did not come directly from the conscious mind.

The trick was to let the conscious mind get out of the way, let the message get through—

In Ben's case, go fishing.

It took him two hours, seven trout, and part of a banana to get the answer he sought.

He had taken a long, cool drink from the stream, cleaned his fish, and was sitting down on a rock to eat the lunch he had packed when the idea came.

He had peeled a banana and taken one bite of it when his mind was triggered by a single, innocuous word:

Banana.

Not just any old banana, of course. A specific one, used for a specific purpose.

Remember?

Charles Darwin and Cleopatra, two chimpanzees in their cages. Charles Darwin pushing his ape brain to the limit to fit two sticks together. Why?

To get a banana.

One lousy banana.

That was well enough, but there was more. Darwin might get his banana, and that was all he cared about. But who had placed the sticks in the cage, who had supplied the banana?

And why?

That was an easy one. It was so simple a child could have figured it out. Someone had given Charles Darwin two sticks and a banana for just one reason: to see whether or not he could solve the problem.

In a nutshell, a scientific experiment.

Now, consider another Charles Darwin, another problem.

Or consider Ben Hazard.

What is the toughest problem a man can tackle? Howells pointed it out many years ago. Of all the animals, man is the only one who wonders where he has come from and where he is going. All the other questions are petty compared to that one. It pushes the human brain to the limit . . .

Ben stood up, his lunch forgotten.

It was all so obvious.

Men had been seeded on the Earth, and a problem had been planted with them—a real problem, one capable of yielding to a true solution. A dazed huddle of human beings had been abandoned by a fire in the mouth of a cave, lost in the morning of a strange new world. Then they had been left strictly alone; there was no evidence that they had been helped in any way since that time.

Why?

To see what they could do.

To see how long it would take them to solve the problem.

In a nutshell, a scientific experiment.

Ben picked up his rod and started back toward the car.

There was one more thing, one more inevitable characteristic of a scientific experiment. No scientist merely sets up his experiment and then goes off and forgets about it, even if he is the absolute ultimate in absent-minded professors.

No.

He has to stick around to see how it all comes out. He has to observe, take notes.

It was monstrous.

The whole history of man on Earth . . .

Ben climbed into his car, started the engine.

There's more. Face up to it.

Suppose that you had set up a fantastic planetary experiment with human beings. Suppose that you—or one of your descendants, for human generations are slow—came back to check on your experiment. What would you do, what would you be?

A garage mechanic?

A shoe salesman?

A pool room shark?

Hardly. You'd have to be in a position to know what was going on. You'd have to work in a field where you could find out the score.

In a word, you'd be an anthropologist.

There's still more. Take it to the end of the line.

Now, suppose that man on Earth cracked the time barrier. Suppose a Temporal Research Project was set up. Wouldn't you be in on it, right at the top?

Sure.

You wouldn't miss it for anything.

Well, who fit the description? It couldn't be Ed; Ben had known him most of his life, known his folks and his wife and his kids, visited the Texas town that had been his home.

It wasn't Ben.

That left Franz Gottwald.

Franz, who had come from Germany and never talked about his past. Franz, with the strangely alien accent. Franz, who had no family. Franz, who had contributed nothing to the project but shrewd, prodding questions . . .

Franz.

The Grand Old Man.

Ben drove with his hands clenched on the wheel and his lips pressed into a thin, hard line. Night had fallen by the time he got out of the mountains, and he drove across an enchanted desert beneath the magic of the stars. The headlights of his car lanced into the night, stabbing, stabbing—

He passed the great New Mexico rocket base, from which men had hurled their missiles to the moon and beyond. There had been talk of a manned shot to Mars . . .

How far would the experimenters let them go?

Ben lit a cigarette, not wanting to fool with his pipe in the car. He was filled with a cold anger he had never known before.

He had solved the problem.

Very well.

It was time to collect his banana.

It was after midnight when Ben got home.

He stuck his fish in the freezer, took a shower, and sat down in his comfortable armchair to collect his thoughts. He promptly discovered yet another fundamental truth about human beings: when they get tired enough, they sleep.

He woke up with a start and looked at his watch. It was five o'clock in the morning.

Ben shaved and was surprised to find that he was hungry. He cooked himself some bacon and scrambled eggs, drank three cups of instant coffee, and felt ready for anything.

Even Franz.

He got into his car and drove through the still-sleeping town to Gottwald's house. It looked safe and familiar in the pale morning light. As a matter of fact, it looked a lot like his own house, since both had been supplied by the government.

That, he thought, was a laugh.

The government had given *Gottwald* a house to live in.

He got out of his car, walked up to the door, and rang the bell. Franz never got to the office before nine, and his car was still in the garage.

His ring was greeted by total silence.

He tried again, holding his finger on the bell. He rang it long enough to wake the dead.

No answer.

Ben tried the door. It was unlocked. He took a deep breath and stepped inside. The house was neat and clean. The familiar books were on the shelves in the living room. It was like stepping into his own home.

"Franz! It's me, Ben."

No answer.

Ben strode over to the bedroom, opened the door, and looked inside. The bed was tidily made, and Franz wasn't in it. Ben walked through the whole house, even peering inside the closets, before he was satisfied.

Franz wasn't home.

Fine. A scientist keeps records, doesn't he?

Ben proceeded to ransack the house. He looked in dresser drawers, on closet shelves, even in the refrigerator. He found nothing unusual. Then he tried the obvious.

He opened Gottwald's desk and looked inside.

The first thing he saw was a letter addressed to himself. There it was, a white envelope with his name typed on it: *Dr. Benjamin Wright Hazard.*

Not to be opened until Christmas?

Ben took the letter, ripped it open, and took out a single sheet of paper. He started to read it, then groped for a chair and sat down.

The letter was neatly typed. It said:

My dear Ben: I have always believed that a scientist must be capable of making predictions. This is not always an easy matter when you are dealing with human beings, but I have known you for a long, long time.

Obviously, you are searching my home, or you would not be reading this note. Obviously, if you are searching my home, you know part of the truth.

If you would like to know the rest of the story, the procedure is simple. Look behind the picture of the sand-painting in my bedroom. You will find a button there. Press the button for exactly five seconds. Then walk out into my patio and stand directly in front of the barbeque pit.

Trust me, Ben. I am not a cannibal.

The letter was signed with Gottwald's scrawled signature.

Ben got up and walked into the bedroom. He looked behind the picture that was hanging over the dresser. There was a small red button.

Press the button for exactly five seconds.

And then—what?

Ben replaced the picture. The whole thing was a trifle too reminiscent of a feeble-minded practical joke. Press the button and get a shock. Press the button and get squirted with water. Press the button and blow up the house—

No. That was absurd.

Wasn't it?

He hesitated. He could call Ed, but then Ed would insist on coming over right away—and Ed had a wife and kids. He could call the police, but the story he had to tell would have sounded absolutely balmy. He had no proof. He might as well recite "Gunga Din."

He went back to Gottwald's desk, found some paper, and typed a letter. He outlined the theory he had formed and wrote down exactly what he was going to do. He put the letter into an envelope, addressed the envelope to Ed, stamped it, and went outside and dropped it in the mailbox on the corner.

He went back into the house.

This time he did not hesitate—not for a second.

He punched the button behind the picture for exactly five seconds. Nothing happened. He went out into the patio and stood directly in front of the barbecue pit.

The wall around the patio hid the outside world, but the blue sky overhead was the same as ever. He saw nothing, heard nothing.

"Snipe hunt," he said aloud.

Then, with breathtaking suddenness, something *did* happen.

There was an abrupt stillness in the air, a total cessation of sound. It was as though invisible glass walls had slipped silently into place and sealed off the world around him.

There was no perceptible transition. One moment the cone of yellow light was not there, and the next it was. It surrounded him: taut, living, seething with an energy that prickled his skin.

He knew that yellow light.

He had seen it once before, in the dawn of time . . .

Ben held his breath; he couldn't help it. He felt strangely weightless, buoyant, a cork in a nameless sea—

His feet left the ground.

"Good God," Ben said.

He was lifted into the yellow light, absorbed in it. He could see perfectly, and it didn't help his stomach any. He could see the town below him—there was Gottwald's patio, the barbeque pit, the adobe house. He began to regret the bacon and eggs he had eaten.

He forced himself to breathe again. The air was warm and tasteless. He rose into the sky, fighting down panic.

Think of it as an elevator. It's just a way of getting from one

*place to another. I can see out, but of course nothing is visible
from the outside . . .*

But then how did I see the yellow light before?

This must be different. They couldn't risk being seen—

Relax!

But he kept going higher, and faster.

The Earth was far away.

It was an uncanny feeling—not exactly unpleasant, but he
didn't care for the view. It was like falling through the sky. It was
impossible to avoid the idea that he was falling, that he was going
to hit something . . .

The blue of the sky faded into black, and he saw the stars.

Where am I going, where are they taking me?

There!

Look up, look up—

There it was, at the end of the tunnel of yellow light.

It blotted out the stars.

It was huge even against the immense backdrop of space itself.
It stunned his mind with its size, that sleeping metal beast, but he
recognized it.

It was the same ship that had landed the first men on Earth.

Dark now, dark and vast and lonely—but the same ship.

The shaft of yellow light pulled him inside; there was no air
lock. As suddenly as it had come, the light was gone.

Ben stumbled and almost fell. The gravity seemed normal, but
the light had supported him for so long that it took his legs a
moment to adjust themselves.

He stood in a cool green room. It was utterly silent.

Ben swallowed hard.

He crossed the room to a metal door. The door opened before he
reached it. There was only blackness beyond, blackness and the
total silence of the dead.

Ben Hazard tried to fight down the numbing conviction that the
ship was empty.

There is an almost palpable air of desolation about long deserted
things, about empty houses and derelict ships and crumbling ruins.
There is a special kind of silence about a place that has once
known life and knows it no longer. There is a type of death that
hovers over things that have not been *used* for a long, long time.

That was the way the ship felt.

Ben could see only the small green room in which he stood and the corridor of darkness outside the door. It could have been only a tiny fraction of the great ship, only one room in a vast city in the sky. But he *knew* that the men who had once lived in the ship were gone. He knew it with a certainty that his mind could not question.

It was a ghost ship.

He knew it was.

That was why his heart almost stopped when he heard the footsteps moving toward him through the silence.

Heavy steps.

Metallic steps.

Ben backed away from the door. He tried to close it but it would not shut. He saw a white light coming at him through the dark tunnel. The light was higher than a man—

Metallic steps?

Ben got a grip on himself and waited. *You fool, you know they had robots. You saw them. Robots don't die, do they?*

Do they kill?

He saw it now, saw its outline behind the light. Twice the size of a man, its metal body gleaming.

It had no face.

The robot filled the doorway and stopped. Ben could hear it now: a soft whirring noise that somehow reminded him of distant winds. He told himself that it was just a machine, just an animated hunk of metal, and his mind accepted the analysis. But it is one thing to know what a robot is, and it is quite another to find yourself in the same room with one.

"Well?" Ben said. He had to say something.

The robot was evidently under no such compulsion. It said nothing and did nothing. It simply stood there.

"You speak English, of course?" Ben said, recalling the line from an idiotic story he had once read.

If the robot spoke anything, it wasn't English.

After a long, uncomfortable minute, the robot turned around and walked into the dark corridor, its light flashing ahead of it. It took four steps, stopped, and looked back over its shoulder.

There was just one thing to do, and one way to go.

Ben nodded and stepped through the doorway after the robot.

He followed the giant metallic man along what seemed to be miles of featureless passageways. Ben heard no voices, saw no lights, met no living things.

He felt no fear now; he was beyond that. He knew that he was in a state of shock where nothing could get through to him, nothing could hurt him. He felt only a kind of sadness, the sadness a man knows when he walks through the tunnels of a pyramid or passes a graveyard on a lonely night.

The ship that men had built was so vast, so silent, so empty . . .

A door opened ahead of them.

Light spilled out into the corridor.

Ben followed the robot into a large, comfortable room. The room was old, old and worn, but it was alive. It was warm and vital and human because there were two people in it. Ben had never before been quite so glad to see anyone.

One of the persons was an elderly woman he had never seen before.

The other was Franz Gottwald.

"Hello, Ben," he said, smiling. "I don't believe you've met my wife."

Ben didn't know whether he was coming into a nightmare or coming out of one, but his manners were automatic.

"I'm very pleased to meet you," he said, and meant it.

The room had a subtle strangeness about it that once more reminded Ben of a dream. It was not merely the expected strangeness of design of a new kind of room, a room lost in the lonely miles of a silent spaceship; it was an out-of-phase oddness that at first he could not identify.

Then he caught it. There were alien things in the room: furniture that was planned for human beings but produced by a totally different culture pattern, carvings that were grotesque to his eyes, rugs that glowed in curiously wrong figures. But there were also familiar, everyday items from the world he knew: a prosaic reading lamp, a coffee pot bubbling on a table, some potted plants, a framed painting by Covarrubias. The mixture was a trifle jarring, but it did have a reassuring air of homeliness.

How strange the mind is. At a time like this, it concentrates on a room.

"Sit down, sit down," Franz said. "Coffee?"

"Thank you." Ben tried a chair and found it comfortable.

The woman he persisted in thinking of as Mrs. Gottwald—though that was certainly not her actual name—poured out a cup and handed it to him. Her lined, delicate face seemed radiant with happiness, but there were tears in her eyes.

"I speak the language too a little," she said hesitantly. "We are so proud of you, so happy—"

Ben took a sip of the coffee to cover his embarrassment. He didn't know what he had expected, but certainly not *this*.

"Don't say anything more, Arnin," Franz said sharply. "We must be very careful."

"That robot of yours," Ben said. "Couldn't you send him out for oiling or something?"

Franz nodded. "I forgot how weird he must seem to you. Please forgive me. I would have greeted you myself, but I am growing old and it is a long walk." He spoke to the robot in a language Ben had never heard, and the robot left the room.

Ben relaxed a little. "Do you two live up here all alone?"

An inane question. But what can I do, what can I say?

Old Franz seated himself next to Ben. He still wore his white suit. He seemed tired, more tired than Ben had ever seen him, but there was a kind of hope in his eyes, a hope that was almost a prayer.

"Ben," he said slowly, "it is hard for me to talk to you—now. I can imagine how you must feel after what you have been through. But you must trust me a little longer. Just forget where you are, Ben—a spaceship is just a ship. Imagine that we are back at the Station, imagine that we are talking as we have talked so many times before. You must think clearly. This is important, my boy, more important than you can know. I want you to tell me what you have discovered—I want to know what led you here. Omit nothing, and choose your words with care. Be as specific and precise as you can. Will you do this one last thing for me? When you have finished, I think I will be able to answer all your questions."

Ben had to smile. *"Be as specific and precise as you can."* How many times had he heard Franz use that very phrase on examinations?

He reached for his pipe. For a moment he had a wild, irrational fear that he had forgotten it—that would have been the last straw, somehow—but it was there. He filled it and lit it gratefully.

"It's your party, Franz. I'll tell you what I know."

"Proceed, Ben—and be careful."

Mrs. Gottwald—Arnin?—sat very still, waiting.

The ship was terribly silent around them.

Ben took his time and told Franz what he knew and what he believed. He left nothing out and made no attempt to soften his words.

When he was finished, Gottwald's wife was crying openly.

Franz, amazingly, looked like a man who had suddenly been relieved of a sentence of death.

"Well?" Ben asked.

Gottwald stood up and stroked his white beard. "You must think I am some kind of a monster," he said, smiling.

Ben shrugged. "I don't know."

Mrs. Gottwald dried her eyes. "Tell him," she said. "You can tell him now."

Gottwald nodded. "I am proud of you, Ben, very proud."

"I was right?"

"You were right in the only thing that matters. The fossils *were* a test, and you have passed that test with flying colors. Of course, you had some help from Edward—"

"I'll give him part of the banana."

Gottwald's smile vanished. "Yes. Yes, I daresay you will. But I am vain enough to want to clear up one slight error in your reconstruction. I do not care for the role of monster, and mad scientists have always seemed rather dull to me."

"The truth is the truth."

"A redundancy, Ben. But never mind. I must tell you that what has happened on Earth was *not* a mere scientific experiment. I must also tell you that I am not only a scientist who has come back, as you put it, to see how the chimpanzees are doing. In fact, I didn't come back at all. We—my people—never left. I was born right here in this ship, in orbit around the Earth. It has always been here."

"For twenty-five thousand years?"

"For twenty-five thousand years."

"But what have you been doing?"

"We've been waiting for you, Ben. You almost did not get here in time. My wife and I are the only ones left."

"Waiting for *me?* But—"

Gottwald held up his hand. "No, not this way. I can show you better than I can tell you. If my people had lived—my other people, I should say, for I have lived on the Earth most of my life—there would have been an impressive ceremony. That can never be now. But I can show you the history lesson we prepared. Will you come with me? It is not far."

The old man turned and walked toward the door, his wife leaning on his arm.

"So long," she whispered. "We have waited so long."

Ben got up and followed them into the corridor.

• • •

In a large assembly room filled with empty seats, somewhere in the great deserted ship, Ben saw the history of Man.

It was more than a film, although a screen was used. Ben lived the history, felt it, was a part of it.

It was not a story of what King Glotz did to King Goop; the proud names of conventional history fade into insignificance when the perspective is broad enough. It was a story of Man, of all men.

It was Gottwald's story—and Ben's.

Ben lived it.

Millions of years ago, on a world that circled a sun so far away that the astronomers of Earth had no name for it and not even a number, a new animal called Man appeared. His evolution had been a freakish thing, a million-to-one shot, and it was not likely to be repeated.

Man, the first animal to substitute cultural growth for physical change, was an immediate success. His tools and his weapons grew ever more efficient. On his home world, Man was a patient animal—but he was Man.

He was restless, curious. One world could not hold him. He built his first primitive spaceships and set out to explore the great dark sea around him. He established colonies and bases on a few of the worlds of his star system. He looked outward, out along the infinite corridors of the universe, and it was not in him to stop.

He tinkered and worked and experimented.

He found the faster-than-light drive.

He pushed on through the terrible emptiness of interstellar space. He touched strange worlds and stranger suns—

And he found that Man was not alone.

There were ships greater than his, and Beings—

Man discovered the Enemy.

It was not a case of misunderstanding, not a failure of diplomacy, not an accident born of fear or greed or stupidity. Man was a civilized animal. He was careful, reasonable, prepared to do whatever was ethically right.

He had no chance.

The Enemy—pounced. That was the only word for it. They were hunters, destroyers, killers. They were motivated by a savage hunger for destruction that Man had never known. They took many shapes, many forms.

Ben saw them.

He saw them rip ships apart, gut them with an utter ferocity that was beyond understanding. He saw them tear human beings to shreds, and eat them, and worse—

Ben screamed.

The Beings were more different from Man than the fish that swim in the sea, and yet . . .

Ben recognized them. He knew them.

They were there, all of them.

Literally, the Beings of nightmares.

The monsters that had troubled the dark sleeps of Earth, the things that crawled through myths, the Enemy who lived on the black side of the mind. The dragons, the serpents, the faces carved on masks, the Beings shaped in stones dug up in rotting jungles—

The Enemy.

We on Earth have not completely forgotten. We remember, despite the shocks that cleansed our minds. We remember, we remember. We have seen them in the darkness that lives always beyond the fires, we have heard them in the thunder that booms in the long, long night.

We remember.

It was not a war. A war, after all, is a specific kind of contest with rules of a sort. There were no rules. It was not a drive for conquest, not an attempt at exploitation. It was something new, something totally alien.

It was destruction.

It was examination.

It was a fight between two different kinds of life, as senseless as a bolt of lightning that forked into the massive body of a screaming dinosaur.

Man wasn't ready.

He fell back, fighting where he could.

The Enemy followed.

Whether he liked it or not, Man was in a fight to the finish.

He fought for his life. He pushed himself to the utmost, tried everything he could think of, fought with everything he had. He exhausted his ingenuity. The Enemy countered his every move.

There was a limit.

Man could not go on.

Ben leaned forward, his fists clenched on his chair. He was a product of his culture. He read the books, saw the tri-di plays. He expected a happy ending.

There wasn't one.

Man lost.

He was utterly routed.

He had time for one last throw of the dice, one last desperate try for survival. He did his best.

He worked out the Plan.

It wasn't enough to run away, to find a remote planet and hide. It wasn't enough just to gain time.

Man faced the facts. He had met the Enemy and he had lost. He had tried everything he knew, and it hadn't been good enough. One day, no matter how far he ran, he would meet the Enemy again.

What could he do?

Man lives by his culture, his way of life. The potential for any culture is great, but it is not limitless. Culture has a way of putting blinders on its bearers; it leads them down certain paths and ignores others. Technological complexity is fine, but it is impotent without the one necessary ingredient:

Ideas.

Man needed new ideas, radically new concepts.

He needed a whole new way of thinking.

Transplanting the existing culture would not do the job. It would simply go on producing variants of the ideas that had already been tried.

Man didn't need transplanting.

He needed a transfusion, a transfusion of ideas.

He needed a brand new culture with fresh solutions to old problems.

There is only one way to get a really different culture pattern: grow it from scratch.

Sow the seeds and get out.

Man put the Plan into effect.

With the last of his resources, he outfitted four fugitive ships and sent them out into the wastes of the seas between the stars.

"We don't know what happened to the other three ships," Franz Gottwald said quietly when the projection was over. "No ship knew the destination of any other ship. They went in different directions, each searching for remote, hidden worlds that might become new homes for men. There is no way of knowing what became of the others; I think it highly unlikely that any of them survived."

"Then Earth is all there is?"

"That is what we believe, Ben—we have to go ahead on that assumption. You know most of the rest of the story. This ship slipped through the Enemy and found the Earth. We landed human beings who were so conditioned that they could remember little or nothing, for they had to begin all over again. We planted the fossils and the apes as a test, just as you supposed."

"But why? There was no need for such a stunt—"

Gottwald smiled. "It wasn't a stunt, my boy. It was the key to everything. You see, we had to warn the men of Earth about what they had to face. More than that, once their cultures had developed along their own lines, we had to share what we had with them. I need hardly remind you that this ship is technologically many thousands of years ahead of anything the Earth has produced. But we couldn't turn the ship over to them until we were *certain* they were ready. You don't give atomic bombs to babies. The men of Earth had to *prove* that they could handle the toughest problem we could dream up. You solved it, Ben."

"I didn't do it alone."

"No, of course not. I can tell you now that my people—my other people—never did invent time travel. That was a totally unexpected means of tackling the problem; we never could have done it. It is the most hopeful thing that has happened."

"But what became of the men and women who stayed here on the ship?"

Franz shook his head. "Twenty-five thousand years is a long, long time, Ben. We were a defeated people. We worked hard; we were not idle. For one thing, we prepared dictionaries for every major language on Earth so that all the data in our libraries will be available to you. But man does not live well inside a ship. Each generation we became fewer; children were very scarce."

"It's like the old enigma of the cities, isn't it?"

"Exactly. No city in human history has ever reproduced its population. Urban births are always lower than rural ones. All cities have always drawn their personnel from the surrounding countryside. The ship was sealed up; we had no rural areas. It was only a matter of time before we were all gone. My wife and I were the last ones, Ben—and we had no children."

"We were so afraid," Mrs. Gottwald said. "So afraid that you would not come before it was too late . . ."

"What would you have done?"

Franz shrugged wearily. "That is one decision I was spared. I did cheat a little, my boy. I was careful to give you no help, but I did plant some projectors near you that kept you stirred up. They broadcast frequencies that . . . ah . . . stimulate the mind, keep it in a state of urgency. Perhaps you noticed them?''

Ben nodded. He remembered the voice that spoke in his skull: *Hurry, hurry—*

''Franz, what will happen now?''

Gottwald stroked his beard, his eyes very tired. ''I can't tell you that. I don't know the answer. I have studied the men of Earth for most of my life, and I still don't know. You are a tough people, Ben, tougher than we ever were. You have fought many battles, and your history is a proud one. But I cannot read the future. I have done my best, and the rest is up to you.''

''It's a terrible responsibility.''

''Yes, for you and for others like you it will be a crushing burden. But it will be a long fight; we will not live to see more than the beginning of it. It will take centuries for the men of Earth to learn all that is in this ship. It's an odd thing, Ben—I have never seen the Enemy face to face. You will probably never see them. But what we do now will determine whether mankind lives or dies.''

''It's too much for one man.''

''Yes.'' Gottwald smiled, remembering. ''It is.''

''I don't know where to begin.''

''We will wait for Edward—he will be here tomorrow, unless I don't know him at all—and then the three of us will sit down together for one last time. We will think it out. I am very tired, Ben; my wife and I have lived past our time. It is hard to be old, and to have no children. I always thought of you and Edward as my sons; I hope you do not find this too maudlin.''

Ben searched for words and couldn't find any.

Franz put his arm around his wife. ''Sometimes, when the job was too big for me, when I felt myself giving up, I would walk up into the old control room of this ship. My wife and I have stood there many times. Would you like to see it?''

''I need it, Franz.''

''Yes. So do I. Come along.''

They walked for what seemed to be miles through the dark passages of the empty ship, then rode a series of elevators up to the control room.

Franz switched on the lights.

"The ship is not dead, you know," he said. "It is only the people who are gone. The computers still maintain the ship's orbit, and the defensive screens still make it invulnerable to detection—you wouldn't have seen it if you had not been coming up the light tube, and there is no way the ship can be tracked from Earth. What do you think of the control room?"

Ben stared at it. It was a large chamber, acres in extent, but it was strangely empty. There were panels of switches and a few small machines, but the control room was mostly empty space.

"It's not what I expected," he said, hiding his disappointment.

Franz smiled. "When machinery is efficient you don't need a lot of it. There is no need for flashing lights and sparks of electricity. What you see here gets the job done."

Ben felt a sudden depression. He had badly needed a lift, and he didn't see it here. "If you'll forgive me for saying so, Franz, it isn't very inspiring. I suppose it is different for you—"

Gottwald answered him by throwing a switch.

Two immense screens flared into life, covering the whole front of the control room.

Ben caught his breath.

One of the screens showed the globe of the Earth far below, blue and green and necklaced with silver clouds.

The other showed the stars.

The stars were alive, so close he could almost touch them with his hand. They burned like radiant beacons in the cold sea of space. They whispered to him, called to him—

Ben knew then that the men of Earth had remembered something more than monsters and nightmares, something more than the fears and terrors that crept through the great dark night.

Not all the dreams had been nightmares.

Through all the years and all the sorrows, Man had never forgotten.

I remember. I remember.

I have seen you through all the centuries of nights. I have looked up to see you, I have lifted my head to pray, I have known wonder—

I remember.

Ben looked again at the sleeping Earth.

He sensed that Old Franz and his wife had drawn back into the shadows.

He stood up straight, squaring his shoulders.

Then Ben Hazard turned once more and looked out into the blazing heritage of the stars.

I remember, I remember—
It has been long, but you, too, have not forgotten.
Wait for us.
We'll be back.

SAIL 25

Jack Vance

Henry Belt came limping into the conference room, mounted the dais, settled himself at the desk. He looked once around the room: a swift bright glance which, focusing nowhere, treated the eight young men who faced him to an almost insulting disinterest. He reached in his pocket, brought forth a pencil and a flat red book, which he placed on the desk. The eight young men watched in absolute silence. They were much alike; healthy, clean, smart, their expressions identically alert and wary. Each had heard legends of Henry Belt, each had formed his private plans and private determinations.

Henry Belt seemed a man of a different species. His face was broad, flat, roped with cartilage and muscle, with skin the color and texture of bacon rind. Coarse white grizzle covered his scalp, his eyes were crafty slits, his nose a misshapen lump. His shoulders were massive, his legs short and gnarled.

"First of all," said Henry Belt, with a gap-toothed grin, "I'll make it clear that I don't expect you to like me. If you do I'll be surprised and displeased. It will mean that I haven't pushed you hard enough."

He leaned back in his chair, surveyed the silent group. "You've heard stories about me. Why haven't they kicked me out of the service? Incorrigible, arrogant, dangerous Henry Belt. Drunken Henry Belt. (This last of course is slander. Henry Belt has never been drunk in his life.) Why do they tolerate me? For one simple reason: out of necessity. No one wants to take on this kind of job. Only a man like Henry Belt can stand up to it: year after year in space, with nothing to look at but a half-dozen round-faced young scrubs. He takes them out, he brings them back. Not all of them, and not all of those who come back are spacemen today. But they'll all cross the street when they see him coming. Henry Belt?

you say. They'll turn pale or go red. None of them will smile. Some of them are high-placed now. They could kick me loose if they chose. Ask them why they don't. Henry Belt is a terror, they'll tell you. He's wicked, he's a tyrant. Cruel as an axe, fickle as a woman. But a voyage with Henry Belt blows the foam off the beer. He's ruined many a man, he's killed a few, but those that come out of it are proud to say, 'I trained with Henry Belt!'

"Another thing you may hear: Henry Belt has luck. But don't pay any heed. Luck runs out. You'll be my thirteenth class, and that's unlucky. I've taken out seventy-two young sprats, no different from yourselves; I've come back twelve times: which is partly Henry Belt and partly luck. The voyages average about two years long: how can a man stand it? There's only one who could: Henry Belt. I've got more spacetime than any man alive, and now I'll tell you a secret: this is my last time out. I'm starting to wake up at night to strange visions. After this class I'll quit. I hope you lads aren't superstitious. A white-eyed woman told me that I'd die in space. She told me other things and they've all come true.

"We'll get to know each other well. And you'll be wondering on what basis I make my recommendations. Am I objective and fair? Do I put aside personal animosity? Naturally there won't be any friendship. Well, here's my system. I keep a red book. Here it is. I'll put your names down right now. You, sir?"

"I'm Cadet Lewis Lynch, sir."

"You?"

"Edward Culpepper, sir."

"Marcus Verona, sir."

"Vidal Weske, sir."

"Marvin McGrath, sir."

"Barry Ostrander, sir."

"Clyde von Gluck, sir."

"Joseph Sutton, sir."

Henry Belt wrote the names in the red book. "This is the system. When you do something to annoy me, I mark you down demerits. At the end of the voyage I total these demerits, add a few here and there for luck, and am so guided. I'm sure nothing could be clearer than this. What annoys me? Ah, that's a question which is hard to answer. If you talk too much: demerits. If you're surly and taciturn: demerits. If you slouch and laze and dog the dirty work: demerits. If you're overzealous and forever scuttling about: demerits. Obsequiousness: demerits. Truculence: demerits. If you sing and whistle: demerits. If you're a stolid bloody bore:

demerits. You can see that the line is hard to draw. Here's a hint which can save you many marks. I don't like gossip, especially when it concerns myself. I'm a sensitive man, and I open my red book fast when I think I'm being insulted.'' Henry Belt once more leaned back in his chair. ''Any questions?''

No one spoke.

Henry Belt nodded. ''Wise. Best not to flaunt your ignorance so early in the game. In response to the thought passing through each of your skulls, I do not think of myself as God. But you may do so, if you choose. And this''—he held up the red book—''you may regard as the Syncretic Compendium. Very well. Any questions?''

''Yes sir,'' said Culpepper.

''Speak, sir.''

''Any objection to alcoholic beverages aboard ship, sir?''

''For the cadets, yes, indeed. I concede that the water must be carried in any event, that the organic compounds present may be reconstituted, but unluckily the bottles weight far too much.''

''I understand, sir.''

Henry Belt rose to his feet. ''One last word. Have I mentioned that I run a tight ship? When I say jump, I expect every one of you to jump. This is dangerous work, of course. I don't guarantee your safety. Far from it, especially since we are assigned to old 25, which should have been broken up long ago. There are eight of you present. Only six cadets will make the voyage. Before the week is over I will make the appropriate notifications. Any more questions? . . . Very well, then. Cheerio.'' Limping on his thin legs as if his feet hurt, Henry Belt departed into the back passage.

For a moment or two there was silence. Then von Gluck said in a soft voice, ''My gracious.''

''He's a tyrannical lunatic,'' grumbled Weske. ''I've never heard anything like it! Megalomania!''

''Easy,'' said Culpepper. ''Remember, no gossiping.''

''Bah!'' muttered McGrath. ''This is a free country. I'll damn well say what I like.''

Weske rose to his feet. ''A wonder somebody hasn't killed him.''

''I wouldn't want to try it,'' said Culpepper. ''He looks tough.'' He made a gesture, stood up, brow furrowed in thought. Then he went to look along the passageway into which Henry Belt had made his departure. There, pressed to the wall, stood Henry Belt.

"Yes, sir," said Culpepper suavely. "I forgot to inquire when you wanted us to convene again."

Henry Belt returned to the rostrum. "Now is as good a time as any." He took his seat, opened his red book. "You, Mr. von Gluck, made the remark, 'My gracious,' in an offensive tone of voice. One demerit. You, Mr. Weske, employed the terms 'tyrannical lunatic' and 'megalomania,' in reference to myself. Three demerits. Mr. McGrath, you observed that freedom of speech is the official doctrine of this country. It is a theory which presently we have no time to explore, but I believe that the statement in its present context carries an overtone of insubordination. One demerit. Mr. Culpepper, your imperturable complacence irritates me. I prefer that you display more uncertainty, or even uneasiness."

"Sorry, sir."

"However, you took occasion to remind your colleagues of my rule, and so I will not mark you down."

"Thank you, sir."

Henry Belt leaned back in the chair, stared at the ceiling. "Listen closely, as I do not care to repeat myself. Take notes if you wish. Topic: Solar Sails, Theory and Practice Thereof. Material with which you should already be familiar, but which I will repeat in order to avoid ambiguity.

"First, why bother with the sail, when nuclear jet-ships are faster, more dependable, more direct, safer and easier to navigate? The answer is threefold. First, a sail is not a bad way to move heavy cargo slowly but cheaply through space. Secondly, the range of the sail is unlimited, since we employ the mechanical pressure of light for thrust, and therefore need carry neither propulsive machinery, material to be ejected, nor energy source. The solar sail is much lighter than its nuclear-powered counterpart, and may carry a larger complement of men in a larger hull. Thirdly, to train a man for space there is no better instrument than the handling of a sail. The computer naturally calculates sail cant and plots the course; in fact, without the computer we'd be dead ducks. Nevertheless the control of a sail provides working familiarity with the cosmic elementals: light, gravity, mass, space.

"There are two types of sail: pure and composite. The first relies on solar energy exclusively, the second carries a secondary power source. We have been assigned Number 25, which is the first sort. It consists of a hull, a large parabolic reflector which serves as radar and radio antenna, as well as reflector for the power generator, and the sail itself. The pressure of radiation, of course, is extremely slight—on the order of an ounce per acre at this distance from the sun. Necessarily the sail must be extremely large and extremely light. We use a fluoro-siliconic film a tenth of a mil in gauge, fogged with lithium to the state of opacity. I believe the layer of lithium is about a thousand two hundred molecules thick. Such a foil weighs about four tons to the square mile. It is fitted to a hoop of thin-walled tubing, from which mono-crystalline iron cords lead to the hull.

"We try to achieve a weight factor of six tons to the square mile, which produces an acceleration of between g/100 and g/1000 depending on proximity to the sun, angle of cant, circumsolar orbital speed, reflectivity of surface. These accelerations seem minute, but calculation shows them to be cumulatively enormous. G/100 yields a velocity increment of 800 miles per hour every hour, 18,000 miles per hour each day, or five miles per second each day. At this rate interplanetary distances are readily negotiable—with proper manipulation of the sail, I need hardly say.

"The virtues of the sail I've mentioned. It is cheap to build and cheap to operate. It requires neither fuel nor ejectant. As it travels through space, the great area captures various ions, which may be expelled in the plasma jet powered by the parabolic reflector, which adds another increment to the acceleration.

"The disadvantages of the sail are those of the glider or sailing ship, in that we must use natural forces with great precision and delicacy.

"There is no particular limit to the size of the sail. On 25 we use about four square miles of sail. For the present voyage we will install a new sail, as the old is well-worn and eroded.

"That will be all for today." Once more Henry Belt limped down from the dais and out the passage. On this occasion there were no comments.

II

The eight cadets shared a dormitory, attended classes together, ate at the same table in the mess-hall. In various shops and laboratories they assembled, disassembled and reassembled computers, pumps, generators, gyro-platforms, star-trackers, communication gear. "It's not enough to be clever with your hands," said Henry Belt. "Dexterity is not enough. Resourcefulness, creativity, the ability to make successful improvisations—these are more important. We'll test you out." And presently each of the cadets was introduced into a room on the floor of which lay a great heap of mingled housings, wires, flexes, gears, components of a dozen varieties of mechanism. "This is a twenty-six-hour test," said Henry Belt. "Each of you has an identical set of components and supplies. There shall be no exchange of parts or information between you. Those whom I suspect of this fault will be dropped from the class, without recommendation. What I want you to build is, first, one standard Aminex Mark 9 Computer. Second, a servo-mechanism to orient a mass ten kilograms toward Mu Hercules. Why Mu Hercules?"

"Because, sir, the solar system moves in the direction of Mu Hercules, and we thereby avoid parallax error. Negligible though it may be, sir."

"The final comment smacks of frivolity, Mr. McGrath, which serves only to distract the attention of those who are trying to take careful note of my instructions. One demerit."

"Sorry, sir. I merely intended to express my awareness that for many practical purposes such a degree of accuracy is unnecessary."

"That idea, cadet, is sufficiently elemental that it need not be labored. I appreciate brevity and precision."

"Yes, sir."

"Thirdly, from these materials, assemble a communication system, operating on one hundred watts, which will permit two-way conversation between Tycho Base and Phobos, at whatever frequency you deem suitable."

The cadets started in identical fashion by sorting the material into various piles, then calibrating and checking the test instruments. Achievement thereafter was disparate. Culpepper and von Gluck, diagnosing the test as partly one of mechanical ingenuity and partly ordeal by frustration, failed to become excited when several indispensable components proved either to be missing or inoperative, and carried each project as far as immediately feasible. McGrath and Weske, beginning with the computer, were reduced to rage and random action. Lynch and Sutton worked doggedly at the computer, Verona at the communication system.

Culpepper alone managed to complete one of the instruments, by the process of sawing, polishing and cementing together sections of two broken crystals into a crude, inefficient, but operative maser unit.

• • •

The day after this test McGrath and Weske disappeared from the dormitory, whether by their own volition or notification from Henry Belt no one ever knew.

The test was followed by weekend leave. Cadet Lynch, attending a cocktail party, found himself in conversation with a Lieutenant-Colonel Trenchard, who shook his head pityingly to hear that Lynch was training with Henry Belt.

"I was up with Old Horrors myself. I tell you it's a miracle we ever got back. Belt was drunk two-thirds of the voyage."

"How does he escape court-martial?" asked Lynch.

"Very simple. All the top men seem to have trained under Henry Belt. Naturally they hate his guts but they all take a perverse pride in the fact. And maybe they hope that someday a cadet will take him apart."

"Have any ever tried?"

"Oh yes. I took a swing at Henry once. I was lucky to escape with a broken collarbone and two sprained ankles. If you come back alive, you'll stand a good chance of reaching the top."

The next evening Henry Belt passed the word. "Next Tuesday morning we go up. We'll be gone several months."

On Tuesday morning the cadets took their places in the angel-wagon. Henry Belt presently appeared. The pilot readied for take-off.

"Hold your hats. On the count . . ." The projectile thrust against the earth, strained, rose, went streaking up into the sky. An hour later the pilot pointed. "There's your boat. Old 25. And 39 right beside it, just in from space."

Henry Belt stared aghast from the port. "What's been done to the ship? The decoration? The red? the white? the yellow? The checkerboard."

"Thank some idiot of a landlubber," said the pilot. "The word came to pretty the old boats for a junket of congressmen."

Henry Belt turned to the cadets. "Observe this foolishness. It is the result of vanity and ignorance. We will be occupied several days removing the paint."

They drifted close below the two sails: No. 39 just down from space, spare and polished beside the bedizened structure of No. 25. In 39's exit port a group of men waited, their gear floating at the end of cords.

"Observe those men," said Henry Belt. "They are jaunty. They have been on a pleasant outing around the planet Mars. They are poorly trained. When you gentlemen return you will be haggard and desperate and well trained. Now, gentlemen, clamp your helmets, and we will proceed.''

The helmets were secured. Henry Belt's voice came by radio. "Lynch, Ostrander will remain here to discharge cargo. Verona, Culpepper, von Gluck, Sutton, leap with cords to the ship; ferry across the cargo, stow it in the proper hatches.''

Henry Belt took charge of his personal cargo, which consisted of several large cases. He eased them out into space, clipped on lines, thrust them toward 25, leapt after. Pulling himself and the cases to the entrance port, he disappeared within.

Discharge of cargo was effected. The crew from 39 transferred to the carrier, which thereupon swung down and away, thrust itself dwindling back toward Earth.

When the cargo had been stowed, the cadets gathered in the wardroom. Henry Belt appeared from the master's cubicle. "Gentlemen, how do you like the surroundings? Eh, Mr. Culpepper?''

"The hull is commodious, sir. The view is superb.''

Henry Belt nodded. "Mr. Lynch? Your impressions?''

"I'm afraid I haven't sorted them out yet, sir.''

"I see. You, Mr. Sutton?''

"Space is larger than I imagined it, sir.''

"True. Space is unimaginable. A good space-man must either be larger than space, or he must ignore it. Both difficult. Well, gentlemen, I will make a few comments, then I will retire and enjoy the voyage. Since this is my last time out, I intend to do nothing whatever. The operation of the ship will be completely in your hands. I will merely appear from time to time to beam benevolently about or, alas! to make marks in my red book. Nominally I shall be in command, but you six will enjoy complete control over the ship. If you return us safely to Earth I will make an approving entry in my red book. If you wreck us or fling us into the sun, you will be more unhappy than I, since it is my destiny to die in space. Mr. von Gluck, do I perceive a smirk on your face?''

"No, sir, it is a thoughtful half-smile.''

"What is humorous in the concept of my demise, may I ask?''

"It will be a great tragedy, sir. I merely was reflecting upon the contemporary persistence of, well, not exactly superstition, but, let us say, the conviction of a subjective cosmos.''

Henry Belt made a notation in the red book. "Whatever is meant by this barbaric jargon I'm sure I don't know, Mr. von

Gluck. It is clear that you fancy yourself a philosopher and
dialectician. I will not fault this, so long as your remarks conceal
no overtones of malice and insolence, to which I am extremely
sensitive. Now as to the persistence of superstition, only an
impoverished mind considers itself the repository of absolute
knowledge. Hamlet spoke on this subject to Horatio, as I recall, in
the well-known work by William Shakespeare. I myself have seen
strange and terrifying sights. Were they hallucinations? Were they
the manipulations of the cosmos by my mind or the mind of
someone—or something—other than myself? I do not know. I
therefore counsel a flexible attitude toward matters where the truth
is still unknown. For this reason: The impact of an inexplicable
experience may well destroy a mind which is too brittle. Do I
make myself clear?''

"Perfectly, sir."

"Very good. To return, then. We shall set a system of watches
whereby each man works in turn with each of the other five. I
thereby hope to discourage the formation of special friendships, or
cliques.

"You have inspected the ship. The hull is a sandwich of
lithium-beryllium, insulating foam, fiber, and an interior skin.
Very light, held rigid by air pressure rather than by any innate
strength of the material. We can therefore afford enough space to
stretch our legs and provide all of us with privacy.

"The master's cubicle is to the left; under no circumstances is
anyone permitted in my quarters. If you wish to speak to me,
knock on my door. If I appear, good. If I do not appear, go away.
To the right are six cubicles which you may now distribute among
yourselves by lot.

"Your schedule will be two hours study, four hours on watch,
six hours off. I will require no specific rate of study progress, but
I recommend that you make good use of your time.

"Our destination is Mars. We will presently construct a new
sail, then, while orbital velocity builds up, you will carefully test
and check all equipment aboard. Each of you will compute sail
cant and course and work out among yourselves any discrepancies
which may appear. I shall take no hand in navigation. I prefer that
you involve me in no disaster. If any such occur I shall severely
mark down the persons responsible.

"Singing, whistling, humming, are forbidden. I disapprove of
fear and hysteria, and mark accordingly. No one dies more than
once; we are well aware of the risks of this, our chosen occupation.

There will be no practical jokes. You may fight, so long as you do not disturb me or break any instruments; however I counsel against it, as it leads to resentment, and I have known cadets to kill each other. I suggest coolness and detachment in your personal relations. Use of the microfilm projector is of course at your own option. You may not use the radio either to dispatch or receive messages. In fact I have put the radio out of commission, as is my practice. I do this to emphasize the fact that, sink or swim, we must make do with our own resources. Are there any questions? . . . Very good. You will find that if you all behave with scrupulous correctness and accuracy, we shall in due course return safe and sound, with a minimum of demerits and no casualties. I am bound to say, however, that in twelve previous voyages this has failed to occur. Now you select your cubicles, stow your gear. The carrier will bring up the new sail tomorrow, and you will go to work."

III

The carrier discharged a great bundle of three-inch tubing: paper-thin lithium hardened with beryllium, reinforced with filaments of monocrystalline iron—a total length of eight miles. The cadets fitted the tubes end to end, cementing the joints. When the tube extended a quarter-mile it was bent bow-shaped by a cord stretched between two ends, and further sections added. As the process continued, the free end curved far out and around, and presently began to veer back in toward the hull. When the last tube was in place the loose end was hauled down, socketed home, to form a great hoop two miles and a half in diameter.

Henry Belt came out occasionally in his space suit to look on, and occasionally spoke a few words of sardonic comment, to which the cadets paid little heed. Their mood had changed; this was exhilaration, to be weightlessly afloat above the bright cloud-marked globe, with continent and ocean wheeling massively below. Anything seemed possible, even the training voyage with Henry Belt! When he came out to inspect their work, they grinned at each other with indulgent amusement. Henry Belt suddenly seemed a rather pitiful creature, a poor vagabond suited only for drunken bluster. Fortunate indeed that they were less naïve than Henry Belt's previous classes! *They* had taken Belt seriously; he had cowed them, reduced them to nervous pulp. Not this crew, not by a long shot! They saw through Henry Belt! Just keep your nose clean, do your work, keep cheerful. The training voyage won't last but a few months, and then real life begins. Gut it out, ignore Henry Belt as much as possible. This is the sensible attitude; the best way to keep on top of the situation.

Already the group had made a composite assessment of its members, arriving at a set of convenient labels. Culpepper: smooth, suave, easy-going. Lynch: excitable, argumentative, hot-tempered. Von Gluck: the artistic temperament, delicate with hands and sensibilities. Ostrander: prissy, finicky, over-tidy. Sutton: moody, suspicious, competitive. Verona: the plugger, rough at the edges, but persistent and reliable.

Around the hull swung the gleaming hoop, and now the carrier brought up the sail, a great roll of darkly shining stuff. When unfolded and unrolled, and unfolded many times more, it became a tough gleaming film, flimsy as gold leaf. Unfolded to its fullest extent it was a shimmering disk, already rippling and bulging to the light of the sun. The cadets fitted the film to the hoop, stretched it taut as a drum-head, cemented it in place. Now the sail must carefully be held edge on to the sun, or it would quickly move away, under a thrust of about a hundred pounds.

From the rim braided-iron threads were led to a ring at the back of the parabolic reflector, dwarfing this as the reflector dwarfed the hull, and now the sail was ready to move.

The carrier brought up a final cargo: water, food, spare parts, a new magazine for the microfilm viewer, mail. Then Henry Belt said, "Make sail."

This was the process of turning the sail to catch the sunlight while the hull moved around Earth away from the sun, canting it parallel to the sun-rays when the ship moved on the sunward leg of its orbit: in short, building up an orbital velocity which in due course would stretch loose the bonds of terrestrial gravity and send Sail 25 kiting out toward Mars.

During this period the cadets checked every item of equipment aboard the vessel. They grimaced with disgust and dismay at some of the instruments; 25 was an old ship, with antiquated gear. Henry Belt seemed to enjoy their grumbling. "This is a training voyage, not a pleasure cruise. If you wanted your noses wiped, you should have taken a post on the ground. And I have no sympathy for fault-finders. If you wish a model by which to form your own conduct, observe me."

The moody introspective Sutton, usually the most diffident and laconic of individuals, ventured an ill-advised witticism. "If we modeled ourselves after you, sir, there'd be no room to move for the whiskey.''

Out came the red book. "Extraordinary impudence, Mr. Sutton. How can you yield so easily to malice?''

Sutton flushed pink; his eyes glistened, he opened his mouth to speak, then closed it firmly. Henry Belt, waiting politely expectant, turned away. "You gentleman will perceive that I rigorously obey my own rules of conduct. I am regular as a clock. There is no better, more genial shipmate than Henry Belt. There is not a fairer man alive. Mr. Culpepper, you have a remark to make?''

"Nothing of consequence, sir.''

Henry Belt went to the port, glared out at the sail. He swung around instantly. "Who is on watch?''

"Sutton and Ostrander, sir.''

"Gentlemen, have you noticed the sail? It has swung about and is canting to show its back to the sun. In another ten minutes we shall be tangled in a hundred miles of guy-wires.''

Sutton and Ostrander sprang to repair the situation. Henry Belt shook his head disparagingly. "This is precisely what is meant by the words 'negligence' and 'inattentiveness.' You two have committed a serious error. This is poor spacemanship. The sail must always be in such a position as to hold the wires taut.''

"There seems to be something wrong with the sensor, sir,'' Sutton blurted. "It should notify us when the sail swings behind us.''

"I fear I must charge you an additional demerit for making excuses, Mr. Sutton. It is your duty to assure yourself that all the warning devices are functioning properly, at all times. Machinery must never be used as a substitute for vigilance.''

Ostrander looked up from the control console. "Someone has turned off the switch, sir. I do not offer this is an excuse, but as an explanation.''

"The line of distinction is often hard to define, Mr. Ostrander. Please bear in mind my remarks on the subject of vigilance.''

"Yes, sir, but—who turned off the switch?''

"Both you and Mr. Sutton are theoretically hard at work watching for any such accident or occurrence. Did you not observe it?''

"No, sir.''

"I might almost accuse you of further inattention and neglect, in this case.''

Ostrander gave Henry Belt a long dubious side-glance. "The

only person I recall going near the console is yourself, sir. I'm sure you wouldn't do such a thing."

Henry Belt shook his head sadly. "In space you must never rely on anyone for rational conduct. A few moments ago Mr. Sutton unfairly imputed to me an unusual thirst for whiskey. Suppose this were the case? Suppose, as an example of pure irony, that I had indeed been drinking whiskey, that I was in fact drunk?"

"I will agree, sir, that anything is possible."

Henry Belt shook his head again. "This is the type of remark, Mr. Ostrander, that I have come to associate with Mr. Culpepper. A better response would have been, 'In the future, I will try to be ready for any conceivable contingency.' Mr. Sutton, did you make a hissing sound between your teeth?"

"I was breathing, sir."

"Please breathe with less vehemence."

Henry Belt turned away and wandered back and forth about the wardroom, scrutinizing cases, frowning at smudges on polished metal. Ostrander muttered something to Sutton, and both watched Henry Belt closely as he moved here and there. Presently Henry Belt lurched toward them. "You show great interest in my movements, gentlemen."

"We were on the watch for another unlikely contingency, sir."

"Very good, Mr. Ostrander. Stick with it. In space nothing is impossible. I'll vouch for this personally."

IV

Henry Belt sent all hands out to remove the paint from the surface of the parabolic reflector. When this had been accomplished, incident sunlight was now focused upon an expanse of photoelectric cells. The power so generated was used to operate plasma jets, expelling ions collected by the vast expanse of sail, further accelerating the ship, thrusting it ever out into an orbit of escape. And finally one day, at an exact instant dictated by the computer, the ship departed from Earth and floated tangentially out into space, off at an angle for the orbit of Mars. At an acceleration of g/100 velocity built up rapidly. Earth dwindled behind; the ship was isolated in space. The cadets' exhilaration vanished, to be replaced by an almost funereal solemnity. The vision of Earth dwindling and retreating is an awesome symbol, equivalent to eternal loss, to the act of dying itself. The more impressionable cadets—Sutton, von Gluck, Ostrander—could not look astern without finding their eyes swimming with tears. Even the suave Culpepper was awed by the magnificence of the spectacle, the sun an aching pit not to be tolerated, Earth a plump pearl rolling on black velvet among a myriad of glittering diamonds. And away from Earth, away from the sun, opened an exalted magnificence of another order entirely. For the first time the cadets became dimly aware that Henry Belt had spoken truly of strange visions. Here was death, here was peace, solitude, star-blazing beauty which promised not oblivion in death, but eternity. . . . Streams and spatters of stars . . . The familiar constellation, the stars with their prideful names presenting themselves like heroes: Achernar, Fomalhaut, Sadal, Suud, Canopus . . .

Sutton could not bear to look into the sky. "It's not that I feel fear," he told von Gluck, "or, yes, perhaps it is fear. It sucks at me, draws me out there. . . . I suppose in due course I'll become accustomed to it."

"I'm not so sure," said von Gluck. "I wouldn't be surprised if space could become a psychological addiction, a need—so that whenever you walked on Earth you felt hot and breathless."

Life settled into a routine. Henry Belt no longer seemed a man, but a capricious aspect of nature, like storm or lightning; and like some natural cataclysm, Henry Belt showed no favoritism, nor forgave one jot or tittle of offense. Apart from the private cubicles, no place on the ship escaped his attention. Always he reeked of whiskey, and it became a matter of covert speculation as to exactly how much whiskey he had brought aboard. But no matter how he reeked or how he swayed on his feet, his eyes remained clever and steady, and he spoke without slurring in his paradoxically clear sweet voice.

One day he seemed slightly drunker than usual, and ordered all hands into space-suits and out to inspect the sail for meteoric puncture. The order seemed sufficiently odd that the cadets stared at him in disbelief. "Gentlemen, you hesitate, you fail to exert yourselves, you luxuriate in sloth. Do you fancy yourselves at the Riviera? Into the space-suits, on the double, and everybody into space. Check hoop, sail, reflector, struts and sensor. You will be adrift for two hours. When you return I want a comprehensive report. Mr. Lynch, I believe you are in charge of this watch. You will present the report."

"Yes, sir."

"One more matter. You will notice that the sail is slightly

bellied by the continual radiation pressure. It therefore acts as a
focusing device, the focal point presumably occurring behind the
cab. But this is not a matter to be taken for granted. I have seen a
man burnt to death in such a freak accident. Bear this in mind."

For two hours the cadets drifted through space, propelled by
tanks of gas and thrust tubes. All enjoyed the experience except
Sutton, who found himself appalled by the immensity of his
emotions. Probably least affected was the practical Verona, who
inspected the sail with a care exacting enough even to satisfy
Henry Belt.

The next day the computer went wrong. Ostrander was in
charge of the watch and knocked on Henry Belt's door to make the
report.

Henry Belt appeared in the doorway. He apparently had been
asleep. "What is the difficulty, Mr. Ostrander?"

"We're in trouble, sir. The computer has gone out."

Henry Belt rubbed his grizzled pate. "This is not an unusual
circumstance. We prepare for this contingency by schooling all
cadets thoroughly in computer design and repair. Have you
identified the difficulty?"

"The bearings which suspend the data-separation disks have
broken. The shaft has several millimeters play and as a result there
is total confusion in the data presented to the analyzer."

"An interesting problem. Why do you present it to me?"

"I thought you should be notified, sir. I don't believe we carry
spares for this particular bearing."

Henry Belt shook his head sadly. "Mr. Ostrander, do you recall
my statement at the beginning of this voyage, that you six
gentlemen are totally responsible for the navigation of the ship?"

"Yes, sir. But—"

"This is an applicable situation. You must either repair the
computer, or perform the calculations yourself."

"Very well, sir. I will do my best."

V

Lynch, Verona, Ostrander and Sutton disassembled the mechanism, removed the worn bearing. "Confounded antique!" said
Lynch. "Why can't they give us decent equipment? Or if they
want to kill us, why not shoot us and save us all trouble."

"We're not dead yet," said Verona. "You've looked for a
spare?"

"Naturally. There's nothing remotely like this."

Verona looked at the bearing dubiously. "I suppose we could cast a babbitt sleeve and machine it to fit. That's what we'll have to do—unless you fellows are awfully fast with your math."

Sutton glanced out the port, quickly turned away his eyes. "I wonder if we should cut sail."

"Why?" asked Ostrander.

"We don't want to built up too much velocity. We're already going thirty miles a second."

"Mars is a long way off."

"And if we miss, we go shooting past. Then where are we?"

"Sutton, you're a pessimist. A shame to find morbid tendencies in one so young." This from von Gluck.

"I'd rather be a live pessimist than a dead comedian."

The new sleeve was duly cast, machined, and fitted. Anxiously the alignment of the data disks was checked. "Well," said Verona dubiously, "there's wobble. How much that affects the functioning remains to be seen. We can take some of it out by shimming the mount. . . ."

Shims of tissue paper were inserted and the wobble seemed to be reduced. "Now—feed in the data," said Sutton. "Let's see how we stand."

Coordinates were fed into the system; the indicator swung. "Enlarge sail cant four degrees," said von Gluck, "we're making too much left concentric. Projected course . . ." He tapped buttons, watched the bright line extend across the screen, swing around a dot representing the center of gravity of Mars. "I make it an elliptical pass, about twenty thousand miles out. That's at present acceleration, and it should toss us right back at Earth."

"Great. Simply great. Let's go, 25!" This was Lynch. "I've heard of guys dropping flat on their faces and kissing Earth when they put down. Me, I'm going to live in a cave the rest of my life."

Sutton went to look at the data disks. The wobble was slight but perceptible. "Good Lord," he said huskily. "The other end of the shaft is loose too."

Lynch started to spit curses; Verona's shoulders slumped. "Let's get to work and fix it."

Another bearing was cast, machined, polished, mounted. The disks wobbled, scraped. Mars, an ocher disk, shouldered ever closer in from the side. With the computer unreliable, the cadets calculated and plotted the course manually. The results were at slight but significant variance with those of the computer. The cadets looked dourly at each other. "Well," growled Ostrander, "there's error. Is it the instruments? The calculation? The plotting? Or the computer?"

Culpepper said in a subdued voice, "Well, we're not about to crash head-on at any rate."

Verona went back to study the computer. "I can't imagine why the bearings don't work better. . . . The mounting brackets—could they have shifted?" He removed the side housing, studied the frame, then went to the case for tools.

"What are you going to do?" demanded Sutton.

"Try to ease the mounting brackets around. I think that's our trouble."

"Leave me alone! You'll bugger the machine so it'll never work."

Verona paused, looked questioningly around the group. "Well? What's the verdict?"

"Maybe we'd better check with the old man," said Ostrander nervously.

"All well and good—but you know what he'll say."

"Let's deal cards. Ace of spades goes to ask him."

Culpepper received the ace. He knocked on Henry Belt's door. There was no response. He started to knock again, but restrained himself.

He returned to the group. "Wait till he shows himself. I'd rather crash into Mars than bring forth Henry Belt and his red book."

The ship crossed the orbit of Mars well ahead of the looming red planet. It came toppling at them with a peculiar clumsy grandeur, a mass obviously bulky and globular, but so fine and clear was the detail, so absent the perspective, that the distance and size might have been anything. Instead of swinging in a sharp elliptical curve back toward Earth, the ship swerved aside in a blunt hyperbola and proceeded outward, now at a velocity of close to fifty miles a second. Mars receded astern and to the side. A new part of space lay ahead. The sun was noticeably smaller. Earth could no longer be differentiated from the stars. Mars departed quickly and politely, and space seemed lonely and forlorn.

Henry Belt had not appeared for two days. At last Culpepper went to knock on the door—once, twice, three times: a strange face looked out. It was Henry Belt, face haggard, skin like pulled taffy.

His eyes were red and glared, his hair seemed matted and more unkempt than hair a quarter-inch long should be.

But he spoke in his quiet clear voice. "Mr. Culpepper, your merciless din has disturbed me. I am quite put out with you."

"Sorry, sir. We feared that you were ill."

Henry Belt made no response. He looked past Culpepper, around the circle of faces. "You gentlemen are unwontedly serious. Has this presumptive illness of mine caused you all distress?"

Sutton spoke in a rush, "The computer is out of order."

"Why then, you must repair it."

"It's a matter of altering the housing. If we do it incorrectly—"

"Mr. Sutton, please do not harass me with the hour-by-hour minutiae of running the ship."

"But, sir, the matter has become serious; we need your advice. We missed the Mars turnaround—"

"Well, I suppose there's always Jupiter. Must I explain the basic elements of astrogation to you?"

"But the computer's out of order—definitely."

"Then, if you wish to return to Earth, you must perform the calculations with pencil and paper. Why is it necessary to explain the obvious?"

"Jupiter is a long way out," said Sutton in a shrill voice. "Why can't we just turn around and go home?" This last was almost a whisper.

"I see I've been too easy on you cads," said Henry Belt. "You stand around idly; you chatter nonsense while the machinery goes to pieces and the ship flies at random. Everybody into space-suits for sail inspection. Come now. Let's have some snap. What are you all? Walking corpses? You, Mr. Culpepper, why the delay?"

"It occurred to me, sir, that we are approaching the asteroid belt. As I am chief of the watch I consider it my duty to cant sail to swing us around the area."

"You may do this; then join the rest in hull and sail inspection."

"Yes, sir."

The cadets donned space-suits, Sutton with the utmost reluctance. Out into the dark void they went, and now here was loneliness indeed.

When they returned, Henry Belt had returned to his compartment.

"As Mr. Belt points out, we have no great choice," said

Ostrander. "We missed Mars, so let's hit Jupiter. Luckily it's in good position—otherwise we'd have to swing out to Saturn or Uranus—"

"They're off behind the sun," said Lynch. "Jupiter's our last chance."

"Let's do it right, then. I say, let's make one last attempt to set those confounded bearings. . . ."

But now it seemed as if the wobble and twist had been eliminated. The disks tracked perfectly, the accuracy monitor glowed green.

"Great!" yelled Lynch. "Feed it the dope. Let's get going! All sail for Jupiter. Good Lord, but we're having a trip!"

"Wait till it's over," said Sutton. Since his return from sail inspection, he had stood to one side, cheeks pinched, eyes staring. "It's not over yet. And maybe it's not meant to be."

The other five pretended not to have heard him. The computer spat out figures and angles. There was a billion miles to travel. Acceleration was less, due to the diminution in the intensity of sunlight. At least a month must pass before Jupiter came close.

VI

The ship, great sail spread to the fading sunlight, fled like a ghost—out, always out. Each of the cadets had quietly performed the same calculation, and arrived at the same result. If the swing around Jupiter were not performed with exactitude, if the ship were not slung back like a stone on a string, there was nothing beyond. Saturn, Uranus, Neptune, Pluto were far around the sun; the ship, speeding at a hundred miles a second, could not be halted by the warning gravity of the sun, nor yet sufficiently accelerated in a concentric direction by sail and jet into a true orbit. The very nature of the sail made it useless as a brake, always the thrust was outward.

Within the hull seven men lived and thought, and the psychic relationship worked and stirred like yeast in a vat of decaying fruit. The fundamental similarity, the human identity of the seven men, was utterly canceled; apparent only were the disparities. Each cadet appeared to others only as a walking characteristic, and Henry Belt was an incomprehensible Thing, who appeared from his compartment at unpredictable times, to move quietly here and there with the blind blank grin of an archaic Attic hero.

Jupiter loomed and bulked. The ship, at last within reach of the

Jovian gravity, sidled over to meet it. The cadets gave ever more careful attention to the computer, checking and counterchecking the instructions. Verona was the most assiduous at this, Sutton the most harassed and ineffectual. Lynch growled and cursed and sweat; Ostrander complained in a thin peevish voice. Von Gluck worked with the calm of pessimistic fatalism; Culpepper seemed unconcerned, almost debonair, a blandness which bewildered Ostrander, infuriated Lynch, awoke a malignant hate in Sutton. Verona and von Gluck on the other hand seemed to derive strength and refreshment from Culpepper's placid acceptance of the situation. Henry Belt said nothing. Occasionally he emerged from his compartment, to survey the wardroom and the cadets with the detached interest of a visitor to an asylum.

It was Lynch who made the discovery. He signaled it with an odd growl of sheer dismay, which brought a resonant questioning sound from Sutton. "My God, my God," muttered Lunch.

Verona was at his side. "What's the trouble?"

"Look. This gear. When we replaced the disks we dephased the whole apparatus one notch. This white dot and this other white dot should synchronize. They're one sprocket apart. All the results would check and be consistent because they'd all be off by the same factor."

Verona sprang into action.

Off came the housing, off came various components. Gently he lifted the gear, set it back into correct alignment. The other cadets leaned over him as he worked, except Culpepper who was chief of the watch.

Henry Belt appeared. "You gentlemen are certainly diligent in your navigation," he said presently. "Perfectionists almost."

"We do our best," greeted Lynch between set teeth. "It's a damn shame sending us out with a machine like this."

The red book appeared. "Mr. Lynch, I mark you down not for your private sentiments, which are of course yours to entertain, but for voicing them and thereby contributing to an unhealthy atmosphere of despairing and hysterical pessimism."

A tide of red crept up from Lynch's neck. He bent over the computer, made no comment. But Sutton suddenly cried out, "What else do you expect from us? We came out here to learn, not to suffer, or to fly on forever!" He gave a ghastly laugh. Henry Belt listened patiently. "Think of it!" cried Sutton. "The seven of us. In this capsule, forever!"

"I am afraid that I must charge you two demerits for your

outburst, Mr. Sutton. A good space-man maintains his dignity at all costs.''

Lynch looked up from the computer. ''Well, now we've got a corrected reading. Do you know what it says?''

Henry Belt turned him a look of polite inquiry.

''We're going to miss,'' said Lynch. ''We're going to pass by just as we passed Mars. Jupiter is pulling us around and sending us out toward Gemini.''

The silence was thick in the room. Henry Belt turned to look at Culpepper, who was standing by the porthole, photographing Jupiter with his personal camera.

''Mr. Culpepper?''

''Yes, sir.''

''You seem unconcerned by the prospect which Mr. Sutton has set forth.''

''I hope it's not imminent.''

''How do you propose to avoid it?''

''I imagine that we will radio for help, sir.''

''You forget that I have destroyed the radio.''

''I remember noting a crate marked 'Radio Parts' stored in the starboard jet-pod.''

''I am sorry to disillusion you, Mr. Culpepper. That case is mislabeled.''

Ostrander jumped to his feet, left the wardroom. There was the sound of moving crates. A moment of silence. Then he returned. He glared at Henry Belt. ''Whiskey. Bottles of whiskey.''

Henry Belt nodded. ''I told you as much.''

''But now we have no radio,'' said Lynch in an ugly voice.

''We never have had a radio, Mr. Lynch. You were warned that you would have to depend on your own resources to bring us home. You have failed, and in the process doomed me as well as yourself. Incidentally, I must mark you all down ten demerits for a faulty cargo check.''

''Demerits,'' said Ostrander in a bleak voice.

''Now, Mr. Culpepper,'' said Henry Belt. ''What is your next proposal?''

''I don't know, sir.''

Verona spoke in a placatory voice. ''What would you do, sir, if you were in our position?''

Henry Belt shook his head. ''I am an imaginative man, Mr. Verona, but there are certain leaps of the mind which are beyond my powers.'' He returned to his compartment.

Von Gluck looked curiously at Culpepper. "It is a fact. You're not at all concerned."

"Oh, I'm concerned. But I believe that Mr. Belt wants to get home too. He's too good a space-man not to know exactly what he's doing."

The door from Henry Belt's compartment slid back. Henry Belt stood in the opening. "Mr. Culpepper, I chanced to overhear your remark, and I now note down ten demerits against you. This attitude expresses a complacence as dangerous as Mr. Sutton's utter funk." He looked about the room. "Pay no heed to Mr. Culpepper. He is wrong. Even if I could repair this disaster, I would not raise a hand. For I expect to die in space."

VII

The sail was canted vectorless, edgewise to the sun. Jupiter was a smudge astern. There were five cadets in the wardroom. Culpepper, Verona, and von Gluck sat talking in low voices. Ostrander and Lynch lay crouched, arms to knees, faces to the wall. Sutton had gone two days before. Quietly donning his space-suit, he had stepped into the exit chamber and thrust himself headlong into space. A propulsion unit gave him added speed, and before any of the cadets could intervene he was gone.

Shortly thereafter Lynch and Ostrander succumbed to inanition, a kind of despondent helplessness: manic-depression in its most stupefying phase. Culpepper the suave, Verona the pragmatic, and von Gluck the sensitive remained.

They spoke quietly to themselves, out of earshot of Henry Belt's room. "I still believe," said Culpepper, "that somehow there is a means to get ourselves out of this mess, and that Henry Belt knows it."

Verona said, "I wish I could think so. . . . We've been over it a hundred times. If we set sail for Saturn or Neptune or Uranus, the outward vector of thrust plus the outward vector of our momentum will take us far beyond Pluto before we're anywhere near. The plasma jets could stop us if we had enough energy, but the shield can't supply it and we don't have another power source. . . ."

Von Gluck hit his fist into his hand. "Gentlemen," he said in a soft delighted voice, "I believe we have sufficient energy at hand. We will use the sail. Remember? It is bellied. It can function as a mirror. It spreads five square miles of surface. Sunlight out here is thin—but so long as we collect enough of it—"

"I understand!" said Culpepper. "We back off the hull till the reactor is at the focus of the sail and turn on the jets!"

Verona said dubiously, "We'll still be receiving radiation pressure. And what's worse, the jets will impinge back on the sail. Effect—cancellation. We'll be nowhere."

"If we cut the center out of the sail—just enough to allow the plasma through—we'd beat that objection. And as for the radiation pressure—we'll surely do better with the plasma drive."

"What do we use to make plasma? We don't have the stock."

"Anything that can be ionized. The radio, the computer, your shoes, my shirt, Culpepper's camera, Henry Belt's whiskey . . ."

VIII

The angel-wagon came up to meet Sail 25, in orbit beside Sail 40, which was just making ready to take out a new crew.

The cargo carrier drifted near, eased into position. Three men sprang across space to Sail 40, a few hundred yards behind 25, tossed lines back to the carrier, pulled bales of cargo and equipment across the gap.

The five cadets and Henry Belt, clad in space-suits, stepped out into the sunlight. Earth spread below, green and blue, white and brown, the contours so precious and dear to bring tears to the eyes. The cadets transferring cargo to Sail 40 gazed at them curiously as they worked. At last they were finished, and the six men of Sail 25 boarded the carrier.

"Back safe and sound, eh, Henry?" said the pilot. "Well, I'm always surprised."

Henry Belt made no answer. The cadets stowed their cargo, and standing by the port, took a final look at Sail 25. The carrier retro-jetted; the two sails seemed to rise above them.

The lighter nosed in and out of the atmosphere, braking, extended its wings, glided to an easy landing on the Mojave Desert.

The cadets, their legs suddenly loose and weak to the unaccustomed gravity, limped after Henry Belt to the carry-all, seated themselves, and were conveyed to the administration complex. They alighted from the carry-all, and now Henry Belt motioned the five to the side.

"Here, gentlemen, is where I leave you. Tonight I will check my red book and prepare my official report. But I believe I can present you an unofficial résumé of my impressions. Mr. Lynch and Mr. Ostrander, I feel that you are ill-suited either for command or for any situation which might inflict prolonged emotional pressure upon you. I cannot recommend you for space duty.

"Mr. von Gluck, Mr. Culpepper, and Mr. Verona, all of you meet my minimum requirements for a recommendation, although I shall write the words 'Especially Recommended' only beside the names 'Clyde von Gluck' and 'Marcus Verona.' You brought the sail back to Earth by essentially faultless navigation.

"So now our association ends. I trust you have profited by it." Henry Belt nodded briefly to each of the five and limped off around the building.

The cadets looked after him. Culpepper reached in his pocket and brought forth a pair of small metal objects which he displayed in his palm. "Recognize these?"

"Hmf," said Lynch in a flat voice. "Bearings for the computer disks. The original ones."

"I found them in the little spare-parts tray. They weren't there before."

Von Gluck nodded. "The machinery always seemed to fail immediately after sail check, as I recall."

Lynch drew in his breath with a sharp hiss. He turned, strode away. Ostrander followed him. Culpepper shrugged. To Verona he gave one of the bearings, to von Gluck the other. "For souvenirs—or medals. You fellows deserve them."

"Thanks, Ed," said von Gluck.

"Thanks," muttered Verona. "I'll make a stick-pin of this thing."

The three, not able to look at each other, glanced up into the sky where the first stars of twilight were appearing, then continued on into the building where family and friends and sweethearts awaited them.

BYE, BYE, BANANA BIRD

Sonya Dorman

There we stood, naked as babies, lined up on the cold tile floor waiting for the doctor. Our first day at the Planet Patrol Academy. We hoped, all eight of us lined up, to become Pippas: P.P.A. rookies. We'd have no rank until we completed our first assignments. Plenty of prestige, and good pay. Only women in top physical condition, between the ages of eighteen and twenty-three, were accepted, and thirty-two was the age at which we retired from active duty, usually to get married and teach at one of the Academies, sometimes to a good job in private industry. We were from several of the ten different Earth Dominions and we spoke the standard British and Swahili, as well as our Dominion dialects.

My friend Merle and I, both from America Dominion, had done a lot of talking before we applied, but the only decision we'd come to was that if we made the grade, we'd stay with it as long as we could.

Merle Rocca was standing next to me, coming out in goose pimples. A nice brunette, with glowing dark skin, and one brown eye. The other eye was a bright blue; she claimed that was why she was called Merle.

"Rimidon," the doctor said, and I stepped forward. I'd grown up in a family that was intense about physical culture, my mother doing her five miles a day on her stationary bike while the small, old-fashioned house shook and resounded to the crash of weights my father was trying to press in the basement gym. My younger brother jogged, ate wheat germ, and went camping with us. It was self-preservation that kept me in good shape.

The doctor did me over from crown to sole: five foot eight, one-thirty-five pounds, no scars, no moles, no serious dental work, vision 20/20, measured out at 36–25–38.

He asked me, "Can't you get a couple of inches off the hips? You'll look like hell in the regulation pantaloons."

"Am I here to be admired?" I asked.

"Shut up," the Sergeant said. She was our housemother. A woman a lot heavier than I was and not as tall, but obviously active duty was behind her. I wondered where she had worked; no one on the staff had less than five years of active duty. Trained troubleshooters, we would go into a central Patrol pool on earth, and then could be called to special duty anywhere, including the colony planets Vogl and Alpha.

Merle was next; heart, lungs, weight, the works. She had that wiry, tireless build which could keep going forever. We both had brains, of course, or we wouldn't be here. Whatever special skills we might be hiding would be developed within the next eight weeks.

Sgt. Mother turned to me and said, "Rimidon, go to room five for a haircut."

I got back into my clothes moodily. I knew my hair would have to go, but I should have done as Merle did, and had it cut short before. You couldn't expect a service barber to do a decent job. "When's lunch?" I asked.

"You just had breakfast when you got here," the doctor said. "No wonder you carry that much weight."

Merle winked at me. I tied my boot laces and went into the corridor. Plain, pale walls; overhead lights behind plastic panels. Couldn't find room five. Four and six were there; also three and seven. On my first day, too. Graduated from college third in a class of two hundred and forty; top of the judo class; long-distance runner; fluent in four languages; played cello, guitar, and nose flute; couldn't find room five.

It was around the end, all by itself in its own little corridor with a tall glass window at the end. I took a glance out at the grounds. They were green and pleasant, set at the base of the mountain range. I was in the central part of the building, three stories high; the dormitory wings spread out at each side, long and lower. From out there on the lawn, the Academy building looked like a large and expensive prep school for unruly children.

"Rimidon, reporting for haircut," I said when I went in. The barber was a tall, middle-aged man, wearing a white jacket and the blackest Vandyke beard I ever saw. Grey eyes, a tender smile.

"Oh, darling," he said as I sat in the chair. "What a headful! How can you bear to give it up."

"I'm willing to make some sacrifices," I said.

While he was chopping off handsful of my honey-yellow hair, I asked him, "Is this all you do, all day, cut off the girls' hair?"

"Don't be silly, darling. I work with Lt. Kimminy in code. I'm also married to her."

He took the clippers and bristled the back of my neck, but then he cut with a razor comb around the ears and front so my hair was shaped into waves and I still looked like the woman I was. "That do?" he asked.

"Lovely," I said. "I never would have hoped."

"Mustn't get discouraged so soon," he said, giving my biceps a squeeze. "Oh! that's good," he exclaimed, for I made him a muscle which must have bruised his hand.

The next two hours were spent in gym, in the swimming pool, and in bolting down a good but entirely inadequate lunch. We'd already taken the psychiatric tests, the achievement and mechanical tests, or they'd never have let us in the door.

We were lined up on hard chairs for a briefing. The colonel, a big, blond man, reminded us that the eight weeks were intended to test, in free situations, our ability to think and react quickly, our persistence in the face of difficulties, and how well we could take care of ourselves in emergencies, physical and mental. The first ten days would be spent primarily in physical training. I had a vision of a nine-foot spiked fence and a pond full of piranhas.

"Remember," Col. Wayser said, just when we thought he had finished, "there is no disgrace in failing. Only about half our rookies graduate and go out on Planet Patrol. You are the cream, the elite, of young women, or you wouldn't have made it this far. For those of you who do not make it into the P.P.A., there are still excellent job opportunities on all the planets. Good luck."

I hadn't paid much attention to him, though there was no escaping the deep rumble of his voice, until he turned his back to look out the window, presumably to show us we were dismissed. He had broad shoulders, broad back, and long, powerful legs. Merle and I exchanged glances, and grinned. Well, would he go for that one blue eye, I wondered, or did he like them tall? Roxy, I chided myself, you mustn't try to make the colonel the first day here.

We were filing out, when Col. Wayser turned back from the window and rumbled, "Rocca. Rimidon." Merle and I turned and faced him.

"I understand you're friends," he said. "Went to college

together. It's customary here to separate friends. We feel they're likely to give each other unwarranted support, or cover up for each other in case of mistakes.''

"Yes, sir,'' we said.

Merle got a room on the ground floor of the west wing, and I had a corner room on the second floor of the east wing. We had wondered if it would be a dormitory set-up, or whether we'd be locked into little cells. What we had were comfortable, fairly large rooms, with a communal shower room on each floor.

Since I'd been up at five in the morning to catch the plane, then the service bus, I was sleepy. I took off my boots and lay down for a nap. On guard, on guard, I said to myself, as my eyes closed. Tarantulas in the washbasin? A colonel in the closet?

An ear-splitting squawk woke me. It was dark, and while I had noticed that grille over the south window, I hadn't really expected anything to issue from it, except perhaps poison gas. It was squawking my name, and instructions to get down to the lounge on the double. I found my boots, put my feet into them, knocked over the lamp and picked it up, got my boots laced and my belt buckled. True enough, I didn't look so great in the blue pantaloons that tucked into the boots. They were cut for thin women and must have been designed by some inactive person. I pulled the belt in another notch to show off my small waist, and went out. The electric clock over the stairway informed me I'd been asleep over three hours. I wondered if my first day at the Academy would be my last.

"Rimidon, this is the service,'' Sgt. Mother said when I entered the lounge. Besides the eight of us who'd arrived in the morning, there were half a dozen men, including the barber who was now in regulation blue uniform. Three of the men looked tough as turnips and mean as mules.

"Yes, madam,'' I said.

"You were on call to be here six o'clock sharp.''

"Yes, ma'am.''

Not a smile showed on any face. Merle carefully looked at the wall. They would throw me to the piranhas, me and my four languages and my nose flute and my mother's hopes for me.

"Siddown,'' she said. There were no chairs left vacant, so I folded my legs gracefully and sat on the floor, sinking down right where I was like a lotus disappearing. One of the mules snorted.

Sgt. Mother gave us the details. "At eight o'clock, four of you are going out on night exercises with your instructors. Rocca and

Sgt. Rhodes. Blitzstein and Cpl. Dale. Hardy and Lt. Fenniman. Rimidon and Sgt. Vichek." The snorting mule looked over all the heads at me, and I looked him back; he was tall, tough, gnarled, and gave off the brotherly warmth of an asteroid.

Merle's Sgt. Rhodes was small, dark, and good-looking, a lovely match for her. I wondered about Blitzstein's Cpl. Dale, who seemed too young to have retired to instructor, but when he moved, I saw that three fingers were missing from his left hand.

Dinner was roast chicken, mashed potatoes, and blueberry pie, but not enough of any of them. Merle was down at the other end of the table, talking with the little blonde Selma Blitzstein. Sgt. Mother was wearing lipstick which made her look a whole lot better, almost as if she could be someone's mother. We had received no instructions about make-up, so a lot of it was apparent; women's bravado, that last smear of color before facing the firing squad. Merle had on gold lipstick and mascara to match; it looked great on her. I hadn't had time to apply any, but I have good skin and large, brown, dark-lashed eyes, so I never favored much extras.

After dinner we had half an hour in which to relax. I was surprised to see Blitzstein sitting with some kind of small tapestry frame, and stood behind her chair to watch those thin, delicate fingers of hers work in red and gold thread, green and peacock blue, a little at a time, slow, easy, with exquisite patience that drew us all to watch, and admire. Gradually, a bird appeared. I'd never seen anything like that work.

By eight, booted and snapped into dark blue jackets, we assembled on the darkening front lawn. A big light blazed over the front door; beyond its illumination the forest lay quiet and black. Sound of water, brook or small river, somewhere. Smell of pine trees. I could feel my senses key up and quiver. Sgt. Vichek took my elbow sternly and turned me toward the woods. "Move," he said.

"Would you like to tell me anything about this patrol?" I asked, walking toward what seemed a solid wall of trees and underbrush.

"Roxy Rimidon," he said. I could have sworn he was grinning, the feel of it lay heavy on my back. "Keep moving."

"Yes, Sgt. Mule," I said under my breath.

I'd spent plenty of time in the woods, growing up, and with my brother, too, on mountain climbs. It must be on my record. None of the forested areas left in this Dominion are completely dense;

there's always a way through. Bonny briar bushes, I realized, getting raked across one cheek. I squinched down to get under some low branches, kept my forearm raised in front of my face, groped with my boots. What if I could lose the mule? How well did he know these woods?

After the first thirty yards or so of thick underbrush, it opened out a little. The trees were large, the smell of pine stronger. I began to move out, conscious of Vichek close behind me, but dropping back a little as I increased my speed. We did about half a mile like that. My eyes now had good night vision, and there appeared to be something unusual about the area we were entering. The openness was all on a lower level; above, it was dense and tangled. Not right. Not nature's way of doing it. Man-made. Look out, Roxy, I told myself, something is either going to drop out of a tree onto your head, or something is going to give way under your feet.

My nerves began to tingle with warning. Vichek was still audible behind me. God, that man had big, heavy feet; he was lumbering along, and snorting now and then as though he had bugs up his nose. The warning tingle rose to a high twang as I swerved, fast, to the right, and plunged into the underbrush. Vichek came to a dead halt and switched on a powerful flashbeam.

Another three feet forward and I'd have walked into a net spread on the ground. Would've been hoisted like a fish. I crouched, invisible, among the saplings and briars. The light danced around as Vichek sought me. I stopped breathing. I practiced not being. There is a way to do it, a way to become leaf, twig, log, bark.

"Rimidon," he said in a soft voice. I was growing a shelf of fungus. My feet had sunk below the leaf mold, seeking a deep grip. He kept the light moving, "Okay," he said, "come on out."

He took a few steps backward and began to search the area. I breathed once. Leaves unfurled from my fingers. His big boots were making a lot of angry noise. Nothing like an angry mule to discourage a person. Inch by inch I moved backward, deeper, into the brush. Vichek swore noisily. He stumbled over something, recovered his balance, and asked God to send him back to active duty on Vogl. By this time I was thirty feet away from him, and wondering how to work my way around behind him, to the path back. Did I dare lose track of him?

Little by little I crawled through. Mosquitoes found me, and feasted; sharp bits of bark got down inside my shirt. I was sticky, tired, and disgusted. What kind of training is this, I wondered?

Why don't they just take us for a good camping trip in the mountains? I made a couple of false starts toward the path and finally found it, though it wasn't cleared enough to be called a path. Before I stood up, I listened, but there wasn't a sound; no boots, no snorts, no mule. To hell with you, I thought. Just the same, I stepped with great care, with great quiet.

Finally, I was close enough to the edge of the woods which fronted the Academy to see the blaze of light over the front door. A horse fell on me. I whipped over as I went down and struck upward, got a good, solid punch landed on his face, and then he had his knee in my stomach and both my arms pinned.

"Give up?" he asked.

"Son of a bitch," I said, and spat out leaf mold. He had a terribly big, bony knee.

"Nah, nah," Vichek said, hauling me to my feet. "I grew up in the Sierras. You gotta admit you met your match."

"You can move quiet when you want to," I admitted.

He snorted a laugh. "Sure I can. I was afraid I was overdoing the noise, on the way out. God, woman, what do you weigh?"

"None of your business," I said, scraping bits of bark off my sweating neck. We went through the last of the woods onto the lawn and came into bright light, where Col. Wayser was standing. Sgt. Mother, a notebook in her hand, looked up at us. She stared at Vichek, so I turned to look, and was delighted to see one of his eyes beginning to swell shut.

"Grade A," Vichek said, looking a little grim. "She's fast as a bobcat for all that weight."

It wasn't bad enough the mule fell on me, but had to remark on my weight in front of the colonel. As if Vichek didn't outweigh me by fifty pounds.

The colonel glanced at me as I went by and I smiled at him, but he only quirked one corner of his mouth a little. Sgt. Mother said, "You're off duty now. You can go to the lounge, if you like."

After I'd shaken the scraps of tree and leaf from my shirt, and combed my hair, I got myself a tall glass of ice water and whiskey, and sat down. Vichek walked in, got himself a stein of beer, and came over and sat beside me on the couch. He took a big swallow of beer, and set the stein down. His eye was shut tight and turning blue. "You coulda belted me on the chin, instead," he said thoughtfully.

"Sorry. You didn't give me a chance to be delicate about my aim."

"No kidding, what do you weigh?"

"One-thirty-five."

"Yeah? I woulda guessed a lot more."

Blitzstein and Cpl. Dale came in, sat down with glasses of beer, and started a chess game. The others slowly appeared, except Merle and her little Sgt. Rhodes. The chess game proceeded. I had another drink, Vichek leafed through a magazine, the p.a. called Merle Rocca and John Rhodes, who were an hour overdue.

"They got the water patrol," Dale said to Vichek.

Merle swims like a minnow. I wondered if she had drowned Rhodes, or if she was sitting in the river with just her nose out to get a breath, while he ran up and down looking for her. Or perhaps Rhodes had drowned Merle.

After I finished the drink I got up. "I'm going to sleep," I said. Vichek didn't move, and I looked down at him. "I suppose you're my instructor for the whole eight weeks?"

"Ain't that our luck," he said, tenderly putting one hand over his black eye. "I'm not allowed to damage you, so you might take that into account, next time."

"Indeed I will," I said with relish. "I won't forget it for a moment."

There was a central stairway, right opposite the big front door, and I was on the first step when the door opened and in came Merle and Rhodes, both of them sopping wet. Sgt. Mother's voice shouting recriminations, threats, and reorientations, followed them in.

"Hi," Merle said when she saw me. Rhodes stood looking downcast and running rivulets onto the bamboo matting.

I said, "Been for a swim? Nice night for it."

Merle glanced back at Rhodes. He raised his dark eyes in supplication to her and she smiled, and started up the stairs with me. "How did you do?" she asked.

"The sergeant won," I said. "What did you do to Rhodes? He looks unhappy." We were on the second floor of my wing by now, and Merle would have to go back to her own quarters. She was pressing the water out of her hair with both hands.

"I'm sorry I didn't realize he'd be faulted for us being so late. Did you ever try to get back into wet clothes after you've taken them off? It takes forever."

"See you at breakfast," I called after her as she ran down the stairway.

We were allowed a night's undisturbed sleep. On waking, I

naturally checked my dreams, found one involving Col. Wayser and shut it off before I arrived at the consequences. I was a rookie, after all. He was head of the Academy, young as he seemed. There were other Planet Patrol Academies, quite a lot of them including the centers where the men studied. But the colonel was the backbone of this one, probably married, certainly used to girls making eyes at him.

Sgt. Mother had breakfast with us, then each of us was assigned to a study course. I drew Transport, of all things. I thought a duller subject would be hard to find, and went looking gloomily for Lt. Nelson's room. First floor, rear, and Lt. Nelson with a pleasant voice, soft temper, and that rare, plum-black skin. The walls were covered with charts; air routes and underground; snow, sand, bog, fen, and mountain tramway. Every means of transport the planets offered were illustrated in her charts. She knew everything about each planet's transport system: the problems, the values, the changes in progress.

Blitzstein and the thin girl Hardy were my companions in this class. We learned how to operate skimmers and how to trap escapees in Vogl's numberless swamps and water byways. Lt. Nelson took us out to a swamp half a mile from the building, put us on Vogl bogshoes, and watched us flounder and splash. My eyes were full of mud, my knees soggy, and my muscles aching, before Lt. Nelson called it a morning. Immaculate in her blue shirt and pantaloons, with polished boots and unmarred make-up, she escorted us back.

She said, "Rimidon, if you'd sweat off a few pounds, you'd be good on those bogshoes, you have remarkable balance."

"Yes, ma'am," I said. "Do you know I can ride a horse?"

She smiled. "They don't use them, except in the resorts. Not for transport. How did you learn?"

"My grandmother was an equestrienne," I said proudly.

"Ah, that's one of our lost arts," she said with sadness. "Why don't you skip dessert at lunch?"

So they began to persecute me, a pound here, a pound there; lean meat and vegetables, fruit juice instead of beer; swim, run, jump, climb, and many an evening trying to get rid of Vichek in woods, hills, and swamps. I never succeeded, though I came pretty close a few times. I learned to respect him a lot; tough as he was, he never pushed it too far, he never lost his temper, and sometimes he even said I was doing fine.

Merle began turning out triumphs in the code-and-computer

department; she was the pet of Lt. Kimminy who headed up C & C, and was married to our barber. They had a son in Patrol on Alpha, and a daughter studying music in Asia Dominion. Lt. Kimminy wore a vague expression and had a soft voice, which disguised a crackling sense of humor and a genius for cybernetics. I liked her, thought I wasn't one of her best students.

"Where did they find all these people?" Merle asked, one of the few times we had a chance to talk. "And it looks like such an innocent building, especially the basement."

The basement was larger than the building on top of it. Lts. Kimminy and Holder worked down there with their computers. One section, at the eastern end, was walled off; a heavy metal door carried a sign which said: Detonation and Deactivation. Selma Blitzstein had disappeared in there the third day and only reappeared at meals. I thought of those thin, precise fingers threading the tapestry bird, treading the little wires, deactivating the little bombs. No question but that her special talent had been discovered.

"I suppose one day we'll be staff," Merle said. "I can't see that far ahead, though. You know, they transferred Johnny Rhodes— they're tougher on staff than they are on rookies."

"I wondered what happened to him."

"I told the colonel it was my fault, but they transferred him out and now I've got Mule Two, that Sgt. Limon." She leaned over and tweaked my sleeve. "Still got your eye on the colonel?"

"Don't see him much. We had the standard interview, I kept a straight face, a stiff upper lip, and my chest out. What do you think he's doing here? He didn't have to retire before thirty-five and he can't be more than thirty."

Merle shrugged. "Maybe he's just recuperating from something. He could go back on active if he applied, I guess."

"He'd have to go all through physical again. Not that I see a thing wrong," I added, and we grinned again at each other.

When Sunday came they promised us the day off, and we had it, but of course we were not allowed to go anywhere. There had been a fire alarm (false) at two in the morning; we fell down rope ladders or tumbled out first-floor windows; none of the lights worked; people yelled; Sgt. Mother called out our names and expected a response. Somewhere, two girls had stayed in bed, and this morning they went home. Leaving six of us.

At three in the afternoon we were called into the lounge for tea. The minute I saw that tray of pastry I felt better. Then I saw the colonel with a woman who must be his wife, not bad looking, but a hopeless case. She simpered when she shook hands, said she was so thrilled to meet us, said she always adored these afternoons on Sunday when she had a chance to see the new cream of the crop, the flower of earthside womanhood. As if she were waiting to see us fed to the Minotaur.

I took a cream puff from the tray, bit out half of it, and looked earnestly at the colonel. He met my eyes, and seemed taken aback. "Rimidon! Aren't you on orders to drop five pounds?"

I swallowed the rest of the cream puff almost whole, and said, "Yes, sir."

Lt. Nelson came to my rescue, saying, "She's already dropped the five pounds, sir."

"Doesn't look it," the colonel remarked, turning away.

"Sir!" I yelled, taking a step forward. Merle caught me by the arm, but I shook her off. I stalked over to Col. Wayser and his lady, who involuntarily turned to face me.

She simpered. "Oh, my dear," she said, "I know those little sweets are so tempting, I don't blame you. I think you look in very good trim."

I look glorious, you skinny little bitch, I thought.

The colonel said mildly, "Rimidon, I didn't intend to be rude."

"No, sir," I said, and went back and took a chocolate eclair from the tray. Sgt. Mother edged me back against the wall. "You don't yell at the colonel," she hissed in my ear.

"Academy colonels don't shame their rookies in public," I hissed back. "Especially in front of their wives."

"Some wife," Sgt. Mother said. "She goes running after every general she sees, a colonel isn't enough."

Chewing the last of the eclair, I turned my head to look into Sgt. Mother's eyes. "What is Col. Wayser doing here, anyway?" I whispered.

She glanced around to make sure no one heard us. Then she answered, briefly, "He was a Zix pilot before they offered him this job."

I should have known. A Zix pilot is done and finished at twenty-five; men older than that are too slow, can't take the stress. Next time I'll smile when I yell at him, I promised myself.

On Monday I crossed the river by tree, leaving Vichek, I thought, on the bank behind me, but he got across in perfect silence and was waiting for me, and yanked me down out of the oak where I had stopped to rest. On Tuesday I walked right into one of those nets and got winched up into the air, while Vichek stood below, and laughed. Early Wednesday evening, Hardy and I were given small backpacks, and Cpl. Dale with Lt. Nelson took us on a terrific, tough climb into the mountains to what looked like the top rock in the world.

There they, along with daylight, left us quite suddenly, with no fire, compass, knives, or coffee pots. Our packs contained one pair of clean socks and a chocolate bar each.

"Oh, hell," Hardy wailed, "I hate camping. I'm a biotronic engineer. And a translator."

Nothing to do, but lie down, with the backpacks for pillows, and to the music of foxes and nightbirds, we fell asleep. Dawn was cool. We put on our clean socks, laced our boots, and ate our chocolate. It seemed easy enough, given the sun for direction, to find our way back. It seemed a pointless exercise, until we heard that *whickoo!* and the crackling ricochet off the rocks at our feet. We both fell flat.

"Oh, hell," Hardy said, "are they going to shoot us before we graduate? Did they give us any weapons?"

"Brains, Hardy. We have brains, muscle, Enovid, lipstick, clean socks, pills for cramps, and the promise of a pension. We can last it out."

Whickoo! Light gauge, one pretty far down the mountain slope at the east, another too damn close, nearly as high as we were, to the left. Can't dig a hole in rock. Nothing but scrub to hide us. The sun was getting higher and hotter.

Hardy said, "I think we ought to figure out what they want us to do, and do the opposite."

"Let's inch back while you're thinking."

It is not easy to inch back up a slope covered with thorn bushes and sharp outcrops, without getting any part of you high enough in the air for a target. Inch for inch, they were coming along with us. *Whur, whur;* the sound of a Clam gun, notable for the burns which it inflicts, as well as for its name which we'd always supposed was a joke: Constant Laser Automatic Motivator.

We sweated in the warming August air. Our clothes ripped, then the skin on our knees and elbows, as we headed for cover.

"They're not going to get me," Hardy muttered.

"Me neither. Costs too much to train us."

We almost achieved the ledge where we'd spent the night when they shot up a whole barrage of rock fragments in front of us. Hardy turned head over heels backward and rolled down the slope, bounced off a boulder and crashed into some bushes. Bounce, roll, crash, I joined her. "Oh, hell," she said when I lay beside her. There was not another sound.

"It's all so pointless," she said. "We've heard gunfire before, what are they out to prove? I should have stayed with Lt. Fennimen, we were just getting into Japanese grammar."

But it wasn't pointless. We found we were limited to about fifteen square feet of the mountain, including our little spiky nest in the bushes. The sun broiled us, though we'd taken off our jackets. Hardy kept covering her nose with one hand; she had very fair skin and it was turning a blistered red.

I'd been thinking about our unseen companies; were they staff, or were they rookies? Not rookies, I decided; surely they wouldn't trust rookies with all that weaponry turned on us.

Hardy suggested, "It's our job to get down past them, and it's their job to keep us here."

"Must be they expect us to wait for dark. I think we better show them how patient and persistent we are, and just do that."

About ten minutes later, Hardy said, "I got to take a leak."

"Go ahead, stand up and find a place."

"You're kidding!" She began to creep around to the other side of the scrub growth. I could hear her mutter, "Eyes, eyes, everywhere, what do they want, I'll burst."

I wished she hadn't mentioned it, because now that she had mentioned it, I had to go too. I pretended I felt empty. After a while, Hardy crawled back, and lay beside me. A half hour later she said, "On the other hand, perhaps they just want us to think they'll wait for us. Maybe all we have to do is find our way down in the dark."

"We could have done that last night. Booby traps?"

"Possibly," she admitted.

By late afternoon it was my turn to crawl around to the other side of the bushes, As soon as it was dark, we'd try to move, and nothing hampers rapid action like a full bladder. There had been no more shots, as long as we stayed put.

"You feel brave?" Hardy asked at dusk. "Want to stand up?"

"You stand up," I said.

She took my hand. "We'll both stand up." We got to our knees first, and peered around, like a couple of rabbits. Silence. A few late birds in the sky. I watched them to see if they avoided any special area, but they did not. We both stood up. Silence. The sun sank. We sat down, looking into the darkness below. "We just walk down, is that it?" I asked.

"Sure, if you can remember how we got up."

Night came up faster and faster along the slopes; ate our boots, eclipsed our knees, swallowed our hearts. "I got a feeling," Hardy said. "I got a strong feeling they're waiting for us to start down."

"So do I."

Night buried our heads and we disappeared.

Hardy asked, "What do you suppose is on the other side of this mountain?"

"The backside," I breathed. "Oh, yes, the backside of the mountain, while they wait for us on the front."

"As I recall, it was much steeper and rougher than the way we came up," Hardy said, and rose to her feet.

So in the darkness we began feeling our way back toward the rocky roof on which we had slept the night before, trying to be quiet. Then slowly, slowly, starting the descent one step at a time. What made us think we could do it quietly, if at all, I can't imagine. We fell over each other, over rocks, bushes, lumps in the ground, ghosts, armies, colonels, and banquet tables. Now and then we sat down and talked about iced tea or beer. Hardy swore she heard a fountain, and I asked her if she'd ever seen the famous ones in Europa Dominion. We went on crashing and thumping, wondering why the waiting group hadn't heard us. Or had they heard us, would they be waiting for us at the bottom?

About midnight we were so exhausted we lay down, and looked at the faint stars in the sky. "Hardy, actually we don't know what's down there at the back of the mountain. We might have to go up over another one, if there's no valley way out."

"I bet there's a river. All along the edges it's got chips of mint-flavored ice and every two feet there's a platter of fried chicken."

"And right in the middle of the river is a little green island made of mattress, and there sits the colonel, brown as a berry and blond on top."

"Rimidon, don't you ever think of anything but the colonel?"

"Seldom," I said. "I'll take a half hour watch and think about him, while you sleep."

I'm proud to say I did stay awake until she'd had her nap, and she stayed awake while I had mine. Too soon, we were stumbling downward again. "We gotta make it before dawn," Hardy kept mumbling.

"Whole thing is stupid," I mumbled back. We were both light-headed. It was a wonder we didn't fall down the rest of the way and lie dead at the bottom. Most of the time we watched our invisible feet. Boulders and shrubs stood out as darker masses so we could avoid them, and in a weary trance we kept going, sometimes sliding yards on our heels and bottoms, sometimes falling into thorny ground pockets.

We started climbing up the next mountain before we were aware that the direction of the slope had changed. "Oh, hell," Hardy chanted, when we found out what we were doing. We went back, left, right, found a kind of rocky channel like a dry river bed, and began to trudge along it. Very gradually it swung around to the north, which should take us back toward the Academy. We stumbled more and more as the sky began to lighten; we went slower and slower. I began to feel it wasn't worth it because there were any number of jobs I could have had without trying this one. I was sure I couldn't make it, but as long as Hardy kept on, I would, too.

She stopped to look at the sky, which was a bright pearl color. "Bet you dropped another five pounds," she said.

I was too tired to answer. Our feet were blistered, and I was thinking of chewing some leaves or bark. Hardy started on once more, and I plodded close behind her. There was a ridge of hill running out from the mountain we had crossed; if we could just get round the ridge, I thought. If we can just hold out until we see what's over there.

After a long time, we made it. Hardy stopped so short I bumped into her. There was a jeep standing there. Vichek was leaning up against it, cleaning his nails.

"Made it, did you," he said, looking up. Hardy staggered over toward him, and I staggered after her.

"Now what would you girls like more than anything else in the world?" Vichek asked, reaching behind him into the jeep.

"Water," Hardy gasped.

I said, "Colonel Wayser," and fell down. But not unconscious. Vichek squatted down and tenderly held the canteen to my mouth while I gulped and spluttered.

"You didn't mean that, did you?" he asked, looking concerned.

"Mean what?" I sat up and held the canteen to my mouth.

"About Ray Wayser."

Hardy was sitting in the jeep eating, so I got to my feet, somehow, and reeled around to the other side to join her. She handed me a sandwich and I fell to. Vichek got in behind the wheel and started the engine. He was smiling to himself, and Hardy asked crossly, "What's so funny?"

"Oh, they were all betting you'd filter down just before dawn, and I swore you'd come over on this side. I had some fight to get out here with a rescue vehicle. You can thank Sgt. Mother for the chow. She was the only one agreed with me that Rimidon had to go over the mountain. Like the bear in the song."

He began to sing as we moved off, bouncing over rocks and ridges. "Oh, the bear went over the mountain," Sgt. Vichek sang, and after another drink from the canteen, and in between bites of her second sandwich, Hardy joined in, and after a while, I did. What else could we do?

There was no one around when we got back. I fell into bed, torn pants, bloody scratches, and all, and slept until dark, when Sgt. Mother woke me. "Come on, Rimidon," she said. "You don't want to miss dinner, do you?"

"Not for anything. Have I time for a shower?"

"Ten minutes." She came on into the room and looked at me reflectively. "Perhaps I should remind you to take your pill?"

"Oh, yes," I said, reaching under my shirt to the waterproof tablet case. "Thank you, Mother. Maybe you better say something to Hardy. It was one thing we forgot."

"You're not supposed to forget anything," she said, and went out, but she paused in the hall to call back, "you and Hardy are the first to go down the other side of the mountain."

I walked to the doorway on my blistered bare feet. "Tell me something. If we hadn't gone down that way, if we'd tried to come down the way we went up, what would have happened?"

"Oh, I'm not allowed to say," she said, looking shocked.

Typical. They never tell you anything. I gulped my hormone tab, took my shower, got into clean clothes, and ran down for dinner.

During the next week classroom studies began to pile up. Ballistics, statistics; voiceprinting, codebreaking, mapmaking; language arts, chess games with the computer; transport, space-sports, mobs: infiltrating of, reducing of, containing of; politics, diplomacy, space law. Our heads nearly burst, and when our brains were so tired we couldn't think any more, we climbed up and down ropes, hiked over more mountains, got out of skintight skirts under water, were strapped into free-fall simulators (Brighton and Krantz got ill and Krantz fainted, both were sent home); and every second day the doctor ran us through for a physical.

I had dropped seven pounds and expected him to be pleased.

"What are you doing, eating on the sly?" he said. "You're still 36–25–38 and look like hell in those pantaloons."

"Wait'll you see me in a dress," I promised.

My evening jaunts into the forest with Vichek were over, fortunately. I didn't see so much of him now, though he took me out on the firing range, where we found out I was a very good shot. I learned to handle some sophisticated weapons with speed and ease. He never said much, except once he asked, "You didn't mean it, about Colonel Wayser?"

"I was delirious," I said sincerely.

Vichek looked me in the eye, like man to man. "The hell you were," he said. "You know how many girls have made passes at the colonel?"

"Hundreds," I guessed.

"Right. So what makes you think you're any different?"

"I'm not, except I'm the worst chess player you ever had here."

We started to walk back from the firing range. Vichek said, "Well, you can't be good at everything."

"I don't seem to have any special talents."

"You got persistence. You and Hardy going down the other side of the mountain. They never thought you'd try it."

"It was Hardy's idea. And I wouldn't have made it, except for following her."

"You don't have to tell anybody that."

"But it's true."

"You don't deserve the colonel," Vichek said.

"The colonel is married."

"The colonel is rumored to be dumping her. Too many generals in the field, I heard. Not that she'd be a loss to us," and he stamped off ahead of me.

Well, that's all very nice, I thought, but I'd hardly go through what I've been through these weeks, just to settle down with the colonel. I intend to see the colonies, and earn my money, before I settle down. I'm only twenty-two. Nearly the age at which a Zix pilot retires, huh? I reminded myself.

All Graduation Day amounted to was that the four of us, me, Merle, Hardy, and Blitzstein, could eat our breakfast in leisure and lounge around speculating on our assignments. Usually, it was six months on jobs, then two months off, then back to work. We also talked about clothes, having been told we could graduate in dresses. The Academies really understood their students very well.

"I'm going to wear the orange one," Merle said, "with those big, black beads from Alpha, and a pint of perfume." Myself, I was fed up with boots and high-necked shirts, so I felt just the way she did. We would have a week in which to visit our families, or go somewhere else to relax, before starting work. I asked Merle if she was going home.

She shook her head. "Johnny Rhodes is teaching at a P.P.A. in Paris. I'm going to fly over to see him."

"Lucky you," Selma Blitzstein said. "I'm going home and be shown off to my relatives."

"Joan?" I asked Hardy. Her nose had finally stopped peeling, and she looked pretty good.

She smiled at us. "Yes, I'm going home for the week; I'll be glad to. Dad's working on a new pulmonary system at the hospital, and he's promised to show me how it is put together."

My things were packed, all but the dress I was going to wear. I took my time with my make-up, and perfume all over, and then the dress, which weighed half an ounce and went on over nothing but my own skin. My hair had grown out a lot, so I gave it a good electric brushing, and then clipped the little diamonds in my ears. They were a present from my mother, though what she thought I'd do with diamonds at the Academy, I can't imagine.

Sgt. Mother was walking the halls, trying to hurry us up. When she saw me, she asked, "What is that?"

"It's my Tucci dress," I explained, "and I'm going to wear it to graduate in."

"I don't believe that's been done before, here, either" she said, and went away.

I waited a little, since I didn't plan to be obscured by the mob. The dress looked like silver fog on me and it ought to be seen in its full effect. All the staff were in the lounge, and the colonel, without his lady. Hardy went in, there was a pause, and I made my entrance. I hadn't counted on the midday sunshine which streamed through the front windows. The dress was opaque in shadow or lamplight, but in bright sunlight it was pure as a pane of glass.

"Rimidon!" the colonel said in astonishment.

"Yes, sir," I said. "As you can see, I've dropped ten pounds."

Sgt. Vichek turned around and pounded silently on the wall with one fist. Sgt. Mother went from window to window, closing the screens. Merle, Hardy, and Blitzstein closed in before me, but I ducked around and stood in line with them.

Lt. Nelson raised her eyebrows, everyone else looked solemn, and Colonel Wayser began to read off our names and assignments.

"Merle Rocca, Waterways Commission, Vogl." He shook her hand, and she stepped back into line.

"Selma Blitzstein, Fringe Patrol, Alpha."

"Joan Hardy, Medical Intelligence, Vogl."

Col. Wayser cleared his throat and went on. "Roxy Rimidon, Island Patrol, Caribbean Area." His handshake was firm, but I got out of it at top speed and stepped back. Caribbean, probably Cuba Dominion, earthside, right here on this planet; routine checking of birds and coconuts, probably. I couldn't have done that badly. Like the others, I'd dreamed of a hard, dangerous job, and all the sights to be seen out there. I'd been through some hard training. I wanted the money, the glory, and most of all, the sense of accomplishment when I got my rank. I could feel the blush spreading upward.

"Rimidon, you're turning red all over," Col. Wayser said, and there was a spark of laughter in his eyes.

When I got that damn dress off, I'd burn it to ashes.

"How bad did I do?" I asked. "What did I flunk?"

Lt. Nelson said, "You did very well. If you'd flunked anything, you wouldn't be here today."

The colonel said, "More than half our graduates get their first assignments here. Earth has eight billion busy people we must keep track of. But if you request reassignment, we will consider it."

"No, sir, I'll take what I get."

"We know you can take it," the colonel said, and his eyes sparked again, though his mouth was sober. "Good luck to all of you," he said.

I went back upstairs, shoved the Tucci dress into a corner of my suitcase, and put on a plain black skater that covered me completely. Merle came in and we gave each other a couple of bear hugs, and danced a couple of wild steps together.

She said, "They've got some volcanic mountains down there on those islands, isn't that nice for you, you can climb them."

"Oh, thanks, Pippa Merle," I groaned.

"Listen, we both made it. When I get back I'll buy you a drink. So long, Pippa Roxy."

"So long. When I'm a lieutenant I'll buy you a whole green jug."

I closed the suitcase and carried it downstairs. Sgt. Mother was there to say goodbye. "It's been a pleasure knowing you, Pippa," she said, and we shook hands.

Outside, we got into the service bus that was waiting to take us to the airport. After I was settled in a seat by the window, I looked out, and saw the colonel, his blond hair blazing in the sunshine. When he saw me watching, he saluted, so I kissed my hand to him. After all, I was off duty.

When I got home, it was so neat and deserted I could tell Mom was off on a visit or tour. I put through a call to her office and Maxine looked out at me. She smiled and said, "Oh, Roxy, Dr. Rimidon's gone to a convention in Honolulu, and then she has a lecture in Helsinki. How long will you be home?"

"Not long. Thanks, Maxine."

"I guess I better call you Pippa now?"

"After all these years, I'd be very offended if you didn't go on calling me Roxy."

There was a pause, while her round and pleasant face continued to shine brightly on the video. "Roxy," she said, whispering. "I'm not supposed to say anything, but your mother's been proposed for head of the Bone Bank."

"No wonder she's busy. I'm leaving Friday, so if she isn't back before that, tell her I hope she makes it."

"Good luck, Pippa."

We signed off, and I sat for a while, thinking about almost nothing in order to rest myself. Then I unpacked my few things, and took my cello out to tune it and practice for half an hour.

After lunch, I took my cello and went down to the Monorail Station. For a little time it was as if I'd never been to the Academy, riding the Monorail with the cello propped lovingly against my thigh, my arm around its neck, close as a pair of lovers, and the roofs and hazy blue sky outside the windows.

I took the walkway over to the Rep Dome, which stood like a black half-melon at the center of the park. Although travel and other expenses were credited to my Patrol card while I was on duty, nothing was free when I was on leave, so I paid my way into the Repertory Dome, the standard fee for performer and spectator alike. The door swished shut behind me and I was in the first of the lamp-lighted halls. This being my home district, I didn't have to look at the directory, but automatically turned into the left-hand corridor. The theatre fronts that faced onto the corridor were composed of Kerr cells; when a performance was in progress or the casting complete, the walls were opaqued and darkened. Set into each of these front walls was the casting plaque, and the first one I passed was blinking on and off: *second violin* (Grady Quartet in G), *second violin* (Grady Quartet in G).

Spoken Arts was at the other side of the dome. As I went down this side, I passed several darkened walls: Mozart Sonatas for Two Hands, Gevenni's Symphony in A.

The next wall was lighted. Aha! The plaque read: Brahms Double Concerto. Coming toward me along the hall was a boy of fifteen, carrying his cello, and we pretended not to see each other, but there was no help for us since we got to the theatre door at the same time.

"Oh, come on," he said to me. "I cut Physics just to get here on time."

The door opened before I could answer and the conductor looked out. It was Maria Guayez, who knew me. "Roxy!" she said. "You're just in time." She smiled at the boy, and said to him, "Georgi, you are not to come during school hours. You know that."

He gave me a very bitter look, picked up his cello, and went away. "Come in, come in," Maria said, taking me by the neck of my cello very tenderly. "I am so glad to see you again. But you have not played for weeks. What must we listen to?"

Several of the musicians were familiar to me, as we had played together under Maria Guayez before. At one time my brother had thought himself in love with her, and instead of going over to the other dome side for the Group Ad Lib cycle, he would sit in the front row and never take his eyes off Maria. She tired of the puppy and sent him away very soon.

For so early in the afternoon the seats were fairly well filled, and it was nice to look down from the stage to the rows of lollipops all intent on us. In the more modern theatres in big Rep Domes, they have your music on a screen in front of your chair; here, we had to use printed music and turn our pages, but most of us were used to it, and I was full of happiness even before we began to make music. Although I'd had no practice for two months, I did not do badly. A couple of times when I came in late, Maria gave me an angry look, and the first violist, who was all of thirteen, stuck her tongue out at me.

Afterward, Maria invited me to dinner. We talked about music, about some of her own compositions, and about the new Block Poetry which was becoming popular. She advised me to spend an evening in the Spoken Arts, and take in some of the poetry readings while I was at it. "What better way to spend your leave?" she asked.

At the moment, I agreed with her, and as it turned out, I spent most of my leave in the park or in various theatres in the Rep Dome. At the end of the week, I packed up, put on my new uniform, and flew down to the Caribbean for my first assignment.

Looking straight up, I could see a little dark bird with rust-red on its breast, clinging to a banana and boring a hole through the peel. It worked hard, and once it had gotten through the peel it began to gorge on the ripening fruit. Most of the banana hands were encased in protective covers, but this one must have been overlooked.

It was early in the morning, and while I lay quite still and looked up into the banana tree, I could feel the night damp through my uniform.

Sgt. Krane was supposed to come up from Roseau to join me. A Cuba Dominion heli had dropped me off on the mountain road, and I'd gone into the plantation a certain distance, keeping out of sight. Here I was lying in wait, for far too long. I'd never met Sgt. Krane and wondered if the person was a woman or a man.

My stomach growled and I envied the bird his breakfast. The whole island was covered with growing fruits, but all I'd had was a thermo-pak of coffee.

Not being sure how the sergeant would arrive, I kept my ears open. There were bird calls, and a little breeze in the big banana leaves, but I never heard another sound until the foot came down on my throat. Not hard, just hard enough to pin me to the spot.

"Hallo," the person said.

I moved my eyes. Tall, with a thin, black, bony face. He wore pale nylon pants and a sleeveless shirt. In one hand he held an island cutlass.

"Good morning," I croaked.

He gazed seriously down at me. The cutlass swung casually as his arm raised a little, then dropped back to his side.

"A nap?" he asked.

"Yes."

"Funny place for it. We have some nice hotels on the island. We don't often get tourists asleep in the middle of a plantation."

"You can see I'm not dressed as a tourist."

"Oh," he said, taking his foot from my throat. "We are seeing people in all kinds of costumes."

Yes, I thought, lying very still; some people have been showing up in Planet Patrol uniforms. That makes lots of trouble for everyone. I measured the distance from the ground to his cutlass hand, and let my muscles go lax, because he had a good eye and could tell if I was lying here all bunched up for a fight.

"You'd better come down to the house with me," he said.

"Whose house?"

"Mr. Marrant's. You're lying under one of his banana trees."

The cutlass had come to full rest. I doubled up like a closing jackknife to get both hands on his cutlass wrist, and kept going, head over heels, flinging him down behind me. I held on until his fingers released the hilt.

Holding the cutlass, I looked down at him. He lay so still I thought I'd damaged him. His eyes were closed. When he opened them I could see how angry he was—his eyes were sort of maroon and his upper lip pulled so tight it disappeared. "Damn neat," he said, but he didn't move.

"Please get up. We'll go down to Mr. Marrant's as soon as the sergeant arrives."

He got gingerly to his feet, rubbing his hip bone where he'd landed. "I think you're a real Patrol. I'm fifty-eight and no one has ever taken my cutlass from me."

One day I'd be fifty-eight and not so full of myself as I was now, and it seemed worth taking a chance. I turned the cutlass hilt first and offered it to him, saying, "I'm sorry, sir. But we're trained for just that kind of thing."

He looked down his nose at my offer. "No, Pippa," he said. "You took it. You keep it until your sergeant comes."

I sat down cross-legged with the cutlass on the ground in front of me, and after a moment, he sat down, too, opposite me. "You're a well-trained young woman," he said.

"Yes, sir. I have to be."

He looked up into the banana tree from which the bird had fled; he looked down at the soft ground where we sat. Sproutlets from old banana roots were up at various levels around us. A hot, dappled sunlight made patterns on our heads and knees.

"The sergeant you wait for is also a woman," he remarked.

The cutlass lay between us on the ground, and I wondered if I should have made that noble gesture. "You have seen her," I said in the same offhand tone.

He looked into my eyes with such sharp intelligence I was sure no imposter could fool him. "At dawn I saw a woman in your blue Patrol uniform walk up into the mountain toward the Three Voices. That is some distance from here."

As far as I knew, Sgt. Krane and myself were the only Patrol members on the island at the time. Either the woman he'd seen was one of the counterfeits, or my sergeant was looking for me somewhere else.

"What are the Three Voices?" I asked.

"Where the waters come down. Our power station is there."

Water power? I was baffled. "Could you direct me there?"

"No," he said. "I could take you there."

In the ensuing silence I wondered if he wished for a bribe, or wanted to see my credentials, or was planning how to do away with me, or if he was merely as mystified as I.

"Tell me, how many of the fake Patrol people have you seen?"

"I have not seen one. I have heard that two men and a woman came in a small boat from the Atlantic side, claiming to be from our own Dominion. They disappeared into the interior," he jerked a thumb over his shoulder to the great mountains behind him, where the clouds were gathering for the daily rain. Three hundred or more inches per year drenched the mountain forests, although the coast had months of clear weather with only an afternoon shower now and then.

Leaving the cutlass on the ground, because I was unwilling to back out from my own fool-hardiness, I stood up. "Will you take me to the Three Voices?"

Leaving the cutlass on the ground, with a glance of utter contempt from its blade to my face, he also got to his feet. "If you wish," he said.

I followed him down the slope, past the trunks of fruiting trees, and new ones rising from the old roots where last year's trees had been cut down after the crop was harvested. When we came to the road I saw a truck of a kind I didn't think still existed. It was powered by combustion; a monster mounted on huge nylon tires. Most of the paint looked as if it had been blasted off. The body was made of bare, splintery boards. He got in behind the wheel and I ran around the truck and got in beside him.

"My name's Roxy Rimidon," I said.

"Yes, Pippa," he answered, and put the truck noisily in gear. It must have had some kind of brakes, but we sailed down the curved road first on one slant and then on another. Now and then chunks of the old road broke off under the wheels and hit the underside of the cab with the sound of a gong. A couple of plantation autogyros flew over us during the ride. We passed through the center of a town, with its palm trees and flowering bromeliads in the central square, and the pale pink and orange houses, with their cool slatted walls, making a geometric print on the hillsides in the bright, hot air.

The road began to curve up again. We passed a similar vehicle on its way down, and both drivers honked a greeting. When we reached the top of the hill, my driver reached under the dashboard and pulled out a speaker in a tangled nest of wires; I never saw anything so unkempt, but it seemed to work.

He spoke patois, which I could not get, except "Patrol" which stuck out like a shout several times. In a few minutes, a heli, with the blue insignia of Cuba Dominion, flew into sight above some cocoa trees and then went on ahead of us, very low. The combined sounds of truck and heli were deafening.

Up one mountain, down the next, into a grey mist. Rain forest appeared around us. There wasn't an inch of bare ground, one plant grew on another; the great limbs of old trees bristled with air plants. Everything dripped and steamed, and I could have sworn I felt mildew in my boots. They were certainly full of sweat.

The heli had come down and was standing in a small, lush valley just below the electric power station with its strange poles and wires and insulators. Two councilmen in beige tropic shorts and shirts were waiting.

"Here she is," my driver said as I got out. "She wants to go up to the Three Voices. She is looking, perhaps, for another Patrol woman."

The two dark men were stiff backed and polite, but nothing more. They turned, and began to climb a steep trail and I followed, hearing the truck roar away behind us.

The trail was rough, jumbled with damp stones, slippery with moss, and soon, almost vertical. There was a dull thunder which increased as we climbed. I began to get the depressed and ominous feeling one gets from subsonics, or the approach of doom, and wondered if just this thundering vibration accounted for it.

Sweat and moisture poured down from my scalp and face, my uniform drenched, the leather of my boots scraped, and stained with moss. The air was so moist it was like breathing through a sponge. The thunder grew so loud it was rumbling and roaring in my chest. The trail took a sharp turn between boulders, and we stood under tremendous cliffs.

I looked up hundreds of feet to where the water began its fall. It came down in three separate places in a foaming, boulder filled pool below us. In the pool, belly up, floated a dead woman in a blue Patrol uniform.

My two companions simply stood looking at her. I went down carefully to the water, where I took off my boots and waded in. The great torrents roared down and a cool mist blew across my face. I caught the body by one leg and pulled it back toward the edge, got an arm under the hips and lifted her out. She flopped wetly, one arm hanging into a crevice. Her cap was missing, but papers in her pocket were orders addressed to Sgt. Ann Krane. When I looked up, the councilmen were watching me suspiciously.

"Ever seen her before?" I asked.

"No," the younger man said. "Never. Is she real Planet Patrol?"

Of course what he meant was: are you real Planet Patrol?

"I'm not sure. Give me a moment more." I pulled her shirttails out of the pantaloons and looked for the featherweight belt at her waist. Strapped to it was standard equipment, including the little container of hormone tabs, and a tiny watertight pouch which held a metal match. Hooked into the breast pocket of her jacket was a steel tube no bigger than a match. I'd never seen one before and took it out to examine it. Something appeared to be inside. I tried to get it apart, but nothing budged. I put my thumbnail into a hairline crack, and for my trouble I got two blue sparks.

If it was a signaling device, which I thought it must be, I had just sent a message. Standing there I listened to the enormous thunder, saw that awesome sight of water pouring down from the tremendous cliffs, and wondered who, or what, might appear in response.

If the corpse was not Sgt. Krane, then she was still around somewhere and I'd better find her.

The older councilman said, "Shall we carry her back?"

"I imagine in a couple of weeks there's be nothing left but a few bones, which will hardly disturb the ecology," I said angrily.

They came down together, picked her up, and began to cart her off down the slippery trail. I hoped she was not my partner, for I didn't feel like going it alone, and felt even less like reporting the murder of a Planet Patrol auxiliary.

The Roseau Council had called for Planet Patrol assistance when the counterfeit Patrol people had appeared, then vanished so suspiciously. At that same time, the young growth from banana roots, wrapped in island soil and packed in life-support crates for shipment to Vogl, had been found destroyed at the airport warehouse. The climate on much of Vogl, though wetter, was similar to that of the Cuba Dominion areas where bananas grew. Because Vogl was our great agriculture triumph, with fast-growing colonies on the waterways and in wet forests, one shipment of new banana trees was to be exported every month for a year.

No one was sure yet how they would take the trip, how they would survive on such a planet, or even at what stage of growth it was best to ship them, but hope of success had been very high. The first shipment was totally destroyed before it even left the island.

We were halfway down the trail, the two men with their dead, wet burden ahead of me, when I heard a small heli coming across from the north of the island. I thought of the signal I must have sent, and called out to them, "Let's get under cover."

We twisted off the path, stumbling among huge roots. My boots slipped in the juice of torn leaves. When I glanced back, before the solid screen of growth could obscure my view, I saw that the men had dropped the body on the trail. Damn fools, to leave it out there in plain view. I kept bulling my way through vines, got cracked across the brow by a branch, and wondered if there were many poisonous insects about. The heli came on over the tops of the trees. There was the sound of triple vanes, the high whine of a beam from a Clam gun, and the backwash of scorching air from where it had hit.

When the sound of the heli grew faint, I began to crawl back toward the path. Where the body had lain, there was a little pile of black ash, with a few wisps of smoke still rising sluggishly in the moist air.

What interested me was the view they may have had from the heli. Did they see only a blue Patrol uniform on a woman, and burn it, of did they know who the woman was? If they held Sgt. Krane, and assumed they had just burned me, the best I could do was get out of uniform and blend into the background. Blending into the background would be a chore; big, blonde, and fair-skinned, I was one out of three or four such women on the whole island.

The two councilmen crawled out to join me. "My God," the young one said.

"A Clam gun," the older one said. "They ought to be banned. Not even Patrol should use them."

Except on special duty, no Patrol member carries a weapon. I looked sharply at the gasgun on his hip, the effective weapon councilmen wore at all times, and he looked away quickly.

Walking onto the trail, I kicked and scattered the pile of ash until nothing could be seen but boot-marks. Taking the lead, I went down, slipping over the wet rocks, with the two men behind me.

They took me to the council office where I should have been able to speak with the council president, but he was off on his boat with some friends.

I left his office, and walked through the old part of town to the more modern area where the hotel was. It had been built recently and was very pleasant, a series of one-room units facing the hot blue Caribbean. The ceilings were high; a band of slat ventilators ran around them at the top. The slats on the sunny side automatically closed when the temperature rose, while those on the shady side opened. Like most of the island buildings, the wall facing the sea was all slatted so that the room could be entirely opened to the sea if the tenant chose. During the rains, and months of high humidity, a switch locked the slats shut and turned on a cooler.

Although it was warm at noon, the humidity was low, so I lay down for a comfortable nap, chuckled to sleep by some bird outside my room in a sweetsop tree. When I woke, it was midafternoon, and the clouds, which always stretched out like Mercator projections at the edge of the sea, were beginning to mass in long horizontals. I had time for a swim. The lava sand, brilliant with grains of silica, was fiery hot, and I ran fast across it to plunge into the water.

When I came out I saw a figure standing in the shade of a cocoa palm. With my feet cool and wet, the return trip over the blazing sand was not as bad. There stood my cutlass-carrying friend of the morning, in a white suit with a bright green scarf at his neck, looking cool in all senses of the word.

"Mr. Marrant would like you to come to his house," he said.

"I must go to the council office this afternoon."

"It is pleasant here on our island, isn't it?" he said, and gave a look at my dripping self, fresh from a swim like a tourist. I could understand that he thought I should be on the job rather than enjoying myself. He went on, "Mr. Marrant has asked you for dinner."

Very good, I thought, because it would give me a place to start. For all I knew, he was harboring Vogl malcontents, an extreme group of the Independents who thought they needed no connection with Earth any more.

"I will call for you at eight," he said.

I thought of the new kyrene dress I'd bought down, and asked in a scandalized voice, "In that truck?"

"No, Pippa, in Mr. Marrant's helicar."

"What's your name?" I asked.

"San' Clement," he said, and turned away, adding something in patois, from which the word "Pippa" burst out with a kind of laugh.

The council president was in his office, a fat man with shrewd eyes and agreeable smile, Ian Toxetl. "Naturally, we think it must be members of the Vogl Independents, who else would do such a thing?" he asked. "Though it is stupid. If they want to be independent and carry on free trade, which they must do for years to come, why wouldn't they welcome a new crop to grow? That is what puzzles us so much. And it's common knowledge that if the banana shipments are successful, next year we'll try cocoa, and perhaps guava too. There are so few native Vogl crops which are edible, they should welcome these shipments."

"If they're fanatics, like that extreme insurrectionist group, there'd be no limit to what they'd try. There's been so much loud talk about the ship space used for food animals or agricultural equipment, and not enough space for people to travel—"

He interrupted me, saying mildly, "But Vogl is an agricultural planet, which the first settlers understood."

"Yes, sir, but here's a second generation. By now, lots of Vogl families would like to send students to our universities. They resent the exclusion of their young people from our Planet Patrol Academies, and the necessity for calling us from Earth to come shoot their troubles for them. Not to mention the exclusion from competition in Games. Though next year they'll be coming in for the first time, for Games."

Mr. Toxetl picked up the carafe from his desk and poured a red drink into two glasses. Ice tinkled in the carafe, and the glasses frosted over. It looked delicious and suspicious. I accepted my drink and sipped it. Sweet and tart, with a faint flavor of nutmeg, and after the sip was swallowed, the small fire of a good rum began to burn.

"This is what you might call a small-town island," he said thoughtfully. "We're happy here, we rarely need to call Patrol for anything. Most of us were delighted to help send banana stock out for experimental growth on Vogl—made us feel we had some part in human progress. You must be aware that the whole shipment was donated by various growers."

"It must make you feel even more bitter about its destruction, then. Just at the moment, though, I'm most concerned with the dead woman. With her identity. If she wasn't Sergeant Krane, I must find out who she was, and where Krane is now."

"Do you want to call your headquarters? We have rather primitive equipment, just the undersea cable, but we can make contact for you—the radiophone is always busy and hardly private."

"If you please. Then we can get on with the job you called us for."

He offered to refill my glass, but I moved it away. "No, thanks, sir, though it's very good."

"Ah, yes, you're from the North," he said whimsically. "I've been there several times. No one drinks in the office. Am I right?"

I couldn't help laughing. "Just about, sir. It's only a matter of local custom."

"So it is," he agreed, and refilled his own glass. Then he turned to the switchboard behind him and began putting through a call. I guessed it would take some time, with such equipment.

In half an hour, I'd made my report, and received instructions to proceed on my own, which is just what I knew they'd tell me. They also gave me the information that two livestock freighters had been impounded at the Vogl spaceport, their crews held as "guests" while Vogl flight engineers and other specialists were taking over. It wasn't yet known whether this was the work of the rapidly growing Independent group, or of some more extreme faction.

"The waterfalls," I said to Mr. Toxetl. "That's a very impressive place."

"Yes, it is, Pippa. Perhaps now that you've seen it, you'll understand why we've resisted the nuclear stations for so long, in spite of being called backward."

"But the nuclear station needn't be put there, sir. I could better be on the coast, or anywhere you please."

He spread his hands. In this century of total mobility, pride of place was a rare thing, but I thought the people of this island felt it strongly. Mr. Toxetl said, "Some of us still believe the Three Voices are meant to supply us with power. A sort of arrangement between those who great-grandparents were born here, and the spirit they believed inhabits the place of the falls."

Having been in the power of that spirit so recently, I knew what he meant. It was not just electricity generated there by that thundering downpour, but something more, intangible though it might be. Once the nuclear station was established, and the power drawn from elsewhere, that part of the interior would be deserted, and the spiritual strength no longer met, and matched, by man.

I went back to my hotel. The tiny patios in front of each unit were filling up with tourists, sipping bright drinks, or eating fruit served in long scoops. One of the scoops had been put on the table on my patio, filled with limes, bananas, and mangoes. A small, dark bird similar to the one I'd seen this morning was drilling a hole through the mango skin. I stood to watch him. He made a fine meal, and wobbled off after he'd stuffed himself. I cleaned out the well he'd drilled in to the mango and ate the rest of the fruit before it could spoil.

After I put on the kyrene dress, which was a changeable red, running through dark orange to scarlet to shades of rose and lavender, I showed off my sophistication by putting in a ruby nose stud. It was uncomfortable, but everyone was wearing them. What bothered me most about it was that in artificial light I kept getting red gleams and flashes from the end of my own nose, and sometimes found myself looking cross-eyed.

San' Clement put the heli down on the hotel lawn at eight o'clock, when the sun was setting over the Caribbean in gorgeous splashes of color. The clouds had turned black and were piling up, though they held no storm as they would have in the North. We lifted up and flew along the coast as the light faded.

San' Clement didn't seem hostile, but he was silent, and during the ride I kept feeling he had to struggle to keep quiet. This conflict he had with himself did nothing to make me feel more secure. He set the heli down on the gentle slope in front of Marrant's house of orange and white slats, with the lamplight shining in stripes across the front of it. He left me at the front door, and vanished into the night.

The door was opened by a small man, a few inches shorter than I. He had amber-colored skin and pure white hair, though he looked no more than thirty-five. "A Pippa!" he said, laughing.

He held the door wide and beckoned me in. I followed him into the big front room opening toward the sea, which was black now, with only a few faint boat lights showing as if they were stars drifting loose in space. Two men and a woman, all casually dressed in light clothing, were sitting around with drinks. They went on chatting as we came in, though the woman looked up at me for a quick assessment. The two men were pale and thin, with that soft, porous look produced by years in a steamy hot climate.

On the coffee table lay the blue cap of Planet Patrol auxiliary. The three silver chevrons on the side of the cap shone in the lamplight. Wherever my sergeant was, she had lost her cap. So had the body in the pool. A moment of outrage and disgust made me speechless.

Then I picked up the cap, and turned it over in my hands.

Marrant said, "One of my men found it this morning."

The woman put her drink down and sat back in her chair, examining my face, my nose stud, with considerable interest. She was about twenty-four and pretty, suntanned, and in good shape like an athlete.

Nothing was said, so I asked, "Who saw the woman in Patrol uniform go up toward the Three Voices?"

"I did," Marrant answered. "San' Clement was driving me down from a neighbor near there, and we saw her. I knew Planet Patrol had been called in, and was glad to see you were on the job, provided she was not one of the people we suspect to be imposters. Isn't it a mystery?" He cocked his sharp white head on one side and looked expectantly at me.

I could feel eggshells crackling under my feet; it was no time to be clumsy. I sat down beside the other woman, and Marrant brought me a drink. It was the same red one Ian Toxetl had given me, but much stronger.

A flash of ruby from my nose made me turn my head slightly, and I had another good look at the woman next to me. Something about the way she sat, the way her clothes fitted her, made me think of Games athletes, who were in perpetual training, and of the Vogl athletes who were already coming in to Earth to train for the next Games. "You're from Vogl."

She picked up her drink and swallowed a mouthful of it. "Yes.

I'm a runner. I'll be at the Games, when we're allowed in, at long last. I came here to train.''

It could be the truth. There was hardly any land on Vogl which was not bog, swamp, water, or wet forest; no good place for a distance runner to train, though some of them managed. "Long distance?" I asked her.

"No. One hundred meters," she said. I knew she was lying. She had the long, slim muscles of a dancer, not the sinewy ropes of a high-speed sprinter.

"I'm Roxy Rimidon," I said, and extended my hand to her. She flinched from me, and to cover it, picked up her drink and finished it off. Sgt. Krane's cap was on my knee. I picked it up and folded it flat. "I'll return it to her family," I said. With a deep breath, I plunged in. "You don't by any chance have her ID? She wasn't wearing it.''

It ran through my mind that last year's proposal to tattoo a Planet Patrol's member's ID number on the inside of the thigh was a reasonable suggestion, even though a total revolt of Patrol members had blown the idea to a powder.

After a shock of hesitation from all of them, except Marrant who gave a cold smile, one of the pale men reached into his pocket and brought out the tag, which he tossed to me. I put it inside the folded cap, and continued to sit there and take little sips of my drink. There were sounds of activity from the kitchen, so I supposed we were going to eat soon. Whether I'd be fed before slaughter was something I'd just have to wait to find out. Meanwhile, I looked around the room.

There was no other door than the one we'd come in by. The slats at the front of the house were sturdy, though I could probably go through them by getting a fast start and using all my weight. Of course no one in the room was going to sit around while I made a hole in Marrant's front wall and escaped.

Marrant was sitting on a formidable lounge in the middle of the room. It was made of white nylon zig-zagged all over with such brilliant turquoise that it was uncomfortable to look at. He sat like a doll, dead-center of the lightning design, still wearing the cold smile.

I asked him, "How did you get her up to the falls, when she was supposed to meet me miles away?"

"It wasn't hard. I pulled over to her on the road to my plantation and said I'd seen a Planet Patrol auxiliary going up toward the falls. She took the bait like a shark.''

I gritted my teeth in disgust. Then I said, "Do you want to tell me what it's about, or shall I just guess?"

"We'd like your cooperation," Marrant said. "I hope you won't be as stubborn as the sergeant. Actually, she was the victim of an accident; we'd much prefer to have her alive and helpful. What kind of training do you auxiliaries get, anyway?"

"Tough," I said. "Long, hard, tough training, and only about forty percent of the Academy students make it. Since we are only allowed to carry weapons on special duty, each individual must consider her whole self a form of weapon. As you must have found out."

Marrant chuckled. "We did, all right. I've one man with broken ribs and another opened up from shoulder to hip with his own knife. As I said, her death was an accident. She was simply uncontainable."

"It was wrong," the woman next to me suddenly said, in a blazing rage. "There was no excuse for killing her."

"She was a good Patrol woman," I said, which was all the epitaph Sgt. Ann Krane would have.

"And you?" the woman suddenly asked, leaning forward. "I hate killing, but it doesn't mean I can't hate you."

"Try me," I told her, and she was halfway out of her chair when Marrant yelled, "Reba, sit down."

She did what he told her. I asked Marrant, "What do you get out of this complicity?"

"Oh, I have some acreage on Vogl."

It made no sense at all to me, Vogl acreage being worth only what you could grow on it, and here he owned a big plantation.

Again I turned to the woman, and I asked, "Are you really a runner?"

"No. I'm one of the Vogl Patrol. We're opening our own Academies. Why should we try to enter yours? We don't need Earth Planet Patrol, half of you fall into our bogs and have to be rescued. We'll have our own, and do a better job. But I don't believe in murder. Your sergeant would still be alive if I'd been in charge."

She looked so murderous I wasn't sure I could believe that. Yet, if she were working with this group and could openly defy them this way, in front of me, she must mean what she said, if only in theory.

Though I had no use for the methods used by these extremists, like many Earth people I did sympathize with the Vogl Independents who wanted their own Planet Patrol. There was no reason they should not have it, and in fact most of us knew it was planned for the future. The Earth Planet Patrol Academies had been established for fifty years, and during that time the best methods of training, mental and physical, had been worked out. Staff must have several years of active duty behind them, and the regulations were tougher on staff than on students; the rule was a good one: don't teach what you don't know or can't do.

The plan on Earth books called for Academy instructors to be sent to Vogl within the next five or six years, when it was expected the ships would have a new drive, making it faster and cheaper to send live cargo back and forth. The instructors would establish Academies in two or three Vogl cities, and train qualified Vogl-born people to staff them.

"Well," I said. "What has all this to do with bananas?"

Marrant got up. He went to a table against the wall, and lifted from it one of the common fruit-scoops. It held what looked like a fruit, large, egg-shaped, with a bluish rind. At one end, a few blue-green fibers sprouted from it. Marrant brought the dish across to me, put it on the table, and began to peel off the bluish rind with a small knife. The pulp was rosy gold. It had a heady fragrance and my mouth watered. I took the fruit and sat looking at it, remembering the Academy sergeant who had said to me: "Your appetite will be the death of you one day."

Today, perhaps? Reba took the fruit from my hand and bit out a large mouthful, chewed it slowly, and swallowed. Then she handed it back to me. "That's a reem, native to Vogl. It grows under the same conditions as bananas, and we can't see any reason for growing bananas, which you have plenty of, when we can grow reems, and export them to you for a lovely high price. Taste it, and you'll see."

I took a bite. It was excellent, sweet as flute music, with the juice like a cool cascade running into the corners of my mouth. I was very hungry, especially since the smell of calalou soup had started to drift out from the kitchen. It took some self-control to put the rest of the uneaten fruit down.

"Do you mean to say you haven't discussed this openly with anyone?" I asked.

Marrant replied, "Sure we have. We, or I should say they, for I'm Earth born no matter where my sympathies lie, were told that Earth would be delighted to make a fair trade. So many crates of bananas for so many crates of reems. And then someone got the brilliant idea of shipping out young banana stock so Vogl could grow bananas for themselves and for export, and doesn't that take care of the value of a crate of reems? And reems, by the way, do not flourish here. I have tried them in my own plantation.''

Reba added, ''And bananas don't travel well. Not like reems. That rind protects them from bruises, and extremes of hot and cold. They're cheaper to ship, easier to harvest, and what's more, we've got all of them, and you don't have any.''

''It seems to me this is a matter for the Trade Councils,'' I said. ''Why impersonate Patrol members, commit murder, destroy a whole shipment of fruit stock? You can't expect us to do business with you now.''

One of the thin men said, ''You've got hundreds of different people and areas growing bananas. The reem crop is in the control of the Independents, and we're in the process of getting it away from them. We'll use it as a political weapon. The Independents have already tried talking fair, and nobody listens.''

At that moment, the door from the kitchen opened and a woman said, ''Dinner's ready.''

Without a glance at me, everyone got up and moved to the table. Marrant stood behind a chair and gestured me over, so I went, and was seated with them. Marrant poured wine into our glasses, the calalou soup was served, and we began to eat. I felt I was sitting with a flock of the banana birds, the spoilers, a gulp here and a bite there, ruining a crop for everyone just to fill their own stomachs. Yet I didn't feel that about Reba, even though she hated me. Of the whole group, she was the only one who seemed to have the genuine motive of wanting to help the people of her home planet.

''If you'd only left Sergeant Krane alone,'' I said all of sudden, surprising myself. ''What the hell do you expect from me now, after you've killed her.''

Reba said, ''I had nothing to do with that, I would have stopped it if I'd been there. I didn't want her killed. We had useful plans for her. Now we'll use you, instead. Even if you don't decide to help us, and I can see you won't. We'll open up your brain with one of our gadgets, and find just what we need for Pippa training.''

Every element of my training was still fresh in my mind. If they had one of the pattern-transfer units—and I was sure they did have one—they could lift it all from my head while I lay unprotesting. It would leave part of my brain blank, and since I was too old for retraining, when I wakened I'd have to find some easy and undemanding job.

"We'd prefer you to help us willingly," one of the men said. The two of them were like twins, thin, pale, with even, soft features. "You'd get the best accommodations, a high rank, and be titular head of the first Vogl Patrol Academy. Not to mention," he smiled and showed sharp, greenish teeth, "many of our farmers would be glad to husband you. In real style."

"Thanks," I said. "If there's anything I like to choose for myself, it's a man." I finished the last spoonful of soup and added, "I suppose your graduates will be known as Vapors."

"Vappas," the man corrected me, with no show of temper.

"And you can't wait a few years for this to come about peacefully, with cooperation between both planets?" I asked.

Reba said passionately, "Don't you think some of us are sick of being farmers? After all, farming has been forced on us for two generations. We've got lots of bright youngsters who want to be radio astronomers, or surgeons, or a lot of things, and very few get the chance. Most of them are packed off to Aggie school and spend their lives tending hybrid goats or tanks of fish eggs. You want to choose a man for yourself, didn't you choose your own job, too?"

Yes, it was a valid argument, and no, they were doing it the worst way possible and would bring nothing but disaster to Vogl. I helped myself from the platter of fried iguana. Marrant went around the table refilling our wine glasses. When he came to my side, he put his hand on my shoulder, and said, "At least think it over. We can use you, and we can offer you a good deal in exchange. If you stay here, you'll never make a high rank before you retire. And don't worry, you can pick your own man, or a dozen of them. The Vogl boys are healthy and good looking."

"More agriculture," I said, pushing away my plate. "Now you're offering me stud service."

Reba threw her wine into my face, and I kicked my chair backward as I got out of it, not without a regret for my kyrene dress which had cost me a month's credit and had never been worn before.

She was as strong as I in her wiry way, though I had ten pounds on her. She had long hair, while my blonde waves had been cut very short before coming down to the tropics, so it didn't give her much to grab hold of. Her training was not as good as mine, but she made up for it with her speed. The skirt of my dress went first, got tangled around my ankles and took me down, while she jumped at me with both feet. I rolled out from under just in time;

we grappled on the floor for a moment before separating and getting up again. I was satisfied to see I'd ruined her dress, too. The bodice hung in tatters around her waist. I bent, and made a feint for her legs, coming up with my shoulder under her chin, and heard her teeth crack together. She spat out blood.

In another moment, we'd stripped each other down to loin pants, and were sweating so we were slippery as eels. She was wearing hard sandals and had a tremendous kick; twice she nearly got me in the face with one heel, but the second time I grabbed hold while her leg was in the air, and she went over backward onto the white and turquoise lounge. I heard a crack as the arm of the lounge gave way, and another crack as I landed full force on her.

Someone pulled me back with incredible strength and held me with a knife at my throat, while the two pale men gripped Reba and held her still. "Damn you," Marrant said into my ear. "I had that lounge shipped from Scandia Dominion and you've ruined it."

My laugh was just a gurgle.

"God, you're conceited," Reba said to him scornfully. "No wonder they found you easy."

"Shut up," one of the men said to her. "He's worked hard and we need him."

"Will you stop fighting?" Marrant said to me.

"If she will."

He released me cautiously. The rags of our clothing lay on the floor and my ruby nose stud was gone, leaving the nostril sore. I looked under my lids at those slats open toward the sea. There hadn't been a sound from outside since I got out of the heli, and it must still be parked out there. It wasn't going to be much fun going headfirst through the front of the house, if San' Clement was guarding the heli, where would I go, in nothing but loin pants?

I twisted away from Marrant, and began to stroll around the room, rubbing spots on my arms and shoulders which hurt. I came to a stop a little to the left, where the slat frame did not cross, and it might be easier to break through. Because I knew I had to get out.

"Here," one of the men said, and tossed his jacket to me. I let it fall to the floor.

"Thanks," I said, "but it's warm."

Marrant eyed me. "Pippa," he said, "if they build them all like you at the Academies, Vogl will have to go some to match you."

I looked sideways at him, as though the compliment had pleased me, and I shifted my weight as though to show myself off. Then I took off from a standing start, headfirst with my shoulders hunched up high. At the last instant I turned my right shoulder to take the brunt of the slats. They gave with a shriek and splintering, and I was upon my feet again and running down the grass toward the shadowy mass of the heli, praying that San' Clement had gone home.

There was the hiss of a gasgun, and the harder sound of some hand weapon, as I ran in front of the heli to get around to the driver's side. The door was open, and as I put my foot on the step, a thin, cold hand, black as the night, took my arm and pulled me up and inside.

I fell across San' Clement's knees as the engine protested, groaned, and was revved up to top speed without mercy. We went straight up, before he worked it into its high speed, going down the coast toward Roseau.

I wriggled over to the other side of the seat. My shoulder hurt and was bloody, and in the night air blowing through the vents my skin chilled quickly. I looked over at San' Clement, but he said nothing.

"Were you waiting for me?" I asked.

"They have another heli. With a Clam gun," San' Clement said. "We have only a little start. Where shall I put you down?"

"Can you get me near the council office?"

"I will try." He was quiet again, and then as the lights of Roseau showed in the distance on the coast, he said, "I worked all my life for Marrant. I'm his foreman."

"Now you're out of a job. What will you do?"

"I have a house, and a few cocoa trees. Four sons and four grandchildren. I am not so bad. If we make it to Roseau."

The lights of the second heli were visible behind us. "Has it got more power than this one?" I asked.

"No. But it has the Clam gun, which they used this morning, you know, to dispose of the sergeant in case the drowning was not enough. The woman was very angry."

"She's still angry," I said "Do you have a transmitter?"

"It is fixed to send and receive only on their wave."

"How far are we now from Roseau?"

"Half a mile, maybe. Look down. You can see it is cleared."

"Then put us down and I'll run for it, and you get under cover. They will follow me, not you."

"You cannot outrun them for half a mile, Pippa."

"I can try," I said.

I saw his teeth shine as he smiled. "Oh, that is good. From the only one who could take my cutlass from me. No one can outrun a Clam gun."

"But they can't afford to burn the town. Put us down, San' Clement, and you take cover. I'll make it somehow."

We started going down. On his side of the seat, San' Clement was going through some vigorous contortions, getting out of his white jacket, and then out of the dark shirt he wore under it. He tossed me the shirt. "Wear it, you show up like a fish belly," he said.

He put the heli down near a group of large, flat-topped trees. The other heli was already coming down after us. We tumbled out. I ran, not toward the trees, which they'd expect me to head for, but across open ground, guessing I wasn't yet in range of their gun. It was a close guess. As I turned into the first street, the Clam gun burst open the ground only a few feet behind me. At least San' Clement had a chance to get out of the way.

The first fence was low and gave me no trouble; then there was a series of them, as I cut along behind the houses, and several of them were high fences with no foothold, which slowed me down. I had tied the ends of San' Clement's shirt around my waist and was unhappily aware of the white flash of my legs going over the tops of fences. The heli was cruising not far away, and they probably had a light which they could use to spot me, if they dared use it right over town.

They dared. They put the spot on, and it made a light like white noon over a fifteen foot area. It began to swing slowly across the grounds in back of the houses, coming closer to where I was. I was at the rear door of a small home; inside, there was music, and people were talking. As the light charged toward my heels, I walked into their kitchen, and right through. The music went on, though the voices stopped dead. I made it to the front door when someone came out of his shock and yelled, and threw a bottle after me. It grazed the back of my neck as I plunged out the front door into the street, ran across and between two houses on the other side.

The swath of light crossed the street just after me, and then swooped back and circled over the house I'd left. When I got into the next street, I looked back, saw the heli low over the roof and someone climbing down the ladder that hung from it into the back yard.

I hit the center of town at a dead run. Startled groups of people dispersed as I came along, heading for the council office. Many of them called after me, but in patois, and there was nothing they could do anyhow. I hoped Toxetl was in.

He was tilted back in his chair taking a snooze when I burst in. At first he had no idea who I was and looked bewildered, then he said, "You're some sight. What has happened?"

"Get me that line through to headquarters, and I'll tell you, or you can listen in," I said. "And I'd like one of those red drinks, I'm so thirsty."

He gestured to the carafe on his desk and I helped myself. His two councilmen ran into the office and skidded to a stop, one on each side of me. Toxetl made a motion which backed them off, and they stood guard on each side of the door.

"Just the two of you in Roseau?" I asked.

"We're enough," the younger one said.

When Toxetl sat back in his chair, waiting for the connection to go through, I gave him the story, tightly condensed. He sent the councilmen out after the man who'd come down from the heli, and they ran out with their gasguns drawn which was enough to alarm everyone in town. "Well, you've had a day," Mr. Toxetl said comfortably. "Why don't you sit down?"

"Got the fidgets, sir, until I make my report, and get this finished. I can't stand to have those people loose. Though no matter what you think, I'd put in a word for the woman Reba. She wasn't responsible for Sergeant Krane's death. And if they're going to have their own Academies, they'll need women like her. Marrant's your charge, I guess."

He lowered his lids, dropped his chin on his chest, and spread out his hands. "Yes, Council will take care of him. They can't get far in such a small heli, only over to another island, or so." He put through a radio call to the office on the Cuba Dominion mainland.

By the time any connection to headquarters came through, the two councilmen were back, with one of the Vogl men between them. He was missing a front tooth.

I was in the middle of my report, having covered the bananas versus reems, and the possibility of leaving Reba out out of it all, when a light started to flash on the board. Mr. Toxetl reached over my shoulder to take out one of the plugs, and when I moved to get out of his way, I also took out the plug in front of me. I'd never seen this kind of communicator, but from the look on his face, I'd done something wrong.

He took his call, saying nothing, and replaced the plug in its socket. He said, "The heli ran out of fuel just short of the next island. The occupants were picked up by a council boat alive and kicking. Whom were you talking to, Pippa?"

"Colonel Cohen," I said.

"Poor Colonel Cohen," Mr. Toxetl murmured. "Bet he never had a Pippa hang up on him before."

"Is that what I did?"

A light was flashing rapidly on the board. Mr. Toxetl moved the plug and took the speaker from me. "Yes," he said into it. "Yes, we've had a lot of trouble on this line, Colonel. Pippa Rimidon's already scolded me for it. Here she is," and he winked at me, and returned the speaker so I could complete my report.

When I'd finished my drink, the younger councilman gave me a ride to my hotel. I was glad to get into the cool, breezy room, and wash the blood from the cuts on my shoulder. It was badly bruised, turning black and yellow, but nothing worse. I'd bled all over San' Clement's shirt, so I washed that out and hung it to dry. Then I turned in and fell asleep between two breaths.

In the morning I ate breakfast on the patio. The little banana bird was there, perched on the back of a lounge. I pushed my plate to his edge of the table, with a slice of banana on it, and watched him hop over. Standing on the rim of the plate, he pecked rapidly at the fruit, now and then giving me a smart look from one eye or the other.

Dressed, with my kit packed, I stopped off at the council office for San' Clement's address. The older of the councilmen gave me a ride to the edge of town, where he dropped me off into the care of his cousin, who had a scooter car. The cousin gave me a long ride and passed me on to his brother-in-law who had one of the old trucks. Little by little I went back into the interior, up through the hills of banana and cocoa plantations, into the misty mountains where the daily rain clouds were gathering.

San' Clement lived in a white and blue house, with a garden of bromeliads surrounding it with orange and red blossoms. The air was full of wet mist and in the near distance a thunderous roar sounded. I took his folded, clean shirt from my kit and carried it up to the door, which San' Clement opened.

"Good morning, sir," I said. "Thanks for the loan of your shirt."

His wife came out and looked at me wide-eyed. "You are young," she said in amazement.

I looked over the roof of their house, towards the towering mountain tops. The Three Voices were over there, and San' Clement lived enclosed within the constant rumble and thunder.

He said, "Yes, the waters come down just over there in back of us. You're welcome for the shirt."

"I wanted to say good-bye, and thanks for your help."

He smiled slightly and turned his head a bit. I knew he was listening to the waterfalls. He didn't say anything else, so I went back to the truck and was relayed down to the coast, where in a few hours I'd get my flight out. Perhaps a few days off, if Colonel Cohen would allow it.

I had a word to say to him about Vogl, and a request to be allowed to speak for Vogl at the next Inter-Dominion meeting, although it was more than two months off. It did seem to me it was time to space-freight a few less dairy goats and sacks of seed, and a few more people, young ones, full of vigor and new ideas, going both ways, to Earth and to Vogl. It was true I was only a Pippa, but everyone is allowed a voice at Inter-Dominion, and I thought it was time some of us got up and spoke.

TEST ULTIMATE

Christopher Anvil

Vaughn Roberts, his muscles tired and sore, stood in the clearing with the other recruits, waiting for the last test to begin. Roberts leaned into the wind that had sprung up, and that made the branches of the trees lift and sway, hiding and then uncovering the dazzling sun. The shifting shadow and glare made it hard to see the guide who had led them almost to the end of the training course, and who now spoke to them from a low platform of logs at the edge of the clearing.

". . . Just one final test, gentlemen," the guide was saying, "and then your training will be over, and you will be full members of the Interstellar Patrol.

"There isn't much to this final exercise, but you must carry it out successfully to pass the course, so you might be interested in a few brief comments.

"To survive, and successfully do his duty, a member of the Interstellar Patrol must make the right use of courage. This quality is so important the final test will emphasize the proper use of courage.

"Now, this is not a complicated test. But it has its points, gentlemen, as I think you will agree after it is over.

"The problem is simply to climb a rock face twenty-five feet in height, onto the ledge at the top. The climb is not difficult, but to get to this rock face, you must first cross a wide, shallow pool. It is a pretty pool, at first glance. But it is stocked with carnivorous fish.

"Remember, gentlemen, this is a test in the proper use of courage. You may not enjoy it, but you must do the best you can to succeed, whatever that may involve.

"To avoid too high a loss rate, the test will be given by

simulator. You will experience a highly realistic illusion, that, to your senses, will be the same as if it *were* real.

"As an aid in learning, a special guide will be assigned to each one of you in this final test."

Roberts abruptly found himself standing in the quiet shade of tall trees, on a stony slope that slanted gradually down to a wide, shallow pool of sparkling, splashing water. Directly across the pool was a narrow border of marsh, rising to a steep forested hill farther back. To Roberts's left, across the length of the pool, was a gray rock face, down which a rivulet of water trickled onto a wide rock shelf, whence it flowed quietly into the pool.

For an instant, the scene seemed pleasant. Then Roberts realized that the sparkle and splash were caused by sleek steel-gray forms that burst up out of the water to snap, and then splatter and splash the surface. The ceaseless flash and snap, and the splatter and splash as the carnivorous fish fell back, now made the pool look to him like a kind of seething hellish cauldron.

Just as the full impact of the scene hit Roberts, a powerfully built figure in the shadows near the edge of the pool turned toward him. Wearing a tight, black one-piece garment, with three rows of ribbons at the left chest, and wide belt bearing knife and fusion gun, this figure was plainly the special guide. Roberts, relieved, waited for instructions.

The guide raised one muscular arm, and swept it out across the pool toward the rock face.

"Don't hesitate. This is a courage test. In you go, and head straight for that rock face!"

Roberts, relieved to have some clear-cut direction, started forward.

Ahead of him, the water seethed.

Roberts fixed his mind on the rock face across the pool, made a rapid estimate of the distance, and then saw with a start that the water was so roiled up that he couldn't see the bottom.

The voice of the first guide, back at the clearing, came to him: "The problem is simply to climb a rock face twenty-five feet in height, onto the ledge at its top."

There across the pool was the rock face and the ledge. But considering that these fish were carnivorous, how could he get through them, across a possibly uneven bottom that he couldn't see, without being eaten up on the way?

Nearby, the special guide called sharply, "Don't hesitate! *Keep moving!*"

Roberts hesitated, then with an effort kept going.

In front of him, the steel-gray forms leaped out, their sharp jaws flashing with a knifelike glint.

The guide, his voice approving, shouted, "Good Lad! Now, *straight for that cliff!*"

Roberts's mind seemed split in halves. Thoughts flashed through his consciousness in a chaotic rush:

"*Don't hesitate! Keep moving!*"

"*There isn't much to this final exercise, but you must carry it out successfully to pass the course . . .*"

"*Don't hesitate. This is a courage test. In you go, and head straight for that rock face!*"

"*The problem is simply to climb a rock face . . .*"

"*. . . Now, go straight for the cliff!*"

"*Remember, gentlemen, this is a test in the proper use of courage.*"

"*Don't hesitate. This is a courage test . . .*"

"*. . . A test in the proper use of courage.*"

Across the pool, the rock face loomed like a mirage over the water. Ten feet out from shore, a big steel-gray muscular form leaped high and fell back, and the splash briefly uncovered a glistening human rib cage.

Roberts stopped in his tracks.

The special guide whirled, put his hand on Roberts's shoulder, and said sharply, "Go straight in! Even if you don't make it, I'll vouch for your courage. *That's all you need to pass the courage test!* Now, *move!*"

He gave Roberts a push to start him into the pool.

Abruptly the two divided halves of Roberts's mind came back together again. He ducked free of the pushing hand, pivoted, and smashed his fist into the guide's muscular midsection.

The guide doubled over, his arms flew out, and he slammed back into some kind of invisible barrier, that recoiled and threw him back toward Roberts. The guide recovered himself, and his hand flashed toward his fusion gun.

Roberts hit him again in the midsection.

The guide went down, and at once came up on one knee, still groping for the fusion gun.

Roberts jerked him to his feet, and knocked him down for the third time.

The guide landed full length on the ground, and Roberts bent, to swiftly take the belt, with its knife and gun. He had hardly straightened, when the guide again struggled to get up, and Roberts cracked him over the head with the gun.

The guide sat back down with a grunt, then started up again.

Roberts stepped back, frowning. He held the gun in one hand, and the belt, with holster and sheathed knife, dangled from the other hand. So far, he hadn't been able to put the special guide down long enough to fasten the belt.

The words of their original guide, back in the clearing, came to him:

"Now, this is not a complicated test. But it has its points, gentlemen, as I think you will agree after it is over."

Roberts glanced out at the seething pool, and back at the grim-faced special guide, just coming to his feet.

Despite the gun, the guide suddenly rushed him. Roberts landed a terrific kick at the base of the chest.

The guide went down, and this time it looked as if he might stay there a while.

Roberts clasped the belt around his waist, looked at the fish springing from the water, glanced back at the motionless guide, then looked around, spotted a length of fallen branch lying on the ground with most of the twigs rotted off. He picked up the branch and swung it over the pool, the far end dipping into the water.

Instantly, the water exploded in gray forms.

Snap! SNAP! Snap!

The branch lightened in his hand as two-and-a-half feet at the far end disappeared.

Roberts glanced around at the guide, already starting to shake his head dazedly. With his thumb, Roberts felt the end of the stick. It was cut off smooth, as if by a sharp curved blade.

The guide sat up, his eyes focused on Roberts. He came to his feet in one fluid motion.

Roberts aimed the gun at the guide's head.

The guide's eyes glinted, and he started forward. His voice had a sharp ring of authority.

"Drop the gun. I'm coming to take it, Mister. *Drop* it!"

Roberts depressed the fusion gun's trigger, and the searing pencil of energy sprang out, missing the guide's head by several inches.

Roberts said flatly, "*Halt!*"

The guide halted, face stern and eyes intent.

"Now," said Roberts, "just back up to where you were."

The guide didn't budge. "You won't get away with this!"

Roberts watched him alertly.

"I won't get away with *what*?"

"Cowardice! You don't show the guts to do as you're told! Now, *drop that gun*!"

Roberts kept the gun aimed at the guide.

"I was told to climb that rock face. I can't climb it if I don't last long enough to get near it. To obey your instructions would guarantee that I wouldn't do what I am supposed to do."

"I told you, Mister, that if you showed courage, I'd vouch for you!"

"That's nice. But that won't get me up that rock face."

The guide's voice came out in a deadly menacing tone.

"Do you question my word?"

"Yes," said Roberts. "As a matter of fact, I question everything about you. I have a suspicion that somewhere there's a complicated little network that projects a mass of muscle, an empty head, and a loud voice, with built-in responses, and that's all there is to you. There's something about you that fits the Interstellar Patrol like oars on a spaceship. Incidentally, I noticed you haven't stepped back. *Back up*!"

Glowering, the muscular figure backed up several feet.

"All right," said Roberts, "turn around."

"Go to hell."

Roberts aimed the fusion gun at the guide's midsection. "Friend, there's a kind of courage that makes sense, and there's another kind that's stupid, even in an illusion. The more I see of you, the more convinced I am that the Patrol would never have let *you* in. It follows that what you really are is a special kind of highly advanced electronic booby trap. You almost got me into that pool, but not quite. That push was too much. If this were strictly a test of raw courage, I'd have had to go in under my *own* power."

"I was helping you."

"That's the point. That help would spoil the test."

The guide spoke in a reasonable, persuasive voice. "I could see you weren't going to make it without help."

"In that case, I'd have been allowed to fail. What's the point of a test if you pass those who should fail?"

The guide now looked sympathetic.

"Lad, I knew a little help at the right time would get you over the hurdle. I never thought you'd show a yellow streak this wide. But I'm still willing to overlook all of this, if—''

Roberts shook his head critically. "Among other things, now you're ignoring the fact that I was given a definite goal, with no set time-limit. Why, should I have to *immediately* jump in with the carnivorous fish? I was told to *cross that pool and climb up that rock face onto the ledge.* That may involve the right *use* of courage, but instant suicide won't accomplish the job."

"Well, now, that about the rock face was only how it was *expressed*. The thing is to *show courage.* That's the test!"

"When you're ordered to attack, the thing to do is to just rush in quick where the defenses are thickest, eh?"

The guide looked reasonable again.

"What do you gain by delay? Sooner or later, you'll *have* to go in. There's a field of force on all sides of us, overhead, and under the ground surface, that leaves just this space between this edge of the pool and the trees. The only opening in the field is toward the pool. *There is no other way out.* What do you gain by putting it off? I'll overlook what you've done if—''

"Turn around," said Roberts.

The guide looked blank, and ignored the demand.

Roberts shifted the gun slightly.

"Turn around."

The muscular figure turned around.

Roberts said, "Lie flat on your face, hands at your sides. Now, keep your arms straight, but work your hands and arms under your body, so your right thigh pins your right hand, and your left thigh pins your left hand. All right, work the whole length of your arms under. Stay that way."

The guide lay flat on his face in the stony dirt.

Roberts walked over.

"Bend your legs slowly at the knee. Raise your feet."

Roberts piled stones on the guide's shoulders, and on the flat soles and heels of the guide's boots.

"Now, don't move, or the stones will fall off, and the clatter will warn me."

Roberts walked back near the water's edge, and looked out over the pool. He had one obstacle temporarily out of the way, but he was still a long distance from that ledge. He carefully felt along the invisible barrier, and, so far as he could judge, it was exactly as described. It felt somewhat like the edge of a kind of large transparent balloon, yielding as he pressed against it, but growing progressively harder to force back as he displaced it. When he stopped pushing, it forced him back.

As he moved around, he glanced repeatedly at the guide, who was cooperating, so far.

There seemed to be no way around the barrier, and very possibly no way to shorten the distance across that stretch of seething water. What the bottom was like was anyone's guess, but it could be uneven blocks of rock, covered with slime, and littered with the skeletons of past victims. From what Roberts had seen, ten seconds in that water would guarantee that he wouldn't climb that rock face.

A dull glint from the direction of the rock face briefly caught his attention, but, when he looked, he saw nothing different, and merely retained the impression of a falling rock. He glanced around.

There *had* to be some way to either get over the pool without going in it, or to deceive or eliminate the fish.

Roberts glanced at his prisoner, then looked at the forest cut off from him by the unseen barrier. Experimentally, he fired his fusion gun. Swinging the beam to be sure he was seeing what he thought he was seeing, he found that the barrier stopped the beam each time. It didn't reflect it. It seemed to absorb it. That meant that he couldn't hope to fell across the pool any of the tall trees beyond the barrier. And where the fusion beam *could* reach, there were no trees close enough to the pool to do any good.

Roberts watched the fish leaping from the water, raised the gun, waited, then aimed at a gleaming gray form, and squeezed the trigger.

A large sharp-jawed fish dropped back, eyes bulging, hit awkwardly on its side, and flopped around on the surface.

All across the pool, the leaping and splashing stopped. The surface of the water roiled in a hundred swift brief currents. The injured fish was jerked, wrenched, and ripped to bits, sharp snouts and sleek flanks showing for just an instant around it.

Roberts aimed carefully, and fired a second time.

A second fish twisted up nearly out of the water, and fell back with a flat splash.

The others at once tore it to shreds.

Roberts fired a third time, at an exposed flank.

A third fish flopped on the surface.

The water around the injured fish was alive with snapping, tearing, steel-gray forms.

Back of Roberts, there was the clatter of a fallen rock.

In rapid succession, Roberts fired at several more fish, then glanced back.

The guide had dumped the stones from one foot, and was carefully lowering the other.

Again, out of the corner of his eye, Roberts sensed motion at the rock face. But there was no time to look in that direction.

He fired carefully, just over the guide's head.

The guide froze.

Roberts turned back, and glanced briefly at the rock face. All that moved there was falling water.

He looked back at the pool, and fired at another fish, and then another.

He kept firing methodically, until suddenly there were no more targets.

A few bits and fragments floated on the surface, but nothing attacked them. The flying insects ranged over the pool unmolested.

Now, supposedly the remaining fish were glutted. If so, it *should* be safe to go across the pool.

Roberts glanced at the rock face to his left, estimated the distance, and blinked.

Down this face of rock, along with the trickle of water, flopped a sleek steel-gray form, bounding and turning, to hit the rock shelf below, where the water flowed out toward the pool, with a loud *splat*.

Roberts abruptly realized what this would do to his plans, and raised the gun.

Behind him, there was a crash of pebbles, and a sudden scramble.

The guide was on his feet, hurtling straight for him.

Roberts sprang aside.

The guide changed direction and slid, then Roberts was back out of the way, and put the thin, dazzling beam of the fusion gun in front of the guide's eyes.

The guide stopped.

Now, Roberts thought, he had survived that.

But, at the same time, that one fish that had come down the rock face had flopped into the pool. And *that* fish wasn't glutted.

Roberts glanced out at the water, and the bits and fragments were no longer floating on the surface. But that little appetizer wouldn't be enough. The fish would still be hungry.

There was a splash, and out of the corner of his eye, Roberts could see the sleek gray form fall back and vanish, after snapping up one of the flying insects.

The guide said, "Drop the gun," and began to slowly walk toward Roberts. "*Drop* it!"

Roberts put the beam of the fusion gun over the guide's left shoulder. Then he put it past the guide's head, over the right shoulder.

The guide grinned, and his eyes glowed.

He kept coming.

From the direction of the rock face, something flashed briefly, falling down the stream that flowed over the rock, to hit with a *splat*.

The guide charged.

Roberts sprang aside, kicked him under the chin, whirled like a ballet dancer, and hammered him across the back of the neck as he passed.

The guide grabbed unsuccessfully at Roberts's leg, then went down on his hands and knees.

Roberts said coldly, "It's a mistake to try unarmed combat on a man armed with a knife and a gun." But he was noting that blows that would have killed an ordinary person were about as effective with this opponent as taps with a length of rolled-up paper.

The guide stumbled to his feet, turned and faced Roberts. "You won't fire the gun or use the knife. Not to kill me. Because you're yellow." He straightened, and his face showed pitying sympathy. "Sorry, lad, but you're yellow."

The guide began walking calmly toward Roberts, his face sure and confident. "Drop the gun. You won't use it. *Drop* it."

Robert aimed at the guide's head.

The guide kept coming, his face reflecting quiet confidence.

Roberts squeezed the trigger.

The fusion beam hit the guide's left eye. There was a dazzling white glow, the flesh peeled back like paper in a fire, and there was a splintering *crack*! Bits and fragments of glass or plastic, glowing redly, flew out in a shower.

"*Halt!*" said Roberts.

The guide halted.

Where the flesh had peeled back to expose the left eye socket, a silvery glitter showed instead of bone.

Roberts reminded himself, all this was taking place in a simulator. But the problem remained.

Roberts studied the motionless roboid "special guide" and said, "I didn't realize the Patrol was so hard-pressed for man power that it was recruiting humanoid robots."

"No, sir."

"How come that now I'm 'sir'?"

"At this stage, sir, I am programmed to so address you."

"You will obey my orders, now?"

"Yes, sir."

"At this stage?"

"Yes, sir."

"So that, if I order you to go over to the water and kneel down you will do it?"

"Yes, sir."

"And if I command you to carry me piggyback across that pool, you will carry me piggyback across the pool."

"I will obey you in this phase, and, at your order, will do *anything* I am capable of doing."

That left unanswered the question whether the robot was capable of carrying him across. It also raised another point. Roberts cleared his throat.

"When does 'this phase' end?"

"When an internal mechanism gives the appropriate command signal, sir."

"When will that happen?"

"I cannot predict, sir. It depends on circumstances."

Roberts nodded. That fit in. The "command signal" would be given at that unpredictable moment when Roberts stuck his neck out far enough for the "guide" to heave him into the pool.

"I see," said Roberts. "Can *you* cross that pool without being attacked?"

"The fish are turned back by a chemical repellent with which my garment has been impregnated. sir. They would otherwise bite me as they would bite you; but they would not ingest my substance, as it is not nourishing to them."

"All right. Go over near the edge of the water, and kneel down."

The robot willingly and obediently went near the edge of the water and knelt down.

Now, thought Roberts, if he climbed on its back, it would take him partway across and then toss him to the fish.

The function of this "special guide" seemed to be to give disastrous advice and murderous assistance. It followed that there was only one thing to do.

Roberts stepped back, aimed deliberately at the base of the robot's neck, and depressed the trigger.

The fusion beam sprang out.

There was a flare of flame, flying sparks, the "head" tilted and separated from the robot's body, and the body rose and wheeled toward Roberts.

Roberts shifted his aim to the lower chest, and the robot fell forward on the sand.

From the rock face to one side a dull flash briefly caught Roberts's attention.

Down the rock face, another steel-gray wetly gleaming length of muscle and hunger tumbled, to land with a *splat*, and flop into the pool.

Roberts wiped the sweat out of his eyes, warily circled the human-like form, and crouched near its feet. Carefully, he undid the boots, and, holding the gun, stood thoughtfully considering the one piece garment. He carefully pulled off the boots, but he had a disinclination to get in reach of the arms, however motionless the robot might seem.

Was the thing out of action, or wasn't it?

He stepped back, found what was left of the long stick he'd held over the water, lightly pressed the end to the edge of the one-piece garment, partway up the back. He moved the stick as if he were tugging at the cloth with his fingers.

Pebbles flew and dust whirled as the headless robot sprang at the stick.

Roberts fired at the robot's lower chest, and again it dropped to the ground.

Now, this time was it finally out of action, or wasn't it?

And what if, in trying to make sure he had hit the control mechanism, he hit the energy-source instead?

Roberts blew out his breath and stubbornly considered the situation.

The obvious thing to do was to get that repellent-impregnated garment.

Roberts raised the gun, and methodically burned the thick arms off the trunk of the mechanism, cut a line across the garment with the fusion beam, warily took hold, and pulled the garment free. A hard kick threw him back and could have knocked him into the pool if he hadn't expected it. But now he had the cut, but still usable, garment. And he could see that he was going to need it.

Down the rock face across the pool, another steel-gray form spun and fell, hit the shelf below with a *splat*, and flopped into the pool.

With an influx like that, there must be some way out for the fish already in the pool. But from where he was, Roberts couldn't see it. He shook his head, put the garment on over his fatigues, put his shoes back on, started for the pool, and then paused, looking at the robot.

The headless, armless torso had rolled toward the place where he would have landed if that last kick had fully connected, and now it was feeling carefully with its feet along the water's edge. Finding nothing, it lay still.

Roberts stood frowning.

Considering the source, how had he come to take *that* piece of information for granted?

He took his shoes off, and pulled off the robot's repellent-impregnated garment. He put his shoes back on, searched along the edge of the invisible barrier, found a second long stick, tied one leg of the garment to the stick, and let the other end of the garment hang free. He walked down near the water's edge, swung the stick out over the water, and dipped about eight inches of the garment into the water.

The stick jerked in his hands. The garment was cut off in a ragged edge half-a-foot above the water, and the steel-gray forms shot up in a boiling froth to snap bits off the part that dangled higher yet.

Roberts straightened.

This was the "repellent-impregnated" garment he had almost relied on.

Roberts glanced around at the robot, saw it was too far away to bother him, drew the fusion gun, lowered the remainder of the garment's dangling leg barely into the water, and shot the first fish to leap out after it.

Other fish attacked that one, and, using his tried and proved method, Roberts reduced their numbers by enough to satisfy the appetite of the remainder.

And once again the pond became placid.

• • •

The robot was now exploring the far edge of the barrier's opening on the pool.

Roberts, thinking over the situation, decided that things were about as favorable as he could hope to get them. Most of the fish in the pond should now be digesting the last meal, and any that might still be hungry ought to be attracted first to the remaining cloth on the end of the stick, rather than to him.

Dipping the cloth in the water, with the stick held in his left hand, Roberts eased carefully into the pool. The fusion gun, he held in his right hand, ready to use in case the cloth were attacked. But when he tried to move forward, his feet at once came up against some obstruction. He tried in a different place, with the same result.

The trip across now turned into a nightmare all on its own. Through the water, still murky, but no longer so badly stirred up, loomed skeletal rib cages and piles of bones. Here and there, a fish hung sluggishly, fins moving spasmodically. Roberts worked his way across, looking up frequently at the rock face, down which from time to time fell a steel-gray form that he had to kill before it got in the pool, because, if he didn't finish it, it might very well finish him.

By the time Roberts was halfway across, the worst of the horror looming up at him through the water had begun to ease off. The bottom was becoming clearer, apparently because most of the victims had never made it this far.

From there on, suddenly it became almost easy, and the bottom was so flat and unobstructed that just a little carelessness on Roberts's part would have dropped him down a narrow vertical cleft not eight feet from the edge of the rock shelf. He got across that with a sense of relief, reached the shelf, and just then something tugged at his shoe.

The cloth on the stick jerked, there was a splash, a sense of something brushing his leg, and when he looked down, the water was stained with red.

He threw the remainder of the "repellent-impregnated" garment into the pool, and pulled himself out on the rock shelf. He moved over near the face of the rock, took off his shirt, and bound it tightly around his badly bitten lower leg.

Now he discovered that the shoe of the same leg had been cut open, and he was bleeding from inside the shoe.

He took the shoe off, clenched his jaw at the sight, tore off strips of his ragged trouser legs, bound his foot, put the cut shoe back on, and laced it tight.

The bandages were turning red, but there was nothing he could do about that. He looked up at the rock face, which was apparently a form of shale, with many little ledges, some of them dry, and some of them, where the water flowed down, wet and mossy. The face wasn't vertical, but if he should slip, there was nothing there to give his bare hands a real hold until he hit the rock shelf at the bottom.

Carefully, he started to climb, clenching his jaw against the pain from his leg. About fifteen feet up, there came a flop-*thump* from above, and one of the steel-gray fish bounced past, snapping at him on the way by.

Roberts began to climb again. When he had almost reached the ledge, he paused, studying the green moss at its rim just above. The moss had little stalks on it, and each stalk had a set of miniature spikes at its end.

What would happen if he touched that? Was it, perhaps, poisonous?

He looked around, then, carefully worked to the side, and now he was on slippery wet rock. There was still moss up above, and he kept moving to the side.

Overhead, an occasional insect flashed out over the edge of the ledge, and then darted back again.

Another carnivorous fish flopped over the edge, and snapped its jaws shut not three inches from Roberts's left shoulder. He kept moving steadily to the side.

Finally, there was no moss up above, and no flying insects darting into view and back again.

Cautiously, he worked his way up onto the ledge.

To the side, where he would have come up if he had climbed straight up, was the edge of a shallow pool into which water flowed from a further, more gentle, incline of rock. Over this pool, flying insects darted irregularly back and forth, to vanish suddenly as the fish shot up and snapped their jaws.

Roberts straightened and drew a deep breath.

Provided he had understood the rules in the first place, he had finally made it.

Abruptly the scene vanished.

The familiar guide—who had been with them throughout the course—looked at him with a smile.

"Well, Roberts, *you* made it."

"Thank you, sir. It's over?"

"It's over. And you are now a full member of the Interstellar Patrol. There will be a little ceremony later on, when the others join us."

" 'The others'?"

"Your fellow basic trainees. I regret to say, Roberts, that even among the best material for the Patrol, there *are* those who believe the sanction of authority is everything. Hence when they are told they will pass the last test if they merely plunge straight in, like so many sheep—Why, they *do* it! Even though it involves the sensations of being eaten alive by carnivorous fish."

"*Don't* they pass the test?"

"Oh, they barely pass the *test*. But the Board of Examiners immediately decides that their action brings into question prior indications of basic suitability for the Patrol. You see, we don't encouraged *unthinking* reliance on authority, or on the appearance of authority. Some of the great defeats and disasters of history have followed from exactly that cause. We have trouble enough without that. So, we pick this last test to give a little reminder that our men should *have the courage to think.* Consider this, Roberts. A recruit in the Interstellar Patrol is given disastrous advice by someone with an air of authority—advice that obviously means the recruit will fail to do what he is supposed to do—and the recruit *does* it! We can't have that."

"What happens?"

"The Board of Examiners grudgingly recommends that the trainee be allowed the opportunity to *repeat the test.* Thus, after having unthinkingly taken his supposed superior's word for it, and having as a result experienced the sensations of being eaten alive by carnivorous fish, the trainee finds himself right back in the same spot all over again, with the same pool, the same fish, and the same electronic boob giving the same worthless advice. What do you *suppose* happens?"

Beside Roberts, his friend Hammell suddenly appeared, his face red, massaging his fists, and feeling tenderly of places low down on his legs.

"Well," said the guide, smiling, "*this* time you made it."

Hammell growled incoherently.

There was another little blink of time, and there stood another friend and fellow trainee, Morrissey, his electric-blue eyes blazing in anger. And there beside him suddenly stood Bergen, his blond hair on end. One after another now, they appeared, until the whole class was there, and then before them appeared a slight well-knit figure with a look of self-discipline and good humor.

"Gentlemen, in the Patrol, thought does not solely radiate from the top down, but takes place on all levels, including that lowest and hence *closest to the facts*. Any time you are tempted to pass the buck upward, or to blindly accept obviously disastrous orders without objecting to them, remember this incident. Possibly by doing so, you may avoid an experience worse than this one.

"Very well, gentlemen, you have now passed the basic training course of the Interstellar Patrol, and you are full members in good standing of the Patrol, with all that this implies. You will now receive your weapons and full issue of uniforms, with appropriate insignia, in the order of your passing out of this course. As I call your names, step forward, salute, and receive your weapons and uniforms.

"Roberts, Vaughn N."

Respectfully, Roberts stepped forward and saluted.

THE STARSLOGGERS

Harry Harrison

I

Bill never realized that sex was the cause of it all. If the sun that morning had not been burning so warmly in the brassy sky of Phigerinadon II, and if he had not glimpsed the sugar-white and barrel-wide backside of Inga-Maria Calyphigia while she bathed in the stream, he might have paid more attention to his plowing than to the burning pressures of heterosexuality. He would have driven his furrow to the far side of the hill before the seductive music sounded along the road. He might never have heard it and his life would have been very, very different. But he did hear it and dropped the handles of the plow that was plugged into the robomule, turned and gaped.

It was indeed a fabulous sight. Leading the parade was a one-robot-band, twelve-feet high and splendid in its great black busby that concealed the hi-fi speakers. The golden pillars of it legs stamped forward as its thirty articulated arms sawed, plucked and fingered at a dazzling variety of instruments. Martial music poured out in wave after inspiring wave and even Bill's thick peasant feet stirred in their clodhoppers as the shining boots of the squad of soldiers crashed along the road in perfect unison. Medals jingled on the manly swell of their scarlet-clad chests. And there could certainly be no nobler sight in all the world. To their rear marched the sergeant, gorgeous in his braid and brass thickly clustered medals and ribbons, sword and gun, girdled gut and steely eye which sought out Bill where he stood gawking over the fence. The grizzled head nodded in his direction, the steel-trap mouth bent into a friendly smile and there was a conspiratorial wink. Then the little legion was past, and hurrying behind in their wake came a huddle of dust-covered ancillary robots, hopping and crawling or rippling along on treads. As soon as these had gone by

Bill climbed clumsily over the split-rail fence and ran after them. There were no more than two interesting events every four years here, and he was not going to miss what hopefully promised to be a third.

A crowd had already gathered in the market square when Bill hurried up, and they were listening to an enthusiastic band concert. The robot hurled itself into the glorious measures of *Star Troopers to the Skies Avaunt*, and thrashed its way through *Rockets Rumble* and almost demolished itself in the tumultuous rhythm of *Sappers at the Pithead Digging*. It pursued this last tune so strenuously that one of it legs flew off, rising high into the air, but was caught dexterously before it could hit the ground and the music ended with the robot balancing on its remaining leg beating time with the detached limb. It also, after an ear-fracturing peal on the basses, used the leg to point across the square to where a tri-di screen and refreshment booth had been set up. The troopers had vanished into the tavern and the recruiting sergeant stood alone among his robots, beaming a welcoming smile.

"Now hear this! Free drinks for all, courtesy of the Emperor, and some lively scenes of jolly adventure in distant climes to amuse you while you sip," he called in an immense and leathery voice.

Most of the people drifted over, Bill in their midst, though a few embittered and elderly draft-dodgers slunk away between the houses. Cooling drinks were shared out by a robot with a spigot for a navel and an inexhaustible supply of plastic glasses in one metallic hip.

Bill sipped his happily while he followed the enthralling adventures of the space troopers in full color with sound effects and simulating subsonics. There was battle and death and glory though it was only the Chingers who died: troopers only suffered neat little wounds in their extremities that could be covered easily by small bandages. And while Bill was enjoying this, Recruiting Sergeant Grue was enjoying him, his little piggy eyes ruddy with greed as they fastened onto the back of Bill's neck.

This is the one! he chortled to himself while, unknowingly, his yellowed tongue licked at his lips. He could already feel the weight of the bonus money in his pocket. The rest of the audience were the usual mixed bag of overage men, fat women, beardless youths and other unenlistables. All except this broad-shouldered, square-chinned, curly-haired chunk of electronic cannon fodder. With a precise hand on the controls the sergeant lowered the background subsonics and aimed a tight-beam stimulator at the back of his victim's head. Bill writhed in his seat, almost taking part in the glorious battles unfolding before him.

As the last chord died and the screen went blank the refreshment robot pounded hollowly on its metallic chest and bellowed DRINK! DRINK! DRINK! The sheeplike audience swept that way, all except Bill who was plucked from their midst by a powerful arm.

"Here, I saved some of you," the sergeant said, passing over a prepared cup so loaded with dissolved ego-reducing drugs that they were crystallizing out at the bottom. "You're a fine figure of a lad and to my eye seem a cut above the yokels here. Did you ever think of making your career in the forces?"

"I'm not the military type, shargeant . . ." Bill chomped his jaws and spat to remove the impediment to his speech, puzzled at the sudden fogginess in his thoughts. Though it was a tribute to his physique that he was even conscious after the volume of drugs and sonics that he had been plyed with. "Not the military type. My fondest ambition is to be of help in the best way I can, in my chosen career as a Technical Fertilizer Operator and I'm almost finished with my correspondence course . . ."

"That's a crappy job for a bright lad like you," the sergeant said while clapping him on the arm to get a good feel of his biceps. Rock. He resisted the impulse to pull Bill's lip down and take a quick peek at the condition of his back teeth. Later. "Leave that kind of job to those that like it. No chance of promotion. While a career in the troopers has no top. Why Grand-Admiral Pflunger came up through the rocket tubes, as they say, from recruit trooper to grand-admiral. How does that sound?"

"It sounds very nice for Mr. Pflunger but I think fertilizer operating is more fun. Gee—I'm feeling sleepy. I think I'll go lie down."

"Not before you've seen this, just as a favor to me of course," the sergeant said, cutting in front of him and pointing to a large book held open by a tiny robot. "Clothes make the man and most men would be ashamed to be seen in a crummy looking smock like that thing draped around you or wearing those broken canal boats on their feet. Why look like *that* when you can look like *this*?"

Bill's eyes followed the thick finger to the color plate in the book where a miracle of misapplied engineering caused his own face to appear on the illustrated figure dressed in trooper-red. The sergeant flipped the pages and on each plate the uniform was a little more gaudy, the rank higher. The last one was that of a grand-admiral and Bill blinked at his own face under the plumed helmet, now with a touch of crowfeet about the eyes and sporting a handsome and gray-shot moustache, but still undeniably his own.

"That's the way you will look," the sergeant murmured into his ear, "once you have climbed the ladder of success. Would you like to try a uniform on? Of course you would like to try a uniform on. Tailor!"

When Bill opened his mouth to protest the sergeant put a large cigar into it, and before he could get it out the robot tailor had rolled up, swept a curtain bearing arm about him and stripped him naked. "Hey! Hey . . .!" he said.

"It won't hurt," the sergeant said, poking his great head through the curtain and beaming at Bill's muscled form. He poked a finger into a pectoral (rock) and then withdrew.

"Ouch!" Bill said as the tailor extruded a cold pointer and jabbed him with it, measuring his size. Something went *chunk* deep inside its tubular torso and a brilliant red jacket began to emerge from a slot in the front. In an instant this was slipped onto Bill and the shining golden buttons buttoned. Luxurious gray moleskin trousers were pulled on next, then gleaming black knee-length boots. Bill staggered a bit as the curtain was whipped away and a powered full-length mirror rolled up.

"Oh how the girls love a uniform," the sergeant said, "and I can't blame them."

A memory of the vision of Inga-Maria Calyphigia's matched white moons obscured Bill's sight for a moment, and when it had cleared he found he was grasping a stylo and was about to sign the form that the recruiting sergeant held before him.

"No," Bill said, a little amazed at his own firmness of mind. "I don't really want to. Technical Fertilizer Operator . . ."

"And not only will you receive this lovely uniform, an enlistment bonus and a free medical examination, but you will be awarded these handsome medals." The sergeant took a flat box, offered to him on cue by a robot, and opened it to display a glittering array of ribbons and bangles. "This is the Honorable Enlistment Award," he intoned gravely, pinning a jewel-encrusted nebula pendant on chartreuse, to Bill's wide chest. "And the Emperor's Congratulatory Gilded Horn, The Forward to Victory

Starburst, the Praise Be Given Salutation of the Mothers of the Victorious Fallen and the Everflowing Cornucopia which does not mean anything but it looks nice and can be used to carry contraceptives." He stepped back and admired Bill's chest which was now adangle with ribbons, shining metal and gleaming paste gems.

"I just couldn't," Bill said. "Thank you anyway for the offer, but . . ."

The sergeant smiled, prepared even for this eleventh hour resistance, and pressed the button on his belt that actuated the programmed hypno-coil in the heel of Bill's new boot. The powerful neural current surged through the contacts and Bill's hand twitched and jumped, and when the momentary fog had lifted from his eyes he saw that he had signed his name.

"But . . ."

"Welcome to the Space Troopers," the sergeant boomed, smacking him on the back (trapezius like rock) and relieving him of the stylo. "FALL IN!" in a larger voice, and the recruits stumbled from the tavern.

"What have they done to my son!" Bill's mother screeched, coming into the market square, clutching at her bosom with one hand and towing his baby brother Charlie with the other. Charlie began to cry and wet his pants.

"Your son is now a trooper for the greater glory of the Emperor," the sergeant said, pushing his slack-jawed and round-shouldered recruit squad into line.

"No! it can't be . . ." Bill's mother sobbed, tearing at her graying hair. "I'm a poor widow, he's my sole support . . . you cannot . . .!"

"Mother . . ." Bill said, but the sergeant shoved him back into the ranks.

"Be brave, madam," he said humbly.

"There can be no greater glory for a mother." He dropped a large newly minted coin into her hand. "Here is the enlistment bonus, the Emperor's shilling. I know he wants you to have it. ATTENTION!"

With a clash of heels the graceless recruits braced their shoulders and lifted their chins. Much to his surprise, so did Bill.

"RIGHT TURN!"

In a single, graceful motion as the command robot relayed the order to the hypno-coil in every boot. FORWARD MARCH! and they did in perfect rhythm, so well under control that, try as hard as he could Bill could neither turn his head nor wave a last good-by to his mother. She vanished behind him and one last, anguished wail cut through the thud of marching feet.

"Step up to count to 130," the sergeant ordered, glancing at the watch which was set under the nail of his little finger. "Just ten miles to the station and we'll be in camp tonight, my lads."

The command robot moved its metronome up one notch and the tramping boots conformed to the smarter pace and the men began to sweat. By the time they had reached the copter station it was nearly dark, their red paper uniforms hung in shreds, the gilt had been rubbed from their potmetal buttons and the surface charge that repelled the dust from their thin plastic boots had leaked away. They looked as ragged, weary, dusty and miserable as they felt.

II

It wasn't the recorded bugle playing reveille that woke Bill, but the supersonics that streamed through the metal frame of his bunk that shook him until the fillings vibrated from his teeth. He sprang to his feet and stood there shivering in the gray of dawn. Because it was summer the floor was refrigerated: no mollycoddling of the men in Camp Leon Trotsky. The pallid chilled figures of the other recruits loomed up on every side. When the soul-shaking vibrations died away they dragged their thick sackcloth and sandpaper fatigue uniforms from their bunks, pulled them hastily on, jammed their feet into the great, purple recruit boots and staggered out into the dawn.

"I am here to break your spirit," a voice, rich with menace, told them, and they looked up and shivered even more as they faced the chief demon in this particular hell.

Petty Chief Officer Deathwish Drang was a specialist from the tips of the angry spikes of his hair to the corrugated stamping soles of his mirror-like boots. He was wide shouldered and lean hipped, while his long arms hung, curved like some horrible anthropoid, the knuckles of his immense fists scarred from the merciless breaking of thousands of teeth.

It was impossible to look at this detestable form and imagine that it issued from the tender womb of a woman. He could never have been born; he must have been built to order by the government. Most terrible of all was the head. The face! The hairline was scarcely a fingers-width above the black tangle of the brows that were set like a rank growth of foliage at the rim of the black pits that concealed the eyes—visible only as baleful red gleams in the stygian darkness. A nose, broken and crushed, squatted above the mouth that was like a knife slash in the taut belly of a corpse, while from between the lips issued the great, white fangs of the canine teeth, at least two inches long, that rested in grooves on the lower lip.

"I am Petty Chief Officer Deathwish Drang and you will call me 'sir' or 'm'lord'." He began to pace grimly before the row of terrified recruits. "I am your father and your mother and your whole universe and your dedicated enemy, and very soon I will have you regretting the day you were born. I will crush your will. When I say frog you will jump. My job is to turn you into troopers, and troopers have discipline. Discipline simply means unthinking subservience, loss of free will, absolute obedience. That is all I ask . . ."

He stopped before Bill, who was not shaking quite as much as the other recruits and scowled.

"I don't like your face. One month of Sunday KP."

"Sir . . ."

"And a second month for talking back."

He waited, but Bill was silent. He had already learned his first lesson on how to be a good trooper. Keep your mouth shut. Deathwish paced on.

"Right now you are nothing but horrible, sordid, flabby pieces of debased civilian flesh. I shall turn that flesh to muscle, your wills to jelly, your minds to machines. You will become good troopers or I will kill you. Very soon you will be hearing stories about me, vicious stories about how I killed and ate a recruit who disobeyed me."

He halted and stared at them. Slowly the coffin-lid lips parted in an evil travesty of a grin, while a drop of saliva formed at the tip of each whitened tusk.

"That story is true."

A moan broke from the row of recruits and they shook as though a chill wind had passed over them. The smile vanished.

"We will run to breakfast now as soon as I have some volunteers for an easy assignment. Can any of you drive a helicar?"

Two recruits hopefully raised their hands and he beckoned them forward. "Alright, both of you, mops and buckets behind that door. Clean out the latrine while the rest are eating. You'll have a better appetite for lunch."

That was Bill's second lesson on how to be a good trooper: never volunteer.

The days of recruit training passed with a horribly lethargic speed. With each day conditions became worse and Bill's exhaustion greater. This seemed impossible, but it was nevertheless true. A large number of gifted and sadistic minds had designed it to be that way. The recruits' heads were shaved for uniformity and their genitalia painted with orange antiseptic to control the endemic crotch crickets. The food was theoretically nourishing but incredibly vile and when, by mistake, one batch of meat was served in an edible state it was caught at the last moment and thrown out and the cook reduced two grades. Their sleep was broken by mock gas attacks and their free time filled with caring for their equipment.

The seventh day was designated as a day of rest but they all had received punishments, like Bill's KP, and it was as any other day. On this, the third Sunday of their imprisonment, they were stumbling through the last hour of the day before the lights were extinguished and they were finally permitted to crawl into their casehardened bunks. Bill pushed against the weak force field that blocked the door, cunningly designed to allow the desert flies to enter but not leave the barracks, and dragged himself in. After fourteen hours of KP his legs vibrated with exhaustion and his arms were wrinkled and pallid as a corpse's from the soapy water. He dropped his jacket to the floor, where it stood stiffly, supported by its burden of sweat, grease and dust, and dragged his shaver from the foot locker. In the latrine he bobbed his head around trying to find a clear space on one of the mirrors.

All of them had been heavily stenciled in large letters with such inspiring messages as KEEP YOUR WUG SHUT—THE CHINGERS ARE LISTENING and IF YOU TALK THIS MAN MAY DIE. He finally plugged the shaver in next to WOULD YOU WANT YOUR SISTER TO MARRY ONE? and centered his face in the O in ONE. Black-rimmed, bloodshot eyes stared back at him as he ran the buzzing machine over the underweight planes of his jaw. It took more than a minute for the meaning of the question to penetrate his fatigue-drugged brain.

"I haven't got a sister," he grumbled peevishly. "And if I did why should she want to marry a lizard anyway?" It was a rhetorical question but it brought an answer from the far end of the room, from the last shot tower in the second row.

"It doesn't mean *exactly* what it says—it's just there to make us hate the dirty enemy more."

Bill jumped, he had thought he was alone in the latrine, and the razor buzzed spitefully and gouged a bit of flesh from his lip.

"Who's there? Why are you hiding?" he snarled, then recognized the huddled dark figure and the many pairs of boots. "Oh, it's only you, Eager." His anger drained away and he turned back to the mirror.

Eager Beager was so much a part of the latrine that you forgot he was there. A moon-faced, eternally smiling youth whose apple red cheeks never lost their glow, and whose smile looked so much out of place here in Camp Leon Trotsky that everyone wanted to kill him until they remembered that he was mad.

He had to be mad because he was always eager to help his buddies and had volunteered as permanent latrine orderly. Not only that, but he liked to polish boots and had offered to do those of one after another of his buddies until now he did the boots for every man in the squad every night. Whenever they were in the barracks Eager Beager could be found crouched at the end of the thrones that were his personal domain, surrounded by heaps of shoes and polishing industriously, his face wreathed in smiles. He would still be there after lights-out, working by the light of a burning wick struck in a can of polish and was usually up before the others in the morning, finishing his voluntary job and still smiling. Sometimes, when the boots were very dirty, he worked right through the night. The kid was obviously insane but no one turned him in because he did such a good job on the boots and they all prayed that he wouldn't die of exhaustion until recruit training was finished.

"Well if that's what they want to say, why don't they just say 'hate the dirty enemy more'," Bill complained. He jerked his thumb at the far wall where there was a poster labeled KNOW THE ENEMY. It featured a life-sized illustration of a Chinger, a seven foot high saurian that looked very much like a scale covered, four armed, green kangaroo with an alligator's head. "Whose sister would want to marry a thing like that anyway? And what would a thing like that want to do with a sister, except maybe ear her?"

Eager put a last buff on a purple toe and picked up another boot. He frowned for a brief instant to show what a serious thought this was. "Well you see, gee—it doesn't mean a *real* sister. It's just part of psychological warfare. We have to win the war. To win the war we have to fight hard. In order to fight hard we have to have good soldiers. Good soldiers have to hate the enemy. That's the way it goes. The Chingers are the only non-human race that has been discovered in the galaxy that has gone beyond the aboriginal level, so naturally we have to wipe them out."

"What the hell do you mean *naturally*? I don't want to wipe anyone out. I just want to go home and be a Technical Fertilizer Operator."

"Well I don't mean you personally, of course—gee!" Eager opened a fresh can of polish with purple-stained hands and dug his fingers into it. "I mean the human race, that's just the way we do things. If we don't wipe them out they'll wipe us out. Of course they say that war is against their religion and they will only fight in defense, and they have never made attacks, yet. But we can't believe them even though it is true. They might change their religion or their minds some day and then where would we be? The best answer is to wipe them out now."

Bill unplugged his razor and washed his face in the tepid, rusty water. "It still doesn't seem to make sense. Alright, so the sister I don't have doesn't marry one of them. But how about that—" he pointed to the stenciling on the duckboards, KEEP THIS SHOWER CLEAR—THE ENEMY CAN HEAR. "Or that—" The sign above the urinal that read BUTTON FLIES—BEWARE SPIES. "Forgetting for the moment that we don't have any secrets here worth traveling a mile to hear, much less twenty-five light-years—how could a Chinger possibly be a spy? What kind of make-up would disguise a seven foot lizard as a recruit? You couldn't even disguise one to look like Deathwish Drang, though you could get pretty close—"

The lights went out and, as though using his name had summoned him like a devil from the pit, the voice of Deathwish blasted through the barracks.

"Into your sacks! Into your sacks! Don't you lousy bowbs know there's a war on!" he rumbled menacingly.

Bill stumbled away through the darkness of the barracks where the only illumination was the red glow from Deathwish's eyes. He fell asleep the instant his head touched his carborundum pillow and it seemed that only a moment had elapsed before reveille sent him hurtling from his bunk.

At breakfast, while he was painfully cutting his coffee-substitute into chunks small enough to swallow, the telenews reported heavy fighting in the Beta Lyra sector with mounting losses. A groan ripples through the mess hall when this was announced, not because of any excess of patriotism, but because any bad news would only make things worse for them. They did not know how this would be arranged, but they were positive it would be. They were right.

Since the morning was a bit cooler than usual the Monday parade was postponed until noon when the ferro-concrete drill ground would have warmed up nicely and there would be the maximum number of heat prostration cases. But this was just the beginning. From where Bill stood at attention near the rear he could see that the air conditioned canopy was up on the reviewing stand. That meant brass. The trigger guard of his atomic rifle dug a hole into his shoulder and a drop of sweat collected then dripped from the tip of his nose. Out of the corners of his eyes he could see the steady ripple of motion as men collapsed here and there among the massed ranks of thousands, and were dragged to the waiting ambulances by alert corpsmen. Here they were laid in the shade of the vehicles until they revived and could be urged back to their positions in the formation with other staggering recruits.

Then the band burst into *Spacemen Ho and Chingers Vanguished!* and the broadcast signal to each boot heel snapped the ranks to attention at the same instant and the thousands of rifles flashed in the sun. The commanding general's staff car—this was obvious from the two stars painted on it—pulled up beside the reviewing stand and a tiny, round figure moved quickly through the furnacelike air to the comfort of the enclosure. Bill had never seen him any closer that this, at least from the front, though once while he was returning from late KP he had spotted the general getting into his car near the camp theatre. At least Bill thought it was him, but all he had seen was a brief rear view. Therefore, if he had a mental picture of the general, it was of a large backside super-imposed in a teeny ant-like figure.

He thought of most officers in these general terms, since the men of course had nothing to do with officers during their recruit training. Bill had had a good glimpse of a 2nd lieutenant once, near the orderly room, and he knew he had a face. And there had been a medical officer who hadn't been more than thirty yards away, who has lectured them on venereal disease, but Bill had been lucky enough to sit behind a post and had promptly fallen asleep.

After the band shut up, the anti-G loudspeakers floated out over the troops and the general addressed them. He had nothing to say that anyone cared to listen to and he closed with the announcement that because of losses in the field their training program would be accelerated, which was just what they had expected. Then the band played some more and they marched back to the barracks, changed into their haircloth fatigues and marched—doubletime now—to the range where they fired their atomic rifles at plastic replicas of Chingers that popped up out of holes in the ground. Their aim was very bad until Deathwish Drang popped out of a hole and every trooper switched to full automatic and hit with every charge fired from every gun, which is a very hard thing to do. Then the smoke cleared and they stopped cheering and started sobbing when they saw that it was only a plastic replica of Deathwish, now torn to tiny pieces, and the original appeared behind them and gnashed its tusks and gave them all a full month's KP.

III

"The human body is a wonderful thing," Bowb Brown said, a month later, when they were sitting around a table in the Lowest Ranks Klub eating plastic skinned sausages stuffed with road sweepings and drinking watery warm beer. Bowb Brown was a thoatherder from the plains, which is why they called him Bowb since everyone knows just what thoatherders do with their thoats. He was tall, thin and bowlegged, his skin burnt to the color of ancient leather. He rarely talked, being more used to the eternal silence of the plains broken only by the eerie cry of the restless thoat. He was a great thinker since the one thing he had had plenty of was time to think in. He could worry a thought for days, even weeks, before he mentioned it aloud, and while he was thinking about it nothing could disturb him. He even let them call him Bowb without protesting: call any other trooper bowb and he would hit you in the face. Bill and Eager and the other troopers from X squad sitting around the table all clapped and cheered, as they always did when Bowb said something.

"Tell us more, Bowb!"

"It can still talk—I thought it was dead!"

"Go on—why is the body a wonderful thing?"

They waited in expectant silence while Bowb managed to tear

a bite from his sausage and, after ineffectual chewing, swallowed it with an effort that brought tears to his eyes. He eased the pain with a mouthful of beer and spoke.

"The human body is a wonderful thing—because if it doesn't die—it lives."

They waited for more until they realized that he was finished, then they sneered.

"Boy, are you full of bowb!"

"Sign up for O.C.S.!"

"Yeah—but what does it *mean?*"

Bill knew what it meant, but didn't tell them.

There were only half as many men in the squad as there had been the first day. One man had been transferred. All the others were sick or in the mental hospital, or discharged for the convenience of the government as being too crippled for active service. Or dead. The survivors after losing every ounce of weight not made up of bone or essential connective tissue, had put back the lost weight in the form of muscle and were now completely adapted to the rigors of Camp Leon Trotsky, though they still loathed it.

Bill marveled at the efficiency of the system. Civilians had to fool around with examinations, grades, retirement benefits, seniority and a thousand other factors that limited the efficiency of the workers. But how easily the troopers did it! They simply killed off the weaker ones and used the survivors. He respected the system. Though he still loathed it.

"You know what I need, I need a woman," Ugly Ugglesway said.

"Don't talk dirty," Bill told him promptly, since he had been brought up correctly.

"I'm not talking dirty!" Ugly whined. "It's not like I said I wanted to re-enlist or that I thought Deathwish was human or anything like that. I just said I need a woman. Don't we all?"

"I need a drink," Bowb Brown said as he took a long swig from his glass of dehydrated reconstituted beer, shuddered, then squirted it out through his teeth in a long stream onto the concrete, where it instantly evaporated.

"Affirm, affirm," Ugly agreed, bobbing his mat-haired warty head up and down. "I need a woman *and* a drink." His whine became almost plaintive. "After all, what else is there to want in the troopers outside of out?"

They thought about that a long time, but could think of nothing else that anyone really wanted. Eager Beager looked out from under the table where he was surreptitiously polishing a boot and said that he wanted more polish, but they ignored him. Even Bill, now that he put his mind to it, could think of nothing he really wanted other than this inextricably linked pair. He tried hard to think of something else, since he had vague memories of wanting other things when he had been a civilian, but nothing else came to mind.

"Gee, it's only seven more weeks until we get our first pass," Eager said from under the table, then screamed as everyone kicked him at once.

But slow as subjective time crawled by, the objective clocks were still operating and the seven weeks did pass by and eliminate themselves one by one. Busy weeks filled with all the essential recruit training courses: bayonet drill, small arms training, short arm inspection, grey-pfing, orientation lectures, drill, communal singing and the Articles of War. These last were read with dreadful regularity twice a week and were absolute torture because of the intense somnolence they brought on.

At the first rustle of the scratchy, monotonous voice from the tape player heads would begin to nod. But every seat in the auditorium was wired with an EEG that monitored the brain waves of the captive troopers. As soon as the shape of the Alpha wave indicated transition from consciousness to slumber a powerful jolt of current would be shot into the dozing buttocks, jabbing the owner painfully awake.

The musty auditorium was a dimly lit torture chamber, filled with the droning dull voice punctuated by the sharp screams of the electrified, the sea of nodding heads abob here and there with painfully leaping figures.

No one ever listened to the terrible executions and sentences announced in the Articles for the most innocent of crimes. Everyone knew that they had signed away all human rights when they enlisted. The itemizing of what they had lost interested them not in the slightest. What they really were interested in was counting the hours until they would receive their first pass.

The ritual by which this reward was begrudgingly given was unusually humiliating, but they expected this and merely lowered their eyes and shuffled forward in the line, ready to sacrifice any remaining shards of their self-respect in exchange for the crimpled scrap of plastic. This rite finished, there was a scramble for the monorail train whose track ran on electrically charged pillars, soaring over the thirty-foot high barbed wire, crossing the quicksand beds, then dropping into the little farming town of Leyville.

At least it had been an agricultural town before Camp Leon Trotsky had been built and sporadically, in the hours when the troopers weren't on leave, it followed its original agrarian bent. The rest of the time the grain and feed stores shut down and the drink and knock shops opened. Many times the same premises were used for both functions. A lever would be pulled when the first of the leave party thundered out of the station and grain bins became beds, salesclerks pimps, cashiers retained their same function—though the prices went up—while counters would be racked with glasses to serve as bars. It was to one of these establishments, a mortuary-cum-saloon, that Bill and his friends went.

"What'll it be, boys?" the ever-smiling owner of the Final Resting Bar and Grill asked.

"Double shot of embalming fluid," Bowb Brown told him.

"No jokes," the landlord said, the smile vanishing for a second as he took down a bottle on which the garish label REAL WHISKY had been pasted over the etched in EMBALMING FLUID. "Any trouble I call the MPs." The smile returned as money struck the counter. "Name your poison, gents."

They sat around a long, narrow table as thick as it was wide with brass handles on both sides, and let the blessed relief of ethyl alcohol trickle a path down their dust-lined throats.

"I never drank before I came into the service," Bill said, draining four fingers neat of Old Kidney Killer and held his glass out for more.

"You never had to," Ugly said, pouring.

"That's for sure," Bowb Brown said, smacking his lips with relish and raising a bottle to his lips again.

"Gee," Eager Beager said, sipping hesitantly at the edge of his glass, "It tastes like a tincture of sugar, wood chips, various esters and a number of higher alcohols."

"Drink up," Bowb said incoherently around the neck of the bottle. "All them things is good for you."

"Now I want a woman," Ugly said and there was a rush as they all jammed in the door trying to get out at the same time, until someone shouted *Look!* and they turned to see Eager still sitting at the table.

"Woman!" Ugly said enthusiastically, in the tone of voice you say Dinner! in when you are calling a dog. The knot of men stirred in the doorway and stamped their feet. Eager didn't move.

"Gee—I think I'll stay right here," he said, his smile simpler than ever. "But you guys run along."

"Don't you feel well, Eager?"

"Feel fine."

"Ain't you reached puberty?"

"Gee . . ."

"What you gonna do here?"

Eager reached under the table and dragged out a canvas grip. He opened it to show that it was packed with great, purple boots. "I thought I'd catch up on my polishing."

They walked slowly down the wooden sidewalk, silent for the moment. "I wonder if there is something wrong with Eager?" Bill asked, but no one answered him. They were looking down the rutted street, at a brilliantly illuminated sign that cast a tempting, ruddy glow.

SPACEMEN'S REST it said. CONTINUOUS STRIP SHOW and BEST DRINKS and better PRIVATE ROOMS FOR GUESTS AND THEIR FRIENDS. They walked faster. The front wall of the Spaceman's Rest was covered with shatterproof glass cases filled with tri-di pix of the fully dressed (bangle and double stars) entertainers, and further in with pix of them nude (debangled with fallen stars). Bill stayed the quick sound of panting by pointing to a small sign almost lost among the tumescent wealth of mammaries.

OFFICERS ONLY it read.

"Move along," an MP grated and poked at them with his electronic nightstick. They shuffled on.

The next establishment admitted men of all classes, but the cover charge was 77 credits, more than they all had between them. After that the OFFICERS ONLY began again until the pavement ended and all the lights were behind them.

"What's that?" Ugly asked at the sound of murmured voices from a nearby darkened street. Peering closely they saw a line of troopers that stretched out of sight around a distant corner. "What's this?" he asked the last man in the line.

"Lower ranks cathouse. Two credits, two minutes. And don't try to buck the line, bowb. On the back, on the back."

They joined up instantly and Bill ended up last, but not for long.

They shuffled forward slowly and other troopers appeared and cued up behind him. The night was cool and he took many life-preserving slugs from his bottle. There was little conversation and what there was died as the red-lit portal loomed ever closer. It opened and closed at regular intervals and one by one Bill's buddies slipped in to partake of its satisfying, though rapid, pleasures. Then it was his turn and the door started to open and he started to step forward. Suddenly sirens started screaming and a large MP with a great fat belly jumped between Bill and the door.

"Emergency recall. Back to the base, you men!" it barked.

Bill howled a strangled groan of frustration and leaped forward, but a light tap with the electronic nightstick sent him reeling back with the others. He was carried along, half stunned, with the shuffling wave of bodies while the sirens moaned and the artificial northern lights in the sky spelled out TO ARMS!!!! in letters of flame each a hundred miles long. Someone put his hand out, holding Bill up as he started to slide under the trampling purple boots. It was his old buddy, Ugly, carrying a satiated smirk and he hated him and tried to hit him. But before he could raise his fist they were swept into monorail car, hurtled through the night and disgorged back in Camp Leon Trotsky He forgot his anger when the gnarled claws of Deathwish Drang dragged them from the crowd.

"Pack your bags," he rasped. "You're shipping out."

"They can't do that to us—we haven't finished our training."

"They can do whatever they want, and they usually do. A glorious space battle has just been fought to its victorious conclusion and there are over four million casualties, give or take a hundred thousand. Replacements are needed, which is you. Prepare to board the transports immediately if not sooner."

"We can't—we have no space gear! The supply room . . ."

"All of the supply personnel have already been shipped out."

"Food . . ."

"The cooks and KP pushers are already spacebound. This is an emergency. All unessential personnel are being sent out. Probably to die." He twanged a tusk coyly and watched them with his loathsome grin. "While I remain here in peaceful security to train your replacements." The delivery tube plunked at his elbow and as he opened the message capsule and read its contents his smile slowly fell to pieces. "They're shipping me out too," he said, hollowly.

IV

Already 89,672,899 recruits had been shipped into space through Camp Leon Trotsky, so the process was an automatic and smoothly working one even though this time it was processing itself, like a snake swallowing its own tail. Bill and his buddies were the last group of recruits through and the snake began ingesting itself right behind them. No sooner had they been shorn of their sprouting fuzz and deloused in the ultrasonic delouser than the barbers rushed at each other and in a welter of under and over arms, gobbets of hair, shards of moustache, bits of flesh, drops of blood, they clipped and shaved each other then pulled the operator after them into the ultrasonic chamber. Medical corpsmen gave themselves injections against rocket fever, space-cafard and the clap, record clerks issued themselves pay books and the loadmasters kicked each other up the ramps and into the waiting shuttle-ships.

Rockets blasted, living columns of fire-like scarlet tongues licking down at the blasting pads, burning up the ramps in a lovely pyrotechnic display since the ramp operators were also aboard. The ships echoed and thundered up into the night sky leaving Camp Leon Trotsky a dark and silent ghost town. Bits of daily orders and punishment rosters rustled and blew from the bulletin boards, dancing through the deserted streets to finally plaster themselves against the noisy, bright windows of the Officer's Club. A great drinking party was in progress there, although there was much complaining because they had to serve themselves.

Up, and up the shuttleships shot, towards the great fleet of deep-spacers that darkened the stars above. It was a new fleet, the most powerful the galaxy had ever seen, so new in fact that the ships were still under construction. Welding torches flared in brilliant points of light while hot rivets hurled their flat trajectories across the sky into waiting buckets. The spots of light died away as one behemoth of the star lanes was completed and thin screams sounded in the spacesuit radio circuit as the workers, instead of being returned to the yards, were pressed into service on the ship they had so recently built.

This was total war.

Bill staggered through the sagging plastic tube that connected the shuttleship to a dreadnaught of space and dropped his bags in front of a Petty Chief Officer who sat at a desk in the hanger-sized spacelock. Or rather he tried to drop it, but since there was no gravity the bags remained in midair and when he pushed them down he rose. (Since a body when it is falling freely is said to be in free fall, and anything with weight has no weight, and for every action there is an equal and opposite reaction or something like that.) The Petty looked up and snarled and pulled Bill back down to the deck.

"None of your bowby spacelubber tricks, tropper. Name?"

"Bill, spelled with two L's."

"Bil," the Petty mumbled, licking the end of his stylo, then inscribing it in the ship's roster with round, illiterate letters. "Two L's for officers only, bowb—learn your place. What's your classification?"

"Recruits, unskilled, untrained, spacesick."

"Well don't puke in here, that's what you have your own quarters for. You are now a Fusetender 6th class, unskilled. Bunk down in compartment 34J-89T-001. Move. And keep that woopsy sack over your head."

No sooner had Bill found his quarters and thrown his bags into a bunk, where they floated five inches over the reclaimed rock-wool mattress, then Eager Beager came in, followed by Bowb Brown and a crowd of strangers, some of them carrying welding torches and angry expressions.

"Where's Ugly and the rest of the squad?" Bill asked.

Bowb shrugged and strapped himself into his bunk for a little shuteye. Eager opened one of the six bags he always carried and removed some boots to polish.

"Are you saved?" a deep voice vibrant with emotion sounded from the other end of the compartment. Bill looked up startled, and the big trooper standing there saw the motion and stabbed towards him with an immense finger. "You, brother, are you saved?"

"That's a little hard to say," Bill mumbled, bending over and rooting in his bag, hoping the man would go away. But he didn't, in fact he came over and sat down on Bill's bunk. Bill tried to ignore him, but this was hard to do because the trooper was over six feet high, heavily muscled and iron jawed. He had lovely, purplish black skin that made Bill a little jealous because his was only sort of grayish pink. Since the trooper's shipboard uniform was almost the same shade of black he looked all of a piece, very effective with his flashing smile and piercing gaze.

● ● ●

"Welcome aboard the *Christine Keeler*," he said and with a friendly shake splintered most of Bill's knuckle bones. "The grand old lady of this fleet, commissioned almost a week ago. I'm Reverend Fusetender 6th Class Tembo, and I see by the stencil on your bag that your name is Bill, and since we're shipmates, Bill, please call me Tembo, and how is the condition of your soul?"

"I haven't had much chance to think about it lately . . ."

"I should think not, just coming from recruit training, since attendance of chapel during training is a court-martial offense. But that's all behind you now and you can be saved. Might I ask if you are of the faith?"

"My folks were Fundamentalist Zoroastrian, so I suppose . . ."

"Superstition, my boy, rank superstition. It was the hand of fate that brought us together in this ship, that your soul would have this one chance to be saved from the fiery pit. You've heard of Earth?"

"I like plain food . . ."

"It's a planet, my boy—the home of the human race. The home from whence we all sprang, see it, a green and lovely world, a jewel in space." Tembo had slipped a tiny projector from his pocket while he spoke and a colored image appeared on the bulkhead, a planet swimming artistically through the void girdled by white clouds. Suddenly, ruddy lightning shot through the clouds and they twisted and boiled while great wounds appeared on the planet below. From the pinhead speaker came the tiny moaning sound of rolling, clashing thunder.

"But wars sprang up among the sons of man and they smote each other with the atomic energies until the Earth itself groaned aloud and mighty was the holocaust. And when the final lightnings stilled there was death in the north, death in the west, death in the east, death, death, death. Do you realize what that means?" Tembo's voice was eloquent with feeling, suspended for an instant in midflight, waiting for the answer to the catachistical question.

"I'm not sure," Bill said, rooting aimlessly in his bag, "I come from Phigerinadon II, it's a quieter place . . ."

"There was no death in the SOUTH! And why was the south spared, I ask you, and the answer is because it was the will of Samedi that all the false prophets and false religions and false gods be wiped from the face of the earth so that the only true faith should remain. The First Reformed Voodoo Church . . ."

General Quarters sounded, a hooting alarm keyed to the resonant frequency of the human skull so that the bone vibrated as

though the head were inside a mighty bell and the eyes blurred out
of focus with each stroke. There was a scramble for the passageway where the hideous sound was not quite as loud and where
non-coms were waiting to herd them to their stations. Bill
followed Eager Beager up an oily ladder and out of the hatch in the
floor of the fuse room.

Great racks of fuses stretched away on all sides of them, while
from the tops of the racks sprang arm-thick cables that looped
upwards and vanished through the ceiling. In front of the racks,
evenly spaced, were round openings a foot in diameter.

"My opening remarks will be brief, any trouble from any of
you and I will personally myself feed you head first down the
nearest fuseway." A greasy forefinger pointed at one of the holes
in the deck and they recognized the voice of their new master. He
was shorter and wider and thicker in the gut than Deathwish, but
there was a generic resemblance that was unmistakable.

"I am Fusetender First Class Spleen. I will take you crumbly
groundcrawling bowbs and will turn you into highly skilled and
efficient fusetenders or else feed you down the nearest fuseway.
This is a highly skilled and efficient technical specialty which
usually takes a year to train a good man. But this is war so you're
going to learn to do it now or else. I will now demonstrate. Tembo
front and center. Take board 19J-9, it's out of circuit now."

Tembo clashed his heels and stood at rigid attention in front of
th board. Stretching away on both sides of him were the fuses,
white ceramic cylinders capped on both ends with metal, each one
a foot in diameter, five foot high and weighing 90 pounds. There
was a red band around the midriff of each fuse. First Class Spleen
tapped one of these bands.

"Every fuse has one of these red bands which is called a
fuseband and is of the color red. When the fuse burns out this band
turns black. I don't expect you to remember all this now, but it's
in your manual and you are going to be letter perfect before I'm
done with you, or else. Now I will show you what will happen
when a fuse burns out. Tembo—that is a burned out fuse! Go!"

"Unggh!" Tembo shouted and leaped at the fuse and grasped
it with both hands. "Unggh!" he said again as he pulled it from
the clips, and again Unggh! when he dropped it into the fuseway.
Then, still Ungghing, he pulled a new fuse from the storage rack
and clipped it into place and, with a final Unggh! snapped back to
attention.

"And that's the way it is done, by the count, by the numbers, the trooper way and you are going to learn it or else.'' A dull buzzing sounded, grumbling through the air like a stifled eructation. ''There's the chow call, so I'll let you break now and while you're eating think about what you are going to have to learn. Fall out.''

Other troopers were going by in the corridor and they followed them into the bowels of the ship.

''Gee—do you think the food might be any better than it was back in camp?'' Eager asked, smacking his lips excitedly.

''It is completely impossible that it could be any worse,'' Bill said as they joined a line leading to a door labeled CONSOLIDATED MESS NUMBER TWO. ''Any change will have to make it better. After all—aren't we fighting troopers now? We have to go into combat fit, the manual says.''

The line moved forward with painful slowness, but within an hour they were at the door. Inside of it a tired looking KP in soapstained, greasy fatigues handed Bill a yellow plastic cup from a rack before him. Bill moved on and when the trooper in front of him stepped away he faced a blank wall from which there emerged a single, handleless spigot. A fat cook standing next to it, wearing a large white chef's hat and a soiled undershirt, waved him forwards with the soup ladle in his hand.

''C'mon, c'mon, ain't you never et before? Cup under the spout, dogtag in the slot, snap it up!''

Bill held the cup as he had been advised and noticed a narrow slit in the metal wall just at eye level. His dogtags were hanging around his neck and he pushed one of them into the slot. Something went *buzzzzz* and a thin stream of yellow fluid gushed out, filling the cup halfway.

''Next man!'' the cook shouted and pulled Bill away so that Eager could take his place. ''What is this?'' Bill asked, peering into the cup.

''What is this! What is this!'' the cook raged, growing bright red. ''This is your dinner you stupid bowb! This is absolutely chemically pure water in which are dissolved 18 amino acids, 16 vitamins, 11 mineral salts, a fatty acid ester and glucose. What else did you expect?''

''Dinner . . . ?'' Bill said hopefully, then saw red as the soup ladle crashed down on his head. ''Could I have it without the fatty acid ester?'' he asked hopefully, but he was pushed out into the corridor where Eager joined him.

"Gee," Eager said. "This has all the food elements necessary to sustain life indefinitely. Isn't that marvelous?"

Bill sipped at his cup then sighed tremulously.

"Look at that," Tembo said, and when Bill turned, a projected image appeared on the corridor wall. It showed a misty firmament in which tiny figures seemed to be riding on clouds. "Hell awaits you, my boy, unless you are saved. Turn your back on your superstitious way. The First Reformed Voodoo Church welcomes you with open arms, come into her bosom and find your place in heaven at Samedi's right hand. Sit there with Mondongue and Bakalou and Zandor who will welcome you."

The projected scene changed, the clouds grew closer, while from the little speaker came the tiny sound of a heavenly choir with drum accompaniment. Now the figures could be seen clearly, all with very dark skins and white robes from the back of which protruded great black wings. They smiled and waved gracefully to each other as their clouds passed, while singing enthusiastically and beating on the little tom-toms that each one carried. It was a lovely scene and Bill's eyes misted a bit.

"Attention!"

The barking tones echoed from the walls and the troopers snapped their shoulders back, heels together, eyes ahead. The heavenly choir vanished as Tembo shoved the projector back into his pocket.

"As you was," First Class Spleen ordered, and they turned to see him leading two MPs with drawn handguns who were acting as a bodyguard for an officer. Bill knew it was an officer because they had had an Officer Identification course, plus the fact that there was a KNOW YOUR OFFICERS chart on the latrine wall that he had had a great deal of opportunity to study during an anguilluliasis epidemic. His jaw gaped open as the officer went by, almost close enough to *touch*, and stopped in front of Tembo.

"Fusetender 6th Class Tembo, I have good news for you. In two weeks your seven year period of enlistment will be up and because of your fine record Captain Zekial has authorized a doubling of the usual mustering-out pay, an honorable discharge with band music as well as your free transport back to Earth."

Tembo, relaxed yet firm, looked down at the runty lieutenant with his well-chewed blonde moustache who stood before him. "That will be impossible, sir."

• • •

"Impossible!" the lieutenant screeched and rocked back and forth on his high-heeled boots. "Who are *you* to tell *me* what is impossible—"

"Not I, sir," Tempo answered with utmost calm. "Regulation 13–9A, paragraph 45, page 8923, volume 43 of *Rules, Regulations and Articles of War*. 'No man nor officer shall or will receive a discharge other than dishonorable with death sentence from a vessel, post, base, camp, ship, outpost, or labor camp during time of emergency' . . ."

"Are you a ship's lawyer, Tembo?"

"No, sir. I'm a loyal trooper, sir. I just want to do my duty, sir."

"There's something very funny about you, Tembo. I saw in your record that you enlisted *voluntarily* without drugs and or hypnotics being used. Now you refuse discharge. That's bad, Tembo, very bad. Gives you a bad name. Makes you look suspicious. Makes you look like a spy or something."

"I'm a loyal trooper of the Emperor, sir, not a spy."

"You're not a spy, Tembo, we have looked into that very carefully. But why *are* you in the service, Tembo?"

"To be a loyal trooper of the Emperor, sir, and to do my best to spread the gospel. Have you been saved, sir?"

"Watch your tongue, trooper, or I'll have you up on charges! Yes, we know that story—*reverend*—but we don't believe it. You're being too tricky, but we'll find out . . ." He stalked away muttering to himself and they all snapped to attention until he was gone. The other troopers looked at Tembo oddly and did not feel comfortable until he had gone. Bill and Eager walked slowly back to their quarters.

"Turned down a discharge!" Bill mumbled in awe.

"Gee," Eager said, "maybe he's nuts? I can't think of any other reason."

"Nobody could be *that* crazy," then "I wonder what's in there?" pointing to a door with a large sign that read ADMITTANCE TO AUTHORIZED PERSONNEL ONLY.

"Gee—I don't know—maybe food?"

They slipped through instantly and closed the door behind them, but there was no food there. Instead they were in a long chamber with one curved wall, while attached to this wall were cumbersome devices set with meters, dials, switches, controls, levers, a view screen and a relief tube. Bill bent over and read the label on the nearest one.

"Mark IV Atomic Blaster—and look at the size of them! This must be the ship's main battery." He turned around and saw that Eager was holding his arm up so that his wristwatch pointed at the guns and was pressing on the crown with the index finger on his other hand.

"What are you doing?" Bill asked.

"Gee—just seeing what time it was."

"How can you tell what time it is when you have the inside of your wrist towards your face and the watch is on the outside?"

Footsteps echoed far down the long gundeck and they remembered the sign on the outside of the door. In an instant they had slipped back through it and Bill pressed it quietly shut. When he turned around Eager Beager had gone so that he had to make his way back to their quarters by himself. Eager was busy shining boots for his buddies and didn't look up from his work when Bill came in.

But what *had* he been doing with his watch?

V

This question kept bugging Bill all the time during the days of their training as they painfully learned the drill of fusetending. It was an exacting, technical job that demanded all their attention, but in spare moments Bill worried. He worried when they stood in line for chow, and he worried during the few moments every night between the time the lights were turned off and the heavy descent of sleep rested upon his fatigue drugged body. He worried whenever he had the time to do it. And he lost weight.

He lost weight not because he was worrying, but for the same reason everyone else lost weight. The shipboard rations. They were designed to sustain life, and that they did, but no mention was made of what kind of life it was to be. It was a dreary, underweight, hungry one. Yet Bill took no notice of this. He had a bigger problem and he needed help. After Sunday drill at the end of their second week he stayed to talk to First Class Spleen instead of joining the others in their tottering run towards the mess hall.

"I have a problem, sir."

"You ain't the only one, but one shot cures it and you ain't a man until you've had it."

"It's not that kind of problem. I'd like to . . . see the . . . chaplain . . ."

Spleen turned white and sank back against the bulkhead. "Now

I heard everything," he said weakly. "Get down to chow and if you don't tell anyone about this, I won't either."

Bill blushed. "I'm sorry about this, First Class Spleen, but I can't help it. It's not my fault I have to see him, it could have happened to anyone." His voice trailed away and he looked down at his feet, rubbing one boot against another. The silence stretched out until Spleen finally spoke, but all the comradeliness was gone from his voice.

"Alright, trooper—if that's the way you want it. But I hope none of the rest of the boys hear about it. Skip chow and get up there now—here's a pass." He scrawled on a scrap of paper then threw it contemptuously to the floor, turning and walking away as Bill bent humbly to pick it up.

Bill went down dropchutes, along corridors, through passageways and up ladders. In the ship's directory the chaplain was listed as being in compartment 362-B on the 89th deck and Bill finally found this, a plain metal door set with rivets. He raised his hand to knock while sweat stood out in great beads from his face and his throat was dry. His knuckles boomed hollowly on the panel and after an endless period a muffled voice sounded from the other side.

"Yeah, yeah—c'mon in—it's open."

Bill stepped through and snapped to attention when he saw the officer behind the single desk that almost filled the tiny room. The officer, a 4th lieutenant, though still young was balding rapidly. There were black circles under his eyes and he needed a shave. His tie, was knotted crookedly and badly crumpled. He continued to scratch among the stacks of paper that littered the desk, picking them up, changing piles with them, scrawling notes on some and throwing others into an overflowing wastebasket. When he moved one of the stacks Bill saw a sign on the desk that read LAUNDRY OFFICER.

"Excuse me, sir," he said, "but I am in the wrong office. I'm looking for the chaplain."

"This is the chaplain's office but he's not on duty until 1300 hours, which, as someone even as stupid looking as you can tell, is in fifteen minutes more."

"Thank you, sir, I'll come back." Bill slid towards the door.

"You'll stay and work." The officer raised bloodshot eyeballs and cackled evilly. "I got you. You can sort the hanky reports. I've lost 600 jockstraps and they may be in there. You think it's easy to be a laundry officer?'' He sniveled with self-pity and pushed a tottering stack of papers over to Bill who began to sort through them. Long before he was finished the buzzer sounded that ended the watch.

"I knew it!" the officer sobbed hopelessly. "This job will never end, instead it gets worse and worse. And you think *you* got problems!" He reached out an unsteady finger and flipped over the sign on his desk. It read CHAPLAIN on the other side. Then he grabbed the end of his necktie and pulled it back hard over his right shoulder. The necktie was fastened to his collar and the collar was set into the ball bearings that rolled smoothly in a track fixed to his shirt. There was a slight whirring sound as the collar rotated, then the necktie was hanging out of sight down his back and his collar was now on backwards, showing white and smooth and cool to the front.

The chaplain steepled his fingers before him, lowered his eyes and smiled sweetly. "How may I help you, my son?"

"I thought you were the laundry officer," Bill said, taken aback.

"I am, my son, but that is just one of the burdens that must fall upon my shoulders. There is little call for a chaplain in these troubled times, but much call for a laundry officer. I do my best to serve." He bent his head, humbly.

"But—which are you? A chaplain who is a part-time laundry officer, or a laundry officer who is a part-time chaplain?"

"That is a mystery, my son. There are some things that it is best not to know. But I see you are troubled. May I ask if you are of the faith?"

"Which faith?"

"That's what I'm asking *you!*" the chaplain snapped, and for a moment the old laundry officer peeped through. "How can I help you if I do not know what your religion is?"

"Fundamentalist Zoroastrian."

The chaplain took a plastic covered sheet from a drawer and ran his finger down it. "Z . . . Z . . . Zen . . . Zodomite . . . Zoroastrian, Reformed Fundamentalist, is that the one?"

"Yes sir."

"Well, should be no trouble with this my son . . . 21 52 05 . . ." He quickly dialed the number on a control plate set in the desk, then, with a grand gesture and an evangelistic gleam in his eye, he swept all the laundry papers to the floor. Hidden machinery hummed briefly, a portion of the desk top dropped away and reappeared a moment later bearing a black plastic box decorated with golden bulls, rampant. "Be with you in a second," the chaplain said, opening the box.

First he unrolled a length of white cloth sewn with more golden bulls and draped this around his neck. He placed a thick, leather-bound book next to the box, then on the closed lid set two metal bulls with hollowed out backs. Into one of them he poured distilled water from a plastic flask and into the other sweet oil, which he ignited. Bill watched these familiar arrangements with growing happiness.

"It's very lucky," Bill said, "that you are a Zoroastrian. It makes it much easier to talk to you."

"No luck involved, my son, just intelligent planning." The chaplain dropped some powdered haoma into the flame and Bill's nose twitched as the drugged incense filled the room. "By the grace of Ahura Mazdan I am an anointed priest of Zoroastra. By Allah's will a faithful Muezzin of Islam, through Yahweh's intercession a circumcised rabbi, and so forth." His benign face broke into a savage snarl. "And also because of an officer shortage, I am the damned laundry officer." His face cleared. "But now, you must tell me your problem."

"Well, it's not easy. It may be just foolish suspicion on my part, but I'm worried about one of my buddies. There is something strange about him. I'm not sure how to tell it . . ."

"Have confidence, my boy, and reveal your innermost feelings to me and do not fear. What I hear shall never leave this room for I am bound to secrecy by the oath of my calling. Unburden yourself."

"That's very nice of you, and I *do* feel better already. You see this buddy of mine has always been a little funny, he shines the boots for all of us and volunteered for latrine orderly and doesn't like girls."

The chaplain nodded beautifically and fanned some of the incense towards his nose. "I see little here to worry you, he sounds a decent lad. For is it not written in the *Vendidad* that we should aid our fellow man and seek to shoulder his burdens and pursue not the harlots of the streets?"

Bill pouted. "That's alright for Sunday school, but it's no way to act in the troopers! Anyway, we just thought he was out of his mind and he might have been—but that's not all. I was with him on the gun deck and he pointed his watch at the guns and pressed the stem and I heard it *click!* It could be a camera. I . . . I think he is a Chinger spy!" Bill sat back, breathing deeply and sweating. The fatal words had been spoken.

The chaplain continued to nod, smiling, half unconscious from the haoma fumes. Finally he snapped out of it, blew his nose and opened the thick copy of the *Avesta*. He mumbled aloud in old Persian a bit, which seemed to brace him, then slammed it shut.

"You must not bear false witness!" he boomed, fixing Bill with piercing gaze and accusing finger.

"You got me wrong," Bill moaned, writhing in the chair. "He's *done* these things, I *saw* him use the watch. What kind of spiritual aid do you call *this?*"

"Just a bracer my boy, a touch of the old-time religion to renew your sense of guilt and start you thinking about going to church regular again. You have been backsliding!" the chaplain roared.

"What else could I do—chapel is forbidden during recruit training."

"Circumstance is no excuse, but you will be forgiven this time because Ahura Mazdah is all-merciful."

"But what about my buddy—the spy?"

"You must forget your suspicions, for they are not worthy of a follower of Zoroaster. This poor lad must not suffer because of his natural inclinations to be friendly, to aid his comrades, to keep himself pure, to own a crummy watch that goes click. And besides, if you do not mind my introducing a spot of logic—how could he be a spy? To be a spy he would have to be a Chinger, and Chingers are seven feet tall with tails. Catch?"

"Yeah, yeah," Bill mumbled unhappily. "I could figure that out for myself—but it still doesn't explain everything."

"It satisfies me, and it must satisfy you. I feel that Ahriman has possessed you to make you think evil of your comrade, and you had better do some penance and join me in a quick prayer before the laundry officer comes back on duty."

This ritual was quickly finished and Bill helped stow the things back in the box and watched it vanish back into the desk. He made his good-bys and turned to leave.

"Just one moment, my son," the chaplain said with his warmest smile, reaching back over his shoulder at the same time to grab the end of his necktie. He pulled and his collar whirred about and as it did the blissful expression was wiped from his face to be replaced by a surly snarl. "Just where do you think you're going, bowb! Put your ass back in that chair."

"B-but," Bill stammered, "you said I was dismissed."

"That's what the chaplain said, and as a laundry officer I have no truck with him. Now—fast—what's the name of this Chinger spy you're hiding?"

"I told you about that under oath—"

"You told the *chaplain* about it, and he keeps his word and he didn't tell me, but I just happened to hear." He pressed a red button on the control panel. "The MPs are on the way. You talk before they get here, bowb, or I'll have you keelhauled without a spacesuit and deprived of canteen privileges for a year. The name?"

"Eager Beager," Bill sobbed as heavy feet trampled outside and two redhats forced their way into the tiny room.

"I have a spy for you boys," the laundry officer announced triumphantly and the MPs grated their teeth, howled deep in their throats, and launched themselves through the air at Bill. He dropped under the assault of fists and clubs and was running with blood before the laundry officer could pull the overmuscled morons with their eyes not an inch apart, off him.

"Not him . . ." the officer gasped, and threw Bill a towel to wipe off some of the blood. "This is our informant, the loyal, patriotic hero who ratted on his buddy by the name of Eager Beager, who we will now grab and chain so he can be questioned. Let's go."

The MPs held Bill up between them and by the time they had come to the fusetenders' quarters the breeze from their swift passage had restored him a bit. The laundry officer opened the door just enough to poke in his head. "Hi, gang!" he called cheerily. "Is Eager Beager here?"

Eager looked up from the boot he was polishing, waving and grinning. "That's me—gee."

"Get him!" the laundry officer expostulated, jumping aside and pointing accusingly. Bill dropped to the floor as the MPs let go of him and thundered into the compartment. By the time he had staggered back to his feet Eager was pinioned handcuffed and chained, hand and foot, but still grinning.

"Gee—you guys want some boots polished too?"

"No backtalk you dirty spy," the laundry officer grated and slapped him hard on the offensive grin. At least he tried to slap him on the offensive grin but Beager opened his mouth and bit the hand that hit him, clamping down hard so that the officer could not get away. "He bit me!" the man howled and tried desperately to pull free. Both MPs, each handcuffed to an arm of the prisoner, raised their clubs to give him a sound battering.

At this moment the top of Eager Beager's head flew open.

Happening at any other time this would have been considered unusual, but happening at this moment it was spectacularly unusual and they all, including Bill, gaped as a seven-inch high lizard climbed out of the open skull and jumped to the floor in which it made a sizeable dent upon landing. It had four tiny arms, a long tail, a head like a baby alligator and was bright green. It looked exactly like a Chinger except that it was seven inches tall instead of seven feet.

"All bowby humans have B. O." it said in a thin imitation of Eager Beager's voice. "Chingers can't sweat. Chingers forever!" It charged across the compartment toward Beager's bunk.

Paralysis prevailed. All of the fusetenders who had witnessed the impossible events stood or sat as they had been, frozen with shock and eyes bulging like hard-boiled eggs. The laundry officer was pinioned by the teeth locked into his hand, while the two MPs struggled with the handcuffs that held them to the immobile body. Only Bill was free to move and, still dizzy from the beating, he bent over to grab the tiny creature. Small and powerful talons locked into his flesh and he was pulled from his feet and went sailing through the air to crash against a bulkhead. "Gee—that's for you, you stoolie!" the miniscule voice squeeked.

Before anyone else could interfere the lizardoid ran to Beager's pile of barracks bags and tore the topmost one open and dived inside. A highpitched humming grew in volume an instant later and from the bag emerged the bulletlike nose of a shining projectile. It pushed out until a tiny spaceship not two feet long floated in the compartment. Then it rotated about its vertical axis, stopped when it pointed at the bulkhead. The humming rose in pitch and the ship suddenly shot forward and tore through the metal of the partition as if it had been no stronger than wet cardboard. There were other distant tearing sounds as it penetrated bulkhead after bulkhead until, with a rending clang it crashed through the outer skin of the ship and escaped into space. There was the roar of air rushing into the void and the clamor of alarm bells.

"Well I'll be damned," the laundry officer said, then snapped his gaping mouth closed and screamed, "Get this thing offa my hand—it's biting me to death!"

The two MPs swayed back and forth, handcuffed effectively to the immobile figure of the former Eager Beager. Beager just stared, smiling around the grip he had on the officer's hand, and it wasn't until Bill got his atomic rifle and put the barrel into Eager's mouth and levered the jaw open that the hand could be withdrawn. While he did this Bill saw that the top of Eager's head had split open just above his ears and was held at the back by a shiny brass hinge. Inside the gaping skull, instead of brains and bones and things, was a model control room with a tiny chair, miniscule controls, teevee screens and a water cooler. Eager was just a robot worked by the little creature that had escaped in the spaceship. It looked like a Chinger—but it was only seven inches tall.

"Hey!" Bill said, "Eager is just a robot worked by the little creature that escaped in the spaceship! It looked like a Chinger—but it was only seven inches tall . . ."

"Seven inches, seven feet—what difference does it make!" the laundry officer mumbled petulantly as he wrapped a handkerchief around his wounded hand. "You don't expect us to tell the recruits how big the enemy really are, or to explain that they come from a 10G planet. We gotta keep the morale up."

VI

Now that Eager Beager had turned out to be a Chinger spy, Bill felt very much alone. Bowb Brown, who never talked anyway, now talked even less, which meant never, so there was no one that Bill could bitch to. Bowb was the only other fuseman in the compartment who had been in Bill's squad at Camp Leon Trotsky, and all of the new men were very clannish and given to sitting close together and mumbling and throwing suspicious looks over their shoulders if he should come too close. Their only recreation was welding and every offwatch they would break out the welders and weld things to the floor and the next watch cut them loose again which is about as dim a way of wasting time as there is, but they seemed to enjoy it. So Bill was very much out of things and tried bitching to Eager Beager.

"Look at the trouble you got me into!" he whined.

"At least close your head when I'm talking to you," Bill

snarled and reached over to slam the top of Eager's head shut. But it didn't do any good. Eager couldn't do anything now except smile. He had polished his last boot. He just stood there now, he was really very heavy and besides was magnetized to the floor. The fusetenders hung their dirty shirts and arc welders on him. He stayed there for three watches before someone figured out what to do with him. Finally a squad of MPs came with crowbars and tilted him into a handcar and rolled him away.

"So long," Bill called out, waving after him, then went back to polishing his boots. "He was a good buddy even if he was a Chinger spy."

Bowb didn't answer him, and welders wouldn't talk to him and he spent a lot of time avoiding Reverend Tembo. The grand old lady of the fleet, *Christine Keeler,* was still in orbit while her engines were being installed. There was very little to do because, in spite of what First Class Spleen had said they had mastered all the intricies of fusetending in a little less than the prescribed year—in fact it took them something like maybe fifteen minutes.

In his free time Bill wandered around the ship, going as far as the MPs who guarded the hatchways would allow him. He even considered going back to see the chaplain so he could have someone to bitch to. But if he timed it wrong he might meet the laundry officer again and that was more than he could face. So he walked through the ship, very much alone, and looked in through the door of a compartment and saw a boot on a bed.

Bill stopped, frozen, immobile, shocked, rigid, horrified, dismayed, and had to fight for control of his suddenly contracted bladder.

He knew that boot. He would never forget that boot until the day he died, just as he would never forget his serial number and could say it frontwards or backwards or from the inside out. Every detail of that terrible boot was clear in his memory from the snakelike laces in the repulsive leather of the uppers—said to be made of human skin—to the corrugated stamping soles tinged with red that could only have been human blood.

That boot belonged to Deathwish Drang.

The boot was attached to a leg and paralyzed with terror, as unable to control himself as a bird before a snake, he found himself leaning further and further into the compartment as his eyes traced up the leg past the belt to the shirt to the neck upon which rested the face that had featured largely in his nightmares since he had enlisted. The lips moved.

"Is that you Bill? C'mon in and rest it."

Bill stumbled in.

"Have a hunk of candy," Deathwish said, and smiled.

Reflex drove Bill's fingers into the offered box and set his jaw chewing on the first solid food that had passed his lips in weeks. Saliva spouted from dusty orifices and his stomach gave a preliminary rumble while his thoughts drove maddingly in circles while he tried to figure out what expression was on Deathwish's face. Lips curved at the corners behind the tusks, little crinkles on the cheeks. It was hopeless. He could not recognize it.

"I hear Eager Beager turned out to be a Chinger spy," Deathwish said, closing the box of candy and sliding it under the pillow. "I should have figured that one out myself. I knew there was something *very* wrong with him, doing his buddies' boots and that crap, but I thought he was just nuts. Should have known better . . ."

"Deathwish," Bill said hoarsely, "it can't be, I know—but you are acting like a human being!"

Deathwish chuckled, not his ripsaw-slicing-human-bone chuckle, but an almost normal one.

Bill stammered. "But you are a sadist, a pervert, a beast, a creature, a thing, a murderer . . ."

"Why, thanks, Bill. That's very nice to hear. I try to do my job to the best of my abilities, but I'm human enough to enjoy a word of praise now and then. Being a murderer is hard to project but I'm glad it got across, even to a recruit as stupid as you were."

"B-but . . . aren't you *really* a . . ."

"Easy now!" Deathwish snapped, and there was enough of the old venom and vileness to lower Bill's body temperature six degrees. Then Deathwish smiled again. "Can't blame you, son, for carrying on this way, you being kind of stupid and from a rube planet and having your education retarded by the troopers and all that. But wake up, boy! Military education is far too important a thing to be wasted by allowing amateurs to get involved. If you read some of the things in our college textbooks it would make your blood cold, yes indeed. Do you realize that in prehistoric times the drill-sergeants or whatever it was they called them, that they were *real* sadists! The armed forces would let these people with no real knowledge absolutely *destroy* recruits. Let them learn to hate the service before they learned to fear it, which wrecks hell with discipline. And talk about wasteful! They were always marching someone to death by accident or drowning a squad or nonsense like that. The waste alone would make you cry."

"Could I asked what you majored in in college?" Bill asked in a very tiny and humble voice.

"Military Discipline, Spirit Breaking and Method Acting. A rough course, four years, but I graduated Sigma Cum, which is not bad for a boy from a working class family. I've made a career of the service and that's why I can't understand why the ungrateful bastards went and shipped me out on this crummy can!" He lifted his goldrimmed glasses to flick away a developing tear.

"You expect gratitude from the service?" Bill asked humbly.

"No, of course not, how foolish of me. Thanks for jerking me back into line, Bill, you'll make a good trooper. All I expect is criminal indifference which I can take advantage of by working through the old boy's network, bribery, cutting false orders, black-marketing and the other usual things. It's just that I *had* been doing a good job on you slobs in Camp Leon Trotsky and the least I expected was to be left alone to keep doing it, which was pretty damn stupid of me. I had better get cracking on my transfer now." He slid to his feet and stowed the candy and goldrimmed glasses away in a locked footlocker.

Bill, who in moments of shock found it hard to adjust instantly, was still bobbing his head and occasionally banging it with the heel of his hand. "Lucky thing," he said, "for your chosen career that you were born deformed—I mean you have such nice teeth."

"Luck nothing," Deathwish said, plunking one of his projecting tusks, "expensive as hell. Do you know what a gene-mutated, vat-grown, surgically implanted set of two-inch tusks cost? I bet you don't know! I worked the summer vac for three years to earn enough to buy these—but I tell you they were worth it. The *image,* that's everything. I studied the old tapes of prehistoric spiritbreakers and in their own crude way they were good. Selected by physical type and low I.Q. of course, but they knew their roles. Bullet heads, shaved clean with scars, thick jaws, repulsive manners, hot pants, everything. I figured a small investment in the beginning would pay rich dividends in the end. And it was a sacrifice, believe me, you won't see many implanted tusks around! For a lot of reasons. Oh, maybe they are good for eating rough meat, but what the hell else? Wait until you try kissing your first girl . . . Now, get lost Bill, I got things to do. See you around.''

His last words faded in the distance since Bill's well-conditioned reflexes had carried him down the corridor the instant he had been dismissed. When the spontaneous terror faded he began to walk with a crafty roll, like a duck with a spring kneecap, that he thought looked like an old spacesailor's gait. He was beginning to feel a seasoned hand and momentarily labored under the delusion that he knew more about the troopers than they knew about him. This pathetic misconception was dispelled instantly by the speakers on the ceiling which belched and then grated their nasal voices throughout the ship.

"Now hear this, the orders direct from the old man himself, Captain Zekial, that you all have been waiting to hear. We're heading into action so we are going to have a clean buckledown fore and aft, stow all loose gear.''

A low, heartfelt groan of pain echoed from every compartment of the immense ship.

VII

There was plenty of latrine rumor and scuttlebutt about this first flight of the *Chris'Keeler* but none of it was true. The rumors were planted by undercover MPs and were valueless. About the only thing they could be sure of was that they might be going someplace because they seemed to be getting ready to go someplace. Even Tembo admitted to that as they lashed down fuses in the storeroom.

"Then again,'' he added, "we might be doing all this just to fool any spies into thinking we are going someplace when really some other ships are going there.''

"Where?'' Bill asked irritably, tying his forefinger into a knot and removing part of the nail when he pulled it free.

"Why anyplace at all, it doesn't matter.'' Tembo was undisturbed by anything that did not bear on his faith. "But I do know where *you* are going, Bill.''

"Where?'' Eagerly. A perennial sucker for a rumor.

"Straight to hell unless you are saved.''

"Not again.'' Bill pleaded.

"Look there,'' Tembo said temptingly, and projected a heavenly scene with golden gates, clouds and a soft tom-tom beat in the background.

"Knock off that salvation crap!" First Class Spleen shouted, and the scene vanished.

Something tugged slightly at Bill's stomach, but he ignored it as being just another of the symptoms sent up continually by his panic-stricken gut which thought it was starving to death and hadn't yet realized that all its marvelous grinding and dissolving machinery had been condemned to a liquid diet. But Tembo stopped work and cocked his head to one side, then poked himself experimentally in the stomach.

"We're moving," he said positively, "and going interstellar too. They've turned on the stardrive."

"You mean we are breaking through into sub-space and will soon experience the terrible wrenching at every fiber of our being?"

"No, they don't use the old sub-space drive anymore because though a lot of ships broke through into sub-space with a fiber-wrenching jerk, none of them have yet broke back out. I read in the *Trooper's Times* where some mathematician said that there had been a slight error in the equations and that time was different in sub-space, but it was different faster not different slower so that it will be maybe forever before those ships come out."

"Then we're going into hyperspace?"

"No such thing."

"Or we're being dissolved into our component atoms and recorded in the memory of a giant computer who thinks we are someplace else so there we are?"

"Wow!" Tembo said, his eyebrows crawling up to his hairline. "For a Zoroastrian farmboy you have some strange ideas! Have you been smoking or drinking something I don't know about?"

"Tell me!" Bill pleaded. "If it's not one of them—what is it? We're going to have to cross interstellar space to fight the Chingers. How are we going to do it?"

"It's like this," Tembo looked around to make sure that First Class Spleen was out of sight, then put his cupped hands together to form a ball. "You make believe that my hands are the ship just floating in space. Then the bloater drive is turned on—"

"The *what?*"

"The bloater drive, it's called that because it bloats things up. You know, everything is made up of little bitty things called electrons, protons, neutrons, trontrons, things like that, sort of held together by a kind of binding energy. Now if you weaken the energy that holds things together—I forgot to tell you that also they are spinning around all the time like crazy, or maybe you already know—you weaken the energy and because they are going around so fast all the little pieces start to move away from each other, and the weaker the energy the further apart they move. Are you with me so far?''

"I think I am, but I'm not sure that I like it.''

"Keep cool. Now—see my hands? As the energy gets weaker the ship gets bigger,'' he moved his hands farther apart. "It gets bigger and bigger until it is as big as a planet, then as big as a sun then a whole stellar system. The bloater drive can make us just as big as we want to be, then it's turned the other way and we shrink back to our regular size and there we are.''

"*Where* are we?''

"Wherever we want to be,'' Tembo answered patiently.

Bill turned away and industriously rubbed shine-o onto a fuse as First Class Spleen sauntered by, a suspicious glint in his eye. As soon as he turned the corner Bill leaned over and hissed at Tembo.

"How can we be anywhere else than where we started? Getting bigger, getting smaller, doesn't get us anyplace.''

"Well, they're pretty tricky with the old bloater drive. The way I heard it it's like you take a rubber band and hold one end in each hand. You don't move your left hand but you stretch the band out as far as it will go with your right hand. When you let the band shrink back again you keep your right hand steady and let go with your left. See? You never moved the rubber band, just stretched it and let it snap—but it has moved over. Like our ship is doing now. It's getting bigger, but in one direction. When the nose reaches wherever we're going the stern will be wherever we were. Then we shrink and bango! there we are. And you can get into heaven just that easily, my son, if only . . .''

"Preaching on government time, Tembo!'' First Class Spleen howled from the other side of the fuserack over which he was looking with a mirror tied to the end of a rod. "I'll have you polishing fuseclips for a year. You've been warned before.''

They tied and polished in silence after that, until a little planet about as big as a tennis ball swam in through the bulkhead. A perfect little planet with tiny icecaps, cold fronts, cloud cover, oceans and the works.

"What's that?'' Bill yiped.

"Bad navigation,'' Tembo scowled. "Backlash, the ship is

slipping back a little on one end instead of going all the other way. No-no! Don't touch it, it can cause accidents sometimes. That's the planet we just left, Phigerinadon II.''

''My home,'' Bill sobbed and felt the tears rise as the planet shrank to the size of a marble. ''So long, Mom.'' He waved as the marble shrank to a mote then vanished.

After this the journey was uneventful, particularly since they could not feel when they were moving, did not know when they stopped, and had no idea where they were. Though they were sure they had arrived somewhere when they were ordered to strip the lashings from the fuses. The inaction continued for three watches and then the GENERAL QUARTERS alarm sounded. Bill ran with the others, happy for the first time since he had enlisted. All the sacrifices, the hardships would not be in vain. He was seeing action at last against the dirty Chingers.

They stood in first position opposite the fuseracks, eyes intent on the red bands on the fuses that were called the fusebands. Through the soles of his boots Bill could feel a faint, distant tremor in the deck.

''What's that?'' he asked Tembo out of the corner of his mouth.

''Main drive, not the bloater drive. Atomic engines. Means we must be maneuvering, doing something.''

''But *what?*''

''Watch them fusebands!'' First Class Spleen shouted.

Bill was beginning to sweat—then suddenly realized that it was becoming excruciatingly hot. Tembo, without taking his eyes from the fuses, slipped out of his clothes and folded them neatly behind him.

''Are we allowed to do that?'' Bill asked, pulling at his collar. ''What's happening?''

''It's against regulations but you have to strip or cook. Peel, son, or you will die unblessed. We must be going into action because the shields are up. Seventeen force screens, one electromagnetic screen, a double armored hull and a thin layer of pseudoliving jelly that flows over and seals any openings. With all that stuff there is absolutely no energy loss from the ship, nor any way to get rid of energy. Or heat. With the engines running and everyone sweating it can get pretty hot. Even hotter when the guns fire.''

The temperature stayed high, just at the boundary of tolerability for hours, while they stared at the fusebands. At one point there was a tiny plink that Bill felt through his bare feet on the hot metal rather than heard.

"What was that?"

"Torpedoes being fired."

"At *what?*"

Tembo just shrugged in answer and never let his vigilant gaze stray from the fusebands. Bill writhed with frustration, boredom, heat rash and fatigue for another hour, until the all clear blew and a breath of cool air came in from the ventilators. By the time he had pulled his uniform back on Tembo was gone and he trudged wearily back to his quarters. There was a new mimeographed notice pinned to the bulletin board in the corridor and he bent to read its blurred message.

FROM: Captain Zekial
TO: All Personnel

RE: Recent engagement

On 23/11-8956 this ship did participate in the destruction by atomic torpedo of the enemy installation 17KL-345 and did in concert with the other vessels of said flotilla RED CRUTCH accomplish its mission, it is thereby hereby authorized that all personnel of this vessel shall attach on Atomic Cluster to the ribbon denoting the Active Duty Unit Engagement Award, or however if this is their first mission of this type they will be authorized to wear the Unit Engagement Award.

NOTE: Some personnel have been observed with their Atomic Clusters inverted and this is WRONG and a COURT-MARTIAL OFFENSE that is punishable by DEATH.

VIII

After the heroic razing of 17KL-345 there were weeks of training and drill to restore the battle-weary veterans to their usual fitness. But midway in these depressing months a new call sounded over the speakers, one Bill had never heard before, a clanging sound like steel bars being clashed together in a metal drum full of marbles. It meant nothing to him nor to the other new men, but it sent Tembo springing from his bunk to do a quick two step Death Curse Dance with tom-tom accompaniment on his footlocker cover.

"Are you around the bend?" Bill asked dully from where he sprawled reading a tattered copy of *Real Ghoul Sexfiend Shocker Comics* with built-in sound effects. A ghastly moan was keening from the page he was looking at.

"Don't you know?" Tembo asked. "Don't you KNOW! That's mail call, my boy, the grandest sound in space."

The rest of the watch was spent in hurrying up and waiting, standing in line and all the rest. Maximum inefficiency was attached to the delivery of the mail but finally, in spite of all barriers, the post was distributed and Bill had a precious special-postal from his mother. On one side of the card was a picture of the Noisome-Offal refinery just outside of his hometown, and this alone was enough to raise a lump in his throat. Then, in the tiny square allowed for the message, his mother's scrawl had traced out: "Bad crop, in debt, robmule has packing glanders, hope you are the same—love, Maw." Still, it was a message from home and he read and reread it as they stood in line for chow. Tembo, just ahead of him, also had a card, all angels and churches, just what you would expect, and Bill was shocked when he saw Tembo read the card one last time then plunge it into his cup of dinner.

"What are you doing that for?" he asked, shocked.

"What else is mail good for?" Tembo hummed, and poked the card deeper. "You just watch this now."

Before Bill's startled gaze, and right in front of his eyes, the card was starting to swell. The white surface broke off and fell away in tiny flakes while the brown insides grew and grew until they filled the cup and were an inch thick. Tembo fished the dripping slab out and took a large bite from one corner.

"Dehydrated chocolate," he said indistinctly. "Good! Try yours."

Even before he spoke Bill had pushed his card down into the liquid and was fascinatingly watching it swell. The message fell away, but instead of brown a swelling white mass became visible.

"Taffy—or bread maybe," he said, and tried not to drool.

The white mass was swelling, pushing against the sides of the cup, expanding out of the top. Bill grabbed the end and held it as it rose. Out and out it came until every drop of liquid had been absorbed and Bill held between his outstretched hands a string of fat, connected letters over two yards long. VOTE - FOR - HONEST - GEEK - THE - TROOPERS - FRIEND they read. Bill leaned over and bit out an immense mouthful of T. He spluttered and spat the damp shards onto the deck.

"Cardboard," he said hollowly. "Mother always shops for bargains. Even in dehydrated chocolate . . ." He reached for his cup for something to wash the old newsprint taste out of his mouth but it was empty.

Somewhere, high in the seats of power a decision was made, a problem resolved, an order issued. From small things do big things grow; a tiny bird terd lands on a snow-covered mountain slope, rolls, collects snow, becomes bigger and bigger, gigantic and more gigantic until it is a thundering mass of snow and ice, an avalanche, a ravening mass of hurtling death that wipes out an entire village. From small beginnings . . . Who knows what the beginning was here, perhaps the Gods do, but they are laughing. Perhaps the haughty strutting peahen wife of some high minister saw a bauble she cherished and with shrewish, spiteful tongue exacerbated her peacock husband until, to give himself peace, he promised her the trinket, then sought the money for its purchase. Perhaps this was a word in the Emperor's ear about a new campaign in the 77sub7th Zone, quiet now for years, a victory there—or even a draw if there were enough deaths—would mean a medal, an award, some cash. And thus did a woman's covetousness, like a tiny bird's terd, start the snowball of warfare rolling, mighty fleets gathering, ship after ship assembling, like a rock in a pool of water the ripples spread until even the lowliest were touched by its motion . . .

"We're heading for action," Tembo said as he sniffed at his cup of lunch. "They're loading up the chow with stimulants, pain depressors, saltpeter and antibiotics."

"Is that why they keep playing the patriotic music?" Bill shouted so that he could be heard over the endless roar of bugles and drums that poured from the speakers. Tembo nodded.

"There's little time left to be saved, to assure your place in Samedi's legions—"

"Why don't you talk to Bowb Brown?" Bill screamed. "I got tom-toms coming out of my ears! Every time I look at a wall I see angels floating by on clouds. Stop bothering me! Work on Bowb—anybody who would do what he does with thoats would probably join up with your Voo-doo mob in a second."

"I have talked with Brown about his soul, but the issue is still in doubt. He never answers me so I am not sure if he has heard me or not. But you are different, my son, you show anger which means you are showing doubt, and doubt is the first step to belief.''

The music cut off in mid-peal and for three seconds there was an echoing blast of silence that abruptly terminated.

"Now hear this. Attention all hands . . . stand by . . . in a few moments we will be taking you to the flagship for an on-the-spot report from the admiral . . . stand by . . ." The voice was cut off by the sounding of General Quarters, but went on again when this hideous sound had ended. ". . . and here we are on the bridge of that gigantic conquistadore of the spacelanes, the twenty-mile long, heavily armored, mightily gunned super battleship the *Fairy Queen* . . . the men on watch are stepping aside now and coming towards me in a simple uniform of spun platinum is the Grand Admiral of the Fleet, the Right Honorable Lord Archaeopteryx . . . Could you spare us a moment Your Lordship? Wonderful! The next voice you are about to hear will be . . .''

The next voice was a burst of music while the fusemen eyed their fusebands, but the next voice after had all the rich adenoidal tones always heard from peers of the empire.

"Lads—we're going into action! This, the mightiest fleet the galaxy has ever seen is heading directly towards the enemy to deliver the devastating blow that may win us the war. In my operations tank before me I see myriad pinpoints of light, stretching as far as the eye can see and each point of light, I tell you they are like holes in a blanket!, is not a ship, not a squadron—but an entire *fleet!* We are sweeping forward, closing in . . .''

The sound of tom-toms filled the air and on the fuseband that Bill was watching appeared a matched set of golden gates, swinging open.

"Tembo!" he screamed. "Will you knock that off! I want to hear about the battle."

"Canned tripe," Tembo sniffed. "Better to use the few remaining moments of this life that may remain to you to seek salvation. That's no admiral, that's a canned tape. I've heard it five times already. They only play it to build morale before what they are sure is to be a battle with heavy losses. It never was an admiral, its from an old teevee program.''

"Yippee!" Bill shouted and leaped forward. The fuse he was looking at crackled with a brilliant discharge around the clips and at the same moment the fuseband charred and turned from red to black. "Unggh!" he grunted, then in rapid succession, "Unggh! Unggh! Unggh!" burning his palms on the still hot fuse, dropping it on his toe, and finally getting it into a fuseway. When he turned back Tembo had already clipped a fresh fuse into the empty clips.

"That was *my* fuse—you shouldn't have . . ." there were tears in his eyes.

"Sorry. But by the rules I must help if I am free."

"Well, at least we're in action," Bill said, back in position and trying to favor his bruised foot.

"Not in action yet, still too cold in here. And that was just a fuse breakdown, you can tell by the clip discharge, they do that sometimes when they get old."

". . . massed armadas manned by heroic troopers . . ."

"We *could* have been in combat." Bill pouted.

". . . thunder of atomic broadsides and lightning trails of hurtling torpedoes . . ."

"I think we are now. It does feel warmer, doesn't it, Bill? We had better undress, if it really is a battle we may get too busy."

"Let's go, let's go, down to the buff," First Class Spleen barked leaping gazelle-like down the rows of fuses, clad only in a pair of dirty gymsocks and his tatooed-on stripes and fouled fuse insignia of rank. There was a sudden crackling in the air and Bill felt the shortly clipped stubs of his hair stirring in his scalp.

"What's that?" he yiped.

"Secondary discharge from that bank of fuses," Tembo pointed. "It's classified as to what is happening but I heard tell that it means one of the defense screens is under radiation attack and as it overloads it climbs up the spectrum to green, to blue to ultraviolet until finally it goes black and the screen breaks down."

"That sounds pretty way out."

"I told you it was just a rumor. The material is classified."

"THERE SHE GOES!!"

A crackling bang split the humid air of the fuseroom and a bank of fuses arced, smoked, burned black. One of them cracked in half, showering small fragments like shrapnel in every direction. The fusemen leaped, grabbed the fuses, slipped in replacements with sweating hands, barely visible to each other through the reeking layers of smoke. The fuses were driven home and there was a moment's silence, broken only by a plaintive bleating from the communications screen.

"Son of a bowb!" First Class Spleen muttered, kicking a fuse out of the way and diving for the screen. His uniform jacket was hanging on a hook next to it, and he struggled into this before banging the receive switch. He finished closing the last button just as the screen cleared. Spleen saluted, so it must have been an officer he was facing. The screen was edge on to Bill so he couldn't tell, but the voice had the quacking no-chin-and-plenty-of-teeth whine that he was beginning to associate with the officer class.

"You're slow in answering, First Class Spleen—maybe Second Class Spleen would be able to answer faster?"

"Have pity, sir—I'm an old man." He dropped to his knees in a prayerful attitude which took him off the screen.

"Get up you idiot! Have you repaired the fuses after that last overload?"

"We *replace,* sir, not *repair.*"

"None of your technical gibberish, you swine! A straight answer!"

"All in order, sir. Operating in the green. No complaints from anyone, your worship."

"Why are you out of uniform?"

"I am in uniform, sir," Spleen whined, moving closer to the screen so that his bare behind and shaking lower limbs could not be seen.

"Don't lie to me! There's *sweat* on your forehead. You aren't allowed to sweat in uniform. Do you see me sweating? And I have a cap on too—at the correct angle. I'll forget it this time because I have a heart of gold. Dismissed."

"Filthy bowb!" Spleen cursed at the top of his lungs, tearing the jacket from his stifling body. The temperature was over 120 and still rising. "Sweat! They have air-conditioning on the bridge—and where do you think they discharge the heat? In here! YEOOW!!" he cried.

Two entire bands of fuses blew out at the same time, three of the fuses exploding like bombs. At the same moment the floor under their feet bucked hard enough to actually be felt.

"Big trouble!" Tembo shouted. "Anything that is strong enough to feel through the stasis field must be powerful enough to flatten this ship like a pancake. There go some more!" He dived for the bank and kicked a fuse clear of the clips and jammed in a replacement.

It was an inferno. Fuses were exploding like aerial bombs, sending whistling particles of ceramic death through the air. There was a lightning crackle as a board shorted to the metal floor and a hideous scream, thankfully cut short, as the sheet of lightning passed through a fusetender's body. Greasy smoke boiled and hung in sheets making it almost impossible to see. Bill raked the remains of a broken fuse from the darkened clips and jumped for the replacement rack. He clutched the 90 pound fuse in his aching arms and had just turned back towards the boards when the universe suddenly exploded.

All the remaining fuses seemed to have shorted at once and the screaming bolt of crackling electricity crashed the length of the room. In its eye-piercing light and in a single, eternal moment Bill saw the flame sear through the ranks of the fusetenders, throwing them about and incinerating them like particles of dust in an open fire. Tembo crumpled and collapsed, a mass of seared flesh; a flying length of metal tore First Class Spleen open from neck to groin in a single hideous wound.

"Look at that vent in Spleen!" Bowb shouted, then screamed as a ball of lightning rolled over him and turned him to a blackened husk in a fraction of a second.

By chance, a mere accident, Bill was holding the solid bulk of the fuse before him when the flame struck. It washed over his left arm which was on the outside of the fuse and hurled its flaming weight against the thick cylinder. The force hit Bill, knocked him back towards the reserve racks of fuses, and rolled him end over end flat on the floor while the all-destroying sheet of fire crackled inches above his head. It died away, as suddenly as it had come, leaving behind nothing but smoke, heat, the scorched smell of roasted flesh, destruction and death, death, death. Bill crawled painfully for the hatchway. Nothing else moved down the blackened and twisted length of the fuseroom.

The compartment below seemed just as hot, the air as bereft of nourishment for his lungs as the one he had just quitted. He crawled on, barely conscious of the fact that he moved on two lacerated knees and one bloody hand. His other arm just hung and dragged, a twisted and blackened length of debris, and only the blessings of deep shock kept him from screaming with unbearable pain.

He crawled on, over a sill, through a passageway. The air was clearer here, and much cooler: he sat up and inhaled its blessed freshness. The compartment was familiar—yet unfamiliar—he blinked at it, trying to understand why. Long and narrow with a curved wall that had the butt ends of immense guns projecting from it.

The main battery, of course, the guns Chinger spy Eager Beager had photographed. Different now, the ceiling closer to the deck, bent and dented, as if some gigantic hammer had beat on it from the outside. There was a man slumped in the gunner's seat of the nearest weapon.

"What happened?" Bill asked, dragging himself over to the man and clutching him by the shoulder. Surprisingly enough the gunner only weighed a few pounds and he fell from the seat light as a husk with a shriveled parchment face as though not a drop of liquid were left in his body.

"Dehydrator ray," Bill grunted. "Thought they only had them on teevee." The gunner's seat was padded and looked very comfortable, far more so than the warped steel deck: Bill slid into the recently vacated position and stared with unseeing eyes at the screen before him. Little moving blobs of light.

In large letters, just above the screen, was printed: GREEN LIGHTS OUR SHIPS, RED LIGHT ENEMY. FORGETTING THIS IS A COURTMARTIAL OFFENSE.

"I won't forget," Bill mumbled as he started to slide sideways from the chair. To steady himself he grabbed a large handle that rose before him, and when he did a circle of light with an X on it moved on the screen. It was very interesting. He put the circle around one of the green lights, then remembered something about a court-martial offense. He jiggled it a bit and moved it over to a red light, with the X right over the light. There was a red button on top of the handle and he pressed it because it looked like the kind of button that is made to be pressed. The gun next to him went *whffle* . . . in a very subdued way and the red lights went out. Not very interesting, he let go of the handle.

"Oh, but you are a fighting fool!" a voice said and, with some effort, Bill turned his head. A man stood in the doorway wearing a burned and tattered uniform still hung with shreds of gold braid. He weaved forward. "I saw it," he breathed. "Until my dying day I won't forget it. A fighting fool! What guts! Fearless! Forward against the enemy, no holds barred, don't give up the ship . . ."

"What the bowb you talking about?" Bill asked thickly.

"A hero!" the officer said pounding Bill on the back, which caused a great deal of pain and was the last straw for his conscious mind which let go the reins of command and went away to sulk. Bill passed out.

IX

"Now won't you be a nice trooper-wooper and drink your dinner . . ."

The warm notes of the voice insinuated themselves into a singularly repulsive dream that Bill was only too glad to leave and, with a great deal of effort he managed to heave his eyes open. A quick bit of blinking got them into focus and he saw before him a cup on a tray held by a white hand that was attached to a white arm that was connected to a white uniform well stuffed with female breasts. With a guttural animal growl Bill knocked the tray aside and hurled himself at the dress. He didn't quite make it because his left arm was wrapped up in something and hung from wires, so that he spun around in the bed like an impaled beetle, still uttering harsh cries. The nurse shrieked and fled.

"Glad to see that you are feeling better," the doctor said, whipping him straight in the bed with a practiced gesture and numbing Bill's still flailing right arm with a neat judo blow. "I'll pour you some more dinner and you drink it right down, then we'll let your buddies in for the unveiling, they're all waiting outside."

The tingling was dying from his arm and he could wrap his fingers about the cup now. He sipped. "What buddies? What unveiling? What's going on here?" he asked suspiciously.

Then the door was opened and the troopers came in. Bill searched their faces, looking for buddies, but all he saw were ex-welders and strangers. Then he remembered. "Bowb Brown cooked!" he screamed. "Tembo broiled! First Class Spleen gutted! They're all dead!" He hid under the covers and moaned horribly.

"That's no way for a hero to act," the doctor said, dragging him back onto the pillows and tucking the covers under his arms. "You're a hero, trooper, the man whose guts, ingenuity, integrity, stick-to-itiveness, fighting spirit and deadly aim saved the ship. All the screens were down, the power room destroyed, the gunners dead, control lost and the enemy dreadnaught zeroing in for the kill when you appeared like an avenging angel, wounded and near to death, and with your last conscious effort fired the shot heard round the fleet, the single blast that disemboweled the enemy and saved our ship, the grand old lady of the fleet *Christine Keeler*.'' He handed a sheet of paper to Bill. ''I am, of course, quoting from the official report, me myself I think it was just a lucky accident.''

''You're just jealous,'' Bill sneered, already falling in love with his new image.

''Don't get freudian with me!'' the doctor screamed, then snuffled pitifully. ''I always wanted to be a hero, but all I do is wait hand and foot on heroes. I'm taking that bandage off now.''

He unclipped the wires that held up Bill's arm and began to unwind the bandages while the troopers crowded around to watch.

''How is my arm, Doc?'' Bill was suddenly worried.

''Grilled like a chop. I had to cut it off.''

''Then what is this?'' Bill shrieked, horrified.

''Another arm that I sewed on. There were lots of them left over after the battle. The ship had over 42 percent casualties and I was really cutting and chopping and sewing, I tell you.''

The last bandage fell away and the troopers ahhhed with delight.

''Say, that's a mighty fine arm!''

''Make it do something.''

''And a damn nice seam there at the shoulder—look how neat the stitches are!''

''Plenty of muscles too and good and long, not like the crummy little short one he has on the other side.''

''Longer and darker—that's a great skin color!''

''It's Tembo's arm!'' Bill howled. ''Take it away!'' He squirmed across the bed but the arm came after him. They propped him up again on the pillows.

''You're a lucky bowb, Bill, having a good arm like that. And your buddy's arm too.''

''We knew that he wanted you to have it.''

''You'll always have something to remember him by.''

It really wasn't a bad arm. Bill bent it and flexed the fingers still looking at it suspiciously. It felt alright. He reached out with it and grabbed a trooper's arm and squeezed. He could feel the man's bones grating together while he screamed and writhed. Then Bill looked closer at the hand and began to shout curses at the doctor.

''You stupid sawbones! You thoat doctor! Some big job—this is a *right arm!*''

''So it's a right arm—so what?''

"But you cut off my *left* arm! Now I have two right arms."

"Listen, there was a shortage of left arms. I'm no miracle worker. I do my best and all I get are complaints. Be happy I didn't sew on a leg." He leered evilly, "Or even better I didn't sew on a . . ."

"It's a good arm, Bill," the trooper said who was rubbing his recently crushed forearm. "And you're really lucky too. Now you can salute with either arm, no one else can do that."

"You're right," Bill said humbly. "I never thought of that. I'm really very lucky." He tried a salute with his left-right arm and the elbow whipped up nicely across his chest and the fingertips quivered at his eyebrow. All the troopers snapped to attention and returned the salute. The door crashed open and an officer poked his head in.

"Stand easy, men—this is just an informal visit by the old man."

"Captain Zekial coming here!"

"I've never seen the old man . . ." The troopers chippered like birds and were as nervous as virgins at a defloration ceremony. Three more officers came through the door followed by a male nurse leading a ten-year-old moron wearing a bib and a captain's uniform.

"Uh . . . hi ya fellows . . ." the captain said.

"The captain wishes to pay his respects to you all," the first lieutenant said crisply.

"Is dat da guy in da bed?"

"And particularly wishes to pay his personal respects to the hero of the hour."

". . . Dere was sometin' else but I forgot . . ."

"And he furthermore wishes to inform the valiant fighter who saved our ship that he is being raised in grade to Fusetender First Class, which increase in rank includes an automatic reenlistment for seven years to be added to his original enlistment, and that upon dismissal from the hospital he is to go by first available transportation to the Imperial planet of Helior, there to receive the hero's award of the Purple Dart with Coalsack Nebula Cluster from the Emperor's own hand."

". . . I think I gotta go to da bathroom . . ."

"But now the exigencies of command recall him to the bridge and he wishes you all an affectionate farewell."

Bill saluted with both arms and the troopers stood at attention until the captain and his officers had gone, then the doctor dismissed the troopers as well.

"Isn't the old man a little young for his post?" Bill asked.

"Not as young as some," the doctor scratched through his hypodermic needles looking for a particularly dull one for an injection. "You have to remember that all captains have to be of the nobility and even a large nobility gets stretched damn thin over a galactic empire. We take what we can get." He found a crooked one and clipped it to the cylinder.

"Affirm, so he's young, but isn't he also a little stupid for the job?"

"Watch that lese majesty stuff, bowb! You get an empire that's a couple of thousand years old and you get a nobility that keeps inbreeding and you get some of the crunched genes and defective recessives coming out and you got a group of people that are a little more exotic than most nuthouses. There's nothing wrong with the old man that a new I.Q. wouldn't cure! You should have seen the captain of the last ship I was on . . ." he shuddered and jabbed the needle viciously into Bill's flesh. Bill screamed, then gloomily watched the blood drip from the hole after the hypodermic had been withdrawn.

The door closed and Bill was alone, looking at the blank wall and his future. He was a First Class Fusetender, and that was nice. But the compulsory reenlistment for seven years was not so nice. His spirits dropped. He wished he could talk to some of his old buddies, then remembered that they were all dead and his spirits dropped even further. He tried to cheer himself up but could think of nothing to be cheery about until he discovered that he could shake hands with himself. This made him feel a little bit better.

He lay back on the pillows and shook hands with himself until he fell asleep.

How easy is the fall from the pinnacle of power to the depths of degradation, for success and failure are but two sides of the same coin, one the obverse and the other the reverse, as the expression goes, and the shaking hand of fate flips this coin and no man knoweth on which side it will landeth.

Fate flipped for Bill. The same fate that had guided his fingers to the trigger that destroyed the Chinger dreadnaught failed one day to guide his fingers on a more mundane mission.

He received his medal—pinned on by the Emperor himself in a heart-warming ceremony—and as soon as the royal cortege had withdrawn the honor guard sprang on Bill and savaged him soundly.

"Sacrilege!" a colonel of marines roared as he sank his heel into Bill's quivering kidney.

"If you were one of my lads I'd have you blown from an atomic cannon!" screeched an artillery major as he mashed a fist against Bill's ear.

Unconscious and bleeding, Bill was finally dragged away by the MPs and locked behind bars. This was only the first of a series of military pokeys through which they shuttled his carcass while trying to make up their minds what to do with him. In transit he brushed against the criminal inhabitants of this secluded world and learned a form of low cunning that enabled him to survive with a minimum of effort. It was a pleasant, easy life, and in all ways superior to his existence as a trooper.

X

The transit stockade was a makeshift building of plastic sheets bolted to bent aluminum frames and was in the center of a large quadrangle. MPs with bayoneted atom rifles marched around the perimeter of the six electrified barbed-wire fences. The multiple gates were opened by remote control and Bill was dragged through them by the handcuff robot that had brought him here.

This debased machine was a squat and heavy cube as high as his knee that ran on clanking treads, and from the top of which projected a steel bar with heavy handcuffs fastened to the end. Bill was on the end of the handcuffs. Escape was impossible because if any attempt was made to force the cuffs the robot sadistically exploded a peewee atom bomb it had in its guts and blew up itself and the escaping prisoner, as well as anyone else in the vicinity. Once inside the compound the robot stopped and did not protest when the guard sergeant unlocked the cuffs. As soon as its prisoner was freed the machine rolled into its kennel and vanished.

"Alright wiseguy, you're in *my* charge now, and dat means trouble for you," the sergeant snapped at Bill. He had a shaven head, a wide and scar-covered jaw, small, close-set eyes in which there flickered the guttering candle of stupidity.

Bill narrowed his own eyes to slits and slowly raised his good left-right arm, flexing the bicep. Tembo's muscle swelled and split the thin prison fatigue jacket with a harsh ripping sound. Then Bill pointed to the ribbon of the Purple Dart which he had pinned to his chest.

"Do you know how I got that?" he asked in a grim and toneless voice. "I got that by killing 13 Chingers single handed in a pillbox had been sent into. I got into this stockade here because after killing the Chingers I came back and killed the sergeant who sent me in there. Now—what did you say about trouble, sergeant?"

"You don't give me no trouble I don't give you no trouble," the guard sergeant squeaked as he skittered away. "You're in cell 13, in there, right upstairs . . ." he stopped suddenly and began to chew all the fingernails on one hand at the same time, with a nibbling crunching sound. Bill gave him a long glower for good measure, then turned and went slowly into the building.

The door to number 13 stood open and Bill looked in at the narrow cell, dimly lit by the light that filtered through the translucent plastic walls. The double-decker bunk took up almost all of the space, leaving only a narrow passage at one side. Two sagging shelves were bolted to the far wall and, along with the stenciled message BE CLEAN NOT OBSCENE—DIRTY TALK HELPS THE ENEMY!, made up the complete furnishings. A small man with a pointed face and beady eyes lay on the bottom bunk looking intently at Bill. Bill looked right back and frowned.

"Come in, sarge," the little man said as he scuttled up the support into the upper bunk. "I been saving the lower for you, yes I have. The name is Blackey and I'm doing ten months for telling a second looey to blow it out . . ."

He ended the sentence with a slight questioning note that Bill ignored. Bill's feet hurt. He kicked off the purple boots and stretched out on the sack. Blackey's head popped over the edge of the upper bunk, not unlike a rodent peering out the landscape. "It's a long time to chow—how's about a dobbinburger?" A hand appeared next to the head and slipped a shiny package down to Bill.

After looking it over suspiciously Bill pulled the sealing string on the end of the plastic bag. As soon as the air rushed in and hit the combustible lining the burger started to smoke and within three seconds was steaming hot. Lifting the bun Bill squirted ketchup in from the little sack at the other end of the bag, then took a suspicious bite. It was rich, juicy horse.

"This old gray mare sure tastes like it used to be," Bill said, talking with his mouth full. "How did you ever smuggle this into the stockade?"

Blackey grinned and produced a broad stage wink. "Contacts. They bring it in to me, all I gotta do is ask. I didn't catch the name."

"Bill." Food had soothed his ruffled temper. "I was sent up on an indeterminate sentence for a crime too hideous to mention."

"What was it?" Blackey licked his lips with anticipation.

"I was given a medal by himself, the Emperor, in person and the ceremony was broadcast live to 967 billion teevee sets."

"So what's wrong with that?"

"My fly was open."

Bill swallowed the last mouthful and wiped his fingers on the blanket. "That was a good burger, too bad there's nothing to wash it down with."

Blackey produced a small bottle labeled COUGH SYRUP and passed it to Bill. "Specially mixed for me by a friend in the medics. Half grain alcohol and half ether."

"Zoingg!" Bill said, dashing the tears from his eyes after draining half the bottle. He felt almost at peace with the world. "You're a good buddy to have around, Blackey."

"You can say that again," Blackey told him earnestly. "It never hurts to have a buddy, not in the troopers, the army, the navy, anywheres. Ask old Blackey, he knows. You got muscles, Bill?"

Bill lazily flexed Tembo's muscle for him.

"That's what I like to see," Blackey said in admiration. "With your muscles and my brain we can get along fine . . ."

"I have a brain too!"

"Relax it! Give it a break, while I do the thinking. I seen service in more armies than you got days in the troopers. I got my first purple heart serving with Hannibal, there's the scar right there," he pointed to a white arc on the back of his hand. "But I picked him for a loser and switched to Romulus and Remus's boys while there was still time. I been learning ever since and I always land on my feet. I saw which way the wind was blowing and ate some laundry soap and got the trots the morning of Waterloo, and I missed but nothing I tell you. I saw the same kind of thing shaping up at the Somme—or was it Ypres?—I forget some of them old names now, and chewed a cigarette and put it into my armpit. You get a fever that way, and missed that show too. There's always an angle to figure I always say."

"I never heard of those battles. Fighting the Chingers?"

"No, earlier than that, a lot earlier than that. Wars and wars ago."

"That makes you pretty old, Blackey. You don't look pretty old."

"I am pretty old, but I don't tell people usually because they give me the laugh. But I remember the pyramids being built, and I remember what lousy chow the Assyrian army had, and the time we took over Wug's mob when they tried to get into our cave, rolled rocks down on them."

"Sounds like a lot of bowb," Bill said lazily, draining the bottle.

"Yeah, that's what everybody says, so I don't tell the old stories anymore. They don't even believe me when I show them my good luck piece." He held out a little white triangle with a ragged edge. "Tooth from a pterodactyl. Knocked it down myself with a stone from a sling I had just invented."

"Looks like a hunk of plastic."

"See what I mean? So I don't tell the old stories anymore. Just keep re-enlisting and drifting with the tide."

Bill sat up and gaped. "Reenlist! Why, that's suicide . . ."

"Safe as houses. Safest place during the war is in the army. The jerks in the front lines get their asses shot off, the civilians at home get their asses blown off. Guys in between safe as houses. It takes 30, 50 maybe 70 guys in the middle to supply every guy in the line. Once you learn to be a fileclerk you're safe. Who ever heard of them shooting at a fileclerk? I'm a great fileclerk. But that's just in wartime. Peacetime, whenever they make a mistake and there is peace for awhile, it's better to be in the combat troops. Better food, longer leaves, nothing much to do. Travel a lot."

"So what happens when the war starts?"

"I know 735 different ways to get into the hospitals."

"Will you teach me a couple?"

"Anything for a buddy, Bill. I'll show you tonight, after they bring the chow around. And the guard what brings the chow is being difficult about a little favor I asked him. Boy, I wish he had a broken arm!" he sighed.

"Which arm?" Bill cracked his knuckles with a loud, rending crunch.

"Dealer's choice."

• • •

The Plastichouse Stockade was a transient center where prisoners were kept on the way from somewhere to elsewhere. It was an easy, relaxed life enjoyed by both guards and inmates with nothing to disturb the even tenor of the days. There had been one new guard, a real eager type fresh in from the National Territorial Guard, but he had had an accident while serving the meals and had broken his arm. Even the other guards were glad to see him go. About once a week Blackey would be taken away under armed guard to the Base Records Section where he was forging new records for a light colonel who was very active in the black market and wanted to make millionaire before he retired. While working on the records Blackey saw to it that the stockade guards received undeserved promotions, extra leave time and cash bonuses for nonexistent medals. As a result Bill and Blackey ate and drank very well and grew fat. It was as peaceful as could possibly be until the morning after a session in the records section when Blackey returned and woke Bill.

"Good news," he said. "We're shipping out."

"What's good about that?" Bill asked, surly at being disturbed and still half stoned from the previous evening's drinking bout. "I like it here."

"It's going to get too hot for us soon. The colonel is giving me the eye and a very funny look and I think he is going to have us shipped to the other end of the galaxy where there is heavy fighting. But he's not going to do anything until next week after I finish the books for him, so I had secret orders cut for us *this* week sending us to Tabes Dorsalis where the cement mines are."

"The dust world!" Bill shouted hoarsely and picked Blackey up by the throat and shook him. "A worldwide cement mine where men die of silicosis in hours. Hell hole of the universe . . ."

Blackey wriggled free and scuttled to the other end of the cell. "Hold it!" he gasped. "Don't go off half cocked. Close the cover on your priming pan and keep your powder dry! Do you think I would ship us to a place like that? That's just the way it is on the teevee shows, but I got the inside dope. If you work in the cement mines, roger, it ain't so good. But they got one tremendous base section there with a lot of clerical help and they use trustees in the motor pool since there aren't enough troops there. While I was working on the records I changed your MS from fusetender which is a suicide job to driver, and here is your driver's license with qualifications on everything from a monocycle to an atomic

89-ton tank. So we get us some soft jobs and besides, the whole base is air-conditioned.''

"It was kind of nice here," Bill said, scowling at the plastic card that certified to his aptitude in chauffeuring a number of strange vehicles most of which he had never seen.

"They come, they go, they're all the same," Blackey said, packing a small toilet kit.

They began to realize that something was wrong when the column of prisoners were shackled then chained together with neckcuffs and leg irons and prodded into the transport spacer by a platoon of combat MPs. "Move along!" they shouted. "You'll have plenty of time to relax when we get to Tabes Dorsalgia."

"Where are we going?" Bill gasped.

"You heard me, snap it bowb."

"You told me Tabes Dorsalis," Bill snarled at Blackey who was ahead of him in the chain. "Tabes Dorsalgia is the base on Veneria where all the fighting is going on—we're heading for combat!"

"A little slip of the pen," Blackey sighed. "You can't win them all."

He dodged the kick Bill swung at him then waited patiently while the MPs beat Bill senseless with their clubs and dragged him aboard the ship.

XI

Veneria . . . a fog-shrouded world of untold horrors, creeping in its orbit around the ghoulish green star Hernia lie some repellent heavenly trespasser newly rose from the nethermost pit. What secrets lie beneath the eternal mists? What nameless monsters undulate and gibber in its dank tarns and bottomless black lagoons? Faced by the unspeakable terrors of this planet men go mad rather than face up to the faceless. Veneria . . . swamp world, the lair of the hideous and unimaginable Venians . . .

It was hot and it was damp and it stank. The wood of the newly constructed barracks was already soft and rotting away. You took your shoes off and before they hit the floor fungus was growing out of them. Once inside the compound their chains were removed, since there was no place for labor camp prisoners to escape to, and Bill wheeled around looking for Blackey, the fingers of Tembo's arm snapping like hungry jaws. Then he remembered that Blackey had spoken to one of the guards as they were leaving the ship, had slipped him something, and a little while later had been unlocked from the line and led away. By now he would be running the file section and by tomorrow he would be living in the nurse's quarters.

Bill sighed, let the whole thing slip out of his mind and vanish since it was just one more antagonistic factor that he had no control over and dropped down onto the nearest bunk. Instantly a vine flashed up from a crack in the floor, whipped four times around the bunk lashing him securely to it, then plunged tendrils into his leg and began to drink his blood.

"Grrrrk . . ." Bill croaked against the pressure of a green loop that tightened around his throat.

"Never lie down without you got a knife in your hand," a thin, yellowish sergeant said as he passed by and severed the vine, with his own knife, where it emerged from the floorboards.

"Thanks, sarge," Bill said, stripping off the coils and throwing them out the window.

The sergeant suddenly began vibrating like a plucked string and dropped onto the foot of Bill's bunk. "P-pocket . . . shirt . . . p-p-pills . . ." he stuttered through chattering teeth. Bill pulled a plastic box of pills out of the sergeant's pocket and forced some of them into his mouth. The vibrations stopped and the man sagged back against the wall, gaunter and yellower and streaming with sweat.

"Jaundice and swamp fever and galloping filariasis, never know when an attack will hit me, that's why they can't send me back to combat, I can't hold a gun. Me, Master Sergeant Ferkel, the best damned flame thrower in Kirjassoff's Kut-throats, and they have me playing nursemaid in a prison labor camp. So you think that bugs me? It does not bug me, it makes me happy, and the only thing that would make me happier would be shipping off this cesspool planet at once."

"Do you think alcohol will hurt your condition?" Bill asked passing over a bottle of cough syrup. "It's kind of rough here?"

"Not only won't hurt it but it will." There was a deep gurgling and when the sergeant spoke again he was hoarser but stronger. "Rough is not the word for it. Fighting the Chingers is bad enough, but on this planet they have the natives, the Venians, on their side. These Venians look like moldy newts and they got just maybe enough IQ to hold a gun and pull the trigger, but it is *their* planet and they're murder out there in the swamps. They hide under the mud and they swim under the water and they swing from the trees and the whole planet is thick with them. They got no sources of supply, no army divisions, no organizations, they just fight. If one dies the others eat him. If one is wounded in the leg the others eat the leg and he grows a new one. If one of them runs out of ammunition or poison darts or whatever he just swims back a hundred miles to base, loads up and back to battle. We have been fighting here for three years and we now control one hundred square miles of territory."

"A hundred, that sounds like a lot."

"Just to a stupid bowb like you. That is ten miles by ten miles, and maybe about two square miles more than we captured in the first landings."

There was the squish-thud of tired feet and weary, mud-soaked men began to drag into the barracks. Sergeant Ferkel hauled himself to his feet and blew a long blast on his whistle.

"Alright you new men, now hear this. You have all been assigned to B squad which is now assembling in the compound, which squad will now march out into the swamp and finish the job these shagged creeps from A squad began this morning. You will do a good days work out there. I am not going to appeal to your sense of loyalty, your honor or your sense of duty . . ." Ferkel whipped out his atomic pistol and blew a hole in the ceiling through which rain began to drip. "I am only going to appeal to your urge to survive, because any man shirking, goofing off or not pulling his own weight will personally be shot dead by me. Now get out." With his bared teeth and shaking hands he looked sick enough and mean enough and mad enough to do it. Bill and the rest of B squad rushed out into the rain and formed ranks.

"Pick up da axes, pick up da picks, get the uranium out," the corporal of the armed guard snarled as they squelched through the mud towards the gate. The labor squad, carrying their tools, stayed in the center, while the armed guard walked on the outside. The guard wasn't there to stop the prisoners from escaping but to give some measure of protection from the enemy. They dragged slowly down the road of felled trees that wound through the swamp. There was a sudden whistling overhead and heavy transports flashed by.

"We're in luck today," one of the older prisoners said, "they're sending in the heavy infantry again. I didn't know they had any left."

"You mean they'll capture more territory?" Bill asked.

"Naw, all they'll get is dead. But while they're getting butchered some of the pressure will be off of us and we can maybe work without losing too many men."

Without orders they all stopped to watch as the heavy infantry fell like rain into the swamps ahead—and vanished just as easily as raindrops. Every once in awhile there would be a boom and flash as a teensie A-bomb went off, which probably atomized a few Venians, but there were billions more of the enemy just waiting to rush in. Small arms crackled in the distance and grenades boomed. Then over the trees they saw a bobbing, bouncing figure approach. It was a heavy infantry-man in his armored suit and gasproof helmet, A-bombs and grenades strapped to him, a regular walking armory. Or rather hopping armory, since he would have had trouble walking on a paved street with the weight of junk hung about him, so therefore moved by jumping, using two reaction rockets, one bolted to each hip. His hops were getting lower and lower as he came near. He landed 50 yards away and sank slowly to his waist in the swamp, his rockets hissing as they touched the water. Then he hopped again, much shorter this time, the rockets fizzling and popping, and he threw his helmet open in the air.

"Hey, guys," he called. "The dirty Chingers got my fuel tank. My rockets are almost out, I can't hop much more. Give a buddy a hand will you . . ." He hit the water with a splash.

"Get outta the monkey suit and we'll pull you in," the guard corporal called.

"Are you nuts!" the soldier shouted. "It takes an hour to get into and outta this thing." He triggered his rockets but they just went pffft and he rose about a foot in the water, then dropped back. "The fuel's gone! Help me you bastards! What's this, bowb-your-buddy week . . ." he shouted as he sank, then his head went under and there were a few bubbles and nothing else.

"It's always bowb-your-buddy week," the corporal said. "Get the column moving!" he ordered, and they shuffled forward. "Them suits weigh 3,000 pounds. Goes down like a rock," the corporal said as he prodded them ahead.

If this was a quiet day, Bill didn't want to see a busy one. Since the entire planet of Veneria was a swamp no advances could be made until a road was built. Individual soldiers might penetrate a bit ahead of the road, but for equipment or supplies or even heavily armed men a road was necessary. Therefore the labor corps was building a road of felled trees. At the front.

Bursts from atom rifles steamed in the water around them and the poison darts were as thick as falling leaves. The firing and sniping on both sides was constant while the prisoners cut down trees, trimmed and lashed them together to push the road forward another few inches. Bill trimmed and chopped and tried to ignore the screams and falling bodies until it began to grow dark. The squad, now a good deal smarter, made their return march in the dusk.

"We pushed it ahead at least 30 yards this afternoon," Bill said to the old prisoner marching at his side.

"Don't mean nothing, Venians swim up in the night and take the logs away."

Bill instantly made his mind up to get out of there.

"Got any more of that joy-juice?" Sergeant Ferkel asked when Bill dropped onto his bunk and began to scrape some of the mud from his boots with the blade of his knife. Bill took a quick slash at a plant coming up through the floorboards before he answered.

"Do you think you could spare me a moment to give me some advice, sergeant?"

"I am a flowing fountain of advice once my throat is lubricated."

Bill dug a bottle out of his pocket. "How do you get out of this outfit?" he asked.

"You get killed," the sergeant told him as he raised the bottle to his lips. Bill snatched it out of his hand.

"That I know without your help," he snarled.

"Well, that's all you gonna know without my help," the sergeant snarled back.

Their noses were touching and they growled at each other deep in their throats. Having proven just where they stood and just how tough they both were they relaxed, and Sergeant Ferkel leaned back while Bill sighed and passed him the bottle.

"How's about a job in the orderly room?"

"We don't have an orderly room. We don't have any records. Everyone sent here gets killed sooner or later, so who cares exactly when."

"What about getting wounded?"

"Get sent to the hospital, get well, get sent back here."

"The only thing left to do is mutiny!" Bill shouted.

"Didn't work last four times we tried it. They just pulled the supply ships out and didn't give us any food until we agreed to start fighting again. Wrong chemistry here, all the food on this planet is pure poison for our metabolisms. We had a couple of guys prove it the hard way. Any mutiny that is going to succeed has to grab enough ships first so we can get off-planet. If you got any good ideas about that I'll put you in touch with the Permanent Mutiny Committee."

"Isn't there *any* way to get out?"

"I anshered that firsht," Ferkel told him and fell over stone drunk.

"I'll see for myself," Bill said as he slid the sergeant's pistol from his holster and slipped out the back door.

Armored floodlights lit up the forward positions facing the enemy and Bill went in the opposite direction, towards the distant white flares of landing rockets. Barracks and warehouses were dotted about on the boggy ground but Bill stayed clear of them since they were all guarded, and the guards had itchy trigger fingers. They fired at anything they saw, anything they heard, and if they didn't see or hear anything they fired once in a while anyway just to keep their morale up. Lights were burning brightly ahead and Bill crawled forward on his stomach to peer from behind a rank growth at a tall, floodlighted fence of barbed wire that stretched out of sight in both directions.

A burst from an atomic rifle burned a hole in the mud about a yard behind him and a searchlight swung over, catching him full in its glare.

"Greetings from your commanding officer," an amplified voice thundered from loudspeakers on the fence. "This is a recorded announcement. You are now attempting to leave the combat zone and enter the restricted headquarters zone. This is forbidden. Your presence has been detected by automatic machinery and these same devices now have a number of guns trained upon you. They will fire in sixty seconds if you do not leave. Be patriotic, man! Do your duty. Death to the Chingers! Fifty-five seconds. Would you like your mother to know that her boy is a coward? Fifty seconds. Your Emperor has invested a lot of money in your training—is this the way you repay him? Forty-five seconds . . ."

Bill cursed and shot up the nearest loudspeaker but the voice continued from others down the length of the fence. He turned and went back the way he had come.

As he neared his barracks, skirting the front line to avoid fire from the nervous guards in the buildings, all the lights went out. At the same time gunfire and bomb explosions broke out on every side.

XII

Something slithered close by in the mud and Bill's trigger finger spontaneously contracted and he shot it. In the brief atomic flare he saw the smoking remains of a dead Venian, as well as an unusually large number of live Venians squelching to the attack. Bill dived aside instantly, so that their return fire missed him, and fled in the opposite direction. His only thought was to save his skin and this he did by getting as far from the firing and the attacking enemy as he could. That this direction happened to be into the trackless swamp he did not consider.

Survive his shivering little ego screamed and he ran on into the swamp.

Running became difficult when the ground turned to mud, and even more difficult when the mud gave way to open water. After paddling desperately for an interminable length of time Bill came to more mud. The first hysteria had now passed, the firing was only a dull rumble in the distance and he was exhausted. He dropped onto the mudbank and instantly sharp teeth sank into his buttocks. Screaming hoarsely he ran on until he ran into a tree. He wasn't going fast enough to hurt himself and the feel of rough bark under his fingers brought out all of his eoanthropic survival instincts: he climbed.

High up there were two branches that forked out from the trunk and he wedged himself into the crotch, back to the solid wood and gun pointed straight ahead and ready. Nothing bothered him now and the night sounds grew dim and distant, the blackness was complete and within a few minutes his head started to nod. He dragged it back a few times, blinked about at nothing, then finally slept soundly.

It was the first gray light of dawn when he opened his gummy eyes and blinked around. There was a little lizard perched on a nearby branch watching him with jewel-like eyes.

"Gee—you were really sacked out," the Chinger said.

Bill's shot tore a smoking scar in the top of the branch, then the Chinger swung back up from underneath and meticulously wiped bits of ash from his paws.

"Easy on the trigger, Bill," it said. "Gee—I could have killed you anytime during the night if I had wanted to."

"I know you," Bill said hoarsely. "You're Eager Beager, aren't you."

"Gee—this is just like old home week, isn't it." A centipede was scuttling by and Eager Beager the Chinger grabbed it up with three of his arms and began pulling off legs with his fourth and eating them. "I recognized you Bill, and wanted to talk to you. I've been feeling bad ever since I called you a stoolie, that wasn't right of me. You were only doing your duty when you turned me in. You wouldn't like to tell me how you recognized me, would you?" he asked, and winked slyly.

"Why don't you bowb off, jack?" Bill growled and groped in his pocket for a bottle of cough syrup. Eager Chinger sighed.

"Well, I suppose I can't expect you to betray anything of military importance, but I hope you will answer a few questions for me." He discarded the delimbed corpse and groped about in his marsupial pouch and produced a tablet and tiny writing instrument. "You must realize that spying is not my chosen occupation, but rather I was dragooned into it through my specialty which is exopology—perhaps you have heard of this discipline?"

"We had an orientation lecture once, an exopologist, all he could talk about was alien creeps and things."

"Yes—well that roughly sums it up. The science of the study of alien life forms, and of course to us you homo sapiens are an alien form." He scuttled halfway around the branch when Bill raised his gun.

"Watch that kind of talk, bowb!"

"Sorry, just my manner of speaking. To put it briefly, since I specialized in the study of your species I was sent out as a spy, reluctantly, but that is the sort of sacrifice one makes during wartime. However, seeing you here reminded me that there are a number of questions and problems still unanswered that I would appreciate your help on, purely in the matter of science, of course."

"Like what?" Bill asked suspiciously, draining the bottle and flinging it away into the jungle.

"Well—gee—to begin simply, how do you feel about us Chingers?"

"Death to all Chingers!" The little pen flew over the tablet.

"But you have been *taught* to say that. How did you feel before you entered the service?"

"Didn't give a damn about Chingers." Out of the corner of his eye Bill was watching a suspicious movement of the leaves in the tree above.

"Fine! Then could you explain to me just who it is that hates us Chingers and wants to fight a war of extermination?"

"Nobody really hates Chingers, I guess. It's just that there is no one else around to fight a war with so we fight with you." The moving leaves had parted and a great, smooth head with slitted eyes peered down.

"I knew it! And that brings me to my really important questions. Why *do* you homo sapiens like to fight wars?"

Bill's hand tightened on his gun as the monstrous head dropped silently down from the leaves behind Eager Chinger Beager. It was attached to a foot-thick and apparently endless serpent body.

"Fight wars? I don't know," Bill said, distracted by the soundless approach of the giant snake. "I guess because we like to, there doesn't seem to be any other reason."

"You *like* to!" the Chinger squeaked, hopping up and down with excitement. "No civilized race could *like* wars, death, killing, maiming, rape, torture, pain to name just a few of the concomitant factors. Your race can't be civilized!"

The snake struck like lightning and Eager Beager Chinger vanished down its spine-covered throat with only the slightest of muffled squeals.

"Yeah . . . I guess we're just not civilized," Bill said, gun ready, but the snake kept going on down. At least fifty yards of it slithered by before the tail flipped past and it was out of sight. "Serves the damn spy right," Bill grunted happily and pulled himself to his feet.

Once on the ground Bill began to realize just how bad a spot he was in. The damp swamp had swallowed up any marks of his passage from the night before and he hadn't the slightest idea in which direction the battle area lay. The sun was just a general illumination behind the layers of fog and cloud, and he felt a sudden chill as he realized how small were his chances of finding his way back. The invasion area, just ten miles to a side, made a microscopic pinprick in the hide of this planet. Yet if he didn't find it he was as good as dead. And if he just stayed here he would die, so, picking what looked like the most likely direction, he started off.

"I'm pooped," he said, and was. A few hours of dragging through the swamps had done nothing except weaken his muscles, filled his skin with insect bites, drain a quart or two of blood into the ubiquitous leeches and deplete the charge in his gun as he killed a dozen or so of the local lifeforms that wanted him for breakfast. He was also hungry and thirsty. And still lost.

The rest of the day just recapitulated the morning so that when the sky began to darken he was close to exhaustion and his supply of cough medicine was gone. He was very hungry when he climbed a tree to find a spot to rest for the night and he plucked a luscious looking red fruit.

"Supposed to be poison," he looked at it suspiciously, then smelled it. It smelled fine. He threw it away.

In the morning he was much hungrier. "Should I put the barrel of the gun in my mouth and blow my head off?" he asked himself, weighing the atomic pistol in his hand. "Plenty of time for that yet. Plenty of things can still happen," yet he didn't really believe it. Suddenly he heard voices coming through the jungle towards him, human voices. He settled behind the limb and aimed his gun in that direction.

The voices grew, then a clanking and rattling. An armed Venian scuttled under the tree, but Bill held his fire as other figures loomed out of the fog. It was a long file of human prisoners wearing the neckirons used to bring Bill and the others to the labor camp, all joined together by a long chain that connected the neckirons. Each of the men was carrying a large box on his head. Bill let them stumble by underneath and kept a careful count of the Venian guards. There were five in all with a sixth bringing up the rear.

When this one had passed underneath the tree Bill dropped straight down on him, braining him with his heavy boots. The Venian was armed with a Chinger-made copy of a standard atomic rifle and Bill smiled wickedly as he hefted its familiar weight. After sticking the pistol into his waistband he crept after the column, rifle ready. He managed to kill the fifth guard by walking up behind him and catching him the the back of the neck with the rifle butt. The last two troopers in the file saw this but had enough brains to be quiet as he crept up on number four. Some stir among the prisoners or a chance sound warned this guard and he turned about, raising his rifle. There was no chance now to kill him silently so Bill burned his head off and ran as fast as he could towards the head of the column. There was a shocked silence when the blast of the rifle echoed through the fog and Bill filled it with a shout.

"Hit the dirt—FAST!"

The soldiers dived into the mud and Bill held his atomic rifle at his waist as he ran, fanning it back and forth before him like a water hose and holding the trigger on full automatic. A continuous blast of fire poured out a yard above the ground and he squirted it in an arc before him. There were shouts and screams in the fog and then the charge in the rifle was exhausted. Bill threw it from him and drew the pistol. Two of the remaining guards were down and the last one was wounded and got off a single badly aimed shot before Bill burned him too.

"Not bad," he said, stopping and panting. "Six out of six."

There were low moans coming from the line of prisoners and Bill curled his lip in disgust at the three men who hadn't dropped at his shouted command.

"What's the matter?" he asked, stirring one with his foot, "never been in combat before?" But this one didn't answer because he was charred dead.

"Never . . ." the next one answered, gasping in pain. "Get the corpsman, I'm wounded, there's one ahead in the line. Oh, oh, why did I ever leave the *Chris' Keeler!* Medic."

Bill frowned at the three gold balls of a fourth lieutenant on the man's collar, then bent and scraped some mud from his face. "You! The laundry officer!" he shouted in outraged anger, raising his gun to finish the job.

"Not I!" the lieutenant moaned, recognizing Bill at last. "The laundry officer is gone, flushed down the drain! This is I, your friendly local pastor, bringing you the blessings of Ahura Mazdah, my son, and have you been reading the *Avesta* every day before going to sleep?"

"Bah!" Bill snarled, he couldn't shoot him now, and walked over to the third wounded man.

"Hello Bill . . ." a weak voice said. "I guess the old reflexes are slowing down . . . I can't blame you for shooting me, I should have hit the dirt like the others . . ."

"You're damn right you should have," Bill said looking down

at the familiar, loathed, tusked face. "You're dying Deathwish, you've bought it."

"I know," Deathwish said and coughed. His eyes were closed.

"Wrap this line in a circle," Bill shouted. "I want the medic up here." The chain of prisoners curved around and they watched as the medic examined the casualties.

"A bandage on the looie's arm takes care of him," he said. "Just superficial burns. But the big guy with the fangs has bought it."

"Can you keep him alive?" Bill asked.

"For awhile, no telling how long."

"Keep him alive." Bill looked around at the circle of prisoners. "Any way to get those neckirons off?" he asked.

"Not without the keys," a burly infantry sergeant answered, "and the lizards never brought them. We'll have to wear them until we get back. How come you risked your neck saving us?" he asked suspiciously.

"Who wanted to save you?" Bill sneered. "I was hungry and I figured that must be food you were carrying."

"Yeah, it is," the sergeant said, looking relieved. "I can understand now why you took the chance."

Bill broke open a can of rations and stuffed his face.

The dead man was cut from his position in the line and the two men, one in front and one in back of the wounded Deathwish, wanted to do the same with him. Bill reasoned with them, explained the only human thing to do was to carry their buddy, and they agreed with him when he threatened to burn their legs off if they didn't. While the chained men were eating, Bill cut two flexible poles and made a stretcher by slipping three donated uniform jackets over them. He gave the captured rifles to the burly sergeant and the most likely looking combat veterans, keeping one for himself.

"Any chance of getting back?" Bill asked the sergeant, who was carefully wiping the moisture from his gun.

"Maybe. We can backtrack the way we come, easy enough to follow the trail after everyone dragged through. Keep an eye peeled for Venians, get them before they can spread the word about us. When we get in earshot of the fighting we try and find a quiet area—then break through. A fifty-fifty chance."

"Those are better odds for all of us than they were about an hour ago."

"You're telling me. But they get worse the longer we hang around here."

"Let's get moving."

Following the track was even easier than Bill had thought, and by early afternoon they heard the first signs of firing, a dim rumble in the distance. The only Venian they had seen had been instantly killed. Bill halted the march.

"Eat as much as you want, then dump the food," he said. "Pass that on. We'll be moving fast soon." He went to see how Deathwish was getting on.

"Badly—" Deathwish gasped, his face white as paper. "This is it, Bill . . . I know it . . . I've terrorized my last recruit . . . stood on my last pay line . . . had my last shortarm . . . so long—Bill . . . you're a good buddy . . . taking care of me like this . . ."

"Glad you think so, Deathwish, and maybe you'd like to do me a favor." He dug in the dying man's pockets until he found his noncom's notebook, then opened it and scrawled on one of the blank pages. "How would you like to sign this, just for old time's sake—Deathwish?"

The big jaw lay slack, the evil red eyes open and staring.

"The dirty bowb's gone and died on me," Bill said disgustedly. After pondering for a moment he dribbled some ink from the pen onto the ball of Deathwish's thumb and pressed it to the paper to make a print.

"Medic!" he shouted, and the line of men curled around so the medic could come back. "How does he look to you?"

"Dead as a herring," the corpsman said after his professional examination.

"Just before he died he left me his tusks in his will, written right down here, see? These are real vat-grown tusks and cost a lot. Can they be transplanted?"

"Sure, as long as you get them cut out and deep froze inside the next twelve hours."

"No problem with that, we'll just carry the body back with us." He stared hard at the two stretcher bearers and fingered his gun, and they had no complaints. "Get that lieutenant up here."

"Chaplain," Bill said, holding out the sheet from the notebook, "I would like an officer's signature on this. Just before he died this trooper here dictated his will, but was too weak to sign it, so he put his thumbprint on it. Now you write below it that you saw him thumbprint it and it is all affirm and legal-like, then sign your name.''

''But—I couldn't do that my son. I did not see the deceased print the will and glmmpf . . .''

He said glmmpf because Bill had poked the barrel of the atomic pistol into his mouth and was rotating it, his finger quivering on the trigger.

''Shoot,'' the infantry sergeant said, and three of the men who could see what was going on were clapping. Bill slowly withdrew the pistol.

''I shall be happy to help,'' the chaplain said, grabbing for the pen.

Bill read the document, grunted in satisfaction, then went over and squatted down next to the medic. ''You from the hospital?'' he asked.

''You can say that again, and if I ever get back into the hospital I ain't never going out of it again. It was just my luck to be out picking up combat casualties when the raid hit.''

''I hear that they aren't shipping any wounded out. Just putting them back into shape and sending them back into the line.''

''You heard right. This is going to be a hard war to live through.''

''But *some* of them must be wounded too badly to send back into action,'' Bill insisted.

''The miracles of modern medicine,'' the medic said indistinctly as he worried a cake of dehydrated luncheon meat. ''Either you die or you're back in the line in a couple of weeks.''

''Maybe a guy gets his arm blown off?''

''They got an icebox full of old arms. Sew a new one on and bango, right back into the line.''

''What about a foot?'' Bill asked, worried.

''That's right—I forgot! They got a foot shortage. So many guys lying around without feet that they're running out of bedspace. They were starting to ship some of them offplanet when I left.''

''You got any pain pills?'' Bill asked, changing the subject. The medic dug out a white bottle.

''Three of these and you'd laugh while they sawed your head off.''

''Give me three.''

''If you ever see a guy around what has his foot shot off you better quick tie something around his leg just over the knee, tight, to cut the blood off."

"Thanks buddy."

"Let's get moving," the infantry sergeant said. "The quicker we move the better our chances."

Occasional flares from atomic rifles burned through the foliage overhead and the thud-thud of heavy weapons shook the mud under their feet. They worked along parallel with the firing until it had died down, then stopped. Bill, the only one not chained in the line, crawled ahead to reconnoiter. The enemy lines seemed to be lightly held and he found the spot that looked the best for a breakthrough. Then, before he returned, he dug the heavy cord from his pocket that he had taken from one of the ration boxes. He tied a tourniquet above his right knee and twisted it tight with a stick, then swallowed the three pills. He stayed behind some heavy shrubs when he called to the others.

"Straight ahead, then sharp right before that clump of trees. Let's go—and FAST!"

Bill led the way until the first men could see the lines ahead. Then he called out, "What's that?" and ran into the heavy foliage. "Chingers!" he shouted and sat down with his back to a tree.

He took careful aim with his pistol and blew his right foot off.

"Get moving fast!" he shouted and heard the crash of the frightened men through the undergrowth. He threw the pistol away, fired at random into the trees a few times, then dragged to his feet. The atomic rifle made a good enough crutch to hobble along on and he did not have far to go. Two troopers, they must have been new to combat or they would have known better, left the shelter to help him inside.

"Thanks, buddies," he gasped, and sank to the ground. "War sure is hell."

XIII

The martial music echoed from the hillside, bouncing back from the rocky ledges and losing itself in the hushed green shadows under the trees. Around the bend, stamping proudly through the dust, came the little parade led by the magnificent form of a one-robot-band. Sunlight gleamed on its golden limbs and twinkled from the brazen instruments it worked with such enthusiasm. A small formation of assorted robots rolled and clattered in its wake and bringing up the rear was the solitary figure of the grizzle-haired recruiting sergeant, striding along strongly, his rows of medals a-jingle. Though the road was smooth the sergeant lurched suddenly, stumbling, and cursed with the rich proficiency of years.

"Halt!" he commanded, and while his little company braked to a stop he leaned against the stone wall that bordered the road and rolled up his right pants leg. When he whistled one of the robots trundled quickly over and held out a tool box from which the sergeant took a large screwdriver and tightened one of the bolts in the ankle of his artificial foot. Then he squirted a few drops from an oil can onto the joint and rolled the pants leg back down. When he straightened up he noticed that a robomule was pulling a plow down a furrow in the field beyond the fence a farmlad guided it.

"Beer!" the sergeant barked, then, "*A Spacemen's Lament.*"

"That's sure pretty music," the plowboy said.

"Join me in a beer," the sergeant said, sprinkling a white powder into it.

"Don't mind iffen I do, sure is hottern'n H— out here today."

"Say *hell*, son."

"Momma don't like me to cuss. You sure do have long teeth, mister."

The sergeant twanged a tusk. "A big fellow like you shouldn't worry about a little cussing. If you were a trooper you could say *hell*—or even *bowb*—if you wanted to, all the time."

"I don't think I'd want to say anything like *that*," he flushed redly under his deep tan. "Thanks for the beer, but I gotta be ploughing on now. Momma said I was to never talk to soldiers."

"Your momma's right, a dirty, cussing, drinking crew the most of them. Say, would you like to see a picture here of a new model robomule that can run 1,000 hours without lubrication?" The sergeant held his hand out behind him and a robot put a viewer into it.

"Why that sounds nice!" The farmlad raised the viewer to his eyes and looked into it and flushed an even deeper red. "That's no mule, mister, that's a *girl* and her clothes are . . ."

The sergeant reached out swiftly and pressed a button on the top of the viewer. Something went *thunk* inside of it and the farmer stood, rigid and frozen. He did not move or change expression when the sergeant reached out and took the little machine.

"Take this stylo," the sergeant said, and the other's fingers closed on it. "Now sign this form, *recruits' signature.*"

"My Charlie! What are you doing with my Charlie!" an ancient, gray-haired woman wailed as she scrambled toward them.

"Your son is now a trooper for the greater glory of the Emperor," the sergeant said, and waved over the robot tailor.

"No—please!" the woman begged, clutching the sergeant's hand and dribbling tears onto it. "I've lost one son, isn't that enough." She blinked up through the tears, then blinked again. "But you—you're my boy! My Bill come home! Even with those teeth and the scars and one black hand and one white hand and one artificial foot, I can tell, a mother always knows!"

The sergeant frowned down at the woman. "I believe you might be right," he said. "I thought Phigerinadon II was familiar."

The robot tailor had finished his job, the red paper jacket shone bravely in the sun, the one-molecule-thick boots gleamed. "Fall in," Bill shouted.

"Billy, Billy . . ." the woman wailed, "this is your little brother, Charlie! You wouldn't take your own little brother into the troopers, would you?"

Bill thought about his mother then he thought about his baby brother, Charlie, then he thought of the one month that would be taken off of his enlistment time for every recruit he brought in and he snapped his answer back.

"Yes," he said.

The music blared, the soldiers marched, the mother cried—as mothers have always done—and the brave little band tramped down the road and over the hill and out of sight into the sunset.

"Fast-paced...realistic detail and subtle humor. It will be good news if Shatner decides to go on writing."—<u>Chicago Sun-Times</u>

WILLIAM SHATNER

_____ TEKWAR _____

Ex-cop Jake Cardigan was framed for dealing the addictive brain stimulant Tek. But now he's been mysteriously released from his prison module and launched back to Los Angeles of 2120. There, a detective agency hires him to find the anti-Tek device carried off by a prominent scientist. But Jake's not the only one crazy enough to risk his life to possess it.

_0-441-80208-7/\$4.50

_____ TEKLORDS _____

Jake Cardigan is back when a synthetic plague is sweeping the city. A top drug-control agent is brutally murdered by a reprogrammed human "zombie," deadlier than an android assassin. For Jake, all roads lead to one fatal circle—the heart of a vast computerized drug ring.

_0-441-80010-6/\$4.99